THE BRIGHT EFFECT

A Novel by

Autumn Doughton and Erica Cope

The Bright Effect
Copyright © 2015 Autumn Doughton and Erica Cope

Cover Design by Okay Creations

ISBN-13: 978-1519115720
ISBN-10: 1519115725

For all the fangirls out there
(You know exactly who you are)

May you always line up for midnight book releases and geek out on Disney songs and scream bloody murder for your favorite band and swoon with your friends over the forever-awesome Mr. Darcy.

And, girls, when someone tries to tell you that you're a joke, go ahead and laugh in their freaking face. Trust us—it's not you; it's them. Because showing the world just how big your love and enthusiasm can be isn't a silly thing.

It's _everything._

This book is also for Jensen Ackles and Jared Padalecki because, well, we wrote it and we can dedicate it to whomever we feel like. And you're never too old to fangirl, are you?

~Autumn and Erica

PART ONE

Tell me, what is it you plan to do with your one wild and precious life?
~Mary Oliver

CHAPTER ONE

Bash

It feels like it never stops. Like no matter what I do, no matter how hard I try, it's never going to be enough. Not ever.

The pulse in my neck pumps hard and fast as I tighten my grip on the steering wheel and let my eyes slide to the clock on the dashboard.

Six seventeen.

Shit.

I should have been at the school seventeen minutes ago, but what could I do when Ron, my milky-eyed boss, insisted I stay late to unload the latest shipment of door hinges? Tell him to go screw himself? Sure, it would have been incredible to see the look on his face but not worth it. I've learned the hard way that a job is a job. Even if it's only part time at a local hardware store working for a half-drunk hick.

Fighting back the familiar frustration, I jerk my car to the curb in front of a two-story white stucco building. Just before killing the ignition, I check the time one last time.

Six nineteen.

"Damn," I mutter as I pocket the keys. I don't bother to lock the doors because no way someone is going to try to steal my beatdown Bronco. The truck is older than me—driven brand new off the lot by my grandparents and guzzling gas and rusting out ever since. One of these days I figure I'll have the money to rebuild it, but until then I'm safe from potential car thieves. You have to know to pump on the clutch to start the thing and beyond that, third gear is sticky as hell.

Outside is as cripplingly hot as it is humid, a normal day in Lowcountry. I take the weathered stone steps two at a time and cross under a faded red and blue sign that declares this the home of the Jefferson Elementary Jaguars.

Mrs. Hopkins, the woman who runs the after school program must hear my work boots thudding against the linoleum because she sticks her head out the cafeteria door when I jog around the corner.

"Good evening, Mr. Holbrook," she says, the skin around her mouth puckering.

"Sorry," I breathe, slowing down. "Work ran late.

"I see that."

"I promise it won't happen again."

"Young man, I know your situation is a unique one," she drawls in a heavy South Carolina accent. "And I do believe that everyone at this school has tried to be understanding and accommodating."

"And I appreciate that," I interject, trying to make my way past her.

"But," she continues with a drawn-out sigh that sets my skin prickling, "you must agree that the school year has taken off like a herd of turtles. Why, it's only September and you've already been late for pick-up at least a half a dozen times."

"And I'm sorry about that, but like I said, work ran late."

Her forehead wrinkles. "We all have our burdens. If you can't make it here on time consistently, you're going to have to find another arrangement for Carter."

As far as another after school arrangement is concerned, there are no options. At least none that I can afford.

"I'll be here on time," I say.

It's clear that Mrs. Hopkins doesn't believe this, but after an uncomfortable pause, she nods her head and pushes the door wider to let me by.

3

The cafeteria reeks of crayons and rubbery hot dogs just like it did when I went to school here. By this time of day the place is mostly deserted and it doesn't take me long to spot Carter. He's sitting with a teacher at one of the long lunch tables. From here I can only see the back of the teacher's head and I wonder if this woman is the reading tutor he mentioned last week. And then I start to wonder if maybe I should know who this tutor is.

A parent knows that kind of thing, don't they? Just like a parent picks up his kid on time and carries around hand sanitizer and helps with homework and has the laundry done and knows what's for dinner.

My aunt and uncle are right. I'm in so over my head it's not even funny.

The sound of Carter's small voice shakes loose the thoughts spinning around my head. "A volcano can t-t-t—"

"Trigger," the tutor offers.

"Trigger floo—"

"That's a tricky one because of the double o. You're going to pronounce it like the 'uh' sound in the word umbrella."

"Okay." Carter is nodding his head. "A volcano can trigger fl-floods, mudslides, r-rockfalls and...and... t-t-tuna—what's that word?"

"Tsunamis."

"And tsunamis."

I'm stunned. This is the first time I've heard him read anything that wasn't written by Dr. Seuss. Carter is a smart kid but since school started he's been struggling to keep up with the other first graders in his class. I've already met with his teacher twice and the last time she even broached the possibility of moving him to a remedial class.

"Great job, Carter. Can you try the next sentence?" she asks gently. Her hair is pulled back into a long, dark braid that falls a few inches past her shoulders. She has one leg bent up under the other and I notice that beneath the simple black

4

dress she's got on, she's wearing leggings colored with swirling stars and planets. Huh.

"Sure," Carter says and finds his place on the page. "There are more th-than 500 a-ac—"

"Active."

"Active volcanos in the world."

When he finishes the sentence, I put my fingers up to my mouth and blow out a shrill whistle. "Awesome job, my man!"

He lifts his head and throws up a maniac gap-toothed smile. "Bash! I'm reading my science worksheet!"

"I see that. And, hey, sorry I'm late," I say. This is the moment the teacher turns around and I realize that it's not a teacher helping him. It's Amelia Bright.

I freeze.

It's not that I've got a problem with Amelia or that I even really know her beyond her face and reputation at school for being rich and a brain. Just seeing her here, ten feet away from me, is unexpected.

Surprise is written all over her face as well. "Sebastian?"

No one has called me that in years. Sometime during fourth grade Sebastian disappeared and Bash took his place. I have to remind myself that the fourth grade was probably the last time Amelia and I spoke.

"What are you doing here, Amelia?" It comes out gruffer than I intend.

She blinks several times. "I volunteer at the elementary school twice a week to tutor kids who need a little extra help with reading. And, um, what about you?"

"I'm here for Carter."

"Oh." I can practically see her doing the math. I'm eighteen and Carter is just about to turn seven so that would make him my...

"He's my brother," I say in answer to her unasked question.

"Oh right." She swallows hard. "Mrs. Hopkins told me his guardian was running late."

"That would be me." I raise my hand.

Confusion flashes in her light brown eyes. "But you said you were his brother."

The last thing I feel like doing after this for-shit day is explaining the situation to Amelia Bright. There's no way that someone like her could ever understand what Carter and I have been through. We might live in the same town and go to the same school, but Amelia and her sister, Daphne, and all of their uppity, porcelain doll friends live on a different planet than we do.

This girl doesn't have the first clue about hard work or real life. She doesn't know how quickly everything you cherish can burn and crumble to nothing but ash.

I cross my arms over my chest and pointedly turn my attention to my brother. "Come on and get your stuff, bud."

But Carter is more generous than I am. As he's slinging his black backpack across his shoulders and reaching for his lunchbox, he tells Amelia, "I live with Bash. He takes care of me."

"I don't understand."

"What don't you understand?" I ask her. "It's not that complicated."

Amelia studies me with a strange look on her face. "You raise your brother?"

For someone who is supposed to be smart, she's being a little a slow on the uptake.

"Yeah."

"But how?"

I shake my head, evading the question, and reach for Carter's hand. "You ready to get out of here?"

Amelia doesn't get that I'm ignoring her or maybe she doesn't care. She stands from the chair and pushes, "How do you raise your brother and go to school?"

Now I'm on the verge of being pissed off. I want to ask her why she thinks this is any of her business, but I remember the way Carter was reading about volcanoes a minute ago and I keep the acidic words trapped in my mouth.

"What about your grades?" she continues, her voice ticking upward. "And what about college next year?"

Jesus, why won't she let this drop?

"I'm already so overwhelmed with everything that they're expecting of us senior year," she's telling me like I care. "I can't imagine."

That's it. That last comment is what does it for me.

"Of course you can't imagine it. You're Miss Perfect, existing in a perfect world where people live in five-bedroom mansions and drive around Green Cove in cars paid for by Daddy. You probably spend your nights on a featherbed dreaming about unicorns and lollipops. I know this is hard for you to believe, but some of us dream about how we're going to scrounge up enough money to pay the electric bill."

Amelia's jaw drops open. "I'm sorry. I didn't mean—"

But I'm not done. "Thank's for helping Carter with his reading," I say snidely. "He sounds great and I'm sure I owe that to you, but don't think that makes it okay for you to look down your nose at us."

"I-I don't... I'm not looking down on you."

Carter makes a sound of protest but I tighten my grip on his hand and pull him toward the door. We don't need this bullshit.

Behind us, Amelia calls out another pathetic apology.

In a steely voice, I send a parting shot over my shoulder. "Just so you know—some things are a lot more important than grades and college."

CHAPTER TWO

Amelia

Daddy likes to say that big decisions all come down to what your gut tells you when everything is on the line.

I prefer to base my life choices on facts, which is why I'm currently sitting in the middle of the bed with my computer balanced on my knees, toggling between school websites and tallying up pros and cons in a spiral notebook. So far, in terms of checkmarks in the pro column, Emory is in the lead and College of Charleston is second. But a quick assessment of my list tells me that Vanderbilt and Wake Forest aren't far behind.

Eyes still on the screen, I reach into the half-eaten bag of Red Vines that's resting against my thigh and fish out a piece of the sugary licorice.

"What are you doing?"

I'm so absorbed in the list that I don't hear her right away.

"Amelia!"

My attention is yanked away from the screen and I see my sister at the edge of my bed, jiggling a little on her toes and flouncing her arms awkwardly like a bird about to take flight. It takes me a second to figure out that she's drying her nail polish.

"Um, hello?" I say, gesturing to the door. No matter how often I ask her to knock, Daphne lives by the *what's yours is mine* mentality. She thinks because we're twins and share genetic code, she has 24-7 access to my room. And to me. "Maybe you've heard of this custom we have called knocking?"

"I asked what you're doing," she repeats, ignoring everything I've just said.

"Oh, the usual. Just trying to plan out the rest of my life. And I know that figuring out which college has a better teacher to student ratio isn't quite as important as researching where to find the biggest yarn ball in America, but we all have to have aspirations."

Daphne hops onto my bed, careful not to brush her nails against the pale floral comforter. She points to the bag of candy and snaps her teeth to let me know she wants a piece. "For your information, the biggest yarn ball isn't even on my list."

"A major oversight," I scoff as I dig out another Red Vine and stick it into her waiting mouth.

Unlike me, my sister hasn't shown a lot of interest in planning for school next year. She'd rather devote all of her brain power to mapping out the road trip she wants to take next summer to get our best friend, Audra, out to California for school.

"What does it say to you that I'm working on a list of colleges and you're working on a list of the wackiest sites in the country?"

"That I'm a lot more fun than you?" she asks as she chews.

I do a yes-no head shake. "Or that you're going to wind up spending your days in a bathrobe and slippers and living on my couch when we're thirty."

"Whatever. You can judge me all you want *if* you do me a big favor."

I raise an eyebrow in suspicion. "What kind of favor?"

"An easy one."

As if I haven't heard that one before. "Like…?"

"Can I borrow your purple dress for tomorrow night?"

I let go of a gusty sigh. "Which one?"

Daphne lifts a hand. "Wait. You have more than one

9

purple dress? Why do I not know this?"

I shrug my shoulders. "I like purple."

She laughs. "I was thinking of the Tory Burch, but I'll take whichever dress is the shortest."

"Daphne!" I scold though I'm not really surprised. Modesty is not really Daphne's thing.

"What?" she feigns innocence. "We were blessed with great legs, Amelia. Just because you've chosen to cover them up with leggings every day—"

"Not *every* day."

"—and socks and God knows what else, doesn't mean that I have to. And, anyway, when I tell you what's happening tomorrow night, you'll understand completely."

I moan but take the bait. "What's happening tomorrow night?"

"Are you sitting down?"

I make a point of looking around my bed. "What kind of question is that? I've been sitting down since you barged into my room."

"Gah, Amelia! It's just an expression," she says, rolling her eyes. "You know Spencer?"

"Spencer McGovern?" A quiver of unease ripples through me as she nods enthusiastically.

"He finally asked me out!"

"And I'm guessing the smile on your face means that you said yes?"

"Are you being for real right now? Of course I said yes. I mean... hellooo?" She shakes her head. "I've been working on him since sophomore year. He's muscly and beautiful. Maybe the most beautiful boy I've ever seen."

This is probably true. With his sculpted features, movie-star smile, and bronze sun-god hair, Spencer McGovern is certainly beautiful. He's also abrasive, self-important, and incredibly rude.

"I don't care how beautiful he is, I wouldn't go out with

him."

Daphne shifts back, her posture going defensive. "Why not?"

"I don't know exactly," I answer honestly. I have nothing concrete against Spencer, I just know that I don't particularly like him. "I had bio with him last year and he was always making obscene gestures behind Mr. Arvesu's back and copying off Andi Wilson. And don't you remember when he shot Maya Schneider's cat with a BB gun when we were in seventh grade?"

"We were twelve and that was an accident!"

"Says who? Spencer?" I retort.

"The cat was in his trash. And, *really*, those are his big offenses?" she asks, tightening her gaze. "Not paying enough attention in biology class and mistaking someone's cat for a rabid raccoon?"

"I don't know, it's more than that. He just seems like the kind of guy who doesn't care about anyone but himself."

Daphne exhales loudly. "Amelia, he's eighteen and just because he's not joining up with Habitat for Humanity doesn't mean that he's not good for a few dates. Can you get out of your head for a sec and try to understand what a big deal this is for me? I was just asked out by arguably the most amazing guy at our school. Just this once, can't you be happy for me?"

"I'm always happy for you."

She frowns and shakes her head. "That's a lie."

"Name another time when I wasn't happy for you," I challenge.

Daphne looks back to me and raises both eyebrows. "Are you kidding? Try every time I mention the road trip with Audra next summer. Or heck, whenever I go out of the house on a school night."

This feels like a familiar argument. The same one we've been having our entire lives.

11

"It's not like I don't want you to have fun," I explain. "I just worry you're not directing your energy in the right place."

"And what about the time I learned to cut hair? You weren't happy for me then."

"That's because you learned on a doll."

"So?"

"It was *my* doll."

Daphne fights a smile. "She looked better with a pixie cut."

"That doll was a limited edition."

"So was the pixie cut."

I can't help it, I laugh.

Daphne grins wryly and scoots off the bed. Her nails must be dry because she grabs ahold of my wrist and pulls me to my feet. When we're eye to eye, she says, "I know you're just doing the protective twin sister move, but in this case I don't think it's necessary. Spencer is a good guy. Daddy and Nancy even know his parents from the Club."

"Well, if they approve it must be love," I snark.

"Amelia, don't be so ornery just because you and Jack didn't work out."

I dart a quick glance at my bedroom door. "Shh!"

She squints and purses her lips in disapproval. "You still haven't told them that you broke up with Jack?"

"No, I did, but let me tell you, they were not happy campers," I whisper to my sister. "I'm still expecting them to try to sign us up for some sort of couple's counseling."

She chuckles because she knows I'm only partly joking. "Trust me, they'll get over it. You only started dating him this summer so they haven't had enough time to get too attached."

I shrug helplessly. "I'm not so sure about that. When Daddy found out Jack's golf handicap was below ten, he was happier than a tornado in a trailer park. And I swear that I caught Nancy browsing floral arrangements on a bridal site last week."

"I could always talk to them and smooth things over for you."

"Could you really?"

Daphne playfully elbows me in the side. "*If* you let me borrow a dress."

"You've resorted to blackmail?"

She cracks a smile. "If that's what it takes."

Begrudgingly, I stalk over to the closet and fling open the door. "Okay," I say, plucking the hangers from the rack, "in the purple dress category, you've got three options."

Daphne quickly dismisses the striped maxi dress I'm holding in my left hand. She takes longer deciding between an A-line Tory Burch and a floral shift.

"That one." She indicates the A-line dress. "The other one looks too churchy."

I hand it over. "Considering the last time I wore that dress was to church, I suppose that's not such a terrible thing."

Laughter bubbles from her mouth as she holds the dress up in front of her body and turns to the full-length mirror beside my dresser.

Watching my sister, I inhale deeply and shake my head. I know it sounds like a cliché, but she really is the pretty twin and that's the hand-to-God truth. Daphne and I might have the same building blocks—slim frames, sloped noses, matching dark brown hair so straight and shiny it slides right out of a ponytail holder, and almond-shaped brown eyes passed on from our father's side of the family—but on her it all fits together differently. People call me *cute*, maybe *charming*. But Daphne, I know, is beautiful.

"That dress is going to look great on you," I tell her truthfully.

"Do you think it will go with those strappy platforms Nancy got me last month?"

"I think so. Very preppy chic." I take a breath and say as

gently as possible, "Just promise me that you'll be careful with Spencer. Maybe I am being over-protective, but I don't want you to get hurt."

Her eyes find mine in the mirror. "Okay, Mommy Dearest."

"I'm serious," I tell her, my voice thin. "Boys are…" Boys are what? I'm not sure what I'm trying to explain. "Boys are a lot of work."

"Is that why you broke it off with Jack? Because he was too much work?"

"Not exactly." The thing about Jack was that on paper he was everything a proper boyfriend should be. Attractive. Attentive. Driven. Sounds like the perfect southern gentleman, right? Except for the part where he was so boring I had to make sure to guzzle a bunch of caffeine before our dates so I wouldn't fall asleep. "Jack was nice, but I've got school to think about. I didn't want to spend my senior year distracted by some boy."

"Amelia, that is the worst excuse I've ever heard. You shouldn't break up with someone to focus on school."

"What about this? Kissing him was kind of like kissing a cricket frog, and I don't mean one that magically turns into a prince."

Daphne spins toward me and screws her face up. "That is nasty."

"*And* he didn't like that I could beat him in tennis. He threw a hissy fit the last time we were on the courts."

"Well now, that's just stupid."

"Tell me about it."

Her eyebrows draw together. "You know, maybe you being single and me finding Spencer could be the start of something new for us."

"Like what? You getting to be Daddy's favorite?"

"Pshhh, bless your heart. Don't you know that I've always been his favorite?"

14

I laugh. "Then what?"

Daphne smiles. "The way I see it, this is our last year in Green Cove together. In the autumn you'll be off to whatever amazing school you decide on and I'm—well, I'm not sure where I'll be yet—somewhere outside of South Carolina on an adventure. But that's not the point. The point is that I don't want either of us have any regrets about senior year."

"What are you implying that I'm going to regret?"

"Being so serious all the time. No one gets old and looks back on high school and says, 'I'm so happy I got such good sleep and turned that essay in on time.' Do you know what I mean? You need to loosen those reins you hold so tightly and live it up."

"I don't want to live it up. All I want is to get an A in AP history."

She points to the bed where my computer screen is still displaying the Emory website. "But you already know you're going to get into any of the schools you want."

"Acceptance is contingent on my grades this year," I remind her.

Daphne groans. "Amelia, there's more to life than grades."

I'm about to shoot back with something sarcastic when my brain gets stuck on something.

Those words. I've heard them before, haven't I?

Suddenly, I'm in the elementary school cafeteria this afternoon and I'm watching Sebastian Holbrook reach for his brother's hand. I'm watching his dark hair graze his chin and his stormy grey eyes move over me. I'm seeing the disgust he can barely hide and registering the defiance that beats just beneath the surface of his skin like a pulse.

Some things are a lot more important than grades and college.

My throat burns and my heart twists painfully in my chest. I want to shout back at him that he has me all wrong. My world isn't perfect. I don't dream about unicorns. I barely sleep. And when I do, I dream about upcoming tests and projects I don't know how I'm going to have time to finish.

I want to yell back at him that almost every night I wake up sweaty and heavy with the weight of all the promises and expectations I'm carrying around.

Sebastian Holbrook thinks that I look down on him? Well, everything he threw at me today proves that it's the other way around.

Back in my bedroom, my sister takes my silence as agreement. She lifts her chin, swings the purple dress over her back and sashays to the door. "See? Amelia, this year is fixing to be the best ever. Don't waste it."

CHAPTER THREE

Bash

On a Friday night, a normal high school senior might be getting ready for a date or going to a football game with friends. But me? I'm at home trying not to burn a box of macaroni and cheese. I swear, I don't know what it was or when I did it, but at some point in this lifetime I must have screwed up and in turn, Karma made me her bitch. Hell, boxed pasta won't even turn out right for me.

I stare down at the charred mess, wondering where I went wrong. Did I add the cheese too soon or leave it on the stove too long? Or maybe I didn't use enough water?

A quick poke with a wooden spoon tells me that most of the noodles and cheese have hardened to the bottom of the pot. But with some effort and a little water, I'm able to scrape together enough for a small bowl.

"Dinner!" I call loud enough that Carter will be able to hear me over the sound of the TV.

I hear the TV click off and a few seconds later, my brother wanders into the kitchen with his nose pinched. His gaze zeroes in on the bowl I've set out for him.

"What's that?"

"It's dinner."

"But what is it?"

"It's macaroni and cheese. What does it look like?"

"Puke."

He's not wrong. Actually, he's probably being too nice. The gloppy orange stuff looks more like insect guts than pasta.

17

I dump the bowl into the sink and head for the tiny pantry. "I think we still have some peanut butter. Maybe even some jelly."

"I've got the bread," Carter chirps.

Then he climbs up onto the counter and we start to build the sandwiches like we're on an assembly line. Bread. Peanut butter. A smear of jelly.

"Can I have some milk?" he asks in between bites.

"Sure thing, hoss," I say, not wanting Carter to know that in my head I'm counting up how much every bite and every sip costs. I can't keep all the fears from him, but food is one thing I don't want him to have to worry about.

The first month we were on our own, I spent almost every minute panicking. Don't get me wrong—I still get that ragged, gnawing sensation in my gut when I think about how low we are on basic things like food and toilet paper and toothpaste, but I've learned to control the anxiety and squeeze every quarter tight. I remind myself that I get paid Tuesday and I'll be able to pay the water and electric bill and should have enough left over to stock up on groceries. Until then, I'll put a brave face on for my little brother and eat dirt myself if that's what it comes to.

I pour out the last of the milk and toss the empty container into the trash bin.

"Here you go, bud."

Carter takes a sip and immediately spits it out, showering me with white spray.

I throw my hands up and jump back. "What the—?"

His face scrunches up. "Gross!"

I pluck the container from the trash and check the date. Sure enough, the milk is expired.

"Sorry," I say, filling a new glass with tap water.

He greedily chugs it down to get rid of the sour milk taste. Then he uses his sleeve to wipe off his mouth. "It's okay."

But it's not okay and I know it. "Some supper I made,

18

huh?"

Carter tilts his head to one side. "It's better than the time we went to that Chinese restaurant over in Jefferson and Mama made me eat algae."

"It was a Japanese restaurant and it was seaweed," I say, laughing. "But, yeah, I remember. It was for her birthday."

He makes a kind of choking noise. "It tasted so bad."

"She was happy that you at least tried it."

"I had to. It was her birthday."

Her *last* birthday. Neither of us says it out loud but we don't have to. The thought reverberates in the air around us.

Carter is the first one to speak. "You want me to show you something?"

I can tell that he's trying to get the conversation away from our mother and right now I'm okay with that. "Sure."

He hops off the counter and goes over to where his backpack and lunchbox are piled on the floor next to my boots. He pulls out a book and brings it back over to show me.

"It's got chapters," he says, excitedly flipping through the pages so that I can see the chapter headings. "I told Amelia that I wanted to try a book with chapters and she brought this to school today. This one is all about different animals who live in a pet store."

For the past week and a half I've tried not to think about Amelia Bright. Looking back at the day we clashed, I figure that I was kind of a dick to her. Yes, she was being nosy, but her questions are the same ones I've fielded a hundred times. *How do you do it? Aren't you tired?*

I get it for sure. When you're in high school and you're raising your little brother, it's only natural for people to be curious.

So why in the hell did I lose it like that?

"Haa-ha-ahh-mmmm-ssstttt-er. Hamster," Carter reads, pointing to a word at the start of a chapter.

"Good job, hoss."

He beams at the approval. "Thanks! Amelia taught me how to stretch out my words. She told me that once I know how to do that I'll be able to read anything I put my mind to."

"She sounds right smart."

In response, Carter nods, but his eyes are on the book. He's slowly following his finger down the page. "Amelia's the smartest person I've ever met."

"Smarter than Mrs. Ruiz?" That's his teacher.

"Yep."

"Smarter than me?"

This one stumps Carter. He doesn't want to hurt my feelings, but it's obvious that he thinks Amelia is indeed smarter. "Well, you're a different-smart," he says diplomatically.

I laugh and ruffle his mop of brown hair. He's going to need another haircut soon. Another thing to add to my always-growing list. "It's after eight—about time for bed."

"But...!" he exclaims, nose still in the book. "Can't I at least finish this chapter?"

"How about this? If you go ahead and brush your teeth, you can read two more chapters in bed. Do we have a deal, bud?"

His grin stretches wide. "Deal!"

***

My fingers are pruny and I'm up to my elbows in soapy water when the doorbell rings.

"Goddamn it all," I mutter. Who rings the doorbell at this time of night when they know a kid is inside?

I grab a dishrag and dry my hands. Then I peek into Carter's room, hoping that the dumbass on the other side of the door didn't wake him up. Everything is good. Carter rolls over in his sleep and I see the blue blanket and big red teddy bear he likes to sleep with clutched tightly in his small hands. Relieved, I close his bedroom door and make my way down the hall to the front door.

Seth Cavanaugh is standing under the yellow porch light in loose jeans and a raggedy baseball cap.

"I've told you not to ring the doorbell at night," I greet him. "It's late and I don't want you waking Carter up."

"Shit, I forgot."

"Sometimes your brain doesn't work. What are you doing here anyway?"

"I didn't feel like going home yet," he says with a shrug.

"Well, I'm finishing up the dishes. C'mon in before we let all the AC out."

"Tonight Monica had some people over," he tells me as he follows me back to the kitchen. "You missed out on a good time."

"Oh yeah?" I don't really care about what I missed at Monica Yancey's house. I'm sure it was the same old crowd doing the same old thing that they're always doing: smoking weed and pretending to want real conversation until someone realizes there's nothing new to talk about in Green Cove and decides to power on the Xbox 360.

He rests his back against the kitchen counter. "Rachel was there."

"Is that so?"

"She asked me about you."

"Mmm."

"Hell, Bash. Don't you want to know what she said?"

Do I? "Not particularly."

Seth doesn't seem to care about my answer. "She's worried about you."

"And why would she be worried?"

"I'd say she's worried because you never go out anymore and because you've stopped talking to anyone but me."

21

"I stopped talking to Rachel because she slept with someone else," I remind him, my patience thinning.

"I get it. Just letting you know it's obvious to everyone who sees you, including me, that you're running on empty."

"I'm fine."

Still leaning against the counter, Seth reaches into his back pocket and pulls out a pack of cigarettes.

"Are you really?" he asks as he smacks the pack against the flat of his palm a couple of times and digs for a lighter. Before he can flick the flint wheel, I'm on him, driving him back to the front door.

"What's the problem?" he cries, scrambling to keep his balance.

"The problem," I say, shoving him beyond the threshold onto the porch, "is that you can't smoke in the house. Remember Carter, the little boy asleep in the next room? I don't want him sucking your second-hand smoke into his lungs and getting this scary little thing called cancer."

Seth doesn't say anything for a second. Then he plucks the cigarette from his mouth and grimaces. "Sorry. I wasn't thinking about—" he points toward the house, "—Carter or... you know."

He means my mother and the ovarian cancer that ate at her from the inside out. "No shit."

He breaks the cigarette in half and slips both parts back into his pocket before dropping onto the ratty wicker loveseat that's pressed up against the side of the house.

I ask, "Why are you smoking anyway?"

"I don't know. Raf said he could get me a carton on the cheap and I didn't want to say no. And I thought it might help with the whole musician bit I'm working on." He shrugs his shoulders. "They're pretty disgusting actually."

"And you're pretty stupid," I say.

"I cannot confirm nor deny that accusation."

The thing is that Seth has been my best friend since before

I could spell my own name. He lives just around the corner from here. He's the kind of guy who puts on a front that he's tough because that's what you have to do to make it sometimes. But on the inside I know he's nothing but softness.

When we were ten, a stray that'd been hanging around the neighborhood for a few months and prowling from house to house got run over. Seth cried about that cat for a week until my mother couldn't take it anymore and went down to the shelter and returned with an orange tabby that Seth named Jinx.

Already, Jinx is on the porch. When she sees Seth, she makes a beeline to him and starts moving in and out of his legs. Next comes the purr, louder than a diesel engine that needs tuning.

"She must have heard you," I say, meaning the cat. "She never shows up for me unless she hears me dumping food into the bowl."

"Jinxy comes to me because she knows she's my best girl and I like to dote on her," Seth replies, picking Jinx up and setting her on his lap.

The purring grows louder.

"Cats," he continues, rubbing two fingers beneath Jinx's chin, "are intuitive creatures so you must give off a stay-away vibe. Kind of like the vibe you give to Rachel."

Flicking a gnat off my arm, I ignore the comment about my ex-girlfriend and slide into the chair opposite them.

Not a lot of people get to see Seth like this—relaxing on a porch with a cat curled up in his lap. But I know he only plays at being a hardass occasionally because he's had a hard life. Maybe even harder than my own.

Like mine, Seth's dad dropped out of the picture a long time ago. His older sister dances for cash at a nightclub near Savannah and his mom spends most of her time getting cozy with her best friend Jack Daniels. The way I see it, the only thing worse than having a mother who's dead, is having one who's still breathing, but cares more about a bottle of whiskey than she does about her own kids.

It probably wouldn't surprise most people if Seth turned into a loser with a record like a lot of the rednecks who grow up here in Lowcountry, but I know he's too smart for any real trouble. Sure, I've accused him of being as stupid as sin and, yeah, he just tried to light up a cigarette in my kitchen, but that's just us. Truth is, Seth's got plans and ideas about having a better life. A life that might take him outside of Green Cove. And if I were going to bet money on anyone making it out of this place, I'd bet on my best friend.

Seth plays the guitar. And I use the word play lightly. It's more like Seth lives the guitar. Tonight, it doesn't take long for him to give in and go into my room to grab the Ibanez he loaned me a couple years ago. That was back when I thought maybe I could learn to play and we could have a band together. Turns out, I'm tone deaf.

We hang on the front porch for a while—him fiddling with the guitar strings, me listening. Then, just before midnight, a white van pulls up to the curb and its brakes are so loud and screechy that Jinx gets scared off.

Seth mutters an oath as he watches the cat dart away and disappear behind the brick pilings that hold up the house.

I look back to the van. It's the kind of generic white van with rust tingeing the bumper that has you thinking of a pervy kidnapper or a shady electrician. Very slowly, the side door slides open and Paul Abbot, my neighbor's son stumbles out. Right away, it's clear that he's three sheets to the wind. Shit, he's so far gone, he can barely keep his head from falling off his neck.

Paul graduated from Green Cove High last spring and since then, I doubt he's seen daylight more than a couple of times. As far as I can tell, he spends the majority of his time sleeping. It's funny because back when he was in school with us, Paul was a big guy—always laughing and lifting weights and working on his tan. Now, he looks pathetic—like a vampire who's been on a hunger strike for three months.

When Paul sees Seth and me outlined in the dim porch light, he pulls up short.

"Yo," he shouts into the dark like we're old friends. But I've never been "friends" with Paul. The entirety of our relationship can be summed up in one story: When he was twelve and I was eleven, he pinned me down in the strip of grass between our houses and shoved a dead lizard into my mouth.

"Hey Paul," I say back just to be neighborly. I'm not afraid of Paul like I was when I was a kid, but I still try to keep things pleasant. Sometimes his mom, Sandra, helps with Carter if I run into a problem with work or school.

Paul heads our way, holding his arms out from his sides to steady himself. When he gets to the porch steps, he has to use his hands and knees to crawl up them like a toddler.

"What's happenin' ya'll?" he slurs out the words and topples onto an open chair.

"Nothing much," I answer slowly. "How about you?"

"Oh—" he waves a hand vaguely "—I've got a couple deals in the pipeline. Just some details to work out and I'll be sittin' on a golden egg. Thinkin' about buyin' myself some sweet wheels when the dust settles. A porsche or maybe one of those Lexus coupes."

"Uh-huh," Seth murmurs doubtfully. "A couple of weeks ago your mom told us you got a job at Office Depot."

"Shit," he says, only it sounds more like *sheeeeet*. "Those fools wanted me to work Saturdays so I told the manager he could find himself another sucker." Then he lurches forward in the chair so suddenly that Seth and I both jump.

"You okay there?" I ask, hoping he's not about to throw up all over my porch.

Paul lifts his chin from his chest and tries to focus his

eyes. Almost like he didn't hear me, he says, "Either of y'all got a smoke?"

Seth rests the guitar between his knees, finds a cigarette, and passes it over.

"Thanks," Paul says, cupping his hand over his mouth as he tries to get the lighter to catch. "That deal I'm a workin' on... We've been lookin' for more guys and I might be able to cut ya'll in. Say, five hundred apiece."

"Who's we?" I ask.

He takes a drag and holds the smoke in his lungs. "Levi Palmerton."

For the first time since he started talking, I think he might be serious and this has me worried. Paul might not be a favorite person in the world, but I still don't want to hear about him being left for dead in some swampy ditch. But if he's really working with Levi Palmerton, there's a good chance of that happening.

Seth's forehead crinkles. "You're not really working with Levi, are you?"

"Sure I am. He's got a hookup with someone in Charleston who needs to unload a lot of product lickity-split. It's just a drop-off and I reckon that makes it easy money."

"It's not easy money if you wind up with two broken legs or dead," Seth says out loud what I'm thinking. "I hear that Levi's a hardcore dealer now and I'm guessing the people he works with are hardcore dealers too."

"Do I look like I'm three pickles shy of a quart?" Paul asks. "I've got myself some terms in this situation. Levi ain't gonna mess with me."

"Whatever you say, man. Just leave Bash and me out of it."

Paul laughs but because he's so far gone, it sounds more like a burble. "You like drivin' around in that piece of shit truck of yours?" he asks me.

"It's not so bad," I say, my eyes looking out to the Bronco

parked in the driveway. "It's rusty but it's got character."

Rolling his eyes, Paul turns his head toward Seth. "How 'bout you, Cavanaugh? You like not having enough money to take your girl out for dinner?"

"I don't have a girl."

This makes Paul laugh harder. "Maybe there's a reason for that," he grunts, hoisting himself up from the chair. Then he takes another long draw off the cigarette and just looks at us for a minute, his body swaying. "If y'all change your minds, you know where to find me."

We watch him go, waiting to see if he'll make it. When Paul gets to his own house without passing out on the sidewalk, Seth smiles crookedly and says, "And you think I'm a cooter?"

I close my eyes and rest my head against the porch rail and think about what Paul said. Easy money or not, I'll admit that it's tempting to take him up on the offer. Just once, I'd like to know how it feels not to worry about how to pay bills or find the money to feed Carter.

In my world, five hundred dollars is a hell of a lot of money. But is it enough to break a promise I made? A promise to always do the right thing for my brother?

"I want to make something of myself and get out of Green Cove as much as everyone else," Seth says, and I hear him adjust the guitar and run his thumb over the strings. "Just not like that."

CHAPTER FOUR

Amelia

So, now I have a problem.

Until two weeks ago, I would have sworn that Sebastian Holbrook touched no part of my life. We don't have friends in common. Our lockers are not next door to each other. And we definitely do not move in the same circles.

Yet, all of a sudden, when I actually want to ignore him, he seems to be everywhere I look. Take, for instance, my Spanish class.

How the heck could I have missed him before?

Is it because he always chooses a desk in the way back and I tend to gravitate toward the front? Or is it because he never seems to raise his hand or participate in the class discussions? No matter what the reason, now that I know he's here, I can't *not* notice him. Trust me—I have tried.

Today, the normally straight rows of desks are in a hodgepodge because the class has split into pairs to conjugate verbs into the past tense. Audra is next to me diligently working to conjugate the -er verbs on our shared list. I'm responsible for the verbs that end in -ir, but I've spent more of the period trying to decode the words inked onto the soles of his sneakers. So far, I've only been able to make out three words.

All your tomorrows

I can't read anything beyond that and it's driving me crazy. I want to go over there, pick his foot up, and demand, "All your tomorrows *what?*"

The sound of Audra's voice snaps my concentration. "Just

remember to pay attention to venir."

"Huh?"

Her blond head is down and she's pointing out one of the verbs on our list. "I'm just remindin' you that venir has an irregular conjugation."

"I know it does."

She glances over and frowns when she sees my mostly blank paper. "Amelia, are you even goin' to do this?"

"Of course I am," I answer tersely, moving my arm so that it's partially blocking her view. "I'm just thinking."

She looks up at my face for a few beats before turning back to her own desk. "Uh-huh."

"What's that supposed to mean?"

The only answer I get comes in the form of an eye roll. *Okay then.*

I clear my throat and attempt to refocus on the assignment, but I can't seem to organize my scattered thoughts. Normally this is the kind of task I could hammer out in ten minutes flat, but today it's like nothing will stick to my brain for more than a second or two. All I'm really doing is wasting time by reading the same word over and over again.

This is seriously no use.

Feeling annoyed and exhausted with it all, I drop my pen and let my eyes wander around the classroom again. Sebastian, I note, is still working on his paper. He's hunched over the desk with his long legs hooked over the rung of his chair and an elbow propped on the corner. Every now and then he pauses in his writing to stretch out the fingers of his hand or push a tumble of black-brown hair off his forehead.

Nancy, with her love for monograms and all things Lilly Pulitzer, would probably label him a miscreant or one of the Methamphetamine Army (her words, not mine). But—I don't know—I think the scruffy jawline and untidy hair curling into his eyes complete the whole I-couldn't-care-less thing he has going on.

I study his wrinkled graphic t-shirt and jeans, faded and worn well past the point of no return. On another boy, those clothes might seem messy, like they'd been slept in or snagged from a pile of stinky laundry. But on Sebastian, they work. And it's not just because he's got a tall, rangy build and broad shoulders. Or because his angular cheekbones and wide-set grey eyes are admittedly fairly gorgeous. It's because there's something unconventional and intriguing about his eclectic mix of country and hipster. He gives off the impression that he'd be just as at home in New York City as he is in Green Cove, South Carolina. And it's like the more I look at Sebastian, the more I *want* to look. God, it's a vicious kind of rabbit hole to fall into.

As soon as I think the last thought, I feel a sharp splintery pain radiate from the sensitive skin just above my elbow.

I whip my head around and glare at Audra. "Owwww! You pinched me!"

She points a manicured finger at me. "Because you're supposed to be workin' on Spanish, not havin' some kind of psycho stare-fest."

"What are you talking about? I am not—"

"¿Amelia, estas bien?"

The question startles me into silence. I look up and see that everyone in the room, including Mr. Gubera, is watching me expectantly.

"¿Estas bien?" he repeats.

Heat floods my cheeks. "Yes, I—uh—bit my tongue."

"En español," he encourages.

I swallow and search the recesses of my head for the right words. "Me mordio la l-lengua."

He smiles. "You just told me that someone else bit your tongue."

Soft laughter fills the room and I want to die. Why oh why did I let Audra talk me into another year of Spanish? I should have switched over to French to finish out my language requirement. Or German even. I'm sure I could *spreche* some *Deutsch.*

"Umm… me mordi la lengua," I try again.

"Excelente," he says, clapping his hands once. Then, like he'd planned it all along, he turns to the whiteboard and picks up a black dry erase marker. "This is probably a fine spot for us to stop and review what you've been working on. I know that using the preterite conjugation can be confusing, but be careful because, as Amelia just demonstrated, one slip-up can change the entire meaning of a sentence."

Oh, good gravy.

***

"I guess I should be askin' you the obvious question," Audra says just after the bell rings. I slip my notebook into my bag and stand up from my desk. "What's that?"

"Am I losin' my ever-lovin' mind or do you have a thing for Bash Holbrook?"

Something warm and fluttery nips at my stomach. "You're definitely losing your mind."

"Am I?" she drawls as we walk into the hall. "Because you spent almost all of Spanish class starin' at him."

"I wasn't staring."

"Then what would you call it?"

"I wouldn't call it anything because it was nothing."

"That was not nothin'. You were starin' at him so hard, I'm surprised there wasn't a puddle of drool on the floor beneath your desk."

"Shut up."

She grins. "Or that the strength of your eyes didn't knock him straight out of his chair."

"Shut up," I say again, but now I'm laughing.

Audra shakes her hair back reminding me that she has

about the best hair I've ever seen. It's long and blond and full of these shampoo-commercial waves that catch the light and look an awful lot like spun gold. Most girls at our school would make a deal with the devil for that kind of hair.

She says, "I can see the headline now: Amelia Bright, Local Debutante and Student Council Treasurer, Takes a Ride on the Dark Side with Bad Boy Bash Holbrook."

I stop in front of my locker. "That's way too long to be a headline."

"Who knows," she muses, "maybe you can get him to take you to Homecomin'. I bet he would be downright yummy in a suit."

I snort. "Yeah right. You are delusional."

"Speakin' of the dance..." She cocks her hip to one side. "You remember Sasha Bartley and I went to that party over in Montclair last weekend?"

"Uh-huh."

"Well, I happened to meet a boy who goes to Middleburg High and I had a feelin' about him."

"And what did that feeling tell you?"

"That I should set y'all up."

I shake my head. "You are not setting me up for Homecoming with some stranger that you met at a party."

"Why not? Because you really *are* interested in Bash Holbrook?"

"Gah, can you please stop yapping about this before someone hears you?"

"Hears what?" Daphne asks, suddenly appearing between us. There's a football game tonight so she's tricked out in her black and gold cheerleader attire, complete with ribbons around her ponytail and a temporary tattoo of a paw print on her right cheek.

"Our girl here is sweet on Bash Holbrook," Audra fills her in with a smile so huge that I can count all of her teeth.

My sister looks ready to keel over. She actually presses a

32

hand into her chest like she's on the verge of a heart attack. "Oh-em-gee—*what?*"

I'm simultaneously wrestling with the release on my lock and shaking my head. "This is exactly how rumors start," I warn them. "I do not like him."

"Could have fooled me," Audra says.

Daphne is grinning goofily. She nudges my shin with the toe of her sneaker and says, "Bash Holbrook? This is so unlike you. I'm impressed."

"You're impressed because I'm unlike myself?" I bristle. "Thanks a lot, Daphne."

"I'm just saying that this is exactly what I've been talking about. You *should* be taking more chances."

"Take all the chances you want," Audra puts in with a sardonic giggle. "Just use protection."

"Trust me, protection is not necessary."

She wrinkles her nose at me. "It is if you know what's good for you."

Daphne laughs. I groan.

"If you two must know the truth," I say rigidly, "I don't like him in the way that you're thinking I like him. I'm simply curious about him."

"*Curious?* Hmm… Is that what the kids are callin' it these days?" Audra jokes.

"Yes," I insist as I shove my Spanish book onto one of the metal shelves and slam the door of my locker closed. This is definitely not the time to confess to my sister and best friend that last week I attempted to stalk Sebastian online but was thwarted by a vague and mostly locked-down profile. The main picture didn't even give me any clues about him; it was just an elongated shadow on a graffiti wall. Cool and kind of artsy, but not exactly a treasure trove of valuable information.

"So," I say, sighing as I turn around and put my back to the locker. "You know how I've been volunteering at the elementary school on Mondays and Wednesdays?"

33

They nod in unison.

"I've been working with Sebastian's little brother."

Daphne's expression wavers. "So, then, why didn't you mention it to us before?"

"Because it was no big deal."

"Yet now you're curious about him?" Audra concludes.

"Well, yes," I admit, feeling something tug inside of me. "Did you know that Sebastian is raising his little brother on his own? How does that work? When does he have time to study or hang out with his friends? And how do you think they support themselves? Do they have money or... I don't know... he must have a job, right?"

"I think he works down at Kane's," my sister offers.

"The hardware store?"

"Uh-huh. Spencer and I stopped there last weekend so he could pick up a refrigerator light bulb for his mom and Bash was behind the paint counter," she explains. "When we left, Spencer mentioned that he probably works there just so he has access to the cans of spray paint."

I shake my head in confusion. "Why would he want spray paint?"

Daphne leans in and confides, "You know, for huffing. That's how they do it."

"He's not like that," I assure her.

"And how do you know what he's like?" Audra asks with one eyebrow raised. "He missed almost *three* months of school last year. Rumor has it that he was expelled for cheatin' and callin' Mrs. Gardner an asshole. It was supposed to be permanent, but the administration ended up lettin' him back in on a technicality.

"I heard he was gone because he got himself into big trouble with the police and was serving time in juvy," Daphne says.

"Juvy? Really, Daphne? I think you've both been drinking a little too much of the Green Cove Kool-aid. Sebastian's just not that way." I don't really know why I'm so quick to defend him. The last time he spoke to me, he practically chewed my head off and spit it out.

She shrugs. "Maybe you want to believe that because he's hot."

"Him being hot has nothing to do with it."

"So you admit it?"

"Admit what?"

My sister's smile goes nuclear. "That you think Bash Holbrook is hot"

"That's not what I said." Flustered, I drop my head and swallow. "If you could have seen the way he was with his little brother, you'd know that there's no way he's into drugs."

"Maybe," Audra says after a pause. "But I still think you're crushin' on him somethin' serious. It's actually kind of adorable. Amelia and Bash sittin' in a tree—"

"Oh, good God," I begin, searching for a way out of this conversation. "You two are off your rockers and I'd love to hang around and hear more of your crazy, but I've got to go or I'll be late to class."

As I zip up my bag and throw the strap over my shoulder, Daphne reminds me that I'm driving her home after school because she'll have a couple hours to waste before the game. Without a word, I nod to her and dash down the hall, weaving in and out of the students moving to and from class. Along the way, I get a lot of smiles and friendly waves, but mostly people wanting something from me. Like Kara Hartman, who needs my approval on some form for the Homecoming committee and Brayden Wright, who goes into a rant about being out of shape from the summer and struggling to maintain strength in his backhand. What it comes down to is that he wants me to organize a voluntary practice schedule for the tennis team.

Fine, I tell him and rush off.

35

I'll get right on that. You know, after I study for next week's big calculus test and finish the essay for my Emory application and send out the requests for the senior class trip and double check to make sure that the Homecoming deejay knows that he's not supposed to play anything by One Direction and confirm that Mr. Brickler has the money student council collected for flood relief.

It's not until I've climbed two sets of stairs and reached D-hall that I finally slow down to catch my breath and realize that in my haste, I stowed my Spanish book in my locker but I never took my history book out.

"Crap on a cracker," I mutter. Of course, I could just leave it, but I know Mrs. Turner. That woman is a stickler for the rules and she's been known to mark off points for students who are unprepared for class. I'm left with two choices: being lost all hour and risk losing points for not having my book with me, or risk losing points for being late.

Decision made, I turn on my heels, bulldoze through the stairwell door and slam right into the person who is coming up the steps. There's a muffled *umph* sound and a stack of books crashes to the ground.

"I'm so sorry!" Breathless, I drop to my knees to help gather up the fallen items.

"It's okay," a deep voice says. "I got it."

I stop mid-reach and lift my face a long, long way up.

Even though I'm still a little dazed, the sight of Sebastian Holbrook's steely eyes looking back causes my heart to spasm inside my chest.

"Hey," he says.

"Hey," I gasp, awkwardly unsticking the strands of hair that are caught on my orange blossom lip gloss. My face is so hot that I can feel the tickle of heat stretching to the back of my neck.

Sebastian picks up the last of his books and stands from a crouched position. As he holds out one hand it occurs to me that even though I've just bodychecked him and sent his stuff flying all over the stairwell, he doesn't seem nearly as grumpy as the last time we interacted.

With my pulse going in overdrive, I repeat my apology and take his hand. Is it weird that I notice how warm and rough his skin is against my own? "I'm sorry. I swear I'm not usually so clumsy."

"I don't know about that," he says, gently releasing his grip. Even though I'm up on both feet, I still barely reach up to his shoulders. "In class you bit your tongue and now this. You should probably be encased in body armor to be on the safe side."

It takes me a second to understand that he's only joking around. "Oh—" I manage a small laugh as I press myself against the wall of the stairwell for balance. "I guess I left my suit of armor at home today."

He glances in the direction I was running. "So where's the fire, Amelia Bright? Or are you hauling butt because you're afraid of missing out on an extra credit opportunity?"

"I forgot my history book back in my locker and now I don't think I can make it even if I run. Mrs. Turner is probably going to take away points from my grade."

"AP American History, right? You're lucky I haven't been to my locker all morning because now you can borrow mine," he says, holding out a familiar-looking book.

I raise an eyebrow. "You take AP History?"

"First period with Turner. Shocking they let in the riff-raff, huh?"

If it's possible, my blush grows even fiercer. "I didn't mean it like that."

"I know you didn't. Shit, that was a really bad joke. The thing is..." He blows out a gush of air and blinks away for a second, almost as if he's nervous. "You've done some kind of job with Carter and instead of thanking you the other day, I acted like a jackass."

"No, you were just—"

"A right jackass," he finishes for me, his grey eyes connecting with mine. "And you didn't deserve it."

I look away and shake my head. "You don't owe me anything if that's what this is about. I volunteer at the elementary school because I want to, not because I'm trying to get people to loan me their schoolbooks."

"Amelia," he says my name slowly like he wants me to pay attention to what he's about to say. "Stop arguing and just take it or you're going to be late."

My thoughts are in a messy tangle, but I'm able to manage a short nod. "Um, okay, thanks. But how will I get it back to you?"

For the first time, the corners of his lips curl upward. It's such a drastic change to his hardened face that my pulse picks up and my stomach does this wild flip flop.

"Don't worry," he says, backing away from me. "I'll find you."

And then, just like that, he's gone.

***

"What do you think about squirrels?" Daphne asks me as we step into the sunlight.

"Squirrels?"

"Yes," she answers, thumbing her phone screen. "Have you ever heard of an albino squirrel?"

"Ummm..." What is she talking about?

School got out a few minutes ago and Daphne and I have already visited our lockers and now we're cutting across the courtyard to get to the parking lot for the daily afterschool gridlock. I'm trying not to be obvious about it, but I'm definitely keeping an eye out for Sebastian.

I'll find you, he'd said. But that was hours ago and I haven't seen him since. I guess there goes my theory that he's suddenly everywhere.

Daphne shoves her phone in my face. "Look at this."

Distracted, my gaze flicks to the phone. "Nice."

"Nice? Amelia, what is your deal right now?" Her tone is indignant. "I just showed you the cutest creature I've ever seen and you called it *nice*. Look at that fluffy tail! That deserves more than nice."

I check the phone again. "Daphne, that looks like a white rat."

"I already told you it's an *albino* squirrel."

"So, basically a white rat," I respond, my voice dripping with sarcasm.

She taps the phone for emphasis. "This is not a white rat, okay? These little guys are sort of a big deal in Olney, Illinois."

"Uh-huh." I'm not sure where she's going with this.

"There are, like, laws preventing tourists from taking them out of the state and everything."

"Wow, that's really cool," I say in a perfect monotone.

"Whatever," she says, shaking her head. The black and gold ribbons that are holding her hair back ripple over her shoulders. "I'm adding Olney to my map as soon as I get home."

My sister has a map tacked up on a bulletin board in her room and whenever she finds a place she wants to visit on her ideal summer road trip, she marks it with one of those tiny post-it strips. At this point, the map is so covered in brightly colored paper it looks like a flattened piñata.

"Is this about earlier?" she asks, latching onto my arm and pulling me in the direction of our car.

I give her a sideways glance. "What do you mean?"

"The Bash Holbrook thing?"

"No, because I already told you and Audra that there is no thing."

"So you're saying that you don't want me to tell you that

he's waiting by the car or that he's looking directly at you?"

My breath hitches and I lift my head. Sure enough, Sebastian is there, leaning back against our silver Prius with both arms crossed over his chest.

When he sees me notice him, he straightens and I catch the faintest of smiles. In the bright afternoon light, his grey eyes look almost blue, and for a moment, I lose myself in them. Then I remember that he's probably just waiting for me to give him back his book and the whole scene reshapes itself in my head.

"I borrowed his history book today," I whisper to Daphne.

She only allows surprise to register on her face for a half a second. Then she squeezes my upper arm and says, "I'm going to go find Spencer for a quick minute while you go on over there and play pretty."

Panic turns my mouth dry. "Don't go."

"Why not? Are you scared?"

"Maybe," I admit.

"Well," Daphne reasons, "usually if you're scared of something, that's a sign that it's worth doing."

What kind of crazy logic is that? "I have no idea what I'm going to say to him."

"You're probably going to thank him for giving you the book."

"And then?"

She smiles and gives me a little shove. "The rest is up to you."

Great. I keep my head down as I dig into my bag and find the book. When I judge I'm a reasonable distance away, I pick up my gaze and force words out of my mouth. "Here's your book. And—uh—thank you so much. You were a lifesaver today."

"That means that you made it to class on time?" he asks, taking the book out of my hands.

40

"Just barely."

"And you learned everything there is to know about U.S. and Mexican relations during the 1830s?"

"Uh-huh." What I don't tell him is that I'll have to review the section tonight because I spent most of the history period flipping through his book, studying the tiny ink drawings he's made on the margins of the pages. "Seriously, I appreciate it. I hate being late and I hate not being ready for class."

The corners of his eyes crinkle. "I kind of picked up on that."

"Right," I say because I can't come up with anything else. Then we stand there just staring at each other and breathing and hovering. God, I wish I were better at this.

Finally, Sebastian tips his stubbly chin a little and says, "So, what I was saying earlier—about that day at the elementary school?"

"Uh-huh?"

He shifts his weight onto one foot, looking uncomfortable. One hand is holding the history book, but the other gets shoved into the pocket of his jeans. "I'm sorry, Amelia."

I shake my head dismissively. "Don't worry about it."

"But I do worry about it. Carter has come a long way and you didn't deserve the heap of shit I shoveled on you. I was having a bad day and I took it out on the wrong person."

"I get it."

"Do you?" The question scratches at something below the surface, something beyond what he's saying out loud.

Suddenly, I want to ask him about the drawings in his book and his little brother and the words he's written on his shoes.

I want to tell him I remember the second grade when he colored me a sympathy card the day I missed school for my grandfather's funeral.

And I want him to know that there are times I think of

41

our middle school trip to the Gibbes Museum in Charleston, and how all the other boys laughed and turned everything into jokes punctuated with farting noises. But I remember that *he* was the one who studied the paintings the most.

Yet, standing here on the sun-beaten asphalt of the school parking lot, I don't know how to say any of this. It's like the words are trapped somewhere between my brain and my mouth and before I can work it all out, Daphne is by my side in her cheer get-up and the moment is gone. I've missed my chance.

"I'll see you 'round, Amelia," Sebastian says as he stuffs the book into a messenger bag hanging from his shoulder. "You have a good weekend."

"Sure thing."

When he's out of earshot, Daphne comments, "At least you talked to him."

"Um, if you call stringing a few words together talking then I guess so." I groan and turn toward the driver's side of our car. "Daphne, I sounded like I fell out of the stupid tree and hit every single branch on the way down. It was completely miserable."

She puts her arm around my back and expertly plucks the car keys out of my right hand. "Nope. It was progress."

CHAPTER FIVE

Bash

Bash: **How is he?**

I send the text off to my Aunt Denise and wait with the phone in the palm of my hand even though there's a handwritten sign taped to the backside of the counter threatening employees not to use phones while at work. The hardware store is in a mid-afternoon lull and there's little chance of me getting caught because Ron, my boss, is in the back guzzling down a bottle of Tennessee whiskey like usual.

Denise: **Carter is fine. He's outside playing catch with Mike. We're taking him for cheeseburgers and a movie tonight and we'll see you tomorrow! Thanks for letting him stay over. You know we love having him.**

As I read her reply I let go of my breath. My brother is spending the weekend thirty miles south in Charleston with our aunt and uncle. Like always, I'm happy that he's having a good time but that doesn't stop me from feeling weird about it.

Playing catch with Mike.

When was the last time I played with him like that or was able to afford a trip to the movies? A sense of shame swells deep in my gut, but before I can examine it too closely, a big guy with tanned leather skin and grease stains on his baggy overalls approaches.

43

"Sir," I say, hiding the phone behind my back and putting on my customer face. "What can I help you with today?"

From his pocket he pulls out a glossy square of orangey-brown paper and sets it down face-up on the paint counter. "How do, son. I'm lookin' to cover about 2000 square feet of exterior with this color. Can you make me a deal if I buy the primer from you at the same time?"

I stow my phone and get to it. I don't have time right now to worry about what kind of job I'm doing raising Carter because it's time to mix up five gallons of Campfire Blaze. "Let me see what I can do."

***

"It's Saturday."

"So I've heard," I say, hefting a second box of hose fittings onto my shoulder.

"And Carter is in Charleston for the weekend." Seth follows me through the swinging black doors of the storeroom back onto the main floor. He's got a bag of chips in his hand and he's chewing them loudly.

"Again—I'm aware of this."

"So what I'm saying is that you don't have to be home tonight to watch him."

I stop halfway down aisle seven and squat to unload the boxes. "True enough."

Seth looks irritated that he has to spell this out for me. "Bash, let's go out and have some fun for a change. I think I can get us into The Tap Room."

"The Tap Room is a piece of shit biker bar."

"Okay then we'll go to Byron's house. Everyone is going to be there."

"Who's everyone?" I ask as I start scooping the hose fittings out and placing them into the right bins.

He stops chewing on the chips and swallows. "Sheyna,

Clay, Monica, Leo… and probably Rachel."

The thought of getting drunk or worse with a bunch of my former friends and my ex doesn't exactly thrill me. "You know I don't talk to them anymore."

"But I do," he says on an exhale. "And, for once, I want to see you acting like normal."

"I act normal."

"No you don't. All you do is work and worry and stress out about stuff that you can't make heads or tails of."

The last of the hose fittings is in place so I pick up the empty boxes and start toward the front of the store. "Seth, I hate to break this to you, but that is my normal now."

"I thought that with Carter gone you could have fun. Like the good ole days."

I don't get a chance to respond because the chime over the main door sounds, indicating that I've got a new customer.

I turn to the left and just about trip over my own feet because Amelia Bright is walking into the store. Today she's got on an olive green dress with loose, kind of hippie sleeves and yellow leggings covered in a geometric print. Not for the first time, I wonder what is up with this girl and leggings.

I exchange a quick glance with Seth, who looks about as bewildered as I feel, and then I rein it in, remembering that she's a customer.

"Hey," I say, shooting for casual as I set the boxes down so they are out of the way of foot traffic. "Welcome to Kane's."

"Um, hey," she says back.

It's strange. How many times have I watched Amelia Bright stand up in front of the entire school and give a speech or ask for donations for one of her causes or inform everyone about a new school policy? But right now she seems nervous as all get out. Her steps are hesitant and she's gripping the strap of her purse like she's passing through a

45

crowd of pickpockets.

A couple seconds pass like this, catapulting us past strange territory and into an awkward lull. Finally, I suck it up and ask, "Was there something I could help you with today?"

Amelia's eyes dart around the store. "Right. Paint. I'm here to get some paint for an accent wall in my bedroom."

"Well, you've come to the right place," Seth says and sweeps his arm to the side like a game show host to point out the paint chips.

His easy tone seems to loosen her up and she even rewards him with a small smile. For reasons I won't try to analyze right now, this irritates the hell out of me so when Amelia turns away, I give Seth a steady look.

What? he mouths back.

I shake my head and try to gesticulate a few choice words. He must take the hint because all of a sudden he acts like he's getting a text on his phone and he makes himself scarce as hen's teeth.

"What color are you picturing?" I ask, trailing behind Amelia.

"Ummm... Maybe white?" she says, chewing on her lip thoughtfully.

"A white accent wall?"

She pauses in front of the display and runs her fingers over the tops of the violet color cards. "Is that silly?"

"Nah, it's just usually people go with a brighter color when they're doing an accent wall. What color is your room now?"

"It's white."

I feel my eyebrows climbing my forehead.

"But it's a totally different shade than what I want to get today. I was thinking more like an off-white. Like a beige," she adds and I can't stop myself from chuckling.

"Whatever you think. You're the customer here."

Her mouth twists into a self-deprecating grimace and she says, "I'm not being very adventurous, am I?"

Shrugging, I tell her, "Everyone has different taste when it comes to home decorating. White is fine if that's what you want."

"Honestly, it might be time for something new; at least, that's what my sister would tell me. But there are so many options. I have no idea how to choose."

I move closer to the samples. "Let's try this: Why don't you describe to me what other colors are in your room? On the bed? Or maybe in the artwork on the walls?"

"Hmmm…" Amelia's eyes fall closed and she takes a deep breath. "My comforter is ivory and it's dotted with soft yellow and teal flowers. There are pale green leaves in the trim and on the pillows."

"Uh-huh," I encourage, selecting a couple of the paint chips.

"And I have a framed poster of a beach sunset above my desk and it has reds and yellows and blues and pastel pink and purple."

I pull a couple more colors then I fan the cards so that she can see. This time when she grins, it's for me. And damn it all if she doesn't have one dimple in the middle of her left cheek.

She delicately rubs her finger across one of the sample cards I've chosen. We're standing so close that I can smell her shampoo and the lotion she uses. I think it's something citrusy. Oranges or maybe lemons.

"Which one would you pick if it was your room?" she asks.

Trying not to think about that dimple or how good she smells, I study the colors and eventually settle on two options: a buttery yellow and a shade of turquoise. "How about one of these? I think both of these would work with whatever you've already got up on the other walls."

Now she goes back to biting her lip. "What are they called?"

I flip the cards over. "The yellow is called Daffodil and the blue is called Sky Magic."

"Sky magic." As she tries it out, the corners of her mouth curl up into a smile as warm as a Lowland summer. "That has to be the one. You can't help but love something called Sky Magic, can you?"

Before I know what's what, my chest is on fire and, like an idiot, I'm smiling back at her. "Definitely not."

***

"You should invite her to come with us tonight," Seth suggests.

From my position behind the paint station I look down the aisle to where Amelia is choosing a 2-inch angled brush and the plastic sheeting that I suggested.

"Why would I do that?"

"Because it's a party and that's what people do when there is a party happening."

"I haven't even said that I'll go with you in the first place."

"Fine by me. I'll go ahead and invite her myself."

With a final rumble, the paint-mixing machine clicks off and I use that as an excuse to sink down to my knees so that I can avoid Seth's gaze. Making an effort to keep my voice steady, I say, "You're not going to invite her."

"Why wouldn't I?"

"Seth, it's not happening so shut it," I warn as I carry the can over to a small rectangular workspace and use the paint key attached to the belt loop of my jeans to open the lid.

"If we invite her, she'll probably bring Audra Singer with her."

"So?"

"So? Audra Singer is fine. Did you get a look at those tight cut-offs she had on this week? She's like a country bumpkin with claws," he says with a smirk. "And have you seen Amelia's sister?"

48

"I have and I think she looks a lot like Amelia."

"They're twins and all, but Daphne is..." He makes a sound of deep appreciation. "She's smokin' hot in that cute little cheerleader uniform she wears around. And, Bash, this could be it. My in with her."

I shake my head. "You're not going to invite Amelia to go to a party because you're hoping it'll somehow land you a spot in her sister's pants."

"Why the hell not?"

"Because it's a shitty thing to do."

"See," he says, cocking his head to one side, "I think it's called thinking outside the box."

"It doesn't matter what you think," I reply, smearing a small strip of paint onto the lid of the can. "Because hanging out at Byron's house with a bunch of crusty rednecks who live on the east end of town is not the kind of thing Amelia Bright and her cheerleader sister or her best friend would ever waste their Saturday night doing."

"What about me?"

I crane my neck to the side and see that Amelia's standing at the counter next to Seth. Her arms are full of painting supplies. I want to laugh when I see that she's got a pack of latex gloves and three different sizes of painter's tape.

"Bash was just saying that you probably wouldn't be interested in going to Byron Scott's party with us tonight."

Her eyes narrow infinitesimally. "Why not?"

"He doesn't think it's your scene."

She looks from Seth to me and squares her shoulders. Aw, shit—this can't be good. I think I've offended her. Again.

"And why isn't it my scene? Let me guess," she says snippily, "I'm too preppy? Too big for my britches to be at a party?"

"That's not what I said."

"Or is it that I'm not enough of a hipster," she presses, "or a punk or whatever I need to be to make your list?"

"I didn't mean it that way," I explain as I grab a nearby rubber mallet to hammer the lid shut. "And there is no list. All I meant is that a party at Byron Scott's, where a bunch of idiots are going to be stupid drunk and will most likely wind up mudding through Westmoreland Field at three in the morning or setting off a shit-ton of fireworks, doesn't seem like your kind of thing."

"Then you might be surprised because Marcel Pruitt mentioned the party to me yesterday and I'm already planning on being there."

The ins and outs of the high school social caste system have long confused me, but this makes no sense at all. *Amelia Bright is going to Byron's party?* It's like finding out that LeBron James is going to be subbing for gym class.

"You're already going?" I ask, my voice leaden with skepticism.

She nods her head vigorously. "I am."

Seth asks, "Are you bringing Audra and your sister with you?"

"Oh, you can count on it," she tells him.

I say, "Then I imagine we'll see you there?"

"That's right—you will," she answers before turning away and striding swiftly toward the front of the store.

When she makes it halfway down the aisle, I stop her. "Amelia?"

She stops abruptly then looks back and lifts one eyebrow in a frank challenge. "Yes?"

Tamping down a smile, I hold the gallon of paint up to eye level and nod my head toward it. "You might want to take this with you. It'll make painting that accent wall a heck of a lot easier."

The blush that spreads from her forehead to her neck could probably power all of Green Cove. She can't even meet my eyes as she scuttles back to the paint station and snatches the gallon can from me. "Oh, right. Thank you."

50

"You're perfectly welcome."

Seth and I watch her struggle to balance and keep hold of all her items. I want to go offer to help her but I'm getting the distinct impression that trying to behave gentlemanly and help her to the front of the store is the last thing Amelia Bright wants right now.

At the cash register, she unceremoniously fumbles everything onto the black conveyer belt. Then she blows her brown hair out of her face and hands Lina, the cashier, a credit card. Not once does she look back at us.

Are you going to tell me what that was all about?" Seth asks meaningfully.

"Hell if I know."

"But I take it you're in for tonight."

Still watching Amelia, I hook my thumbs into my back pockets and nod my head. "I'm in."

CHAPTER SIX

Amelia

This was such a bad idea.

Country-pop is blaring from the sound system in twangy, stomach-churning thumps. The whole house reeks of a noxious mixture of liquor and what I'm guessing is weed. A string of blue and green Christmas lights tacked unevenly between the wall and the shoddy aluminum ceiling is the only source of light in here.

Crowded. Chaotic. Dark.

Despite the fact that I'm walking with my arms out in front of me, every few steps I bump into something new. This time it's some girl's leg. She lets out a howl and glares up at me from under the rim of a camo-print hat. She's got on a red halter, dusty cowboy boots on her feet, and a micro jean skirt that makes Daphne's sense of style look like it was developed in a nunnery.

"Sorry, I'm just trying to get back to my friends," I mumble, pressing my hand to the corner of a cheaply-made end table so that I don't topple over. What I should have said was, *What did you expect to happen when you decided to sit on the floor in the middle of a packed room?*

Basically, this party meets all of my criteria for a nightmarish situation. And the worst part is that I put on this kelly green low-cut blouse myself, piled on my favorite Kendra Scott jewelry, and came here willingly. To what? Prove a point? Well, the joke's on me because it doesn't look like Sebastian is even here.

At least my sister seems to be enjoying herself. She was

pleased as punch when I told her this afternoon that I wanted to go to a party and immediately started calling up everyone in her massive social sphere and telling them to meet us. And the minute we walked through the door, she grabbed three cups from some guy I'm positive she'd never seen before and shoved one in my face and handed another to Audra.

I tried to tell her I didn't want it but she insisted, swearing up and down that hard lemonade is good for the soul. Then Audra promised to only have one and be in charge of the keys and my fate was sealed.

Forty miserable minutes later, here I am, nursing the same drink, trying to avoid most conversation, and wishing I could spontaneously teleport to my bed. Or maybe even a bookstore. The new mystery I've been waiting on for the past four months came out earlier in the week and it's killing me to know that I could be snuggled up under my covers right now with that book but, instead, I'm at this awful party.

Lord, what was I thinking? Sebastian was absolutely right when he said this place wasn't going to be my scene. It's soooo not my scene.

I finally clear the rest of the obstacle course that is the living room and find Audra leaning against a wall.

"Where's Daphne?" I ask, trying to peer out into the darkness.

Audra points in the direction of the back porch. Through the window, I can just make out my sister sitting on top of Spencer McGovern's lap. He's wearing his football jersey and jeans, and to my total and utter disgust, there's a cigar hanging out of his mouth.

"Joy," I mutter. "I'm so glad that she invited him and all his football team friends to come out with us tonight."

"Okay, spill it," Audra says. "What on God's green earth has Spencer done to make you dislike him so much?"

"I don't know," I start, reluctant to put it into words. "Can't I just not like him?"

"Sure you can because I don't like him much either. It just doesn't seem like you is all and it has me thinkin' there's somethin' I don't know."

I shrug. "Let's just say that Spencer gives me the heebie jeebies. It's almost like he has an imbalance of neutrons or protons or something."

This gets a laugh out of her. "Amelia, did you just up and compare your sister's boyfriend to an unstable atom?"

"We're talking about radionuclides in chemistry and I guess I have them on the brain."

She shakes her head. "We're at a party—the first one you've attended all year I might add—and you're talkin' about chemistry."

"I'll stop."

She laughs some more. "Amelia, I don't think you can stop even if you want to and that's one reason I love you. Girl, if you hate the party as much as your face tells me you do, let's just hightail it out of here. Truth is, I'm not feelin' things either."

"We could go over that Homecoming action plan again," I suggest. "I promised Mr. Brickler that I'd turn it in on Monday."

"*Or* we could pop on over to Cacciatore's to pick up a large pizza with extra cheese and binge on Netflix and junk food for the rest of the night."

Half-laughing, I concede, "Your plan sounds better."

"Of course it does." Audra smiles. "Just think, I might even let you have a go at one of my Twizzlers."

"Or maybe I'll treat you to the superior candy. Red Vines."

"In your dreams, Sugartits."

Laughing, I look over my shoulder to where Daphne is now full-on making out with Spencer. *That was fast.* "As tempting as that sounds, we can't go just yet. Daphne is... in the middle of something. Or I guess I should say that her tongue is in the middle of something."

"Keep tellin' yourself that there has to be somethin' great about him if she likes him this much."

"Yeah, his pretty face."

"C'mon now, she is not that shallow."

"You do realize who we're talking about?" I ask on a laugh. "But you're probably right. Daphne is a lot of things but dumb isn't one of them, so maybe there's more to Spencer than what I'm seeing."

"Couldn't hurt to keep an open mind," Audra says, bobbing her head to the side. "And, speakin' of an open mind... Looky looky who just walked in."

From her teasing tone, I know it's going to be Sebastian Holbrook before I even turn my head. Still, I'm somehow surprised when my gaze skips across the dark room and crashes directly into his. Surprised and maybe a little terrified. It's a crazy feeling. All night I've been expecting to see him— waiting for it even—yet now that he's actually here, I have no idea what to do with myself or how to act.

"Wave him over here so that he can check you out in that hot-as-hell skirt. Maybe he'll be so blinded by the shape of your butt that he won't even notice you've paired a perfectly good outfit with those ridiculous leggings," Audra says.

My fizzy nerves snap. "What? I'm not going to wave at him or show him my skirt. He'll think I'm a lunatic."

Not having it, she grabs my hand and flaps it for me.

"Audra!"

She laughs as I flash an awkward smile at Sebastian then drop my face in embarrassment.

"It worked," she rasps in my ear. "He's definitely checkin' you out."

"You're imagining things."

"I'm not," she insists. "And, let me tell you, the boy's game is on fleek tonight. How have I not noticed those arm muscles before? Or that sexy mouth?"

55

"Audra."

"It's true. And, holy hell, I think… Yes!"

"What is it?"

"He's headin' over here," she whispers fervently.

"No." There's a quaver in my voice.

"He is!"

"He can't be."

"Obviously he can because it's happenin' right now, Amelia."

This time I take a peek from under my hair. Sure enough, Sebastian's eyes are on me and he's threading his way through the living room, squeezing past the drunken couples gyrating on the makeshift dance floor and stepping over a minefield of discarded red plastic cups. I'm not sure whether I want to throw up or cheer.

"Good luck," Audra coos as she dislodges herself from the wall.

I grab for her arm, desperate and suddenly way too hot. "Where do you think you're going?"

"To—um—see about the ladies' room," she says with a wry smile.

"You can't just leave me here!"

"Amelia, it's for your own good. I'll catch up to you later, okay?"

What can I say to that? It's not like I can keep my friend hostage because I'm afraid of what stupid thing I'll do without a chaperone present. "Fine," I mumble, reluctantly releasing the death grip I have on her forearm.

"You'll be all right," she assures me. "Just remember to breathe."

And then she's gone and I am left alone and exposed. Forget about breathing; it's like I can't even swallow. I've never felt so hot or inadequate in my life and… well, it sucks more than a little.

And why is he even coming over here? Doesn't Sebastian

have better things to do than watch me embarrass myself again? Or maybe that's exactly what he's after. Maybe he's developed a fondness for seeing me squirm.

Under the blue-green glow of the Christmas lights, Sebastian's features are blurry—almost like I'm looking at him through shallow water—but the closer he gets, the more solid he becomes. I start to make out the shine of his grey eyes, buffered beneath a fringe of black lashes, the shape of his jaw, and, of course, the downward curve of his lips.

When he's less than an arm's length from me, I straighten my spine and push my hair away from my eyes. *Battle stations at the ready.*

"Hey," he says casually, like we do this all of the time.

"Hey," I choke out. It's not much but considering it feels like my mouth fills with glue whenever I'm around him, it'll have to do.

"You came."

Aiming for cool and collected, I shrug one shoulder. "I told you I was going to be here, didn't I?"

Sebastian runs a hand through his messy hair as he warily surveys the party. "And are you having fun yet?"

"Totally. Best night ever." I lift my cup in a mock toast and make myself take a sip of the lukewarm liquid.

He watches me and his cheek muscle twitches like he's trying hard not to smile. "Yeah, I can tell. You look completely at ease."

"Uh-huh."

"It's in the way you're standing kind of like this," he teases, scrunching his shoulders up to his ears. "And how you seem to love that drink." He winces in what I assume is supposed to be an imitation of me. "You look pleased as a pig in shit, Amelia."

I'm not prepared for his dry sense of humor and I can't help but break into embarrassed laughter. "Ugh! You know, I was going to try really hard to be mad at you tonight after the way you made fun of me this afternoon."

"And how's that working out for you?"

"Not so well. And just so we're clear—*this*," I point to my cup, "tastes like lemon-flavored cough syrup."

"Sounds delicious." He claps his hands with faux excitement. "Can you please point me in the direction of the cough syrup bar?"

Despite all of my earlier tension, I laugh some more. "I think it's over there by Weedy Wallows," I say, gesturing toward the couch where a few of my classmates are now crowded around a guy who seems to be showing off the contents of a small plastic bag.

"Nice." Sebastian takes a step closer so that his mouth is only a couple of inches from my ear. "So, what else have I missed? Keg stands? Body shots? Has Monica Yancey started one of her strip teases yet?"

"What?" I sputter.

He pulls back to meet my eyes and I feel a tingle slide down the length of my spine. "If I remember correctly, it happens at every one of these things. By the fourth drink, she's taking off her shirt and flashing everyone."

"If you remember correctly?"

For a second, he just looks at me. Then he tilts his chin away. "I don't have a lot of time for this kind of thing anymore. I've got Carter to think about."

Right.

"So, where—" The moment the words slip out of my mouth I immediately wish I could press the rewind button. Sebastian has made it perfectly clear that his home life is none of my business, hasn't he?

"What?"

I shake my head. "Nevermind."

"Were you wondering where he is? Because he's staying with my aunt and uncle this weekend."

I want to ask him more about his aunt and uncle, but

Byron Scott, inexplicably dressed in nothing but a pair of plaid boxer shorts and a black pirate hat, runs into the living room and starts yelling, "Beer pong tournament in the barn! Five minutes!"

"A beer Pong tournament?"

"You'll see."

"Honestly, I'd rather not," I say just as someone jostles me from behind, pushing me into Sebastian.

"Sorry!" I try stepping back but my way is blocked by the wave of people trying to move past me to get to the back door.

"Christ. It might be better to just go with it," he says, looking over the top of my head. One of his hands is still cupped around my waist, steadying me and that small bit of contact sends a warm current whisking through my body.

"Okay." I duck closer to him as we move through a tiny galley kitchen and out the back door into the hot and sticky night. Sebastian's body is strong and solid beside me and for a couple of seconds, I don't even mind that we're practically being trampled so that a stampede of buffoons can get a front row look at a beer pong tournament.

"Amelia!" my sister shouts, grabbing onto my arm and trying to hoist herself onto my back like when we were kids and took turns giving each other piggyback rides around the backyard.

"Well, hello to you."

"Did someone say beer pong?" she squawks directly into my ear. And man, does she smell like she's been dunked into a swimming pool of hunch punch. Even in the open air, the stench is so strong and sickeningly sweet it makes my stomach do a somersault.

"Daphne, you're pulling on my hair," I say, carefully extricating her from my back and dropping her onto the damp grass.

She doesn't seem to mind. Not missing a beat, she skips

around to my side and pops her arm over my shoulder. "Oh-my-God. You know Bash Holbrook?"

"Um, yeah...?" I glance at him.

"Don't look," Daphne warns, her eyes huge.

Sebastian, who can hear her also, shoots me a confused look.

"But—"

Daphne puts her hand over my mouth and says dramatically, "Shhhh! He. Is. Right. Next. To. You."

I feign surprise. "Oh my God, really?"

"Mm-hmm!" She squeals and nods enthusiastically, not catching on.

"Heads up, you know, since he's right next to me, he can actually hear you," I whisper back at her in a mocking way.

Her mouth forms an o-shape. "He can hear me?"

Good gravy, how much has she had to drink?

"Yes, Daphne. There are these things called sound waves," I say the words deliberately like I'm talking to a four-year-old and, let's face it, a four-year-old probably has more common sense than an intoxicated Daphne.

But she isn't listening to me anymore. She's sidled up to Sebastian and is smiling at him like he's the best thing she's ever seen. It's completely mortifying.

"Just so you know," she says, flirtily batting her eyelashes at him. "I'm totally down with Amelia taking a walk on the wild side, if you know what I mean. My sister is in desperate need of living it up and I think *you*—" she pokes him in the chest with her finger, "—might be just the guy for the job."

Then she winks at him before disappearing into a wooden barn with the rest of the herd. Like, she actually winks and it's so awful I think that I might die of embarrassment. It's at times like these that I wish I was a turtle so I could hide inside a protective shell.

I cover my face with my hands. "I am so sorry."

Sebastian ignores my apology. "Is she always like that?"

I sigh. "Embarrassing and over exuberant to the extreme?"

Amused, he nods.

"Yep. That's Daphne for you. You could say that she lacks a filter."

"Yeah, I'm picking up on that."

We enter the barn and find an open spot not far from the door. It smells familiar and comforting, like sawdust and hay in here, and I start to relax again.

"In the past," I tell him, "I've tried to act like I don't know my sister, but the matching face makes that a little difficult."

He laughs then gestures to the center of the barn where a long folding table has been placed between two empty horse stalls. "So do you play?"

"Play what? Beer pong? Um, no."

"It's a sport with a lot of nuance."

I take in the set-up. A crooked chalk line has been sketched across the table, dividing it into two equal sides. On either end, ten red plastic cups have been hastily arranged to create a triangle like in bowling. "I can see that."

Sebastian bends closer and explains, "Each side tries to land a ping pong ball into one of the opposing team's cups."

"And if they get it?" I ask, suddenly becoming aware of how little space there is between us. I can feel the heat from his body burning through my shirt and the press of his arm against mine.

"Then whoever's playing has to drink the beer in the cup." He slowly turns his head toward me and I feel that little electric charge again. Almost like a hiccup in my pulse. "Just think of it as the redneck version of table tennis."

Unnerved by my reaction, I make myself blink and look away. "Got it."

Across the barn I easily spot Audra chatting up a tall guy in a yellow polo shirt but I have to stand on my toes to find Daphne. She's on the second level of the barn, leaning against

Spencer's back and looking at her phone while he huddles with his friends around an upended barrel. It looks like... well, I can't be positive from way down here, but it looks like he's trading a plastic bag filled with tiny capsules.

Spencer says something to one of the guys he's with, laughs, then picks a pill from the bag and pops it onto his tongue.

What in the actual hell?

No. Just no.

This can't be what I think it is because Daphne wouldn't be mixed up with someone who's taking drugs.

Would she?

My stomach twists angrily.

"Amelia—you good?" It's Sebastian and his eyes are narrowed in seriousness.

Willing myself not to jump to anymore conclusions or full-on freak out until I've had a chance to talk to my sister about this, I take a shaky breath and say, "Yeah, I thought I saw something, but... it's nothing."

"You sure?"

"I'm sure," I say, wanting to drop this thread.

In front of us, the beer pong game is in full swing. This round Byron is teamed up with Cole Greene and they're losing terribly to Leo Herman, who I know vaguely from my math class last year, and Seth Cavanaugh.

"Your friend," I comment. "He's pretty good."

"Don't tell him that."

"Why not?"

Sebastian gives me a sideways look. "Seth doesn't need an ego boost."

I laugh and this is when I notice that several girls are staring at me. Or more accurately, they're staring at Sebastian and, by extension, me. The glare that one red-haired girl is giving us is so intense that I wonder if I should hold up a hand and tell her, *Don't worry—it's not what you think.*

"Especially," he continues, not noticing the girls at all, "not coming from you."

"What's that supposed to mean?"

He turns his head so that he's looking at me. "It means that girls like you are the whole package."

"The whole package?"

He shrugs. "You know what I'm saying. Beautiful, smart, and popular. And Seth is but a mere mortal. You'd eviscerate him."

Smart I'm used to, but *beautiful* is a new one. "I think," I say slowly, "you're confusing me with someone else."

"Nah, I don't think so. Aren't I speaking with the student body treasurer and a past winner of the best attendance award?"

I make a face. "How could you possibly remember that? I won that award in the seventh grade."

He shakes his head, evading the question. "Face it, Amelia—you're perfect and everyone in Green Cove knows it."

"I'm not perfect."

"Really?" The corners of his mouth tip up. "Could have fooled me."

Embarrassed by the direction of this conversation, I look back to the game just in time to see the ping pong ball leave Leo's fingers and sail into the last cup. A deafening cheer rises up as Byron tips his head back, chugs the beer, and throws the empty cup onto the dirt floor of the barn.

"Who's next?" Leo shouts as he beats on his chest with a closed fist. Lord, he's acting like such a jock. Looking at his body language and the cocky grin plastered on his face, you'd think he just won the World Series, not a game of beer pong in a barn.

This whole thing is stupid.

Of course, the moment I think this, guess who stands up and volunteers to play next?

"Me! Me!" Daphne is literally jumping up and down and waving her hands in the air.

"One thing I will give your sister," Sebastian says dryly, "is that she's a happy drunk."

"She's happy in all things," I say, watching Daphne, who's clearly trying to get Spencer to play on her team. She giggles and grazes her lips over his cheek, but he shrugs her off and turns back to his friends.

God, this guy…

When it becomes clear that he's not going to give in, Daphne pouts her lips in disappointment and I have the real urge to walk over there and tell Spencer McGovern exactly what I think of him. But before my brain can get my feet moving, Seth Cavanaugh steps in.

"I'll play with you," he offers, tossing the white ping pong ball back and forth between his hands.

My sister smiles hopefully and slings herself under one of the balcony rails to the ground level. "You will?"

"Of course."

For his part, Leo looks annoyed by the loss of his teammate, but not nearly as annoyed as Spencer, who seems to have suddenly realized that his girlfriend is not an accessory attached securely to his belt loop.

The first couple minutes of the game pass without much drama, but then Daphne lands a ball into a cup and in her excitement, throws her arms around Seth's neck.

And, like he's been waiting for this chance, Spencer explodes from his stool and bellows, "What the hell, Daphne?"

Then it's like everything is happening at once. A bunch of guys are squaring off, about to get in a fight or at least pretending to, and in the background, girls are hysterically shrieking their heads off.

Through the chaotic haze of it all, I see my sister grappling with Spencer and I can tell that she's simultaneously crying and apologizing. He leans close and says something to her before shoving her toward one of the horse stalls and storming off through the open barn door.

I silently beg Daphne to look at me, but she doesn't. Instead, she hides her red face, turns and runs, disappearing into the night.

There's not even a question—I follow and find her on the side of the barn boxed-in by two rusted out cisterns. Her head is bent and I can tell even from this angle that her face is wet and blotchy from crying.

"What was all that about?" I ask, refilling my lungs with the humid air.

"I don't know..." She gulps and brushes at the tears clinging to her eyelids. I think I'd been expecting her to shake it off, put on her famous Daphne smile and give Spencer the bird, so I'm more than a little disappointed when she follows this with, "But I really screwed up."

"I was there, Daphne. You didn't do anything."

She hiccups. "Spencer accused me of flirting, but I swear I wasn't."

"I know you weren't," I console her.

"It doesn't matter because I've ruined everything."

"What are you talking about? He's a jerk and if he—"

"Stop it!" She pops onto both feet, her chin jutting out at me in that stubborn way of hers. "I'm sick of you saying things about my boyfriend and acting like you're allowed to. Just because it never works out with you and guys, doesn't mean that it has to be the same for me!"

We have gained an audience. Audra is next to me, and a few paces away, I barely make out Sebastian hanging back in the shadows.

"Daphne..." I reach for her hand.

"Let me go," she yells, pulling back hard and almost tripping.

"You're drunk and acting crazy," I rationalize.

"Like usual, you don't understand anything," she accuses. Then she swipes the back of her hand across her face and tears across the tall grass in the direction of Byron's house.

I start to chase her, but Audra stops me. "Just stay here. I'll go."

"But I need to talk to her."

"I'll take care of her and make sure that she gets home safe."

"But—"

Audra doesn't give me another chance to argue with her before she takes off into a sprint. Feeling lost, like I've forgotten the words to a favorite song, I stand there and watch them both go.

Several hollow seconds later, Sebastian asks, "Are you okay?"

I simply shake my head. *No, I'm not okay. Not even a little bit.*

"Do you want a ride?"

It occurs to me then that I probably do need a ride. I came with Daphne in Audra's car, but after what happened I'm not sure...

"I don't know," I say haltingly as I swallow back the hurt that's bubbling up inside of me.

"Where do you live?" he asks.

"Out on Hickory Road. Down past where the railroad tracks cut south."

"Not the old Parker Plantation?"

Yes, my house has a name, and, yes, it was once considered a plantation. Now the fields have given way to trees and wild grasses and the house is just a house. A big one at that, but still just a house.

"That's it. My father's mother was a Parker."

He looks at me for a moment and whistles. "That's quite a home."

Home. I definitely don't want to be here anymore, but I don't feel like being there either. Not with Daphne one room

66

away and still fuming at me.

Sebastian must read something into my silence because he says, "Look, I don't have to take you home, Amelia. I'm sure I could find someone else to drive you if that's better."

"It's not that," I reply, wrapping my arms securely over my chest. "I was just thinking about being home right now with Daphne still mad at me."

He considers this. "So if you could be anywhere in the world, where would it be?"

I don't even think about my answer. "The beach."

"Let's go then."

"What?" I almost laugh at the absurdity.

"Let's go," he repeats and this time it dawns on me that he's being dead serious.

"Right now?"

"Why not?"

"Because…" I trail off, unable to come up with a real answer. None of my normal excuses seem to apply here and the truth of the matter is that, in this whole mess of a night, the idea of getting in Sebastian Holbrook's truck and going to the beach is the only thing that makes any kind of sense.

So I end up shrugging helplessly and saying the only thing I can think of when faced with the prospect of a road trip at eleven o'clock at night with someone I barely know.

"Your music or mine?"

CHAPTER SEVEN

Bash

"I can't believe this."

"What can't you believe?" I ask, taking a step toward her. There are no lights out here, but I have no problem seeing her clearly. The moon and the stars are hanging low over the Atlantic, reflecting off the black water and lighting up the whole night with a phosphorescent glow.

Amelia balances on one leg and twirls herself on the sand. "I can't believe that we're at the beach. That we actually left the party and drove out here."

I shake my head. "We live in the Lowlands. Haven't you ever been to the beach before?"

"Obviously I have. But never at night... and never 'just because' and with no real plan."

She slips off her loafers, deposits them in a pile just past the craggy shadows of the tall grasses that line the sand dunes and skips down to the shore. When she hits the spot where the beach goes smooth, she stops to roll the bottoms of her leggings up to her knees. Then she steps forward and when the salty water washes over her toes, she throws her head back and lets out a giddy laugh. Instantly, I love the sound of it and decide that seeing her like this—happy and unencumbered—was worth the price of the gas it took to get here. Especially after how upset she was at the party.

"Are you coming?" she asks, looking back.

Crouching low, I quickly untie my sneakers and get them off my feet. I leave them beside her shoes and crunch my way through the cool, damp sand to the edge of the water.

When I reach Amelia's side, her eyes flicker to mine and that little movement reverberates deep in my gut.

"It's so beautiful," she muses. "But at the same time, doesn't it seem almost dangerous? The way the water is so dark and you can't see what's moving under the surface of it."

I don't respond. I know we're supposed to be talking about the ocean, but my eyes are on her and I can't seem to drag them away. And I wonder if she senses it—the way I'm looking like I've never dared to look before.

Can she feel me tracing the outline of her lips? Memorizing the shape of her eyelids and the slope of her chin? Or noticing how sexy her shoulders look in that shirt and how it fits her tightly in all the right places?

If I didn't let myself really understand it before, I understand it now.

Amelia is beautiful. And not in a way that's fake or overly made-up like most of the girls I come across. She's herself and, really, that's enough.

"Thank you for bringing me here," she says, gaze still on the water. "I wouldn't have known."

Eventually, I make myself speak. "Wouldn't have known what?"

She wraps her arms over her body and shivers. "That it could be like this."

"Like what?"

"Like magic."

I chuckle.

"You're making fun of me," she says flatly.

I shake my head. "I'm not."

"But you're laughing," she points out.

"It's not that I'm laughing *at* you. It's that I've never known someone to get so poetic about the beach. I can't imagine what your reaction would be if I had driven you all the way to Disney World."

69

"Disney World is overrated," she says. "Well, except for the teacups. I love the teacups and anything that spins."

I snort. "Any kind of spinny ride makes me hurl."

Now it's her turn to laugh.

For a while after that, we leave our bare feet in the water, letting the salty ocean air whip into our faces and sting our eyeballs, and we talk. Well, mostly Amelia does the talking. She tells me about vacations she's been on and explains that her family goes skiing someplace new every February. What eventually comes out is that she's been on mountains all over the world—Switzerland, Japan, France. Impressed, I intentionally don't admit that I've only been out of South Carolina twice in my life.

And in those few sacred minutes, I discover Amelia and the stuff that you can't tell when you see her in the hallways at school or look at her yearbook photo.

I find out that she wishes she could play an instrument, and that she danced—as in ballet—for her whole life until sophomore year when she decided that it was taking up too much time after school. And she's not as into tennis as she used to be, but she feels like she has to stay on the team because she already made a commitment and being team captain senior year looks good to colleges. And, most surprisingly, that she doesn't see herself as popular.

"Audra's really my only friend," she says, shrugging. "And, of course, Daphne when she's not furious with me."

By this point, we've trudged back up the beach and are sitting on the sand next to our shoes.

"Everyone in the entire senior class, if not the whole school, is your friend," I contend. "And you can't deny it because I've seen you in the hallways and in the cafeteria surrounded by your many admirers."

"Those people aren't my friends," she maintains. "They act like they care because their daddy knows my daddy. Or maybe they want me to do something for them like allocate more of the class budget for their club or be a go-between with one of the faculty advisors on vending machine issues."

"Vending machine issues?"

"Like, what candy bars to stock and whether or not it's necessary to have two flavors of Fanta."

"Which, obviously, it is."

She smiles but it doesn't reach the rest of her face. "But, see… that's not friendship. That's nothing but a business transaction, which is how all my daddy's so-called friendships are. It's all, 'you rub my back and I'll rub yours.' I might play along for now, but that's not what I want for my own life. I want something different."

"Like what?"

"Something *real.*"

I wince at my own ignorance. My life is all about keeping up and juggling responsibilities, so how is it that I never once considered the possibility that Amelia's life is like that too?

"Up there!" Amelia's body jerks into mine, breaking into my thoughts. "It's a shooting star."

I look to where she's pointing at an object blinking in the sky. "I think that's a satellite."

"Hmmm… And I guess you can't make a wish on a satellite?"

"Only if you're wishing for better cell phone reception."

This makes her crack up and it's so big and loud and unexpected that I start laughing too.

When our eyes are wet and our stomachs are sore, she clears her throat and asks me, "So, what does it say?"

At first I think she's talking about the satellite and I'm confused. Then I see that she's holding up one of my sneakers and I realize she wants to know about the quote on the sole of my shoe.

"All your tomorrows start here."

She rubs her thumb over the words. "It's cool. Did you write it?"

71

"No, it's a Neil Gaiman quote."

As anticipated, she gives me a blank look. Unless Amelia is into fantasy or graphic novels, she has no idea who I'm talking about.

"He's my favorite writer," I tell her. "When my mom was sick, I had to take a bunch of time off of school to help get her to and from her chemo appointments in Columbia."

"That's why you were gone for so long last year?"

I nod. "Yeah, it was a lot of hours waiting around the hospital and I was bored so I started to read a lot. She found me a signed copy of *Fragile Things* at a used bookstore." I shrug and look to the dark water, which is just about to crash onto the sand. "Anyway, I guess I read it so often that this line stuck with me. And when she died, it became our motto—Carter's and mine. We had no idea what was going to happen, but every minute was a chance to start over and have the rest of our lives in front of us. And, for me, it's a double meaning."

"How so?"

I pause to take a breath and reorder my thoughts. "When I agreed to be Carter's guardian, I basically told my mom that all of my tomorrows were going to be about him."

"Did you ever consider not taking him?"

I would be lying if I told her *no, the thought never crossed my mind*. "We have an aunt and uncle who live in Charleston and they wanted him," I say. "For a while that was my mother's plan. But after going through the treatments and all of that, things changed. We wanted to be together in our own small family and keep hold of something that we knew. It was hard at first and it can still get frustrating at times, but I have to remember that every moment from here on out starts and ends with him. I have to do right by the promise I made."

"All your tomorrows..." she murmurs, a small smile touching her lips. "I like it."

I decide that it's only fair if I get to ask her a question.

"My turn."

"Your turn?"

"Mm-hmm." I nod. "What's with the leggings?"

Her forehead rumples in confusion. "What about them?"

"Well, let's see," I say, using the tip of my finger to brush the sand off of the leggings in question. "What's on those?" I squint. "Are those supposed to be monkeys?"

"Those are not monkeys! They're sloths!"

Her feisty outrage is adorable. "Sloths?"

"Yes, though I do have a pair of monkey leggings," she admits.

I snicker. "C'mon. I know there has to be a story there. Half of you looks like every other wannabe sorority girl or doctor's wife in Green Cove and the other half looks like you've got a different mind about things."

"It's silly."

"It's not silly," I reassure her.

"It is actually, but since you saved me from that party and my sister's wrath and brought me out to the beach, I'll tell you anyway." She sweeps her glossy brown hair out of her eyes before continuing. "When Daphne and I turned fourteen, in addition to the usual bookstore gift certificate, our grandmother bought us each a subscription to a legging-of-the-month club."

"Legging-of-the-month? Be serious," I chide just to piss her off. Because, if I'm honest, I'm starting to like it when she gets worked up. "That does not exist."

"Oh, it exists," she scoffs. "I know this because I'm a member."

"Do you guys have membership cards and secret handshakes and stuff like that?"

"If I told you that, I'd have to kill you."

I laugh. "Okay, I'm hooked. Tell me more about the leggings."

"Well," she says on a sigh, "predictably, Daphne hated

them. And I don't know... I guess I started wearing them around the house at first because they were comfortable, and then I did it as a joke to prove a point to my sister. But eventually I liked them just for me."

"What's not to like? They're soft. They're stretchy. And they're covered in sloths."

"Exactly," she replies, a subversive grin stretching across her face. "And in a weird way, maybe wearing leggings is my idea of rebelling. Everyone thinks..." The smile fades and Amelia turns so that all I can see is her profile haloed by the silvery moonlight. Like this, you would almost think she was lit up from the inside. "They think that I'm a perfect southern belle or an uptight daddy's girl or whatever, and the leggings are just the tiniest way that I can do the unexpected. Does that make any sense?"

"It does," I say, my mind straying to what I said earlier. I called her perfect, didn't I?

"I know that it's a lame rebellion, on par with refusing to eat my green vegetables, but it drives Nancy crazy so it must be working a little bit."

"Who's Nancy?

She's quiet for a second and I notice how her fingertips burrow into the sand. "Nancy is my stepmom."

"Your parents are divorced?"

Again, she doesn't speak right away and I wonder if I've overstepped—gotten too personal for her. But then she says, "No, my mother died from complications when Daphne and I were born."

The revelation hits me with the force of a truck. "What?"

Amelia concentrates on the water and pulls her legs into her chest and hugs her knees. "Yeah. I'm fuzzy on the details because my dad doesn't talk about it much. Obviously I don't remember her the way you remember your mom. I only know her through pictures, so it's strange to miss someone I never met. Still... I do in my own way."

She pauses and I hear her breathing change, get less even. "Sometimes when I'm not sure how to feel about it, I think about my father and what it must have felt like for him. Can you imagine? When he left for the hospital with my mom, he must have had so much hope. Like, everything was on the horizon for both of them. And then suddenly he was alone, coming home with two daughters and no wife."

My throat has gone dry. *Say something you prick*, I tell myself and I open my mouth but nothing comes out.

Amelia lowers her head and for a moment, I can't see her face in the darkness. "Then he met Nancy when Daphne and I were two and… well, I don't want you to get the idea that she's awful. She's not like a stepmother in a bad story or anything like that. She has high expectations and they can be hard to live up to, but she loves us. And, really, she's the only mom we've ever known."

There's so much to say but I have no idea how to begin. All this time I've assumed Amelia's life was what it seemed like on the outside. Easy. Simple. Uncomplicated.

But she's turning out to be the same as one of those puzzles—those optical illusions—where the longer you stare, the more the lines slant and the picture changes. And I don't know much, but I do know that I want to stick around and solve the puzzle.

"I'm sorry," I say finally, my voice croaky.

"I'm sorry too."

And then she looks at me and I get this feeling—this *I'm screwed* feeling—like I'm standing on a high ledge and I know there is a choice to be made here. I can either back down off the ledge or I can jump. Either way, I'm about to lose my place.

"Do you think there's something out there?" she asks, voice solemn. "I mean, after?"

"I honestly don't know, but I hope so."

Amelia lets that sink in. "Daphne thinks that it's

impossible so we have to get all our living in while we can."

"What do *you* think?"

"I'm not sure but, like anything that exists, we're all just atoms, right? We're pretty much the same as the stars or sand," she says, lifting her hand and letting the sand on her palm fall between the cracks of her fingers, "or leaves on trees or water or sky, so I guess we can't disappear completely. It could be—" she pauses and takes a breath, "— that we just become something different."

Maybe it's weird to think about kissing Amelia when we're sitting on the beach at midnight talking about our dead mothers and whether or not there's an afterlife, but with the night winding its spell around us and my heart beating a rhythmic chant in my chest, that's exactly what I'm doing. And when she turns to me and her face is so close to mine that I can make out the freckles dusting the bridge of her nose, the impulse hits me so hard that it almost hurts.

"Does that sound crazy?" she asks me in a small voice.

"No, that sounds right to me," I tell her as I look away and try to unravel the tight feeling in my abdomen.

I don't want to like her. I don't want to feel anything like the way I'm feeling because I already know where it's going to lead. No way does a girl like Amelia Bright ever choose me and my complicated life.

Not ever.

CHAPTER EIGHT

Amelia

It's funny how the ride out to the beach seemed to go by so fast, rushing by in clips of black sky and shadowy fields, but the ride home is slower, heavier somehow.

Or maybe I'm imagining it's that way because back at the beach was one of the best times of my life and I'm nervous that Sebastian doesn't think the same thing. And then I start wondering why I'm so concerned with what he thinks about it or me or anything else for that matter. It's not like this is a date. This is… actually, I'm not sure *what* this is.

Fifteen minutes into the drive home, if I'm going by the clock on my phone, he clicks his blinker on and pulls off the road into a deserted parking lot in front of a run-down gas station.

"Sorry," he says, yanking the parking brake, "I'm going to have to grab some caffeine to stay up. Do you want anything?"

Sure. How about a clue as to what you're thinking?

But I don't say this. Obviously.

I just nod my head and follow him into the empty gas station. The place is far too bright and smells like boiled peanuts. Buried behind the counter there's an old guy reading a fishing magazine. He eyes us with suspicion for a second and then seems to decide that we'll do and goes back to his lures and hooks. I leave Sebastian by the humming freezers and meander toward the row of candy.

"Red Vines?" Sebastian balks when I set my bag up on the register counter next to the energy drink he grabbed.

"Uh… is that not okay?" I ask, feeling terrifically self-conscious.

"No, it's fine," he says hastily. "But most people go for Twizzlers."

"That's because they can't appreciate the sweet, plasticky awesomeness that is Red Vines."

He laughs and I realize how much he's smiled and laughed tonight. Because of *me*. And that knowledge has me feeling weird and almost giddy.

After we pay, we sit in the car for a bit, not going anywhere, just passing the bag of Red Vines back and forth and talking. Sebastian plays songs for me on his phone—mainly 70s punk bands that I've never heard of—and tries to teach me some of the lyrics.

And then the dashboard clock flips to three in the morning, and he turns to the cracked vinyl steering wheel and says, "I should get you home. Your parents are probably going to go batshit."

"I'm sure they went to bed at ten and have no idea that I'm not there. And Daphne would have called if there was a problem," I say, checking my phone just to be sure I haven't missed anything. "She might be mad, but she wouldn't let me get into trouble. It's twin code."

"You're not worried about a middle of the night bed check?"

I laugh. "Daddy might wake up on occasion to check on Daphne, but I've never given him a reason to worry."

"So none of the guys you've dated have kept you out all night plying you with Red Vines?"

It comes off as a joke, but I get the sense that there's an underlying question there. He wants to know about my lovelife or lack thereof.

"There haven't been that many guys," I tell him, trying to keep my tone level as I reach into the bag of Red Vines. "And they all preferred Twizzlers."

He chuckles.

"Plus I've been kind of turned off men since one lost me the three-legged race on Field Day."

Sebastian shakes his head and drums his fingers on the gear shift. "I was wondering if you remembered that."

"Of course I remember it! I was so mad."

"Amelia, we were nine," he reminds me.

I shrug and twirl the twisty red piece of candy between two fingers before biting off one end. "Still, I hated losing."

"I could tell and I figured that's why you never talked to me again."

I pause, wondering if a small part of him actually believes that. "Well, I'm talking to you now."

He stretches back in the seat, tilting his head so that his grey eyes are still on me. *God*, he's hot. Like, three-alarm fire hot. "I know. And have I mentioned yet that I like it?"

"Not exactly."

"Well, I do."

"Me too."

We fall into one of those quiets where it's apparent that both people are thinking about something but don't want to say it out loud. Me? Well, I'm thinking about how close we're sitting and about how mesmerizing the shape of Sebastian's mouth is and how even in the dark confines of the truck, I can see the little hairs on his jaw and neck and how I've never kissed a guy with stubble before.

"I should warn you," he says, and I have a momentary freakout that I've verbalized this last thought—you know, the one about kissing him—but then Sebastian clears his throat and keeps talking. "I don't know how to do this."

"Do what?"

His hand flops back and forth between us.

Oh. *Oh.*

"I mean, we don't have to…" Uncertainty oozes out of all of my pores. *I have completely misread the situation.*

"No, it's not like that." He closes his eyes and shakes his head. "Let me explain. I don't want you to think I was saying that I'm not having a great time, but you should know that things in my life aren't easy. After everything that happened with my mom last year, almost every one of my friends bailed. My girlfriend disappeared faster than you could say 'kegger on the beach' and most of the guys I grew up with couldn't get a grip on how different things became for me. They still wanted to party and hang out and plan how they're going to get into the bars in Summerville with their fake IDs and that wasn't my life anymore."

"It's not mine either," I point out.

"What I'm trying to tell you," he says, scrunching his forehead, "is that I got used to everyone fading away. Seth is the only person who's stuck through it all with me and I'm not sure if it's because he likes being my friend or if it's because he's got a thing for my cat."

"Your cat?"

He nods. "Jinx."

I smile.

"Anyway," he continues with determination like the words are pressing on him, "the others come around from time to time to ask how I'm doing. They pretend to care, but I can tell that it's mainly pity." Here, he pauses and in that pause, I can hear what he's not saying. *Don't you dare pity me.*

"I don't pity you, if that's what you're thinking," I reply as gently as I can. I so want to reach over and grab hold of his hand, but we're not ready for that. Not yet. "Just because your life isn't like the life of every other student at Green Cove High doesn't mean that your life is bad. I happen to admire what you're doing with Carter."

He swallows and shifts his jaw.

"And if we're being honest about things, there's something I should probably tell you."

"What is it?" he asks, frowning. A few strands of his dark

hair have fallen in front of his eyes and it's taking all my willpower not to reach over and push them back and run my fingers over his sharp cheekbones.

"I'm allergic to cats."

This makes him laugh, and I mean *really* laugh, and the tension cocooning us shatters. I'm still not entirely positive I know what our conversation was truly about—whether Sebastian had been trying to say in a roundabout but polite way that he doesn't have any interest in dating me or if we really were talking about forging a friendship—but either way, I guess I can live with it.

I draw in a breath, my heart twisting to say this. "So... friends?"

Sebastian looks at me for a long moment and I feel it again—that uncanny pull, like the ocean on the sand—winding its fingers through my ribcage and tugging.

"Friends," he says.

***

Somewhere between midnight and sunrise, time and reality lost all real meaning to me. But now that Sebastian is gone and I'm standing in salt-stained clothes on my own downy bathroom rug with a toothbrush in my hand and my flushed reflection staring back, it all floods back in.

I replay that awful party and my fight with Daphne and I start to feel sick.

Most people would probably say that it's completely normal for sisters to get into arguments, but for my sister and me it's definitely not normal. Sure, I might tease her about being careless and she's always giving me a hard time for being so serious, but to actually get in a real fight like that and walk away angry? Yeah, it just never happens.

Almost shyly, I creep in through her bedroom door. Early dawn light is streaming in through the sheer curtains, washing the entire room a soft, pearly blue. As expected, my sister is completely zonked out. Her dark hair is a rat's nest around her face and she's snoring softly into her pillow.

"Daphne?" I touch her shoulder. I'm not sure what I plan to say, but I need to make sure we're okay. "Daphne?"

"Amelia?" She groggily blinks her eyes open. "Why are you up so early?

"I'm not. I haven't even gone to bed."

She starts to sit up, alarm erasing the sleep from her features. "Why? What happened?"

"Shhh," I say quietly. "I'll tell you later, but... can I sleep here with you? I know you're mad at me, but I don't want to be alone."

In answer, Daphne pulls the bed sheets back and scoots over to make room for me. Relieved, I crawl under the blanket and curl my body into hers.

"I'm sorry," I whisper after a second.

She rolls onto her side so that we're facing each other. "I don't want you to be sorry. I'm the sorry one."

"Does that mean..." I'm almost afraid to ask. "You and Spencer?"

She shakes her head. "No, we're fine," she says, her voice thin. "But I don't want to fight with you about him. I don't want to fight with you about anything."

"I don't want that either," I say, reaching beneath the covers to give her a hard hug.

She takes the embrace for a moment but, too soon, winces and pulls away from me.

"What's wrong?" I ask, worried all over again.

"I fell into a door," she says, sheepishly rubbing her arm. "That was after you left."

I give a soft laugh. "You were *so* drunk."

Her grin is a little sad. "I know and I swear that it's never going to happen again."

"Never is a long time," I say.

"Okay, at least not until next weekend," she rectifies as she slips one hand beneath her pillow and shakes out her hair so that it's not caught beneath her shoulder. "Tell me—did you really leave the party with Bash Holbrook? Because that's what Audra said."

I nod in silent confirmation.

"What's he like?"

"He's…he's not the way everyone says he is. You know how he missed all that school last year and people think he got in trouble?"

"Yeah?"

I shake my head weakly. "He wasn't expelled or on the run from the police. His mother was dying and he was shuttling her back and forth to doctor appointments."

"Wow," her voice wavers. "I don't even know what to say."

"I know. And tonight he drove me out to Murrels Inlet and it was… well, it was kind of incredible."

Daphne's eyes grow big and earnest. "Tell me everything."

"I will, I will," I reply on a yawn. "But not right now, okay? I swear if I don't go to sleep in the next thirty seconds, I'm going to start hallucinating."

She laughs. "At least tell me if you guys are, like, together."

"It's not like that with him," I insist, maybe trying to convince myself as much as her. "We're just friends."

She gives me a skeptical look. "Friends who go to the beach in the middle of the night?"

"Well... yeah."

She sighs wistfully. "If you say so."

"I say so."

"M'kay. Night." And with that, my sister turns over and snuggles into her side of the mattress.

"Night, Daphne. I'm glad we're okay."

"Me too."

83

"Love you."

"Love you more," she whispers back.

I close my eyes in contentment and exhale slowly, letting my body settle into the quiet. And just as the deep recesses of sleep grab my ankles and drag me under the surface, I have one last thought. I wonder if maybe, just maybe, my dreams will be filled with marshy grasses, dark waves, and flickering starlight and, best of all, Sebastian Holbrook.

CHAPTER NINE

Bash

"It's been nine days and counting," Seth says as he scoops up a massive amount of tater tots and deposits them in a shallow bowl on his cafeteria tray.

I follow him down the lunch line and reach for one of the sesame bagels that's been shoved up next to a pile of watery-looking cantaloupe chunks. "Since what?"

"Since Byron's party and this unlikely friendship you've got going on with Amelia Bright," he says, moving on to the corndogs. He grabs two of them and coats them with a river of artificial cheese. Since we've been kids, Seth's appetite has fascinated me.

"What's that supposed to mean?"

"Dude, for one, you left the party with her, which you still haven't told me a thing about. Though," he continues with a wicked grin, "I gotta tell you, my imagination has filled in a lot of the blanks."

"Your imagination is misguided."

Seth ignores this. "And now you're talking to her in the halls between classes and bringing her gifts."

"I am not bringing her gifts," I say stiffly.

"Then explain what happened during morning break yesterday."

"I gave her a bag of Red Vines."

"Red Vines," he repeats in wonder like I've suddenly started speaking in tongues and he finds it astounding.

I give a small shrug. "She likes them."

He shakes his head and hands over his student card to Evelyn, the lady who runs the cafeteria register. "Bash, bringing a girl candy is the equivalent of tattooing her name in a heart on your arm and posting that shit on Instagram."

Jesus, is that true? "It's not like that with us."

"Then what's it like?"

"She's... cool."

This appears to mystify him more than the Red Vines. "She's *cool*? No shit she's cool. That's all you're going to say about it?"

"I'm not sure what else you want from me."

"I want details and by 'details' I mean that I need to know if her ass is as perfect as I think it is," he presses, winking at Evelyn when she flashes him a disapproving glare.

"I wouldn't know anything about her ass." Except that it looked great in the jeans she wore to school on Monday—an observation I'm not about to share with Seth.

"Fine, fine... don't tell me everything yet. But at least assure me that this means that you're getting out of your slump."

"My slump?"

"The sad and romantically tortured state you've been in since last year."

"The only thing that I would classify as torture is being forced to have this conversation with you," I say definitively. "And Amelia and I are friends. End of the story."

"Friends?"

"Friends," I repeat. And it's the truth. Well, at least, I *think* it's the truth.

"Mmm-hmm."

"Don't *mmm-hmm* me. It makes you sound like a girl."

"What's wrong with sounding like a girl? Don't be such a misogynist."

"Me?" I choke out. "You were the one who was asking about asses, dillweed."

"That was for research purposes," he tells me like this makes perfect sense. Then he balances his lunch tray in one hand and points across the cafeteria. "And if you really are such great buds with Amelia, let's go over there and eat lunch with her today."

"Did you get high during fourth period or something? We're not eating lunch with her."

"Why not?"

"Because."

It's one thing to talk to Amelia when it's just the two of us at the beach at night or to chat her up for a few minutes in the quad before the bell rings. But it's a different thing to go sit down at her lunch table under the watch of a couple hundred classmates who seem to be able to see through my skin all the way to my bones.

"She looks lonely," he comments.

Amelia is sandwiched between Audra Singer and her sister, Daphne, who is talking to them both animatedly. She looks about as lonely as a sardine crammed into a can and I tell Seth this.

"I still think she could use the company," he says, eyeing Daphne.

"Is that what this is about? Her sister?"

Seth smiles wolfishly.

"You realize that Daphne Bright has a boyfriend? And that he plays on the football team and drives a BMW. You can't compete with that, Seth."

"A man can still dream, can't he? And I don't see any sign of that douchebag right now, do you?"

It's true that Spencer McGovern is nowhere in sight. "It doesn't matter. We still can't just walk on over to their table."

"Why not? You said you were friends with her. Friends eat lunch together.

"There's a social order."

"Who are you—Miss Manners? Social order my ass," he

mutters, cutting across the tiled floor in the direction of Amelia's table.

"Don't you fuc—" But it's too late. Seth is already slamming his tray down on the table.

The three girls jump in surprise.

"Hello," he says, leaning forward into their space.

Audra looks vaguely annoyed by the interruption but Daphne is giggling. I'm not sure what the hell Amelia is thinking. Her face has gone a soft shade of pink and her eyes are downturned.

Seth isn't backing off. "Bash here was just talking about you and it became clear that he wanted to lunch with you but was too much of a pansy to ask himself."

Nice.

"Don't listen to anything he says," I tell them as I start to lead Seth away by the collar of his t-shirt. "He's recently checked himself out of a psych unit against doctor's orders."

"No, it's fine," Amelia replies, scooting her chair over and nudging Daphne in the process. "You're welcome to sit with us if you want to."

"Of course he wants to," Seth answers, shoving me down into a seat and plunking himself next to Daphne.

Before he can get too happy about this arrangement, Spencer McGovern, using pantomimes to keep us all quiet, sneaks up to the table and starts to tickle Daphne. She squeals with laughter and winds up in his lap with her arms draped over his shoulders. A couple of Spencer's jock friends sit down as well. I don't know their names so I decide to think of them as Dick #1 and Dick #2.

Seth looks ready to stab someone between the eyes and I get it. Watching Daphne nuzzle into her boyfriend's neck and listen to Dick #2 tell the story of how he ordered a gallon's worth of lube and had it shipped to our principal's condo, is not on either one of our bucket lists. But in terms of uncomfortable situations, I guess it could be worse. I could always be chosen by a gameshow host to sing a Journey song karaoke-style or forcibly strapped down to a table to have my testicles waxed.

"Are you having fun yet?" Amelia asks quietly when Spencer starts to regale us with stories about the time he stole his dad's yacht. Yep, this prick is actually using the word "yacht."

"Am I being that obvious?"

"It's the way you're sitting kind of like this," she says, hunching over and making a dejected face. "And how you seem to love that bagel so much."

I realize that she's echoing what I said to her that night at Byron's party and I start to laugh.

This draws Daphne's attention. She gets her face out of Spencer's neck, untangles her fingers from his hair, and asks, "Bash, where all did you get that shirt? I love it."

I look down because I've forgotten what I'm wearing. It's a dark blue shirt with a graphic that depicts a bunch of cell phones arranged into the shape of a massive chair. I remember that I drew it one night when I was in the middle of a *Game of Thrones* marathon. It was modeled after a marketing poster for the show and had been a play on the words. Get it—*Game of Phones*. Probably stupid, but it made me chuckle at the time.

"He designed it," Seth answers for me.

I shoot him a look of irritation. He knows I don't like to talk about this part of my life.

"He did mine too," he continues, pointing to his shirt with it's a drawing of the earth wearing horn-rimmed glasses. Across the top in a chunky font, it says, *World's Okayest Student.*

"You drew these?" Amelia asks. Then she bends to get a better look at the design on my chest. I catch the smell of her shampoo and my head gets buzzy.

"How did you do that?" Audra asks, leaning in as well.

"I use paint or charcoal for the basic image and then a computer program to digitize it and finalize the design."

Amelia is still staring at my shirt. "Wow, you're really talented.

"You are!" Daphne gushes. Behind her, Spencer is glowering at me and I figure the guy is pissed that he's lost the spotlight.

"My boy has mad skills," Seth says as he chews on a corn dog. "He's got a whole closet full of designs."

Amelia blinks up at me. "Truly?"

"It's not a big deal," I say. "Just a couple t-shirts."

I'm hoping the topic will die a quick death but Seth has other plans. Now he's got his phone out and is showing pictures of designs I've done. "They're categorized newest to oldest," he tells them, smiling a little too long at Daphne.

Amelia takes the phone from him and scrolls through the gallery, stopping occasionally to enlarge a design. "Is this what you want to do when you graduate?"

I shrug. "Nah, it's only for fun."

"You could probably get into a really good school with these designs," she says.

"See? Thank you, Amelia." Seth is grinning. "I've been telling him for a while that he should try for art school."

"I'm not going to art school," I say, annoyed.

Amelia's eyes narrow. "Why not?"

"Because those are t-shirts, not actual art."

"You could always go to fashion school like a faggot," Spencer mutters loudly.

Dick #1 and Dick #2 think this is the funniest thing they've ever heard and start to guffaw uncontrollably, blowing potato chip crumbs and Mountain Dew through their lips.

"You two are disgustin'!" Audra shouts, throwing down a couple of napkins to wipe up the mess.

"She's right. You're worse than a litter of untrained

puppies," Amelia snaps. "And, Spencer, you can go to hell."

Spencer makes a fake pouty face at her. "Ooooh, did I offend your delicate sensibilities? Does that mean you're a fashion lover or a fag lover?"

"For your information, I'm both," she retorts and I'm so impressed I want to reach over and slap her on the back.

"Guys…" Daphne complains. "Please don't fight again."

"We're not fighting, babe," Spencer says, patting her thigh. "Your sister and I are just poking a little fun at each other."

Audra rolls her eyes. "Yeah, if you call actin' like a bigoted meathead fun."

Before Spencer or either of his friends can think of a worthy comeback to this, the warning bell rings, signaling it's almost time for fifth period, and the cafeteria goes into cleanup mode.

"I hope you don't take them seriously," Amelia says as we gather up our trash and take it to the nearest garbage can. "I'm not sure that any of them could even recite the alphabet all the way through let alone tell you anything about art."

"I learned a long time ago not to let assclowns like Spencer McGovern get to me. By the way, do you always eat lunch with them?"

"Not if I can help it. Tomorrow, I'm planning to fast and hunker down in the library during lunch so that I can study for that Spanish test. You're welcome to join me."

"Yeah?" I ask, surprised at the invitation.

"Sure. I'll even share my index cards with you."

I laugh. "Index cards? Now you're pulling out the big guns."

"I try," she teases, smiling as she puts her lunch tray on a shelf above the trashcan. "But hey, earlier, you know that I was serious, right? You could do it."

"Do what?"

She tugs at the bottom of my shirt. "Do *this* in college."

"College isn't in the cards for some of us."

"You mean you haven't thought about it?"

"It's not that I haven't *thought* about it. But Carter is my top priority and I don't see how me going off to school fits in with his life. Not to mention that tuition and books and rent aren't exactly free."

"Crap—what am I trying to say? I know it's not any of my business." She shakes her head and bites down on her lip self-consciously. It's damn cute. "I didn't mean to be insensitive."

"Don't apologize," I say. "If things were different, I don't know, maybe I would want to look at schools. But with the way things are right now, I can't. I have to take it one day at a time."

She nods then notices Seth waiting for me by the door to the stairwell.

"We've got next period together," I tell her.

"Okay, well…" She backs away from me slowly and asks, "Will I see you this afternoon?"

I'm confused, or maybe I'm distracted by the way her legs look in the skirt she's wearing. She's ditched the leggings and loafers in favor of simple leather sandals today and it's the first time I've seen her toes in bright light. I can't quite get over that they're painted purple.

"What?" I ask dumbly.

"This afternoon? Carter and tutoring? Will I see you?"

I was actually going to ask Seth to pick my brother up today so I could offer to stay late at work and earn another couple of hours, but now I'm trashing that plan and mentally rearranging my schedule.

"You will definitely see me."

***

I'm not late for pick up.

Actually, I get to the elementary school fifteen minutes

early, and don't think I miss the look of surprise on Mrs. Hopkins' face when she sees me walk through the door.

Carter and Amelia are sitting together at one of the back tables and I know the moment I register the off-kilter expression on his face that something isn't right.

"What's wrong?"

"He's had a bad day," Amelia answers, rubbing his back.

I sit down on the bench beside him and drop my keys onto the table. "Are you going to tell me what happened?"

With a mournful sigh he says, "Brecken was mean to me at lunch today. He called me a stupid head because I'm in the last reading group and he told everyone that I don't even know how to do multiplication."

"Bud, you're in the first grade. I don't think any of the kids in your class can multiply yet. Sounds to me like this Brecken kid was just messing with you."

"And you have to remember that with the all the hard work you've been doing lately, you're going to be moving up to the next reading group very soon," Amelia says.

Carter sniffles. "It's not just that! Brecken wouldn't let me play on his team at recess because I'm too small. He said I'm a baby and I probably still wear diapers."

"Hey, hey," I soothe. "You're not a baby and I know for a fact that you don't wear diapers."

"Then why would he say that?"

"Because..." My eyes go to Amelia. I need help and I need it badly.

"If you ask me," she says confidently, "Brecken sounds like a bully and that means that for whatever reason it makes him feel better to make you feel bad."

"But that doesn't make any sense," he whines, shaking his head so hard that dark brown hair flops into his eyes.

"I know it doesn't, which is why you can't let what he thinks bother you so much."

His little shoulders move up and down. "I guess."

"Amelia's right. It's tough but you've got to try to ignore this kid," I tell him. "And forget about the baby comment. You're going to grow up just like me and I don't look like a baby, do I?"

He tilts his head to the side and scrutinizes me. "Does that mean I'm gonna get hair on my face too?"

I scratch my chin, feeling the prickly hairs on my fingertips. "Do you want hair on your face?"

"Of course I want hair on my face. Then no one will call me a baby," Carter answers seriously.

"Why wait?" Amelia hands me a black marker and adds in a whisper that Carter can't hear, "It's washable."

I steady my brother's head and draw a thick handlebar mustache above his upper lip, making sure to add dramatic fringed wingtips to the ends. He looks ridiculous, like a cartoon villain, and it takes everything I've got to keep a straight face when Amelia holds out a small mirror she's pulled out of her purse and asks him, "Better?"

Carter turns his head from side to side, carefully studying his reflection. Then his face explodes into a grin and he throws his arms around my waist. "You're the best!"

"You're *really* going to love me when I tell you what else I have planned for today."

"What? Tell me! Tell me!"

I put my hand on my head to make a fin. "Da-da-da-duh," I sing out an off-key rendition of the *Jaws* theme song.

"You're taking me shark hunting!" He shouts, jumping to his feet and clapping his hands together.

Amelia is appalled. "You guys are going to hunt *sharks?*"

"No," I say through my laughter. "We're going to look for shark *teeth.*"

Her expression calms. "Okay, that makes a little more sense. So you're going out to the beach?"

"Nope," Carter says. "We go to look for them in the creeks near our house. You can find them anyplace that used to be underwater."

"We can do it as long as we hurry," I tell him. "We still have to run home and grab your mud boots and make it out to Blackwater Creek before dark."

Pulling his twisted backpack straps over his shoulders, he says to Amelia, "One time Bash found a tooth this big in Blackwater Creek." His arms go out as wide as they can go.

"It was more like this," I amend, holding my thumb and index finger about an inch and a half apart.

She laughs. "You guys have a good time."

"You could come with us," Carter says, his eyes squinting with hope. "I can show you exactly what to look for because I'm really good at it."

"I would love to but unfortunately I have to go to a banquet thingy for my student government group. Next time?"

"Okay, maybe we could even take you to the beach. Bash says you can find the best ones at low tide."

Amelia tilts her face to me. I don't know what's going on in her head, but I'm thinking of our night together and of the way her skin smelled and how her soft brown eyes flickered with moonlight.

"I'd like that," she says, blinking and breaking our connection. "I'd like it a lot."

***

"Carter, you need to sit still," I remind him. He's so excited to go look for shark teeth that he's bouncing in his booster chair and kicking the back of my seat.

"How many do you think we'll find today? Maybe a million!"

"A million? You really think so?"

"Yep! Do you know how many zeros are in one million?"

"How many?" I ask.

"Six!" he tells me proudly. "One, zero, zero, zero, zero, zero, zero."

"Wow." I shake my head back and forth.

"I know! And I think I can even count the zeros in one *billion*."

"No way," I say, glad that he seems to have forgotten all about the kid that was giving him shit today.

He starts counting off on his fingers. "One, zero, zero, zero, zero, zero, zero, zero, zero, zero. That's nine!"

"Good work."

"How big of a jar do you think we'd need to hold a billion shark teeth?"

I chuckle. "I have no idea."

"Maybe as big as the car."

"I guess it would depend on the size of the teeth," I say as we pull onto our street.

Carter unbuckles his seatbelt and climbs over the console into the front seat. "If we found a billion megalodon teeth we'd probably need a jar the size of the house."

"Probably so." I throw the car into park and see that there is a petite woman hovering near the front door of the house. *Great,* she's probably here trying to sell us a vacuum or a Bible.

Carter wrinkles his forehead. "Who's that lady?"

"I have no clue, bud, but we'd better go find out."

"She looks like a teacher."

Or a funeral director, I think, taking in her briefcase and serious pantsuit. She certainly seems out of place on this side of town where most everyone works with their hands and doesn't have an extra pot to piss in.

"Whatever it is you're selling, lady," I say as we crunch our way across the oyster shell driveway to the front porch. "Sorry for your trouble but we're not buying."

The woman crooks her eyebrows and looks between my brother and I, her eyes lingering on the marker mustache on his face.

"I'm not here looking for a sale. Can I ask if you always allow this child to ride in the front seat of your truck?"

Carter tells her, "I'm only allowed when we're on our street."

I place my hand on his shoulder and force him back a step. "Not to be rude, but this is none of your concern."

"Actually, it is," she tells me with a reedy smile. "I'm with the Green Cove County Department of Children and Family Services."

What the hell?

My guts turn over and I know Carter can't be doing much better. Hell, I can *feel* the way he's looking at me and the anxiety rolling off of his little body in waves.

"Carter," I say to him quietly. "Can you go back to the Bronco and grab your lunch box. I think you left it in the backseat."

He swallows and nods, his eyes dark with worry.

When we're alone, the woman holds out an ivory-colored business card that I'm too shaken to read. "I'm Elaine Travers," she says. "And you must be Sebastian Holbrook, the legal guardian of Carter Holbrook?"

A hundred thoughts tumbling around my head, I nod.

"We received a complaint about the minor's living situation and I am here for a surprise inspection of the premises."

"You got a complaint? From *who?*"

"I'm not at liberty to say." Her gaze sweeps from me to the door. "If you agree to let me have a look inside, this should be fairly quick and simple."

"And if I don't let you in?"

"Then I would have to contact my office and let them know that you are not cooperating. And things... well, they would become more complicated."

Complicated is not something I want. "What will you need

97

to look for?"

"This is a general inspection of the premises to make sure that the house is clean, food is available, and there are no signs of any illegal activity."

I nod, silently thanking whatever instinct had me go to the grocery store yesterday. At least we have the basics.

"I've already checked Carter's school attendance records and spoken to his teachers," she says, surprising me. "If you're not hiding anything here at the house, you should have nothing to worry about. Your brother's teacher reports that he's making strides with his schoolwork."

"Okay," I say, putting my key in the lock. I'm too sick to my stomach to follow her through the door so I stand there on the front porch, watching her move around the living room with her briefcase in one hand and a clipboard in the other.

"Bash?" Carter whispers, coming up the steps behind me and slipping his hand into mine. His skin is hot and sweaty. "We're not going to go on a shark hunt tonight, are we?"

I look down at him and tighten my grip. "No, bud. I don't think we are."

"Is something bad happening?"

Anger spears my chest. *Who would do this to us?*

"No. Everything is going to be fine," I say, more determined than ever to make this work. "I promise."

CHAPTER TEN

Amelia

"Are you okay?" I ask, flipping back the page of my notebook and using a pink gel pen to underline one of the vocabulary words that keeps tripping me up.

"Hmm?" Sebastian grumbles, not looking up from the textbook spread open in front of him.

It's Thursday and we're spending the lunch period in the back corner of the library studying for Spanish class. "I asked if everything is all right."

"Things are fine and dandy, Amelia," he says.

The curiosity that's been bothering me for the past ten minutes presses harder against my breastbone. "Really? Because you seem kind of—I don't know—*off.*"

He glances up at me, black hair falling down over his eyes. "It's nothing."

"Is that why you've read the same page at least a hundred times?"

His eyebrows come down and a look of annoyance moves across his face. "I'm studying. Isn't that why we're here, Amelia?"

I feel a prickle of heat in my cheeks and drop my head halfway. "Sorry, I shouldn't have asked."

"No... it's me. *Shit,*" he says, his chest rising slowly as he sucks in air. "I'm not used to explaining myself to anyone."

"You don't have to explain anything you don't want to." Good gravy, why am I so dumb? I sound like a public service announcement made by a guidance counselor to fend off peer pressure. *You don't have to do anything you don't want to.*

"But I want to," he says.

I nibble a little on my lower lip. "Okay?"

"It's about Carter."

A bolt of concern snakes its way through my body. "What's wrong? Are you worried that kid is bothering him still?"

"It's not like that. When we got home yesterday, there was a woman waiting for us from social services."

"*What?* Why?"

"A spontaneous inspection of the house," he says. "Someone filed an anonymous complaint."

"About you and Carter?" I ask, thinking that I'm not understanding him right.

He nods his head. "She went around making sure that it was a safe place for a kid to live. She said she'd have to file an official report but that everything seemed okay so I hope we're in the clear."

"How's Carter?"

"The whole time he was scared out of his mind and I'll tell you, I wasn't far off," he says and I can hear the fury in his voice. "I'm trying to get this all straight in my head, but I can't make sense of who would report us."

"Someone who doesn't know you very well."

He looks at me. "Or someone who knows me too well."

"I don't believe that. I've seen how you are with Carter. You love him."

Sebastian clears his throat and tips back in his chair. "I do, but that's not all it takes."

"It's a good start."

"Maybe." He shakes away a thought and refocuses his eyes on me.

"Can I ask you something I've wondered before?"

Sebastian lifts an eyebrow. "Shoot."

"Where's your father?"

I see a tick in his jaw. "No longer in the picture. And that's for the best."

"Oh."

"He was a drunk who used to get his kicks beating up on my mom and me."

"So what happened?"

"Nature."

"What do you mean?" I ask, confused.

"About three years ago, I was finally bigger than him. So one night when things got real bad, I knocked him down and told him we were better off without him and to turn tail and never show his ugly face again." He shrugs. "So far he hasn't."

I don't know how to respond. I open my mouth to say something—anything—but nothing comes out. The bell sounds then and I can't help but think, *saved by the bell*.

"Thanks for listening to me, Amelia," he says, slipping a pencil in between the pages of his book to hold his place. "I'm sorry we didn't get much Spanish done."

"It doesn't matter," I say, meaning it. "I'll just study at home this afternoon. You know you're welcome to join me if you're free."

"At your house?"

I nod, a nervous feeling flowing through me.

"Won't your parents mind?"

"My father will be at work and my stepmother has her sewing circle this afternoon."

He grins. "Okay then. I'll bring the Red Vines."

***

Sebastian Holbrook is in my house.

I repeat this sentence like a mantra as I rush around my room, looking for anything that might cause embarrassment. Frére Jacques, the stuffed rabbit that usually sits on my bed, is the first victim of my cleaning frenzy. With a quick kiss on his pilly forehead, I stuff him inside my nightstand and then I'm on underwear patrol, looking on every surface to make sure that there is not one scrap of offending lace in sight.

I'm a pretty clean person so this is quick work, which is lucky because I've left Sebastian downstairs with Daphne and there's no telling what will come out of her mouth if given enough time. My one consolation is that Nancy isn't home this afternoon. It's hard to imagine her having anything good to say about Sebastian and his messy hair and frayed jeans.

Again, the thought overwhelms me: *Sebastian Holbrook is in my house!*

Panting and wiping my palms on the thighs of my black leggings, I hurl myself down the stairs and fly into the kitchen. He's sitting on one of the stools in the breakfast bar, eating a rice crispy treat, and listening to Daphne describe (in excruciating detail) the dress she just bought for the Homecoming dance.

"—and then it comes down in the back like this," she says, spinning around and showing him with her hand how low the dressline dips. "And it's got this completely perfect chiffon rose that hides the zipper. I know how it sounds but I promise that it's not too schmaltzy."

Sebastian nods along like he's following every word and I smile to myself. Honestly, if it weren't for the mildly glazed look in his eyes, I might even think he found my sister's opus to her new dress interesting.

"Hey, you ready?" I ask, thinking how weird it is seeing him here, in my space, with Nancy's china collection displayed on the wall just over his head.

"Sure am," he says, almost leaping off the stool.

"Well you two have fun." Daphne sighs and leans up against the granite countertop. "Bash, if you want, I can finish telling you about the dress later."

He looks so horrified by the prospect, I almost burst out laughing.

102

"Um," he says, picking up the pace but trying not to be obvious about it. "That would be great, Daphne. Really great."

"Thank you," I whisper to him when we're on the stairs.

"For what?"

"For humoring her. I understand the self-control it takes because I've been listening to her describe *the dress*," I say, using air quotes, "for two days."

He says, "She's very pro-chiffon."

"And tulle."

"And ruching—whatever that is."

"Don't leave out the sequins."

"Like I would or *could* forget the sequins."

By the time we reach my room, we're both laughing. I swing the door open and step back to let him pass by.

Sebastian Holbrook is in my room!

Nervous, I watch him circle my bed, taking in all the little pieces of me. My old ballet shoes and jewelry hanging on a peg board near the closet. The mason jar full of seashells that Daphne and I collected three summers ago from Pine Island in the Outer Banks. The small collection of music boxes lined up along the back of my desk like a train. The framed photos next to my bed and the pillows piled beneath the window.

"What's with all the pillows?" he asks, stopping beside my bookcase.

"I like to study and read under the window for the light."

He doesn't answer right away, just peers into a shelf, examining a rainbow of worn book spines. "You have a lot of books. Have you read all of them?"

"Not *all* of them."

He looks at me with that half smile I'm starting to get to know. "But you've read most of them, haven't you?"

I scrunch up my nose. "Probably, though I don't have as much time to read as I want to lately."

"There's always time for books," he says. "And now that I

know how much you like to read, I'll have to introduce you to Neil Gaiman."

I remember that he told me Neil Gaiman was his favorite author. "I'd like that."

"So which one is your all-time favorite?" he asks, pointing to the shelves.

Asking a reader to pick *one* book is a nearly impossible thing. I scan the shelves for a minute, pausing on one of my favorite Sherlock Holmes mysteries and a book about a woman who is trained from childhood as a Geisha, before finally deciding. I pull out the book—one that had originally been my mother's when she was in college—and show him the cover.

"*Wuthering Heights?*"

I nod.

Sebastian considers this and says, "So you're a romantic."

"No one has ever called me a romantic before. A planner, an overachiever maybe... not a romantic."

"Any girl who chooses Heathcliff and Catherine out of all the characters in the world is either a romantic or mighty depressed."

I shrug. "Then maybe I'm depressed."

"I remember how you were at the beach so I'm leaning the other way."

I have no idea what to say to this so I awkwardly change subject. "So... Spanish?"

Sebastian knows what I'm doing but plays along and we each take a floor pillow and start to go over our notes and quiz each other on vocabulary words. It turns out that Sebastian is not the slacker I originally thought he was and just because he sits in the back of the classroom doesn't mean he's not following Mr. Gubera's lessons. His notes are actually more helpful than mine and I use them to make a new set of study cards.

"Amelia?"

At this point we've been studying for about an hour. "Yeah?"

"Something is bothering me."

My stomach tightens as I look up from the index cards I'm working on. There's something in his voice that lets me know his question has nothing to do with Spanish. "What is it?"

"Where's your Sky Magic wall?"

"Oh…" I look around at the familiar dryer lint colored walls. "I haven't gotten to it yet."

"It's been weeks."

"I know but I've never painted before and I wasn't sure what I was doing, so…"

"C'mon," he says, standing up from the floor and stretching his arms over his head. "It's not that hard and I'll help you do it. Where's the paint?"

"You want to paint the wall right *now?*"

"I'm here, aren't I?"

"But… but…" I sputter. "Don't you have to get Carter from school?"

Sebastian shrugs. "Seth already picked him up for me because I told him we were studying. He texted me ten minutes ago to let me know they were going to go get lost at the arcade for the next couple of hours so I'm good."

"What about Spanish?"

"I figure with how we've been going, we're both primed to ace the hell out of the exam," he says. "Now, where's that paint?"

Reluctantly, I show him the can of paint and the supplies hidden under the dust ruffle of my bed. The brushes are still in the plastic bags I brought them home in.

"You don't have to do this," I tell him as we lay protective sheeting over the carpet in my room. We've already moved my desk and knick knacks away from the wall.

"Actually," he says, surveying our work, "I think I do need

to do this for my own sanity. Exactly how long have you had this paint now?"

"Point taken," I say, finding a ponytail holder and securing my hair into a messy bun.

Sebastian gives the can a good shaking before opening the lid and carefully setting it aside. "You'll do tape and trim and I'll roll," he tells me and hands over a roll of blue painter's tape.

It takes longer than I think it will to get the tape right, but eventually I'm standing on a chair with a brush in my hand and Sebastian is walking me through the process. At first, I get too much paint on the brush and have to hurriedly clean up my drips, but after a couple of tries, I get it right. Or, at least, Sebastian seems satisfied enough with my work to leave me on my own.

"What do you have going on a week from Saturday?" he asks me, rolling the blue paint all the way to the ceiling with one confident pass. "Carter has a sleepover at his friend Nathan's house and Seth is playing a show down at The Biltmore. I was going to see if you wanted to check it out with me."

These words dangle in the air for a moment until he follows them up with, "Or not."

"No, I was just thinking that it's the same night as Homecoming."

He balls his left hand into a fist and rubs it over his face. "Oh right."

"Yeah..." I keep my eyes on the paintbrush, making sure to get a clean line. "I'm on the committee so I at least have to put in an appearance. And Daphne is on the court this year and she would probably murder me in my sleep if I miss her big moment. Or should I say—the dress' big moment?"

He laughs and I suck in a breath and continue, "Otherwise, I would have loved to go with you. I didn't even know that Seth was in a band."

"He *is* the band. There will be a guy to come in on drums when he needs them, but it's really him and his guitar."

Sebastian tells me a little more about Seth and how he's been playing since he was nine and is hoping to make an album of original songs in the next few years. As we talk, the wall begins to fill in with the new color, casting my entire room in cool bluish light. It's not even done and I can already tell that I love it. Wiping my hair from my forehead, I step back to appreciate our work.

"It looks amazing."

Sebastian is using the roller to reach the tape along the baseboards. He looks at me over his shoulder and laughs.

"What?" I ask, biting down on my lip.

"You have blue all over your forehead."

I look down and see that my hands are splattered with paint. "Ughhh! I must have smeared it with my hands."

"It will come off."

"As long as I can get paint free by Homecoming I'm okay."

He turns, plunking the roller into the pan to soak up more paint. "I didn't ask you before—who's your date?"

"I don't have one," I say, feeling inexplicably awkward to be answering this question. Sebastian and I have been beating around this whole friendship bush awhile now, but other than that first night at the beach, neither of us has brought up our dating lives. At all.

"You're not going with anyone?"

"A lot of people go alone. And Audra had wanted to set me up with some guy she knows from Middleburg High, but then she said he kept asking how tall I am and whether or not I was going to be wearing heels and, if so, how high..." I inhale deeply. "Anyway, I decided that the whole thing was becoming too much of an ordeal and I don't want to spend my night with some guy who may or may not be battling a Napoleon complex."

"Probably a sound plan."

I smile.

He glances over, catches me smiling then looks away. "I could always go and we could hit up Seth's show afterward. He doesn't go on until after ten."

There is a little silence before I manage to pull my head together and say, "You want to go to Homecoming?"

"*Want* might be a stretch." He shrugs his shoulders.

"I get it. It's not really your kind of thing."

"It's not, but I am curious considering that I've never been to a school dance."

"Not one?"

He shakes his head. "Nope."

"And you're thinking maybe you should do it before it's too late and you've missed out on your chance to experience all that taffeta and bad dancing?"

"Something like that."

"Because God forbid you miss out on teachers requesting that the Deejay play the *Cha-Cha Slide*. Not to mention the spiked punch or the cookie table."

He arches an eyebrow. "There's going to be a cookie table?"

"With three kinds of cookies," I tell him smugly. "Chocolate chip, snickerdoodle, and oatmeal raisin."

He's smiling widely now and it's impossible for me not to smile back.

"Damn, that settles it. What time should I pick you up?"

***

"That Spencer really is a nice boy," Nancy says, drizzling dressing over the olive salad.

"He sure is," Daphne responds as she digs into the risotto.

"I saw his mother this morning and was reminded what a lovely woman she is. Daphne, she told me that Spencer hopes to attend Georgetown next fall and that he just sent in his application. Maybe his college aspirations will rub off on you, sweetpea." Nancy gives her a pointed look.

"Guess what? Amelia's finally got a Homecoming date," my sister announces crudely. I kick her under the dining room table to let her know I don't appreciate being thrown under the bus like this. Of course I had planned to tell my parents about Sebastian and Homecoming. Just not right this minute.

Daddy looks up from his plate. He's an attorney and spends most of our family meals deep in thought or grumbling to himself about cases and clients who are pestering him. Only occasionally does our conversation draw his interest like this.

"That's wonderful, dear," Nancy says, smiling at me. "Now tell us—who's the lucky young man?"

Daphne answers, "Bash Holbrook."

Now we really have Daddy's attention. "*Bash?* And what kind of name is Bash?"

"It's short for Sebastian," I explain, starting to become uncomfortable. "Like a nickname."

"I see," Nancy says, her mouth tilting dubiously. "Amelia, can you tell us anything more about this Bash? Do we know the boy?"

"Well, he's a senior."

They both nod.

"And we've gone to school together since elementary school so you've probably seen him before, but I don't think you've been formally introduced."

Dad frowns. "At least we'll meet him when he comes to pick you up for your date."

Nancy says, "Actually, we have the Perry's fundraiser that night, but I can cancel if you think it's best to be here and meet Amelia's date."

I have to struggle to keep from shouting. "Um, no. You

don't need to cancel for me. It's not even a real date. We're just going together because it's convenient."

"And Bash is a really cool guy," Daphne says, flashing me a look of regret. *That's right, sister, you should be sorry for bringing this up!* "He works at Kane's Hardware."

"Isn't that interesting," Nancy says. "Is Bash on a sports team at your school?"

"No, he's not the sporty type."

"Well, is he in one of your clubs?"

"No."

"What about colleges. Do you know which ones he's considering for next year?" she tries.

"I... uh... I don't think he's decided yet," I answer, shoving a bite of chicken picatta into my mouth and chewing aggressively. I am *really* disliking this conversation.

"What do his parents do? Do we know them?" These are usually the kinds of questions they reserve for Daphne's dates.

"Nancy, why does that matter what his parents do? Are you going to ask me for his fingerprints also?" I ask defensively.

"Amelia Laine!" Dad reprimands. "There is no need to sass your stepmother. We're curious about your date because the world is a dangerous place. We only want what's best for our girls. That's fair, isn't it?"

"Yes, sir," I mumble, cowed by his use of my middle name like I'm six years old again.

He picks up the glass of sweet tea near his plate and swirls the straw around the glass before taking a sip. "And truth be told, Amelia, we've picked up on some changes in you recently."

Nancy nods her head in agreement and that fidgety feeling in my belly grows stronger. *Where is this going?*

"Like what?"

"Mostly small things," Nancy starts.

"Like what?" I repeat.

"You seem distracted and I've certainly noted a decline in the amount of time you're spending on schoolwork."

"That's because I've been busy helping plan things with the Homecoming committee," I contend, my face flushing. "Not to mention that I've got volunteer commitments and the tennis team breathing down my back and Mrs. Kyle is already asking me to organize a food drive for the holidays. But I won't let my grades suffer. I promise."

Daddy says sternly, "You haven't let me look at your Emory essay as of yet."

"Because I haven't written it!"

He just looks at me. "That's exactly what we're talking about, darlin'. If I'm remembering things correctly, you had planned to have all of your college essays completed last Friday."

"And your room, dear," Nancy adds.

"What about my room?"

"You didn't even ask if you could paint it and yet I leave for a few hours for my sewing circle and when I come home, you've painted a wall blue in your room."

I feel a lump rise in my throat, thick and painful. "It's just paint. If you don't like it, I'll change it back."

"I'm not arguing that I don't like it; I'm simply pointing out that this sort of behavior seems out of character for you, Amelia."

"Darlin'," Daddy says, "we don't want you to lose sight of the finish line when you're this close to getting what you want. We're not criticizing you. We're nudging."

Nudging? It feels more like a hammer hitting me over the head. Repeatedly.

I stare down at the fork balanced on the edge of my plate not knowing how to respond. *Have I been distracted? Am I really letting things slip?* I *did* allow my self-imposed deadline for college essays to come and go.

111

"Hey, did I tell you guys that I'm thinking of getting a tattoo?" Daphne blurts out, breaking the terrible silence. "A bird or maybe a star or something else right along here." She lifts up a hand showing us the pale skin on the underside of her wrist.

My mouth flaps open in surprise. Nancy and Daddy both turn to Daphne, their eyes bulging from their heads. And, like that, my interrogation is over.

CHAPTER ELEVEN

Bash

It doesn't seem to matter that Elaine Travers cleared us almost as soon as she walked into our house last week. I still feel like she and the entire Department of Children and Family Services are looking over my shoulder. Watching me. Taking notes. Judging me.

Because of this, I've been trying to take special care with things, like packing healthier lunches and making sure to pick Carter up on time. But it's not like I can control everything.

Which is precisely what I'm thinking when my cell phone rings in the middle of class and Mr. Gubera loses his cool.

"Mr. Holbrook, I think you are aware of my no cell phone policy," he scolds, glaring at me from over the thin metal rims of his glasses.

"I am," I say, checking my phone anyway. Shit, I missed a call from Carter's school.

"I don't think it's too much to ask you kids to keep your cell phones on vibrate, is it?"

"It's not, but..." I point to my phone. "I might have an emergency."

"Fine. At least take it outside so you don't disturb the rest of the class," he says, gesturing to the classroom door.

"Thanks. And I'm sorry," I say, stuffing my notebook into my bag and slipping out of my chair. Amelia catches my eye as I head out the door. *You okay,* she mouths. *I don't know,* I mouth back.

In the hall, I play the voicemail.

This is Susan Knowles, the nurse at Green Cove Elementary. I've got Carter Holbrook in my clinic and it appears he's come down with a stomach bug that's been circulating the primary grades. I've given him some fluids and let him rest on one of my beds, but I think he'd do a lot better at home. If you could call the school and arrange for pick up, I'd greatly appreciate it.

So Carter's sick. I'll have to miss the test in my economics class this afternoon, but at least I'm sure I can get Mrs. Martin to give me a make-up.

I make a quick stop in the office and let Ms. Hanson, the lady who guards the admission desk know why I'll be gone. Then I haul ass out to the parking lot and get into the Bronco and—SHIT.

The thing won't start.

I turn the key again. The engine screeches like it wants to turn over, but it dies out before it catches.

"Come on!" I beg, simultaneously punching the steering wheel and twisting the key.

Nothing.

"Great," I mumble as I reach over into the passenger seat to find my phone. I'll have to get Seth's help and if that doesn't work out then I'll call my Aunt Denise.

As soon as my fingers wrap around the phone, it starts to ring in my hand. Thinking it's Carter's school, I don't even bother looking at the screen.

"I'm on my way," I say.

A pause. "On your way where?"

It takes me a second to make out who the voice belongs to. "Amelia?" We traded numbers when we studied together but this is the first time she's used it.

"Yeah, hi. I was just checking to make sure that everything is okay because you never came back to Spanish class."

"The nurse from Carter's school called. I need to go pick him up but my truck won't start."

"Where are you?"

"I'm sitting in the parking lot trying to figure out what to

114

do next," I tell her. "Thanks for checking in, but I've got to go so I can text Seth. I think he might be able to give me a ride out to the elementary school and hopefully home."

"Oh, okay," she replies slowly. "Or you could get that girl walking toward you to help."

"What?"

"The brown-haired one with the purple backpack. Do you see her?"

I pick up my head and spot Amelia walking out the main doors of the school. "What are you doing, Amelia?"

"Helping out," she says into the phone.

"But you've got class," I remind her when she reaches the edge of the parking lot. "Isn't this your AP History period?"

I see her shrug her shoulders. "I'll just tell Mrs. Turner that I had to work on important Homecoming stuff."

I chuckle in disbelief. "You're going to lie to one of your teachers?"

"I don't know if I would call it a lie."

"Then what would you call it?"

She's almost to my car. "Bending the truth."

"I don't want you to get in trouble for me. I know school's important to you."

Amelia dangles her keys and says into the phone. "I've heard that some things are more important."

Our eyes meet through the windshield and something razor-sharp inside of me wrenches free. Have I been kidding myself this whole time? I never wanted to fall for Amelia Bright, but now I know I was just fooling myself. I can't *not* fall for this girl.

It's impossible.

***

"Now you're all set," Amelia says as she swings a plastic grocery bag up onto the kitchen counter.

After we got Carter from school, she insisted we stop at the store so she could run in and pick up a "magic cure," which as it turns out consists of peach popsicles, ginger ale, and five cans of chicken noodle soup.

"Where do these go?" she asks as she pulls the cans of soup from the bag.

"I've got them," I say, acutely aware that this is the first time that Amelia has been to my house. It's nothing like her place and I'm wondering what she makes of the low ceilings, the peeling kitchen wallpaper, and the well-used furnishings.

"Carter," she calls, poking her head around the hallway corner, "what do you want, sweetie?"

Predictably, he says, "A popsicle."

"How about some soup and then a popsicle?" I shoot back.

Amelia grins at me. "That sounds fair. The magic cure doesn't really work unless all three ingredients are combined."

I open the cabinet above the sink. "I'll pour him a ginger ale."

While I get the soup going, Amelia entertains Carter in his room. He introduces her to our cat, Jinx, and she tells him that she's allergic but should be fine as long as she doesn't pet her.

"You can't pet cats?" he asks.

"If I do my eyes get red and I start to sneeze."

"That's *sad*."

"I agree. It is sad."

I'm pouring the steaming soup into a bowl when I hear Carter ask her, "Can you read me a story?"

"Sure thing," she answers instantly. "Which one?"

Carter must be pointing to a book. He says, "Mama said that one was Bash's favorite."

It must be *Where the Wild Things Are*. When I was a kid, I made her read that one a thousand times.

"That makes sense," Amelia says. "In the book, Max

reminds me a bit of Sebastian."

"Yeah. They're both grumpy sometimes."

"True. But both Max and Sebastian are good guys."

"Why do you call him Sebastian?" Carter asks.

"Isn't that his name?"

"Everyone else calls him Bash. Only Mama called him Sebastian."

Amelia hesitates. "Well, I think it's a great name. It's no wonder your mother wanted to use it."

Carter yawns. "Are you his girlfriend? Is that why you call him that?"

Shit.

"I'm a friend who's a girl," Amelia says carefully, "but I'm not his girlfriend in the way that you're thinking."

"I didn't like his last girlfriend. She was icky." This is news to me. I always thought that Carter and Rachel got on pretty well.

"Oh?" she asks as I creep closer to the bedroom door.

"Yep. She was always rolling her eyes at me or talking to me like I was stupid. You're much better."

Amelia gives a soft laugh. "Thank you."

"And it would be okay with me if you were Bash's girlfriend. Then you'd get to spend even more time with me and that would be good."

I think that's my cue. I loudly enter Carter's room and set a glass on the small table next to his bed. "Here's your ginger ale."

Jinx is curled up on the foot of the bed and Carter is buried beneath his favorite blue blanket. It's sort of dingy but the kid fights me every time I try to wash the thing.

"Thank you," he says, sitting up and taking a sip from the glass. "Amelia is going to read to me."

"Amelia probably needs to get back to school, bud."

"No way. Not until I read this story," she says. "Carter tells me it's your favorite."

117

"What else did he tell you?"

"Secret stuff," Carter answers, twisting his fingers around the blanket and pulling it up to his chin.

"Oh yeah? Well, the soup is probably cool enough now. If you eat it all up, I'll let you have one of those popsicles Amelia got you."

Carter gives me a weak salute. "Aye aye, Captain."

"Let me help you with the soup," Amelia says, standing from the bed and setting the book aside.

"No, I can get it," I start to tell her, but she's already in the hall.

"Bash, can I have some crackers too?" Carter asks.

"You got it."

"And cookies?" he asks hopefully.

"Don't push your luck there, hoss."

"It was worth a try," he sighs and lets his eyes flutter shut. He really does look pale and tired. I hope he'll get some sleep after he has the soup and popsicle.

In the kitchen, Amelia is blowing on the soup. "I think this should be fine," she says, glancing at me over one shoulder.

"Good. The little man is exhausted. I hope this magic cure of yours does the trick."

That dimple in her cheek makes an appearance. "Trust me, his fever is going to break by tonight and he's going to feel much better."

I pick up the bowl of soup and reach around her to rip a paper towel off the roll. She moves to the side so I can get past, but I'm still close enough to smell her skin—that intoxicating blend of citrus and soap.

"About my name..." I say.

"Y-yes?" she stammers awkwardly, probably realizing that I was listening in on her and my brother and I overheard the girlfriend question.

"It's true what Carter said. You are the only one who calls

me Sebastian now."

She shifts in place uncomfortably. "I can stop if you don't like it."

I make sure that our eyes hold when I tell her, "Don't stop. I like it."

Her mouth falls a little and her breathing changes. I can actually see her chest pumping faster and her eyes flick to my lips, which I think is a good sign. Is it possible that she's thinking of me the way that I'm thinking of her?

Testing the waters, I lean in and tilt my upper body more fully to her. Her eyebrows furrow and she takes a deliberate breath like she's deciding something. Damn, maybe it *is* possible...

"Bash?" I hear from Carter's room.

A frustrated sound escapes my throat. Not taking my eyes off Amelia, I call out, "Yeah?"

"Can you find Red Dead Fred for me? He's hiding."

"Red Dead Fred?" Amelia whispers.

"That's his bear," I whisper back, feeling the corners of my mouth crook. "Don't ask me how he came up with it."

"Got it." She takes the bowl and paper towel from me. "So, you go find the bear and I'll carry the soup."

"Kay." Then louder, I call out. "I'm coming, bud. You know Red Dead Fred can't hide from me."

I don't have to look back to know that Amelia is watching me go.

Game on.

CHAPTER TWELVE

Amelia

"Too much, too much!" I moan, staring at myself in the mirror.

Daphne pops her head into the bathroom. She is struggling with one of her earrings. "What is it—*ooooh!*"

"I was going for the smokey eye look," I tell her, frantically rubbing at my face. "But I may have gotten a little overzealous with the eyeliner."

It's an understatement. Right now there's so much black stuff rimmed around my eyes that I could pass for a raccoon.

"This is no biggie," Daphne says, setting down her necklace next to the sink. She reaches for a washcloth and pumps a dollop of face wash onto it.

"No biggie? If Nancy was home, she would tell me I look like the Bride of Frankenstein!"

"Then lucky for you that they're at a charity dinner," she says as she slaps my hands away from my face and gently dabs at my eyes. "And for the record, you do not look like the Bride of Frankenstein. You're way more mermaid than zombie. I love that dress."

"It's *your* dress."

She gives me a cheeky smirk. "See? I just knew someone with impeccable taste picked it out."

I laugh. "So can you really fix me up in time?"

"Of course I can." She dries my face with the other end of the washcloth and then looks through our makeup bin, selecting a tube of foundation, a light powder, and a shimmery dark grey eyeshadow. Turning back to me, she says, "Let me work a little magic and, trust me, your man won't know what hit him when you walk down those stairs."

At the mention of Sebastian, the butterflies trapped in my stomach burst into a frenzied flight. "You don't think I'm overdoing it? We're only going as friends and I'm afraid that *this*—" I indicate the silky turquoise dress I'm wearing and my hair, "—is sending the wrong message."

"What are you going on about? Are you worried that he's going to show up here in those old jeans he wears or those God-awful sneakers?"

I love those sneakers. "No, I'm sure he'll dress up a little. At least... I guess he will. We didn't talk about it."

"I'm sure he'll be passable and you, sister dear, look mighty fab-u-lous. Your hair is exquisite and I'm convinced poems will be written about it."

Earlier, she wove my hair into six uneven braids and looped them at the crown of my head in an intricate knot that she finished off with tiny black pearl bobby pins.

"I'm not saying that I don't love it. I'm just worried that it's too... too..."

"Gorgeous?"

"I guess." I fiddle with the loose strands around my face and frown. "I don't want Sebastian to think that I'm trying to come on to him."

"But aren't you?" she asks as she dusts my nose with powder.

"No."

"And why is that, Amelia? You're single and he's single... You're attractive and he's attractive... For the life of me, I can't see what the problem is."

"There isn't a problem." I close my eyelids so that she can apply the eyeshadow. "I just don't think he likes me like that."

"That's crap."

"It's not," I maintain. "I've already told you that the night

121

we drove to Murrels Inlet, he said all this stuff and made it perfectly clear to me that there's not a snowball's chance in hell of things between us heading in that direction. He said that his life is too complicated."

Of course, the other day when Carter was sick, I could have sworn that he was about to kiss me. Even now, I can almost *feel* how his big body felt pressed ever so slightly against mine and the way his warm breath misted over my lips and eyelids. Just the memory of it makes me get all shivery and anxious.

I've got it so bad.

Assessing me, Daphne picks up a tube of mascara and unscrews the cap. She plunges the wand back and forth a few times to make sure the brush is evenly coated. "People change their minds. And do you want to know what I figure?"

I laugh nervously. "I'm not sure I do."

"I'll tell you anyway. I think you already like him. *A lot.* And I think you're just fooling yourself by pretending this isn't a real date," she says, daubing my lips with a reddish gloss. "Think about it: Sebastian Holbrook is going to our school's Homecoming. For *you*."

"But…"

"Relax a touch," she commands.

"I can't. It's scary."

"Well, you know what I think about that," she says. "If something scares you then it's probably worth doing, and that goes double for boys. And why are you so nervous anyway? It's not like you haven't spent time with him. I swear, lately that's *all* you've been doing. If I weren't so self-assured that you love me best, I'd be green with jealousy."

"Sebastian isn't the only reason I'm on edge. What if something goes wrong tonight—you know, with the dance and everything?"

"Amelia, you know this thing is going to go off without a

hitch. There's no other option with you in charge." She smiles confidently and picks up the large powder brush. "And when yours truly takes the stage to accept the crown for Homecoming Queen, not one streamer or paper lantern will be out of place."

"Are you mocking me?"

"No, I'm mocking *me*. I know that Homecoming court is cheesy but I'm still excited about it."

"You should be. You're going to win."

"Eh, if I don't…" She shrugs as she applies a swipe of ivory powder across my forehead and down the bridge of my nose. "We'll still have fun tonight. Did I tell you that I think Spencer has something big planned for me after the dance?"

"What is it?"

She pulls in a breath and releases it slowly. "I can't be sure but he mentioned taking me down to his daddy's boat and I think he might tell me that he loves me."

I meet her eyes in the mirror. "What will you say?"

"That I love him back."

"Do you?"

"I don't know for sure, but I *want* to be in love. Isn't that enough for tonight?"

"I guess," I say and swallow down my doubts about Spencer McGovern. I might not like him, but it's obvious that Daphne does. She might even *love* the guy.

"And I think we might…" her voice trails off.

"You might what?"

She waggles her eyebrows and understanding dawns. *So the V card is in play?*

Truthfully, I have no idea what to think. For all of our lives, as different as we are, Daphne and I have always done the big things in tandem. Our first steps were within hours of each other. Dad took the training wheels off our bikes at the exact same time. The summer after we turned seven, I was waiting on the ladder for my turn when my sister went off the diving board into the deep end of the pool. We had our first kisses only three days apart.

And yet now she's telling me that she's batting for a home run while I'm still in the dugout munching on a box of Cracker Jacks.

The telltale sound of an engine rumbling up the long drive makes both of our eyes go wide.

Daphne drops the makeup brush with a squeal and rushes over to the small bathroom window. "It's Sebastian!"

"No, no, no! He can't see me like this."

"Shhhh… calm down." Daphne chuckles to herself. "Geesh, when did you think I'd be the one telling you to calm down?"

"But I'm not ready!"

"I will go downstairs and let your date in and I'll even entertain him until you finish. One more coat of mascara and some bronzer should do it. Oh, and shoes. Don't forget your shoes."

"Thank you. Did I mention that you're the best sister in the world and you look beautiful?"

She smooths down her shiny brown waves and does a playful curtsy. Then she grabs her necklace off the counter. "See you in a minute. And just remember—you've got this completely covered."

The chime of the doorbell echoes throughout the house. My heartbeat skips wildly and I can almost *hear* the blood rushing through the veins in my body. *Relax, Amelia.*

Daphne's footsteps pound on the stairs. "I'm coming!"

Inhale, exhale. I blow out a gush of air and force myself to take in another deep calming breath as I finish my makeup exactly like Daphne told me.

Now I can make out voices. Daphne loudly compliments Sebastian on "how well he cleans up," and I get the feeling that she's hoping I'm listening, which only makes me that much more nervous to see him.

Inhale, exhale.

Trying to keep my heartrate under control, I walk into my room and slip on the pretty silver heels resting on the foot of my bed. Then I turn to the long mirror on the back of my door for one last look.

A couple of strands of brown hair are falling into my eyes and I try to sweep them to the side, but they fall right back. But overall, I suppose I don't look too terrible.

The dress hugs me tighter than anything I've ever worn before. It's long and sleek with barely-there sleeves that fall off my shoulders. I run my fingers over the soft turquoise fabric and twist around so that I can see what I look like from the back. Daphne and Audra are always telling me to play up my butt and I'm hoping this is what they meant.

The doorbell rings again. Great, that has to be Spencer. It's probably unfair after everything Daphne's told me, but I'd been hoping to avoid a run-in at the house. My sister might just love the guy, but when it comes to Spencer McGovern, less is definitely more in my book.

"Come on in, honeydew!" Daphne yells.

Honeydew? Ugh, gag me.

The front door opens and slams closed. I take one more breath as I grab my purse from the knob of my closet door and double-check that I've got lip gloss and money. But before I can even turn around, a savage commotion assaults my ears. My insides rattle as I abandon my things on the bed and run toward the noise. "Is everything…?"

In an instant, I take in the chaotic scene unraveling below me in the foyer. The antique umbrella holder that belonged to my grandmother is overturned and Nancy's favorite lamp is smashed. Tiny ceramic bits lay scattered between the front door and the landing.

"Daphne?"

She is cowering against the door that opens into Daddy's office, covering her face with her hands to protect herself from Spencer and Sebastian, who are currently in an armlock.

"You asshole," Spencer growls out as he tries to head butt Sebastian. Sebastian ducks and they both skid into the wall, knocking down a black and white portrait of my grandfather. *No, not Pops!*

I grip the railing with sweaty fingers and scream, "Stop it! Stop!"

Sebastian jerks my way and Spencer uses the distraction to get a jab in. Sebastian grunts in pain but manages to wrench himself free and seize hold of Spencer's clenched fist. In one powerful and swift move, he hooks Spencer's arm behind his back and knocks him to the floor.

"Stay down!" he yells in Spencer's ear.

"What is going on?" I gape, horrified.

Sebastian is breathing hard. He positions his knee dead-center on Spencer's spine and wipes at his hair and I see a trail of blood from his temple to his chin. "This piece of shit tried to attack Daphne."

I can't even process this. "*What?*"

"I did no such thing. You are out of control," Spencer spits out nastily, continuing to struggle. "Why don't you tell Amelia how you had your filthy hands inside her sister's dress!"

"Shut your mouth!" Sebastian orders and presses his knee down harder. "Have you lost your mind? I was helping her with her necklace."

Bewildered, I look at Daphne, who is still slumped forward gently rocking herself. The strap of her dress—the dress she's been worshiping for weeks—is torn and hanging loose from one shoulder.

Could Spencer have done that?

I look back to where he's panting on the floor. His handsome face is red and twisted with rage.

Yes, he absolutely could have.

"Get out," I say just above a whisper.

"Thank you," Spencer grunts, kicking his feet out in frustration. "You heard her, monkey boy. Now, if you'll get the fuck off me and go back to the projects where you belong."

"I meant *you*, Spencer."

"You're kidding, right?" he asks me as Sebastian pulls him to his feet.

"No…" My voice is trembly. "I think you should go."

"This is wrong," he snaps at me and then twists his head around. "Daphne, you know how I feel about you. Baby, straighten out your sister and tell her to call off her guard dog."

In reply, Sebastian shoves him harder toward the door.

"Not necessary," Spencer sneers resentfully. Then he lifts his wide shoulders and brushes off the front of his suit jacket. "I can see myself out. But do not think for one minute that my father will not be hearing of this."

"Wait!" Daphne shouts, acting quickly and all but lunging at Spencer. "H-he didn't mean anything by it. Please!"

I look at her hard. "What are you doing?"

"It's a mistake, Amelia," she cries, clumsily grabbing hold of Spencer's hands and dragging her body toward his. "Really! You have to believe me."

"I don't…" I rasp, my voice catching in the back of my throat. Everything is moving too fast and I can't seem to catch up. "You're sure?"

Her nod is as frantic as her expression.

"See?" Spencer gives me a scornful look as he runs a hand through his curling dirty blond hair to smooth it down.

I ignore him and move toward my sister. Uncertainty is knotting up my stomach and sending mixed signals to my brain. "But," I say to her, "look at your dress."

She awkwardly tugs the loose strap onto her shoulder and tries to keep it in place by tucking it into the fabric under her armpit. "The dress will be fine. *I'll* be fine. It was just an

127

accident."

"An accident?" Sebastian asks tightly. "I saw him and it looked like he pushed you into that wall."

"No one wants your opinion, Holbrook," Spencer says smugly. "By the way, are you even housebroken? Shouldn't you be sniffing ass on the other side of town with the rest of the hicks?"

Sebastian balls his fists. "You push your luck, McGovern."

"Do I?" he scowls, but he backs away.

Like I'm in a dream, I watch Daphne shake out her hair and wipe at the skin beneath her eyes where her mascara has dripped. Spencer bends to pick up the pieces of the broken lamp and straighten the umbrella holder. He scoops up her necklace from where it landed by the curving legs of the hall table then slips it over her head and fumbles with the latch. If I wasn't so focused on my sister right now, I might miss the way she flinches when his hands move on her neck, but I *am* watching and I see it plain as day.

My breathing gets heavier as I start thinking back over the past month or so, to that party at Byron Scott's house and how Daphne and Spencer had that fight and how later she'd told me that she hurt her arm falling into a doorway. Was that even true? Is *anything* true?

"Your arm." The words are out of my mouth before I can stop them.

Daphne's eyes dart cagily from Spencer to me. "What?"

"Has Spencer hurt you like this before?"

She rears back like I'm the one who pushed her. "*God*, Amelia! It was an accident. I already *told* you—this was nothing but a huge misunderstanding."

"How can you say that?" I ask, overwhelmed by the throbbing sense of danger. "You're confused. I think I should call Nancy and Daddy."

"Amelia, stop!" she bellows, squeezing her eyes shut and punching her hands over her ears. "I don't want to hear that

I'm confused when I'm not. And if you call our parents, just know that I will never *ever* speak to you again."

My throat is burning—dry and hot—and I wonder then if I'm about to cry. "Daphne, *please*," I gasp, unsure of what to do or how to do it. "Just give me a minute to think about things."

"She can't give you a minute because we're going to be late," Spencer says, wrapping his arm around my sister's waist and pulling her into his side.

I blink at Daphne, stunned, and draw in a sharp breath. "You still want to go to Homecoming?"

Her mouth twists to the side. "Why wouldn't we?"

Why wouldn't we?

Spencer sees the expression on my face and says, "Amelia, you need to stop being so pissy. Despite what your juvenile delinquent here wants you to think, I did not and would not hurt your sister."

"He's right," Daphne agrees, pasting on a bogusly bright smile. Her eyes go to the mirror above the hall table and she carefully spreads her shiny, chestnut hair to one side, covering up the broken dress strap. "This is a really big night for you and for me. Let's try to forget about all this messiness and go have fun."

Have fun? Is she kidding?

"Daphne, *please*?"

"Don't, Amelia," she warns, waving me off as Spencer tugs her toward the door. "I'll see you there, okay? Everything is going to be great. You wait and see."

With my brain and body frozen somewhere between disbelief and defeat, I watch them leave and climb into Spencer's cherry red BMW.

Inhale, exhale.

Dusk creeps in through the thin, arching windows that crown the front door, making fiery orange bands across the thick Persian rug. In the quiet, I dimly hear the rumble of the

129

ice maker coming from the kitchen and the sound of the hall clock clicking away the seconds.

Finally, Sebastian's deep voice breaks through the stillness. "Are you okay?"

I come close to telling him that I'm fine because that's my programmed response when someone asks me how I'm doing. But then I think better of it. The truth is that I'm not fine. Not by a long shot.

"Not really."

"Do you want me to leave?"

"No."

"Do you still want to go to Homecoming?"

The thought of Homecoming has me so nauseated I can almost taste the bitter on my tongue. *All those people...* But that's the life I signed up for. As Daddy likes to say, *I've made my bed and now I have to lie in it whether I want to or not.*

"I can't skip it."

"Why not?"

"Because—" I turn from the door and stop short. I've been so upset, I haven't allowed myself to really take a look at Sebastian.

He's got on a black two-button suit over a crisp white shirt. He's not wearing a tie, but he doesn't need one to look great. I mean, I've already discovered that he's hot in his daily uniform of holey jeans, sneakers, and the t-shirts he designs, but *like this?*

Even though he's roughed-up from his brawl with Spencer, I can tell that he took the time to do his hair and shave. And with his dark hair slicked back from his forehead and his face clean-cut and completely visible, it becomes obvious that all this time he's been playing down his looks.

Sebastian isn't just attractive or passable. He is *unbelievably* gorgeous.

He takes a sharp breath in through his nose and his hard, grey eyes tighten. "Amelia? What is it?"

130

My hands fly to my face to hide my blush as I try to regain my train of thought. "I... I can't just not go to the dance. I'm one of the planners and people are counting on me. *Daphne* is counting on me."

"You think it will make a difference?"

"I don't know what happened here, but I can't just let it go. I have to try to talk to her again."

He nods in understanding. "She's your sister."

Inhale, exhale. "No matter what."

CHAPTER THIRTEEN

Bash

I'm so focused on Amelia and how she's handling what happened back at her house that I don't notice it right away. It's not until we've been at the dance for almost an hour that I start to pick up on the whispers and furtive glances being thrown in our direction.

There's a big part of me that wants to think these people, the ones we see in the halls every day at school, are admiring Amelia with her hair up and away from her face and her body looking perfect in that blue dress. I would understand because tonight, even after everything that went down, she's amazing and it's got my brain going in so many directions I can't tell up from down.

But I know that's not why everyone is looking over here and talking low behind their cupped hands. The fact is that no one sees Amelia looking beautiful or the way she's making sure this dance goes off without a hitch. They don't witness her running around in high-heeled shoes, stocking the punch table with plastic cups or checking in with the deejay to remind him what songs to play. Nope, they don't see anything real about her. They are too preoccupied with the way she's standing next to me.

Because it doesn't matter that I'm dressed up in a stuffy rental suit or that I shaved and used Seth's gel to tame my hair back. Or that I'm raising a kid and working to support us both. It doesn't count that I'm going to make the honor roll this term, or that I haven't so much as smoked a joint or sipped a beer since my mother was diagnosed over a year ago.

To this crowd—Amelia's crowd—I'm nothing but a shady kid who grew up on the wrong side of town and that's all I'll ever be.

I'm no-good Nick Holbrook's kid. Elected most likely to... *Be a drunk. A degenerate. A loser. Get a girl pregnant.* Take your pick.

"What's wrong?" Amelia asks.

"Nothing," I say, tensing and clenching my hands into tight fists. "I should probably be asking you that same question."

"Because of Daphne?" Amelia glances over to where her sister and Spencer are laughing and holding court with their whole crew at one of the round banquet-style tables. She furrows her forehead and says, "I don't know what to do about this, Sebastian. She won't even *talk* to me so I don't think I'm going to be able to get her away from him unless I drag her behind me kicking and screaming the whole way out of here."

"And that's out of the question?"

At least that gets a small smile out of her even if she bites it back. "It's like, why isn't she willing to have a conversation with me? What the heck did *I* do wrong? She should be mad at Spencer, right? Instead she's acting like she's angry with *me*."

"Your sister is embarrassed or scared. Or probably a little bit of both," I say, thinking back on Mama and how she'd get when my father was in one of his moods. Thank Christ it hadn't gone that far with lousy, fucking Spencer McGovern. Still, I see the potential and the danger there and it's got my guard way up.

"Maybe it really was a misunderstanding or whatever and we don't know the whole story," she says, worrying on her bottom lip.

"It didn't look that way to me. He walked into your house and went straight for her."

"But Daphne's not like that," she tells me and I can see how much she wants to believe the truth in her own words. "I mean, she might be into Spencer but she's not one of those girls. If I could just get her alone for a minute then maybe I could reason with her."

"*There* you are!" Audra Singer comes up behind Amelia. She's wearing a short yellow dress and heels that add about four inches to her tiny frame. Her bright blond hair is arranged in a halo of curls around her face. "Amelia, you keep runnin' off when I'm wantin' to get a group photo!"

Amelia shakes her head in apology. "Sorry, I guess I've been distracted tonight."

"I'll say," Audra responds, laughing and draping an arm over Amelia's shoulders. "Looksy, I'm tryin' to get a shot in before they announce the court. I heard from Chad Wooten, whose girlfriend was in charge of countin' up the votes, that the happy couple won this thing by a landslide."

Amelia's face crumples. "They did?"

I follow her gaze to the *happy* couple. Spencer is holding Daphne possessively against his chest as he leans in and kisses her neck. No wonder Amelia looks like she's about to be sick.

"Mr. Brickler is goin' to announce the king and queen in like ten so let's get Daphne and Spencer and—wait. Amelia, what in the world is the matter with you?"

Amelia doesn't answer. She's crying and shaking her head.

Audra glares over at me. "Did you do somethin' to her, Bash Holbrook? Because I swear to all that is holy, if you hurt my best friend, I will tear your freakin' balls off so fast you won't be able to squeal."

"It's not Sebastian!" Amelia sobs.

"What's wrong then?"

"It's just—" She doesn't finish. She picks up the hem of her blue dress and takes off, disappearing through the closest exit.

Audra turns to face me. "Did I say somethin' wrong?"

"No, she's just... upset."

She pops her hip and gives me an annoyed look. "Really, Sherlock? Like I couldn't tell that Amelia is upset about somethin'. Jeez Louise—*what* is the problem?"

"It's sister stuff," I say vaguely and hope that Audra doesn't push me. I'm not sure it's my place to tell her about what is going on between Amelia and Daphne.

"Sister stuff," she repeats slowly, holding up her hands. "Okay... so then why aren't you goin' after her like your life depends on it?"

I eye her, wary. "Maybe she needs to be alone. Or maybe she'd rather talk to you."

Audra flicks her wrist impatiently. "Are you stupid or somethin'? Don't you see how that girl looks at you? Trust me, there is no one else on God's green earth that Amelia wants to go to her right now."

I look off, considering things. Shit, if what Audra is saying is right then I am being a complete fool. "Do you think so?"

Here comes an eye roll. "Of course I think so. Go on and get your head out of your ass and chase her down already."

I swallow thickly and take a deep breath before pivoting around. "Thanks."

"Well," she yells after me, "you better be believin' you owe me one, Bash Holbrook!"

The door Amelia ran through leads to a dim and sterile hallway that circles around the back of the school gym. I have no idea which direction she went so it takes me a minute to spot her crouched in the shadows the way she is.

"Amelia!"

She spins toward me. Her chest is heaving and the skin on her neck is red and splotchy. "Did you see that back there?"

"Yes."

"Did you see the way Daphne was with him?"

I nod. "I did."

135

"I can't be here!" She's almost vibrating with emotion. "Not with the way my sister is acting! I can't... I can't watch her and Spencer kissing and cuddling like everything is just fine. It makes me sick to my stomach!"

"Then let's go," I say, carefully stepping closer.

Tears threaten to spill over. "Just leave Homecoming?"

"Yep. We can walk right out of here and go to Seth's show."

"I don't know that I'm the best company right now," she cries, her shoulders trembling. "I just... I'm not sure I'm fit to be around people."

"Then we'll skip the show. We'll leave the dance and go someplace just the two of us. Hell, I'll take you straight home if that's what you want."

"You make it sound simple, but it's not, Sebastian. I can't just leave."

"Why not?"

"Because of Daphne."

"I hate to be the bearer of bad news, but you're not exactly doing your sister any good crying back here," I say. "Amelia, I'm the first to agree that you need to have a good talk with her, but maybe this isn't the right time or place."

She gives a frustrated sigh and shakes her head. "You don't understand."

"What don't I understand?" I ask, stalking even closer. "Explain it to me."

"Everyone is expecting me to be here and to act a certain way. They want me to be student government Amelia or tennis team Amelia. They want me to be Daphne's smiling sister, standing up on that stage when they choose her for Homecoming Queen. And I know they'll talk about me if I disappear."

I shrug. "So what? Don't you know that everyone was talking about you the minute you walked through the door with me?"

She sniffles and manages a crooked smile. "I mean... you kind of have a point."

"Amelia, you don't have to stay here with these people because of a one-sided obligation. Christ, you don't have to stay anywhere you don't want to be." I tuck my finger under her chin and lift her face to mine. "So let's leave."

She blinks those soft brown eyes at me. "Where would we go?"

Wiping her tears away with my thumb, I say, "I have an idea."

CHAPTER FOURTEEN

Amelia

By the time we pull off of Route 321 and start up a rough dirt road toward the old water tower, it's full night. The sky is black and cloudy, punctuated only by the murky outline of a partial moon.

I have no idea why we're here or why we stopped by the hardware store where Sebastian works. I'm also clueless as to what's in the plastic shopping bag he carries with him as we get out of the truck and make our way toward the abandoned structure.

"You're not going to tell me anything? Even now?" I ask, using my phone as a flashlight to shine a light in front of my feet. Tufts of yellow grass cover the ground where I step.

"Just wait," he says, giving me some eyebrow action. "You know, I thought you'd be a lot more patient than this."

"That's because you've never seen me on Christmas morning."

He laughs then drops the bag and tells me to wait where I am for a second. I watch him scale a cinderblock wall and skip over one of the metal rungs of the water tower. He disappears from my sight and a few seconds later, a flood light comes on, illuminating the bottom of the tower and the wall, which I now see is covered with graffiti.

I gently pull aside a leafy green kudzu vine so that I can get a better look at one of the portions of the wall. "I never knew this was out here," I say in amazement.

Sebastian hops down and picks up the bag and I finally get

138

a glimpse of what's inside.

"So that's why you stopped? To pick up paint?"

"My boss is a grade-A dick who drinks way too much whiskey, but he lets me have the damaged paint cans. That's one of the reasons I stay at the job," he says with a shrug. "I also picked up some sample-sized latex paints and brushes. Thought they'd be easier for you to handle than the spray cans."

"Won't we get caught?" I ask, looking over my shoulder, half expecting a dozen police officers in full SWAT gear to jump from the shadows of the pine trees that surround the water tower.

"Nah, I wouldn't take you someplace that would get you into any kind of trouble. The cops know that a couple of us come out here sometimes and no one seems to care. This water tower hasn't been used in over a decade."

"Oh."

"In the winter when it's not so hot, I come down here a lot," he says. "It feels good to lose myself for a time."

I watch with interest as he pulls a couple of cans of spray paint from the bag and shakes them up. Then he passes the bag to me.

"Um, what am I supposed to do with this?" I ask, gazing down at the contents.

"Paint."

Right. Just paint like it's no big deal.

I feel downright useless as I take out the paints and make myself a little spread on the flattened shopping bag. I'm no artist and I have zero idea what I'm doing or how I should get started.

I glance over at Sebastian, who has taken up a post about fifteen feet away from me. He's removed his jacket and button-down shirt and is now in a pair of black pants that hang low on his narrow hips and a thin white tank top that only highlights his tanned arms and muscular chest.

Gawd.

I breathe in, seeking equilibrium, and turn back to face the wall. This portion is layered with splatters of orange and green. There's a black slash of spray paint cutting across the center. Just below it someone has scrawled words I can't quite read and then finished it off with *SCREAM DONKEYS SCREAM.*

Donkeys? Talk about weird. *Of course, screaming might feel pretty good right about now,* I think and a memory rises to the top of my mind.

The summer after seventh grade, we'd all gone with Daddy on a business trip to San Francisco. While he was in meetings, Nancy took us sightseeing. We did the normal stuff—Fisherman's Wharf, Alcatraz, the Ghirardelli chocolate factory. And then on the last day she packed us into the rental car and drove us north of the city, along the coast. Then she pulled over and told us to climb out. For a fraction of a moment, I wondered if she was going to leave us there in the middle of nowhere like kittens she didn't want to take care of any more.

But she didn't. She walked us to the edge of that cliff and we all stood there with the sun shining brightly into our eyes. I don't know what was going on in Nancy's head, but all I could think was that it felt like I was about to jump off the edge of the world and sail through the sky. And then Daphne had grabbed onto my hand and she'd started howling and, in a fit of recklessness, I'd joined in. And I remember how Daphne's scream had turned into uncontrollable laughter and she'd collapsed to the ground beside me with her head thrown back and her eyes glowing with sunshine.

It's a good memory.

Buoyed, I unscrew the cap on one of the jars of blue paint and I dip the brush in. I push aside the niggling worries about my sister and Spencer and the Homecoming dance and I set in on the wall, finding a rhythm I can keep and only allowing myself to think of that long ago summer day in northern California.

Endless moments later, I drop the brush to the plastic bag and tilt my head to the side. It's not exactly a Matisse, but it's not *terrible*.

Wiping my dripping fingers together so that the paint balls up, I start to back away from my painting. I bump into something and give a frightened jump.

"Whoa," Sebastian says, steadying me with his hands. His bare arms press against mine for a second too long. He pulls away and juts his chin forward. "What is it?"

I flush, maybe because he's asking about my mural or maybe because he's standing so close I can feel him breathing.

"It's kind of abstract I guess. Like a memory," I say but it actually comes out more like a question. "When Daphne and I were in middle school, our step-mom took us to this cliff overlooking the Pacific Ocean and we screamed our heads off until we had nothing left in our lungs."

Out loud it sounds stupid.

"It's the sky?"

I nod, embarrassed.

Sebastian walks closer but he doesn't touch the wall because he knows the paint is still wet and I'm guessing he doesn't want to smear it.

"And this is the sun?" he asks, pointing to the yellow and pink pinpricks I've painted in a kind of swirling vortex. Now that I look again, it's more like a pastel tornado than a sun.

"Sort of," I say, trying not to notice a bead of sweat dripping down his neck or the rock-hard chest that his tank top is doing little to conceal. "Now that I've showed you mine, it's only fair for you to show me yours."

Ack, that did not sound so dirty in my head.

Hiding a grin, he leads me down the wall. I turn to look and my breath catches.

In front of me is a dark, secretive ocean and a black sky filled with stars. A somber moon bathes the entire scene in ghostly light.

My heart stutters, each new beat coming faster than the last.

That's *our* moon.

Sebastian has painted *our* night at the beach. And it's utterly beautiful.

With wonderment, I blink and say to him, "How did you do this? The stars look iridescent."

"It's just paint, Amelia."

I'd always thought of spray paint as sort of clunky and crass but this is... It leaves me breathless, almost haunted.

"It's not *just* paint."

He gives an embarrassed laugh and rakes a hand back through his long hair.

"I mean it," I tell him, wanting to reach out and touch the painted black edge of the water just to hold onto the feeling that's burning through my veins for a little longer. But I refrain because I don't want to ruin Sebastian's work. "I wish I could make something out of nothing."

"Who says you can't?"

I shrug and turn away from the wall to face him head on. "I'm not talented. Playing a decent game of tennis and getting good grades in school is not the same thing."

"I wasn't thinking of tennis or school," he says cryptically. And then he changes directions, tipping his face to the night. "So that cliff story? Does that mean you aren't afraid of heights?"

"Why?"

Sebastian looks at the old water tower and back to me.

"You want to climb it?" I ask in disbelief. "Is it even safe?"

"Mostly."

I can tell that he doesn't really expect me to go along with this idea because his face is transformed by surprise when I bend down to unstrap the heeled sandals on my feet and gather up the bottom of the turquoise dress.

"You're doing it?"

"I'm doing it," I answer, leaving the dress in a loose knot that hangs at the side of my thigh.

Sebastian lets me go up the ladder first, which turns out to be a good move. The climb is scarier than I even anticipate and I'm only able to manage it because I know he's just behind me, his face level with my calves and his outstretched arms primed to catch me should I stumble.

"You're almost there," he urges as my hands grip the curve at the top of the ladder.

There is an instant of panic when my bare foot slips on the slick surface of the last rung, but Sebastian is already pushing up from behind, steadying me with his hard chest and strong arms.

"You got it, Amelia."

"Um, thanks," I mumble, drawing in a relieved breath and trying not to let myself press against him or notice the quick, fiery sensation that is traveling up the length of my spine like a lit fuse.

"There's a platform just that way. It's only about ten feet," he says, encouraging me.

Ignoring the pulsating of my body, I cautiously step onto the curved and narrow walkway that hugs the belly of the water tower.

Ten feet or not, progress is slow. I'm careful not to focus on the dizzying distance between myself and the ground. Sebastian stays back, patiently waiting as I plan out each step and scoot along, squeezing the rusty metal rail so tight with my fingers I know my knuckles must be white.

"It's not a cliff looking out over the Pacific," he says in a fading voice. Up here, I note, the wind sucks up sound, scattering it in every direction like confetti.

"It's still beautiful," I say, the sight of the slanting and boundless landscape below driving away my fear and replacing it with euphoria.

Then I must shiver or give some clue that I'm suddenly feeling the chill in the air because Sebastian tells me to sit against the water tower to block the rushing breeze.

"I should have brought my jacket up here," he says, looking apologetically at his chest, which even in the dim light, is on full display in his practically see-through white tank.

"I'm fine," I say and my heart flutters. Stupid, idiotic heart.

"You're not, but we're all the way up here now. Actually, I should have taken you home to change entirely. That dress is speckled with paint."

"It's Daphne's and she'll just have to get over it," I tell him as I swing my legs under the railing so that they dangle off the corrugated steel platform. "I guess this whole night isn't what you thought it would be when you put a suit on and came to pick me up, is it?"

He smiles as if to himself. "Nope. It's better."

I purse my lips. "*Better*? Which part did you like the most—when you had to wrestle my sister's boyfriend to the ground or when I made you leave Homecoming early? Or— ooh, I know—it was when I kept you from your best friend's concert, wasn't it?"

"Amelia, I'm sitting here with the best view in all of Green Cove and I promise you that Seth will have other shows," he says. "And you have got to already know that I never cared about the dance."

"I thought you wanted to eat cookies," I joke even though his expression is serious.

He looks at me. Just *looks* and I could swear that there is something in that look. Something bigger than what I'm grasping.

"I never gave a lick about cookies," he says quietly, his

144

chiseled features stern in the shadowed moonlight. "I only wanted a claim on that time. With *you*."

Swallowing down a lump in my throat, I say, "Me?"

Amazingly, his eyes drop to my mouth and then come back up and I finally allow myself to see that they are scorching hot and full of want.

Is this actually happening?

Is he going to kiss me?

Do I *want* him to kiss me?

Yes, says a voice in my mind, faint at first but growing stronger. *Yes.*

Out loud, I hear myself say, "But I thought…"

Sebastian scratches the back of his neck and I watch with fascination as his shoulder muscles flex and the Adam's apple in his throat bobs. He's nervous. Because of *me*.

"I like you, Amelia."

My breath hitches. It's such a simple thing to say, but I can't help but think how hard that must have been for him. How those few small words are tangled up inside of my own head, twisting and gnawing at me.

But if he can be brave, I can be brave too. So with my pulse beating madly in the palms of my hands, I lean in to close the distance between us. His grey eyes narrow and flicker over every inch of me, setting the air around us ablaze.

Yes.

Emboldened and pretending not to be afraid of the pressing intensity of that gaze, I take my index finger and gently stroke the side of his face, just below his ear where his jaw meets his neck.

For a long moment, Sebastian is ridiculously still. And then, like a breath that can only be held for so long, his whole body shudders.

"I was sure you would never give me a chance," he says, capturing my hand and pressing it over his chest where his unyielding heart drums like thunder. "But, Amelia, I don't want this if it's only for tonight."

"That's not what I want either."

"You're in?"

"I'm in," I whisper back.

This is the answer he was hoping for. His mouth curves and he leans down to me. I part my lips, tilting my head back to welcome him, and that first touch explodes quickly through my body.

Yes.

My heart races and I kiss him back with a pleasure and a strange kind of possessiveness that goes deeper and seems older than anything I've ever known. I've done this before, yes, but never like *this*. Like I'm opening up someone's soul and jumping inside to have a look around.

And that feeling, unstoppable as the wind whistling up through the spindly pine trees and forcing the black, black clouds across the sky, goes both ways. I know this with the same certainty I know day from night.

Sebastian's hands tighten on me and slide down to my waist to knead at my hips. My heart trips as I think of that night at the beach and how I'd told him that I wanted something real.

This. This is real.

CHAPTER FIFTEEN

Bash

It's a Saturday morning and I'm sitting next to one of the most beautiful girls I've ever seen in my life. She's shaking out her long hair and separating it into three sections so that she can braid it, and while she does this, she talks about a movie she watched last night as she was falling asleep. Yellow sunlight plays up her delicate features and the faint smattering of freckles on her nose. Her legs are crossed primly over each other and she's got an English lit textbook in her lap. Every now and then, she stops talking, looks over, and gives me a shy smile.

That's it. The look that gets me every single time.

Unable to help myself, I shove away my economics book, wrap my arms across her middle, and pick her up from the couch. Then I fall backward, cradling her on top of me as we crash into the loose throw pillows.

"Stop!" she cries out and tries to push away, but she's laughing along with me.

I brush her hair back, careful not to mess up the fresh braid, and draw her face closer to mine. Her eyes fall closed and she gives a soft, vulnerable sigh, opening her mouth for me. Like always, my chest tightens and I feel an electric jolt running through my entire body.

My fingers slowly trace the waistband of her navy blue skirt as I kiss her lips and the sweet, hot skin that spans from her jaw to her collarbone. When I get to the tiny buttons that are keeping her shirt together, she exhales almost like she's melting into my hands, and whispers directly in my ear, "We can't. *Carter.*"

"He's playing with Legos in his room," I argue, trying not to stare at the tiny strip of bra my exploration has uncovered. *Pink lace.*

"And he might get bored with them and come out here any minute."

She's right. I know she's right, but that doesn't stop me from groaning in agony as I lift her off of me and the pink lace disappears from my line of sight.

"Plus," she says smartly, "we're supposed to be studying."

"And one of these days the stars and the scheduling gods will align and we'll be studying all alone."

She gives me that pensive smile, nearly killing me right then and there. "What will you do then?"

Her boldness raises my eyebrows. "I haven't gotten past the being alone part, but I think I can figure it out. And in two weeks that might happen."

"Is that so?"

"Carter is supposed to stay with our aunt and uncle in Charleston."

She stares at me.

"What is it?" I ask her.

"Two weekends from now I'll be in Columbia for a student government trip."

"Student government? Damn it all to hell. This is exactly what's wrong with politics."

She laughs and once again, I'm like a moth to the flame. I lean in and cup the back of her neck.

"Forget the shitty timing of the trip and come here," I say, dragging her close and grazing my lips against hers.

See, I'm allowed to do things like this because the beautiful girl happens to be my girlfriend.

My *girlfriend.*

How's that for Karma?

"I used to wonder about this," she murmurs.

"Wonder about what?"

Her thumb trails along my chin. "This," she whispers. "What it would be like to kiss you with your scruffy jaw."

"And?"

She laughs against my mouth. "Isn't it obvious?"

My heart goes a little berserk over her admission and I make a snap decision. "Amelia, I want to show you something."

"What is it?" she asks.

Hating to put distance between us but needing to reach my bag, I hold her hand on top of my thigh as I bend down and grab my cracked black leather notebook. It feels damn heavy in my hands and I wonder if that's simply a side effect of my nerves.

I've never let anyone look at my sketchbook before. Not Seth. Not Carter. Not Rachel back when we were a thing. Not even my mother.

Amelia takes the notebook from me and rests back on the couch. I know the moment she realizes what she's looking at because she stops and her eyes come to mine with a question.

I nod, trying not to show her how anxious I am, and it must work because she turns the page and studies the first drawing.

It's a hand facing palm side up. Simple enough, except that when you get to the wrist, you see the craggy veins, weaving across pale skin like the lines on some outdated road map. And then there are the thick IV lines marking out the territory like grim-looking flags.

"Your mom?" she asks, running her index finger over the bottom of the page.

"Yeah."

She moves slowly through the book, stopping occasionally to ask me a question or make a comment. Most of the drawings are messy or unfinished. Some are funny ideas I started for t-shirts and some are rough landscapes I've drawn

149

from memory or imagination. She goes a little moony over the one of Carter sleeping with his favorite bear and blanket tucked under his chin. And finally, she gets to the first one of herself.

"When did you draw this?" she asks me, her voice filled with something like awe.

"September."

I can tell that this astonishes her because those maple syrup eyes of hers get impossibly big. "But we weren't even talking then."

"That doesn't mean I wasn't looking," I tell her. "It was the day after I found out you were tutoring Carter. I drew you while we were in Spanish class."

"I never knew," she says, shaking her head and looking back at the sketchbook.

"That was the idea."

She flips through a couple more pages until she gets to one of my favorites. She stares at it, not saying a thing for the longest time. So long that my pulse starts to buzz disturbingly.

"And this one?" she finally asks.

It's a pencil sketch of her and her sister stretched out on the grass of the main courtyard at school. Daphne has on bulky sunglasses that block out most of her face. Amelia's eyes are closed and her face is tilted up to the sky, soaking up the warmth.

"I saw you two like that during lunch one day and…" I can't believe I'm about to tell her this. I'm going to sound like a stalker and, hell, I probably deserve the label. "I took a picture on my phone so I wouldn't forget and then I drew it after work later that afternoon."

"I love it," she says even as her expression darkens. I know why. Every time her sister comes up, her face shutters, like a cloud passing in front of the sun. It's been like that for weeks

150

"Still not talking?"

A tiny muscle on the left side of her face clenches. "I've tried so many times but she refuses to discuss Spencer. She says I'm crazy and that you were confused about what happened."

"Amelia, I'm sorry."

"It's not your fault that things are so strained," she says with a sigh. "Honestly, Nancy and Daddy don't even notice the tension. Audra, on the other hand, says she's giving us exactly one more week to work our crap out. Or else."

"What happens in a week?"

A small smile dances over her mouth. "With Audra I don't know, but I don't want to find out either."

I laugh. I can see that. Audra Singer is a take-no-prisoners kind of girl. "You and Daphne are going to figure it out."

"You know, sometimes I think she's playing like she's still mad at me because she's really mad at herself," she says quietly, her teeth sliding over her bottom lip. "Or maybe that's just what I'm hoping is true."

"Nah, it makes sense. Have you talked to your parents about Spencer yet?"

"Not yet. She made me promise not to say anything and I just...I..."

"You don't want to go back on that?"

She swallows and nods. Amelia knows how I feel about this because we've been over it already, but I don't want to be the one pushing her into a decision she's not ready for.

"Either way it doesn't feel right," she says, her face pinching.

I thread our fingers together and guide her to my chest. Even though I've been doing this same move every day since Homecoming, it still amazes me how well she fits with my body. That she *wants* to be like this with me.

"If I talk to them then I'm doing it behind Daphne's back," she goes on, "And if I don't talk to them... well, that feels wrong too. I swear that anything I get in my head to do hurts."

Pressing my mouth to her forehead just below her hairline, I say, "Maybe promises are supposed to hurt a little. Keeping them and breaking them."

"Sebastian, I don't want you to think Daphne is weak or stupid because she's not."

"I know," I say, thinking of my own mother and how for years she struggled to find it inside of herself to leave my father, bastard that he was. "It's not just about strength or smarts."

"Daphne's lost right now. Or something." Amelia shakes her head and holds up my sketchbook. "But enough of that. Let's talk about *this*."

"What about it?"

She tips her head back so that she can meet my eyes. "I already knew you were good, but these are incredible."

"I don't know about incredible."

"Well, I do. Sebastian, you have to *do* this."

"You mean like for a job?"

She nods. "Or for school. You know... Emory probably has a good art program."

"Emory? Isn't that in Atlanta?"

Again, she nods. "But it's not that far. I mapped it the other day and it's only a five-hour drive from here to there."

I start to wonder why she was looking at the map between Green Cove and Atlanta, and then with a sick and sudden force, it becomes clear. "Is that where you're going next year?"

"Maybe. I'm still deciding between there, Vanderbilt, Wake Forest or maybe College of Charleston or Tulane. And, obviously I still have to get in."

"You'll get in."

She shrugs and chews on her bottom lip. I've always known that Amelia would be leaving Green Cove for school, but sitting here on my couch with the taste of her still fresh on my lips, I start to think about what that means for me.

Logically, we haven't been together long enough for me to care. Still... I care.

"Sebastian," she says, her voice wobbly as she flips back through the pages of the sketchbook, "there are a lot of great scholarship programs. If you let people see these drawings the way that I'm seeing them, they would sit up and take notice."

"Amelia, I've told you already. Guys like me don't go to college. We don't become graphic designers or artists."

"Why?"

"Because I'm not from London or New York. I'm just a poor kid from the middle of nowhere South Carolina who's trying his hardest to raise a little boy up to be something other than an asshole. I'll be lucky if I can get a job as a mechanic or as the produce manager at the Piggly Wiggly when we graduate."

"You don't see yourself clearly."

"And you do?"

An inadvertently sexy smile twists at her lips. "I'm starting to."

"And?"

She leans in closer—so close that I can feel her breath on my neck and the little tiny hairs that have fallen from her braid tickle my face. "I want to see more. I want to *know* more."

"More?"

"Everything," she says, softly kissing my jaw.

"Everything?"

"Mmhmm..." Her eyes search mine. "For starters—Coke or Pepsi?"

I crack a smile. "Coke."

"Pancakes or waffles?"

It takes me a second to choose this one. "Both are damn

good but I'll go with waffles."

"Tattoos or piercings?"

"Piercings," I say, eyeing the small gold studs in her earlobes.

"Roller skates or rollerblades?"

"Neither."

Laughing, Amelia tells me, "That's not an acceptable answer."

"Well, can I say skateboard? Does that count?"

"Okay, just this once, the judges will make an exception and take skateboard."

"Good. So is it my turn yet?"

"Go for it."

"Okay…" Damn, coming up with these is harder than I thought it would be. "Day or night?"

"Night."

"Sweet or sour?"

She makes a face. "Sweet. Is that even a real choice?"

I laugh, point taken. "Lake or beach?"

"Are you going to be at this beach with me?"

"If you want me to." Even I hear the uncertainty in my voice—it's still hard to believe that *this girl* is actually mine.

"Then I'm definitely going with the beach," she says, flicking her tongue into my mouth and driving me over the edge.

Sliding my hands around her waist, I anchor her to my chest and kiss her back with all of the longing pent up inside of me. She meets me there, kissing me hard and running her hands down my back to my hips almost feverishly.

This surprises me because up until now, aside from our teasing and a couple of PG-13 moments, Amelia and I have been taking things slow. And I'm good with slow. But I'm good with this too.

Hell, with Amelia, anything and everything works for me.

The kiss deepens as she climbs onto my lap and moves her

hands up the nape of my neck into my hair. She's not wearing her customary leggings and her skirt is bunched up, showing areas of her thighs that I've never seen before. I feel desperate, almost shaky as I touch her there, letting my fingers explore her warm skin until I can hardly breathe.

There is one question I have to ask her. I think I know the answer and it's hella awkward to put it out there, but I need to be positive. Her heart is beating so fast and hard that I can feel it beneath my fingers.

"Amelia, have you ever—"

"Look at me!"

Shiiiiit.

Amelia's muscles tense, her head snaps back, and she scrambles off of me as Carter runs at us from his room at full speed repeatedly yelling, *Look at me! Look at me!* from behind a red and gold plastic mask.

Your timing could not be worse, bud," I pant, adjusting my position on the couch and sucking in a tight breath for composure.

"Bash, this outfit is so cool. I haven't tried to fly but I might be able to!"

"What are you?" Amelia asks, discreetly rearranging her skirt so that nothing is out of place.

Carter puts one hand out and puffs his chest out in his best superhero impression. "I'm Iron Man."

"Carter, we're not going trick or treating until after dinner. Not even if you start to fly."

"But why can't we go now? I'm ready."

"It's not even lunch yet and no one starts handing out candy until after dark. You've got hours until showtime."

He tugs the mask off, showing us his pink and sweaty face. "Amelia, are you coming trick or treating with us?"

"Do you want me to?"

He jumps up and down in excitement. "Yeah! What's your costume?"

"Umm... Do I need one?"

His face changes and he wrinkles up his nose. "Of course you need a costume. They won't give you any candy if you go out in your regular clothes."

"I guess I could wear my candy corn leggings."

I laugh.

Her forehead creases. "What?"

"Only you would have candy corn leggings," I say, lifting my hand and touching the pink that blossoms on her face.

Carter shakes his head. "Leggings aren't going to get you the good candy."

"Well, what about you?" she questions me.

"Bash is boring," Carter tells her with superiority. "And he's wearing the same thing as last year. It's just a shirt that says 'Nudist on strike.' I don't even know what that means. It's so dumb, but I know you can do better, Amelia."

"Well..." She looks at me for help but I'm not going to get her out of this. I would pay good money to see what Amelia Bright comes up with for a Halloween costume at the last minute.

"Yeah, Amelia," I say, grinning in amusement. "What's your costume?"

"I don't think I can tell you because it's top secret."

"Top secret?" I ask, pretending to be impressed. "That sounds serious."

She arches an eyebrow at me. "Oh it is. Just you wait."

CHAPTER SIXTEEN

Amelia

"What is this?"

"Huh?" I spin away from the bed and see Daphne peeking her head into my room. "What's what?"

She sucks her cheeks into the sides of her mouth and takes a tentative step across the threshold. "Is Nancy doing a charity clothing drive that I don't know about?"

"Oh." I sigh and take in the mound of discarded clothes on the floor by my feet. It's like my closet got sick and threw up. "Sebastian's little brother invited me to go trick or treating with them so I'm raiding all my stuff to find something brilliant for a costume tonight."

She sits on the edge of my bed. "That sounds fun."

I shrug. "It will be if I can figure out what to wear."

Daphne laughs, but it's a tired and distracted sound. "So you guys...?"

"You mean Sebastian and me?"

"Yeah? Seems like you're pretty into him."

"I like him. A lot." Truly, *like* doesn't cover it. Every single moment I spend with Sebastian makes my heart crack open a little wider. Pretty soon I figure he'll be able to move in and make a home for himself there. "He makes me feel—God, I don't know how to describe it."

"Happy?" she supplies.

"The happiest."

"That's really good."

"I never thought I'd be one of those girls but it's *right* with him. And even though it's been less than a month it somehow seems like things have always been this way. I didn't think that could ever happen to me."

"Amelia, your voice is gooey and you're dangerously close to swooning."

"I might be."

"He gives you butterflies?"

"More like a tornado."

"*Sa-woon.*" My sister smiles at me and it suddenly hits me that we're having a real conversation.

"Daphne, are we talking again?" I ask cautiously.

"I want to be talking."

"I want that too," I say, sinking down beside her on the bed. "I'm sorry about the way things have been with us. I think about it all of the time, but I don't know what to *do* to fix it."

"No, it's me, Amelia. I've been such a brat."

"You're not a brat."

Her voice becomes heavy, "No, I am. And I don't know...it's just...I think you might have been right about Spencer."

My ribcage compresses, squeezing my lungs. "Did he hurt you again?"

She blinks and recoils. "Not physically."

"Then what happened?"

"I kinda, sorta, maybe hijacked his phone two nights ago while he was in the bathroom."

"So you snooped?"

"I snooped," she admits. "And I found out that he's been texting this girl, Maggie. I think it's the same Maggie who graduated a couple of years ahead of us."

"Maggie Fitzpatrick?"

"That's her. At least, I think that's who it is."

"No way."

"Yes way."

"Were the texts—you know—*damning?*"

"It could've been nothing. I didn't get a chance to read all of the messages before he got back, but there was enough there that I've got a really bad feeling about the whole thing."

"I'm sorry."

"Don't be." She takes a quick breath for courage. "I didn't want to tell you this before but Spencer has gotten into some stuff that I don't want to be a part of."

"Drugs?"

"I think so. Steroids or pills or... something. I'm not sure."

"I kind of knew but I didn't want to believe it was true," I tell her. "So, what are you going to do now?"

"I'm going to do the same thing I've been doing since Thursday night. I'm going to avoid his calls and all of his fake excuses."

"You two are done?"

"We're done." She sounds so self-assured that I almost believe her.

"You seem confident about it."

"I am," she says. "I feel better than I have in a long time. I feel like *me*. Spencer can take his popularity and his adoring fan club with him. I won't miss it one bit."

"Wow. That's.... just wow. Good for you."

She laughs at my shock. "But enough about Spencer. He's taken enough time and I don't want him to suck up another second of my life," she says, sitting up straighter. "And it sounds like you and I have super important things to discuss."

"Like what?"

Daphne points an accusatory finger at the pile of clothes. "Like, what's your costume going to be?"

"Um, at this point I'm thinking nothing."

"Are you saying you want to be completely naked or just Lady Gaga naked? My guess is that Sebastian will be into it either way."

159

I laugh. "You know that's not what I meant."

"You could wear my cheerleading outfit," she suggests.

"I'm not sure your cheer outfit is much better than being naked."

She rolls her eyes. "We'll have to go shopping."

"But the only costumes left will be the sexy nurse or stripper fairy get-ups and neither of those sound remotely appealing. Not to mention that I'm taking a first grader trick or treating," I point out. "I don't want him to be faced with lacy garters and ridiculous cleavage the entire night."

"Then we have to get a little more creative."

"Um, what do you have in mind?"

In answer, she just flashes me a mischievous smile.

"Seriously, Daphne. What are you planning?"

***

An hour later, I'm standing on a scratched-up wooden platform in the dressing room at the back of a local thrift store wearing a smelly wedding dress. It's so frothy that it could put a cappuccino to shame.

"Ugh, now I really do look like the Bride of Frankenstein. You can't even deny it."

Daphne turns around and inspects my reflection in the mirror. "True, but that's what we're going for this time. See," she says, lifting up the hem of the dress and fluffing it out even more, "we'll pick up some fake blood and white stage makeup and *voila!* It's your monster wedding day."

I pull at one of the enormous white satin bows attached to a bell-shaped sleeve. "I don't know about this."

"Okay, I get that it might be too much," she says as she backs away. "Just give me another minute. I haven't even browsed the sleepwear section yet."

"Oh God, sleepwear? What could there possibly be for me to try on in *sleepwear?*"

As it turns out, Daphne thinks there's a lot. First she dresses me in a pair of flannel footie pajamas thinking that she'll send me out tonight as one of Santa's elves or Outdoorsy Barbie. When that doesn't pan out, she forces me into a sheer nightie that she's matched with lime green pleather leggings.

"And what's this look supposed to be?"

"Maybe an eighties rocker?"

I guffaw. "It's more prostitute than rocker."

"Well, what about—ohmigod, I have an idea!" She drops the canary yellow bathrobe and insane cat slippers she's carrying and dashes from the fitting room.

"Daphne?" I'd chase after her, but I'm still wearing the nightie and I am not about to show the other shoppers what my bra looks like.

Crap.

Daphne lets out a loud and gleeful whoop when she resurfaces from the racks of junk and musty coats.

"Check it out!" She's holding up some old hunk of black metal that upon closer inspection I realize is a Polaroid camera. An ancient one.

"Is that for my costume?"

"No, it's for me. *This* is for you," she says, handing me an ugly black and white patterned dress.

"Are those cats?" I ask, eyeing the dress with suspicion.

"Yes! I spotted it earlier but I couldn't think of how to use it in a costume. Then when I saw the yellow bathrobe and those perfect cat slippers, I just knew."

"Knew *what*?"

"Crazy. Cat. Lady."

"You're joking."

"Why would I joke? This idea is both appropriate *and* hilariously hideous."

"Couldn't I just be a hobo?"

"Nope. Cat Lady all the way. You're doing this, Amelia."

"Well, I do have cat leggings. They're rainbow colored."

"See? I can't even handle it." Daphne drapes the bathrobe over my shoulders and pretends to snap my picture with the old camera. "Also, I think I need to buy this thing."

"It's so old you could probably donate it to the Smithsonian."

"A camera like this doesn't belong in a stuffy museum. It belongs with me, taking pictures of the world like it was meant to. It's *special*."

"How do you know it works?"

"I don't, but it's *fun* regardless. And since it's only like four dollars, the upside completely outweighs the downside."

"Even if it does work, you'll never be able to find film for it," I predict.

"Just watch me. It'll be perfect for our road trip," she says, putting the strap over her neck and pulling her phone from her purse. "Hey, do you want me to text Audra to see if she can meet us at Annie May's for coffee?"

"And a pumpkin cream cheese muffin?"

"Now you're talking. I'm going to get two of those muffins."

"Two?"

"They're seasonal and I'm recovering from the demise of a bad relationship," she reasons with a shrug as she sends the text.

Audra's lightning fast response makes Daphne laugh.

"What did she say?"

She shakes her head and passes the phone to me. "See for yourself."

Audra: **Wooohoo! The band is back together. You bitches are not allowed to break up again. GET IT?**

And a second text sent right after the first.

162

Audra: And YES to Annie May's. Order me one of those whipped cream deals and tell them I want extra whipped cream. Actually, just get me a huge cup of nothing but whipped cream. And I want a chocolate muffin. I srsly deserve it after dealing with you 2 fools. SEE YA in 10!

CHAPTER SEVENTEEN

Bash

My aunt and uncle live on the northern end of the Charleston peninsula where the rambling historic mansions that you would see in the touristy carriage rides below Broad Street give way to smaller craftsman style houses and carriage homes hidden from the street by azalea bushes and flourishing Crepe Myrtles.

Real estate in this part of town has to be expensive, but Mike and Denise are both software designers and from what I can tell, they do well for themselves. A few years ago they discovered a boarding house that had been converted into trendy, high-end townhomes and they unloaded Mike's fishing boat so that they could put a downpayment on the three-story unit right there on the end.

These days Mike bikes to work and my aunt stays home and works from an office she set up on the third floor. Last fall they adopted a golden retriever from a shelter and named him Dakota and Mike decided to add a fence and paint the boards white. Now all they need is two point five kids and they'll be living out the American Dream.

"Bash, you're here." Denise has the forest green front door open before I can step from my truck to the curb. "I'll tell Mike to put on the hamburgers."

Her head disappears for a moment and when she comes back, I ask her, "How's Carter? Did he have fun?"

"Yes!" It's the little man himself, barrelling out the front door and flying down the uneven brick walkway.

I catch him with my arms and swing him around. "I missed you, bud."

"I was only here for two days."

"I can still miss you," I say, releasing him. "It's lonely at the house when you're gone."

"Wasn't Amelia with you?"

"Nope. She had to go with her student government group to Columbia for a symposium on school voting," I remind him as I stoop down to kiss Aunt Denise on the cheek. She's dark-haired and petite just like my mother was.

"Oh right."

Denise beams at me. "Amelia is the girlfriend we've heard so much about from Carter?"

"That's her," I reply.

"You'll have to tell us even more about her," she says, directing both of us into the kitchen. "Carter already told us that she's tutoring him and that she has brown hair and a nose."

"Nice call on the nose, bud."

Carter shrugs. He's jumped onto one of the brass-backed counter stools and is eating carrot slices off of the cutting board Denise is using to chop for a salad.

"He also told us that she smiles a lot and loves cats."

I laugh, thinking about her Halloween costume. "She's actually allergic to cats but she seems okay around Jinx. And she does smile a lot."

"Maybe it's rubbing off on you," she says. "I haven't seen you looking this happy in a while. And I'll tell you that Carter seems to think this girl hung the moon in the sky."

"We don't have proof of that but we're not ruling anything out."

Denise chuckles and the sound is so much like Mama that for an instant I lose control of my breath.

"Burgers ready in fifteen!" Mike calls from out on the back patio.

The kitchen erupts into activity then. Denise takes a position at the stove, mashing a pot of potatoes while managing to direct Carter and I to finish the salad and set the round table with plates and silverware.

"Bash, I'm glad you could stay for dinner," Denise says when all of the plates are loaded and we are sitting down.

I finish adding lettuce to my hamburger and squash the bun down hard so the thing doesn't fall apart on me. "Thank you for the invitation. I'm not one to turn down food and I know this guy isn't either."

Carter's head bounces up and down. There's already a ring of smeared ketchup around his mouth.

The rest of the dinner conversation is easy. Mike tells us about a project he's trying to deal with at work—something about a phone app glitching on him. And Denise asks us questions about school and Amelia.

When all the burgers are eaten and I'm so full that I have to lean back in my chair and cross my arms over my abdomen, Denise tells Carter to go get his stuff together and he bolts up the stairs to the room he uses while he's here.

"So, your aunt and I've been talking a lot lately," Mike says.

"Uh-huh?" I mutter, trying my damndest not to burp out loud.

"And..." He and Denise share a look. This is when I realize that she's tense.

"We were wondering how would it feel to get your life back?" she asks me.

I snort. "My life? What are you talking about?"

My aunt shifts in her chair as she eyes me warily. "Well, you're a senior now."

I'm nodding along. "I am."

"And now that you have a serious girlfriend, I can't imagine it's easy to behave like a normal teenage boy."

"It's not but I manage it."

166

"Should you have to manage it?" Mike asks and I see the way he scoots closer to Denise and covers her hand with his own. This small move puts my senses on high alert.

"What are you talking about?" I ask, looking back and forth between them.

Denise pulls in a breath. "Taking care of a seven-year-old is too much responsibility for a kid your age."

My brain snaps to the day last month when Elaine Travers swooped in to check on Carter and me. Sitting here at my aunt and uncle's kitchen table, I have that exact same gnawing, scare-the-shit-out-of-me feeling.

Could Social Services have contacted Denise and Mike to let them know about the investigation? Is that allowed?

"Where is this coming from?" I ask them.

Mike answers me in a steady, deliberate voice. "Your aunt and I have been doing a lot of soul searching these past months. When your mother passed, we didn't push the issue because everyone was in turmoil. Denise had lost her big sister and you boys… you'd lost so much already." My aunt is starting to tear-up. Hell, I'm starting to tear up. "But now that the dust has settled," he says grimly, "we both think it would be best for all parties if we took over primary guardianship of Carter."

I'm listening but the words don't make sense to me right away. When they finally bore through the side of my skull and hit home, I jump up from the table. "*What?*"

Denise is crying now. "You know that after your mama died, we wanted you both to move in with us."

"Then you must remember that we both wanted to stay in Green Cove," I yell at her. "It's what *she* wanted for us."

"Is it?" Mike throws out.

"What are you implying?" Do they know something I don't? Did my mother talk to them about this before she died?

"I know what it's like to grow up in Green Cove and feel

stuck there," Denise sobs. "Your mama went through it and she never got out because she stayed behind with your father. I went through the same thing, but I fought my way into college and a different kind of life. Now it's your turn, Bash. You don't want to be stuck there forever, do you? And I know you don't want that for Carter."

"Why is this happening now?"

"Because we want you to think about letting your brother start school here at the beginning of next term," Mike says calmly. "We'd like you to be here also, but we would understand if you want to finish out your senior year in Green Cove."

Denise nods and sniffles, getting her tears under control. "We thought you boys could have one last Christmas in the house and then Carter could get a fresh start in Charleston in the new year."

"That's not going to happen."

"Just think about it, son," Mike says.

"I'm not your son."

He sighs in a way that has me thinking he knew I was going to say that just like he knows I can't take care of my brother. "You need to start thinking about what's best for Carter."

"I am thinking about it. I think about it every damn day."

"We don't want for things to get ugly," my aunt says, her grey eyes wet and pleading. Those are my mother's eyes. My eyes. Carter's eyes.

"Then don't make them ugly." It's both a question and a statement.

"It's not that easy, Bash. We aren't just going to give up on this and walk away. Too much is at stake."

"But that's how I feel," I say, my fingers squeezing the chair back. "I promised her I would take care of him and now you want to make me break my word."

"I would never want to go against Jean Anne's wishes, but

I honestly think she was confused toward the end. She was trying her best to make good out of a bad situation, but this arrangement is not appropriate. It's too hard when it doesn't have to be that way. You need to live the life of a young man and not be saddled with the care of yourself *and* a small child."

"It's not like that," I say and my voice cracks. "I need Carter as much as he needs me."

"Bash, hon, Mike and I are going to do whatever it takes to set this right. Do you understand that?"

My tongue is so dry that it feels tacky against the roof of my mouth. "You *can't* do this to us."

"You're not being reasonable," Mike says, shaking his head.

"Because you're asking my permission to walk into my life and blow it up."

Denise looks at me. "But you have to see where we're coming from. We do have options."

"What's that suppose to mean?"

"Just that we've talked to several attorneys."

My abdomen clenches tight as I wait for the other shoe to drop. I guess I've known it was coming since Mike cleared his throat and told me that he and my aunt have been *doing a lot of talking.* It's still weird how all the pieces come together at once and I can see this family portrait for what it is.

"Are you the ones who called Social Services?"

Neither Mike nor Denise move, but I see the guilt on their faces. It's fucking blinding.

"How could you do it?" I ask.

"Bash, we were worried and we thought it was the right thing to do for everyone," Denise explains.

"You know what? Save it for someone who wants to hear. I'm done with this conversation and you," I say darkly as I move toward the stairs. I need to get Carter and get out of this house. *Now.* "Carter, hurry up!"

Denise follows me. "Think about this, Bash. Who do you think a judge is going to side with? The 18-year-old kid working at a hardware store after school or the two adults who can provide Carter with a financially secure and stable life?"

"Is that a threat?"

Carter appears at the top of the stairs. His backpack is in one hand and Red Dead Fred is in the other.

"I don't want to threaten you," Denise says quietly so that Carter won't hear her. "But please understand me when I tell you that Mike and I *will* do whatever it takes to ensure what's best for that little boy."

I look away. "So will I."

***

"I understand. Thank you for your time," I say, pressing the end button to finish the call.

That was the fifth lawyer I've talked to this afternoon and every conversation went about the same way.

Interesting case. Let me pass you along to my paralegal who can explain what my retainer is.

The minute I tell them I can't pay a retainer, my case gets a lot less compelling and schedules are too full to take me on.

You'd think by now, I would be used to taking the shots that come at me, but they still draw blood. Every single time. People like to say that money can't buy happiness, but it sure as hell can buy peace of mind in the form of legal representation.

According to my Google search, there is one other lawyer around Green Cove who might take the case, but I just can't bring myself to make that last call. The two times we've met, it's been more than obvious that Bill Bright doesn't like me around his daughter. He can hardly look me in the eye so I do not think he's going to up and volunteer to be my attorney out of the kindness of his heart.

Maybe I'm also avoiding the call because if I tell Mr. Bright that I'm being sued for custody by my aunt and uncle, then I have no choice but to tell Amelia. The last three days, I've kept her in the dark, chucking up my sour mood to bad sleep. I don't know how much longer I can keep the act up, but once I say it out loud and she hears it, all of this becomes real.

What am I going to do?

Bottom line is that Mike and Denise are royally screwing me. They can pretend it's for my own good, but I know a beatdown when I see it. And the worst part is that their predictions are coming true. I can't compete with them when it comes to financial stability. Hell, I can't even hire myself a real lawyer. And even if I talk to my boss about picking up extra hours at Kane's, I don't think it will make a difference. What's a few hundred dollars more when I need five *thousand*?

"Bash? You at home?"

There's a shadow at the screen door.

"In here."

Paul from next door lets himself in. "Mom's on another one of her butter kicks," he says, dropping a casserole dish on the sofa table and making himself comfortable. "She made y'all some kind of shrimp thing. I think there's rice and sweet carrots in it and she said to let it cool down and stick it the refrigerator. Y'all can nuke it if you want or eat it cold."

"Thanks. Carter loves shrimp."

"Who doesn't?" Paul asks, stretching his arms over his head and kicking his feet up on the table. "So, whatchya doin'?"

I indicate the phone in my hand. "Calling attorneys, trying to get one to work for me for free."

"You in trouble?"

"Nah, I just have something to work out."

"I was gonna say that I can still get you that sweet deal I

171

mentioned awhile back."

I'm impressed that he even remembers that night. He was so wasted I figured his brain had turned to grits and everything was forgotten.

"I don't think so."

Paul's yellow-green eyes narrow. "Just sayin' that things are going well for me. You saw my car?"

I did. It was hard to ignore when he drove that shiny new sports car up the street. The engine was louder than fireworks on the Fourth of July.

"It's a beauty," I tell him.

"You could have a matchin' one."

"I'm not going to transport drugs for you."

"It's not like that," he says, breathing in through his open mouth. "It's not even a transport because I do that end. All you would need to do is let us use your place."

"For what?"

"That's for me to know and you to never find out."

I think I've heard of this before. Meth dealers rotate houses to cook in so that they won't get caught. "You want me to let you make drugs here?"

He lifts his shoulders in a way that could mean yes or no. "All you'd have to do is clear out of your humble abode for a time and when we're finished, you clean up and make it like we were never here."

"That's all?"

"Piece of cake, man."

"I don't know, Paul."

"Do you remember when we used to get high with everyone at the quickie mart before first period?"

Paul and I were never friends even when he was a student at Green Cove High, but we did run in the same circles.

"That was a long time ago."

"I'm just sayin' that you used to be fearless and what I'm presentin' to you is less risky than gettin' high with a bunch of teenagers before school. And you can make *good* money this way, Bash. I'm talkin' thousands."

Thousands? As tempting as the offer sounds—especially now when I *need* that extra cash—I don't know if I can go there. Letting strangers in the house where Carter and I sleep so that they can cook up meth in our kitchen?

Shit, it sounds really bad even in my own head. And Social Services has already sent someone to the house once. I don't have any assurances that won't happen again.

On the other hand, I reason, *I might actually get away with it.* Then I'd have the money I desperately need to fight my aunt and uncle for Carter. With that kind of cash I'd be able to keep our little family together in the way Mama wanted. Hell, with *thousands* I could even take a look at schools.

College. The word reverberates throughout my entire body. With everything I've had to juggle in my life, I never thought of it as a real possibility. But maybe with the right resources it could become a reality.

And, if what Paul is telling me is true, I wouldn't technically be the one dealing in the illegal shit. I'd just be cleaning up afterward.

"I'm tellin' you," Paul says, putting an end to my wild thoughts. "It's easy money, man. Easy as pie."

CHAPTER EIGHTEEN

Amelia

Amelia: **Summer or winter?**

Bash: **Summer of course. Katy Perry or Taylor Swift?**

I giggle as I tap out a response.

Amelia: **T Swift all the way. LOL**

Bash: **Should've guessed that one :P**

"Are you going to do that all day, Amelia?"

I blink up at my sister. "Huh?"

"You know, text with Lover Boy while I shop over here and talk to myself?"

"I'm not—"

"Oh, what-the-frick-ever," Daphne says but her expression is soft. "You are so gonzo over there, Nancy might be able to get you in something smocked with a monogram without you even knowing it."

We're at the mall two towns away with our stepmother, who had insisted that our fall and winter wardrobes needed a little padding.

"Smocking and a monogram?" I hiss at Daphne. "I might be texting with my boyfriend but I am not *that* far gone."

She groans and looks away. Then she lets loose a thrilled squeal and pulls out a burgundy strapless dress with delicate-looking silk bows at the neckline. Gathering it to her chest, she exclaims, "This is perfect for Thanksgiving! Nancy, what do you think?"

Our stepmother pauses her methodical perusal of the clothing racks and looks up. She hums while she studies the fabric in Daphne's hands. "It's lovely but I preferred the hunter green one. It's a better choice with your coloring."

Daphne twists her mouth and considers this before draping the dress over her arm and giving me a secret smile. "I'll still try this one on. It's going to look great with hoop earrings and my suede peeptoes."

My phone buzzes in my hand and I can't help myself. I love playing this game with Sebastian.

Bash: **Tacos or Burritos?**

This one is easy for me.

Amelia: **Shrimp tacos with slaw and lots and lots of sour cream**

I wait, hoping that he'll respond right away. My heart flutters when the little dots begin to move across my screen to let me know that he's writing out a text.

Bash: **Those sound a lot like shrimp tacos from LeRoy's**

Amelia: **Probably because they are.**

Bash: **Those are my favorite too. Want to go get shrimp tacos with me on Friday night?**

Amelia: **Are you asking me on a date?**

Bash: **As long as you don't mind if I bring along a 7 y.o. who will want to talk superheroes and Legos the whole time.**

Amelia: **Superheroes and Legos? Count me in!**

"Amelia, are you still texting with that boy?"

I tear my eyes away from the phone and see that Nancy is frowning at me.

Daphne shoots me her favorite I-told-you-so-look. "Don't be too hard on her, Nancy. She's living in La-la-land and it's simultaneously adorable and disgusting."

I drop the phone into the side pocket of my purse. "Sorry. It was a homework question from Audra."

Daphne, who clearly doesn't believe this, rolls her eyes. "I'm going to try these things on, okay? Be ready to help me decide."

We watch her struggle with the many items she'd found and close herself in a dressing room. When we're alone, Nancy says to me, "You two have been spending an awful lot of time together lately. Is it serious?"

I wince in response. This is so not the Saturday afternoon conversation you want to have with your stepmother.

"I'll take that as a yes," she concludes.

"Nancy, I've only been with him for about a month so I don't think it can be classified as serious quite yet."

She sighs as though she disagrees with my assessment. "Are you still getting your schoolwork done?"

"Yes."

"Tennis season is just around the corner," she says as if I don't know this. "Soon your time is going to be fully occupied with practices and team responsibilities. Will he understand?"

"Of course he will. He's got work and school and plenty of things that keep him busy."

"And this boy—this Bash... he isn't trying to pressure you into anything?"

I look up as a flood of heat rushes to my face. *Pressure me?* "Umm... What do you mean, Nancy?"

"College, dear. Being with him isn't going to change your plans, is it? Your father and I worry that after all your hard work over the past few years, your decision making might be clouded by this new relationship."

"I'm not going to give up on my future for a guy if that's what you're worried about."

"All the same, we'd like to see you finish up those college applications and get them in the mail," she says with a pointed look.

"I will."

"Hey, what about me?" Daphne shouts through the dressing room door. I can hear her wrestling with clothes in there. "Why aren't you worried about a boy distracting me?"

"Oh, Daphne," Nancy chuckles. Then to me, she murmurs, "I hope she chooses the green for Thanksgiving."

"The burgundy was nice too."

"Amelia, I'd like for you to put some effort into your appearance as well. Your father has invited his business partners to join us."

"I didn't really see anything that I liked," I mumble.

"I saw a fantastic shirtdress made by Tory Burch," she suggests. "As long as you don't try to pair it with anything else—" she casts a skeptical look at the leggings I'm wearing, "—it would be very flattering."

"Nancy, about Thanksgiving," I start because I've suddenly had an idea. "Sebastian and his little brother don't have any plans this year. Actually, during our last tutoring session, Carter let it slip that they're talking about getting Chinese take out and having a Marvel movie marathon this year." I give an uncomfortable laugh. "But I don't think that it counts as a Thanksgiving plan unless there is turkey and stuffing involved."

Nancy just stares at me, not taking the hint, so I continue. "So... I was wondering if maybe they could join us for dinner? There's always plenty of food and I thought it might be a nice way for you and Daddy to get to know Sebastian better."

"And his brother?"

"Well, yeah. He can't exactly leave Carter behind."

"And these boys don't they have *any* family of their own to spend the holiday with?"

"They have an aunt and uncle in Charleston, but they aren't spending the holiday with them." I honestly don't know what the real story is there, but the last time I asked, Sebastian told me that they weren't going to be seeing them for a while.

She shakes her head. "I'm not sure that's such a good idea on Thanksgiving, Amelia."

"Why not?"

"It's quite a bit of extra work to have more guests."

It's a blatant excuse, and a bad one at that. "I thought... You're always saying that you enjoy hosting for the holidays."

"I already told you that your father has invited his business partners to join us," she says like this explains everything.

"And you don't want Daddy's partners at the firm to meet Sebastian?"

The corners of her mouth crease in disapproval. "Along with his little brother? I hardly think it's appropriate for a holiday dinner, do you, Amelia?"

I blanch. I don't know what I'd been expecting but it's not this. This dismissal from my stepmother feels like a slap to the face.

Daphne interrupts my tumultuous thoughts by emerging from the dressing room in the burgundy dress. "Hey—what do you guys think?"

"I love it," I say, trying to school my expression.

More frowning from Nancy. "I thought you were going to

try on the green one."

"I grabbed that one too," Daphne explains. "And I think you're right about it for Thanksgiving, but can I get this dress for Audra's party? It's perfect."

"Of course, dear. Now remind me why Audra is having a party."

"It's a big thing her parents are throwing for her eighteenth birthday," I explain.

Daphne nods. "Yep. Her dad rented out the clubhouse and is, like, flying in a whole band or something. It's going to be the party of the entire year if not the decade."

Looking up from where she'd been inspecting the length of Daphne's hemline, Nancy says smoothly, "That sounds lovely. When is this party?"

"The weekend after Thanksgiving," Daphne answers, twirling and watching her reflection in all the different angles of the oversized dressing room mirrors.

Aiming for casual, Nancy asks, "And will Spencer be there?"

Daphne abruptly stops spinning. "Um… well, *everyone* is going to be there so I guess so."

"Don't you know?" she coaxes.

"I told you that we're taking a little breather, that's all."

A breather? What does Daphne mean by that? She assured me that she and Spencer were a thing of the past. Is she beating around the bush for Nancy's benefit or is something going on?

"You did say that. I was only hoping you two would work things out. You know how much your daddy and I like him. Spencer is a real catch."

Goosebumps of disquiet break out over my skin when Daphne smiles slyly at Nancy and shrugs her shoulders.

Clearing my throat, I mumble, "I thought you told me that you and Spencer broke up?"

She won't look at me. "I mean… yeah, Amelia. But we've

179

talked some and who knows what will happen? Never say never."

"Always wise," Nancy says heartily.

I open my mouth to speak and then close it.

Now we're back to *Spencer*? The druggie? The potential cheater? How does that make any kind of sense?

I don't care how cute he is, how much people seem to like him, or what kind of car he drives. Daphne has to know that she's so much better off without him in her life.

And why is this just coming out now? How could she keep this huge thing from me?

I knew she was texting a lot yesterday because I could hear her phone going off all night, but I'd assumed it was Audra or someone from the cheer squad. But I'm starting to think those texts might have been from Spencer.

"Here's that shirtdress, Amelia," Nancy says, pushing something blue and black and floral at me.

Without a word, I take the dress and turn to escape into the solitude of the dressing room.

"You could wear it with simple flats," Nancy calls through the door.

"Or I could let you borrow my black leather ankle boots," says Daphne.

Leaning into the cool surface of the mirror, I close my eyes. I need a second to sort through the sharp and almost painful emotions rocketing around inside of me.

God, Daphne and I might share a face, but lately, it's like we are so disconnected. I used to be able to know exactly what she was thinking and gauge her state of mind with just one glance. There was no one in the world I trusted more than her. But now... I have no idea where Daphne and I stand or what's happening with her.

Every day it's like the wall of secrets that's been piling up between us grows higher and higher and I have no idea how to knock it down or climb over it to reach her.

CHAPTER NINETEEN

Bash

Amelia: Unicorns or rainbows?

Bash: What kind of question is that? I guess unicorns because the whole horn thing is kind of badass.

Amelia: LOL. Jeans or shorts?

Bash: Leggings. My turn.

Amelia: Shoot.

Bash: I know about your Red Vines addiction, but I have more candy questions. Chocolate or gummy bears?

It doesn't take her long to think of an answer that makes me smile.

Amelia: Chocolate covered gummy bears FTW!

Bash: Ice cream or fro-yo?

Amelia: Hello? I'm a southerner. ICE CREAM! Speaking of... There better be ice cream at this party or I am staging a rebellion.

I laugh as I write her back. I've never been much of phone guy, and I definitely wouldn't consider myself a texter, but with Amelia, it's fun.

Bash: **Not that I'm complaining about talking to you, but shouldn't you be paying attention to your best friend instead of texting me? It is her birthday.**

Amelia: **Audra doesn't know I exist tonight. Her cousin is here and he's brought his college roommate and Audra has determined that HE is going to be her birthday present.**

I drag a hand through my hair. Shit. As long as Amelia isn't interested in this college kid.

Bash: **But are you having fun?**

There. That doesn't sound like it came from an obsessive boyfriend who needs to rein in his shit.

Amelia: **Define fun**

Bash: **Are you having a good time?**

It kills me to wait for her answer. What if Amelia and I aren't really on the same page and I'm just deluding myself? What if she decided while she's at Audra's party that we don't mesh? What will I do when she realizes that she can do a hell of a lot better than me?
Damn it.
Maybe she isn't answering my question because she really is having a good time and she doesn't want to hurt my feelings. Or, I think, my hands involuntarily balling into fists, *maybe she actually did meet someone else.*

"Amelia?" Seth asks me. He's on the broken recliner in my living room, petting Jinx, who's taken up a sentry post on his lap, and flicking through TV channels. We don't even have cable so the options are a rerun of *Supernatural* or *Antiques Roadshow.*

"Yeah," I say, dropping my phone onto the coffee table and scratching a hand down over my face. I have got to get myself under control. "She's at a party for Audra Singer's birthday."

"Heard about it at school," he says. "Why aren't you there with her?"

"I've got Carter."

"You know I would have watched him for you if you'd asked."

I shrug. "I've got work tomorrow."

"Still not an answer, Bash."

"Audra's party is not my kind of thing."

He narrows his eyes at me. "I'm thinking that wherever Amelia Bright is at is exactly your kind of thing."

I swallow hard. He's got a point but I'm not ready to admit it out loud. "Not tonight. She should be with her friends. I don't want her worrying about whether or not I'm fitting in with everyone that's there. I want her to have fun."

"Fun, huh?"

"Of course." *What do you think I am—a shitty and jealous boyfriend?*

"Is that why you look like someone just kicked you in the balls or did I miss something?"

I shake my head in defeat. "Shit, Seth... There are guys at the party who don't have to worry about finding a babysitter or fitting in. Guys who go to college. Guys with a future laid out in front of them. I can't help but think what will happen when Amelia finally figures out that's not me."

"I don't think Amelia cares about any of that, but if you're worried she does then why don't you change it?"

"What do you mean?"

"Damn it, Bash," he groans. "How many times have I told you to look into scholarships? If you don't want to do it for yourself then maybe you'll do it for Amelia."

"How would we live? *Where* would we live?"

"You'll rent this place and use the money for an apartment or a dorm or however people do it."

"I don't know," I say, suddenly feeling restless. My thoughts are uncomfortable—veering in so many directions that I'm having a hard time processing it all. "Things are…"

"Things are *what?*"

I throw my hands up and abruptly stand from the couch to pace the living room. Seth watches me without speaking.

"My aunt and uncle are suing me for custody of Carter," I tell him finally.

He blinks slowly. "What?"

"My aunt and uncle—"

"I heard you but I thought… *How?*"

I dig out the certified letter I got two days ago. "They're saying that my mother wasn't in her right mind when she made the decision to make me his guardian. They're asking a judge to grant them full custody."

"Shit."

"No kidding," I say, falling back to the couch. "It's a bunch of legal bullshit and it makes me sick to read it."

Seth is squinting down at the letter in his hands. "What did Amelia say?"

"I haven't told her yet."

"What the hell, man?"

I hesitate, wondering about it myself. Why haven't I told her about the custody dispute? "I guess I'm embarrassed."

He shakes his head and holds up the letter. "So are you going to get yourself a good lawyer?"

"I called a bunch of them but they all cost money that I don't have." I stare at him for a long moment before quietly admitting, "Paul talked to me again."

Seth straightens in the recliner. "Do not go there, Bash. There has to be another way."

I still can't shake the thought that I'd only need to do it once and Carter and I would be set. I'd be able to hire a real lawyer to look at my case.

"I don't know that there is another way. I feel like every damn day I'm fighting a losing battle."

"You're not going to lose anything," he says confidently. "And, dude, this is even more reason for you to look at schools."

"How do you figure?" I ask.

"You want to impress a judge? Show that you're building a life. Show that you can take care of a kid, work a job, graduate from high school, *and* go to college."

On the coffee table, my phone lights up and starts buzzing.

Amelia: This band is so loud it's making my brain hurt. Everyone is drunk and disgusting.

Another text from her comes in almost immediately and I stare down at it, thinking of Amelia and how she has her future planned out and wondering where I fit in her plans—if I do at all. Maybe it wouldn't be such a bad thing to form some plans of my own—other than working at the hardware store for the rest of my life. I want more than that of course. I just never saw it in the cards for me, but Seth does and so does Amelia.

Amelia: **I miss you. I wish you were here.**

Bash: **I wish YOU were HERE**

"Okay," I say to Seth as I pocket my phone. "Let's do it."

***

"This one looks good." Seth angles the laptop toward me so I can look at the university website he's got pulled up.

"Does it have family housing?"

He clicks around the website. "Hmmm, I don't think so."

"That's a no go then."

"Back to Google I go."

"Thanks for helping me do this."

"No problem. Hey—what about the University of Florida?" Seth asks. "They have a good art program and I'm seeing a bunch of scholarship options."

"Family housing?"

"Yeah, the school is huge and it says here that they have housing for students with dependents."

"Really?" I lean over so that I can read the information for myself. "Florida. I guess I could live in Florida."

"I wonder how the music scene is down in Gainesville?"

I lift my eyebrows in interest and ask him, "You thinking about tagging along?"

Seth gives a noncommittal shrug. "I'm not staying in Green Cove—that's for sure. You know college isn't on my agenda but I've got to play my music someplace. And why not Florida?"

My phone vibrates from my back pocket, only this time from an actual call, not just a text.

"That Amelia?"

"Yeah," I say, an uneasy feeling sliding around my middle as I watch her name move across the screen. Why is she calling instead of texting from the party? I don't know what it is, but something isn't right.

"Amelia?" I answer.

"Sebastian?" I can barely hear her over the loud music and commotion in the background, but—*shit*, is she crying?

"What happened? Are you hurt?"

186

"No..." She fades out for a second and then comes back. This time her voice is clearer so I think she must have moved into a quieter room. "It's Spencer. He's completely lost it."

I curse under my breath. "What did he do?"

"He and my sister—I'm not sure... It's all so confusing."

"Amelia," I say firmly. "Tell me what he did."

"He's freaking me out!"

My heart stumbles and I squeeze the phone a little tighter. "How?"

"Daphne was talking to some guy and Spencer got mad. He started saying crazy things and threatening the guy." She pauses to draw in a shaky breath. "Daphne isn't taking it very seriously, but I think I've convinced her that we need to leave anyway."

"That's good, Amelia."

"I... I saw his face, Sebastian. He was mad and he's completely smashed and—Oh God, I'm not sure what to do because we got a ride here and now we're stuck. I know it's a lot to ask, but our parents aren't home and, even if they were, I don't know what I would say to them. And Audra's got a whole party full of people here and... I wasn't sure who else to call."

"You did the right thing," I tell her, rubbing at my forehead and trying to get my erratic heartbeat under control.

"What's going on?" Seth whispers.

"Amelia's in trouble. Or her sister is," I answer him. "I don't really know. And—" I glance down the hall to where Carter is sleeping. *Damnit.* I can't just leave him while I help Amelia.

Seth seems to understand my dilemma because he says, "Go. I'll stay here with Carter."

"Sebastian? Are you still there?" Amelia asks, panic making her voice shake a little. "Hello? Can you hear me?"

I'm already reaching for my keys when I confirm with

187

Seth, "You sure?"

He nods. "Yes. *Go.*"

I turn back to the phone. "Amelia?"

She exhales, relieved. "I'm here!"

"Where are you?"

"Daphne and I are out in front of the club near the tennis courts."

"I'll be there in ten minutes. You and Daphne just stay where you are and whatever you do—don't try to deal with Spencer. You got that?"

"I got it," she answers obediently. "And Sebastian?"

"Yeah?"

"Thank you. Just… thank you."

CHAPTER TWENTY

Amelia

I wait, shivering as the wet chill of the night sinks into my bones. The muffled sounds of the party trickle past the lobby of the club and the paned glass windows to my ears.

Audra texts me again. *Where are you?* And, again, I ignore it. I really don't want to ruin her big night if I don't have to. It will be easier for us to leave the party and deal with the fallout tomorrow.

"We could just go back inside," Daphne squeaks from behind me. She's bouncing around on her toes and rubbing the tops of her arms. That strapless dress might look good on her, but it's not doing much to block out the cool November air.

"I told Sebastian we would wait until he got here."

"And I told *you* that you're probably overreacting. Spencer was acting nuts, yeah, but I'm sure he's passed out in some corner by now."

"God, Daphne—we're not going over this again," I complain. "We're going to wait right where we are and then we're going home. End of discussion."

"I know... I swear that I've never seen him like that, Amelia."

"But you finally agree with me that Spencer is bad news?"

She closes her eyes. "I agree that I don't want to deal with it anymore."

"Good. Then we stay outside and wait."

"Even if that means we end up with frostbite?"

I roll my eyes. "We're not going to get frostbite."

The glow of headlights bumping down the long gravel drive that leads up to the club captures my attention. I hold my breath watching the truck clear the last turn.

It's him! My heart lifts as I race down the steps to meet him.

Sebastian doesn't look for a real parking spot. Instead, he just stops the Bronco in the circular drive that loops by the tennis courts and jumps out.

The steely look in his eyes brings me up short. "Are you okay?" he asks me, his voice hard as stone as his gaze bounces between Daphne and me.

"We're fine," she answers. "Just a little shaken up."

He turns to me. "Amelia?"

"I'm sorry," I say hastily. "Earlier, I was scared. But I know you have Carter to worry about and you don't need me to pile on even more..."

He grabs hold of my shoulders and looks me up and down slowly like he's making sure that I actually am okay. "You stayed out here and waited for me?"

God, how is it that I'm so much calmer just having him touch me like this?

Giving into the sensation, I rest my head against the hollow point between his chest and neck and wrap my arms across his middle. Slowly, I press my lips to his skin where his pulse thrums. "I told you we would," I say, breathing out.

"Good girl."

"I'm sorry," I say again.

Sebastian backs away and ducks so that we're the same level. Then he touches my face, rubbing the heels of his hands over my cheeks. "Shit, don't be sorry for anything. I was so worried..." A single muscle ticks in his jaw. "But it's going to be all right now. I'm going to make sure of it."

"But—" I begin.

"Shhhh..." With a tender kiss to my forehead, he whispers, "And I'm not going to let anything bad happen to you, Amelia. I can promise you that."

***

The house is dark and empty when we walk in. I fumble along the wall, searching for the light switch.

"Where are your parents?" Sebastian asks in a hushed tone.

"Daddy has a hunting camp just north of Waccamaw. They won't be home until Monday."

I finally find the switch and the foyer is diffused with balmy orange light. Daphne walks in behind Sebastian and blinks at me.

"Do you want me to get you something?" I ask her.

She shakes her head. She hasn't said much since we left Audra's party.

"You sure?"

This time, she nods in answer.

"Not even a mug of hot chocolate?" I push. When we were younger, even if it was in the heat of summer, hot chocolate was always the go-to panacea for every ailment. It wasn't necessarily about the drink. It was more about the ritual of Nancy setting us up on the bar stools in the kitchen and talking to us while she made it.

"Come on, Daphne," I coax, remembering how we'd make our stepmother count out the marshmallows in each mug so that we could be sure we had the exact same amount. "It will make you feel better."

And we can talk, is what I don't say out loud.

"Hot chocolate sounds good to me," Sebastian says, catching on that I want to get Daphne comfortable and talking.

"See?" I turn and look at Daphne.

"Okay," she relents with the smallest hint of a smile. "But I want ten of those tiny marshmallows."

Despite how I'm feeling, I chuckle. "Of course you do."

A couple of minutes later, I set down three steaming mugs of hot chocolate onto the counter that separates the kitchen from the breakfast nook. Daphne picks up one of the mugs and counts all ten marshmallows—making sure I didn't gyp her—before taking a sip.

"Daphne, we need to talk," I say lightly.

Sebastian meets my gaze and an understanding passes between us. "Where's the bathroom?"

I point him in the right direction.

"There's not much to talk about, is there?" Daphne says as soon as Sebastian excuses himself.

"Tonight with Spencer—"

"Spencer and I are done," she says over me.

"You've said that before," I argue. "You told me he was with another girl and that he was into drugs and you didn't want anything to do with him. And then I turn around and you're talking to him and acting like you might want to get back together."

Daphne winces, chastised, as she pokes her fingers at the marshmallows in her cup. "I know."

"So what am I supposed to believe? What is going on with you?"

"I wish you could understand," she murmurs before taking a tentative sip of the hot chocolate.

"Maybe I will if you tell me."

"Okay." She sucks in a big breath and continues, "Spencer might be a jerk, but people pay attention to him."

"He's popular," I surmise. "Which, I already knew. And, God, *you're* popular, Daphne."

She shakes her head. "Not like him. I've always had to work at it, but Spencer is golden. He's doesn't even have to think to make people notice him. He's like... like a god."

I lift an eyebrow in skepticism. "A god?"

"You know what I mean. He could have anyone... any

192

girl," she says, getting a desperate look in her eyes. "And he still chose *me*. Do you know how that feels?"

I think of Sebastian and how it feels to know that I'm the one he chose to share a part of himself that no one else gets to see. "I guess I do."

She manages a faint smile. "It's addictive—being admired like that. It makes you feel special. And having Spencer think about me and look at me like he couldn't stop even if he wanted to... I've been afraid to lose that. What if there isn't anybody else after him? What if he's all there is?"

"We're seventeen, Daphne," I remind her.

She tucks a stray piece of brown hair behind her ear. "I know, but nothing is a certainty, you know? After this year everyone is going to spread out and things are going to change. You'll leave Green Cove for college, but what about me?"

"If you're afraid then come with me."

"You know that I'd never get into the schools that you're going to get into."

"You might."

"Amelia," she says simply.

"I don't even know where I'm going yet and you've got the road trip with Audra," I remind her.

"I know." She shrugs and then takes another sip of hot chocolate. "And I'm excited about it, but I think part of me is planning such a different future from you because deep down, I know that I can't compete."

"What are you talking about, Daphne? We're not in a competition."

"But sometimes it feels like that. Even Daddy and Nancy don't take me seriously. They're always pushing and encouraging you to work harder. But me? They think all I can do is pick out clothes and paint my nails like a pro."

"They don't think that."

Again, she shrugs. "Maybe—maybe not. But, Amelia,

you're special and I... well, I don't want to be the one left behind."

"I'm not going to leave you behind," I tell her.

My sister drops her face and in a very small voice, says, "But you *are.*"

Tears pool in my eyes but I refuse to let myself cry. Daphne needs me to stay strong. She needs me to take charge and fix this. It's what I do. It's who I am.

"Daphne, look at me."

She picks her head up. Her brown eyes are dark and shiny with emotion.

"I'm not going to go off and forget about you, okay? I couldn't even if I wanted to."

"Promise?"

"Promise."

"Thanks, Amelia. And for tonight." She tilts her head and smirks. "Considering all things, you might not believe this, but it really is over with Spencer."

"For good?" I question.

"Yes," she says on a sigh. "Tonight was different. Tonight was kind of scary."

I close my fingers around the warm ceramic handle of my mug. "I know you probably don't want to hear this, Daphne, but I think we should tell Nancy and Daddy."

"But tell them what? Spencer just yelled at me a lot. He's jealous, but I don't think he's actually dangerous."

"I disagree," I say, shaking my head. "He threatened you."

"I don't think he meant anything by it, Amelia. He was just drunk and acting like a fool."

I cross my arms across my chest. "I'd still feel better if you told them about what happened."

"I don't know—it might be weird, " she contends. "Daddy knows his father through work and Nancy still thinks that Spencer is perfect."

"Because you haven't told her what he's really like."

"Maybe you're right but I can't do anything about it tonight, can I? I'll talk to them on Monday after they get back from their trip."

"You will?"

"Yes," she says adamantly enough that I believe her.

Coming in from the hallway, Sebastian clears his throat and asks, "Am I interrupting?"

"No," Daphne and I say at the same time and laugh.

"Jinx. Owe me a Coke."

I roll my eyes. "Tomorrow, you're on."

She drains the last of her hot chocolate and slams down the empty mug. "I'm actually going to go to bed."

Sebastian shifts his weight. "You don't have to go because of me."

She flaps a hand and opens her mouth in a lazy yawn. "No, I'm zonked. You two... do what you do," she says, sliding off the bar stool and smoothing down her wrinkled dress. "You certainly don't need an audience while you get all mushy."

Good grief, Daphne. I roll my eyes at her retreating back. "Night," I tell her. "Love you."

"Love you more!"

When we can hear Daphne's steps on the staircase I let go of a long breath.

Sebastian walks all the way into the kitchen and asks me, "Everything good with her?"

"I think so. And, by the way, thanks for giving us a chance to talk."

"Of course," he says, looking at me. Even now, after this crazy night, I could get lost inside those eyes. "Are you guys going to be okay tonight?"

His hot chocolate is probably cold by now, but I pick up the mug and hand it to him anyway. "We'll be fine."

He takes a sip then says, "Because I'll stay if you need me to. I can always call Seth and see if he'll spend the rest of the

195

night with Carter."

My skin heats just from thinking about him staying over. *Where would he sleep?* Oh God, *would we even sleep?*

"No, it's okay. I know that you have to work tomorrow—" I glance at the clock above the stove and see that it's after midnight. "Actually, in a few hours I guess. God, Sebastian, I'm so sorry about all of this."

"Don't be sorry for calling me," he replies, stepping closer. "I *want* to be the one that you call."

"Right. I'm sure you loved having your Saturday night interrupted with the whole damsel in distress routine," I joke.

He places the mug of hot chocolate on the counter and then he turns so that we're facing each other.

"Amelia, you can do the damsel in distress thing with me anytime you want. Hell, you can call me if you need someone to open a jar of mayonnaise for you."

I smile. "Thanks, but I can usually handle jars on my own."

He rolls his shoulders. "How about spiders? Can you handle spiders on your own?"

"They aren't so bad," I say, laughing softly.

"Thunder and lightning?"

I roll my eyes, but my smile remains in place. "Are you kidding? I love storms."

His dark eyebrows compress. "Snakes?"

"Okay, you win. Snakes are the worst."

"So you'll call me if you stumble upon a pit of vipers?" He strokes his knuckles down the side of my face.

"I'll call," I whisper.

We're quiet for a long moment, each of us staring intently. Finally, Sebastian drops his head against mine and says, "I was worried tonight."

"I know."

His gaze darts to my lips and my breathing grows shallow. *Kiss me,* I silently beg.

"Before, I thought that I had all that I could handle and that worrying about someone else would be unneeded stress."

"Oh..?" I murmur, backing up until I can feel the edge of the granite counter bumping my spine.

"Let me finish, Amelia," he says with a shuddering breath. "I used to think that because another person meant another thing that I couldn't control. Another thing that owned me. But now..." He leans in, caging me in with his arms. "I want to have that with you. I *need* to feel that."

"That I own you?"

I'd said it to tease him, but Sebastian's face remains serious, like he's just confessed his deepest, darkest secret to me.

Oh. My heart is slamming against my chest.

"It goes both ways," I whisper. "That feeling."

Sebastian swallows.

I lick my lips.

The air around us is charged with everything we've said and everything that we haven't said.

"Amelia, I think..."

Fingers touch my face. Breath brushes my skin. And the taste of him—warm and chocolatey and perfect—fills my head.

I break away, just barely. "Sebastian, about tonight—"

"Yeah?" His voice is strangled.

I press even closer, feeling the delicious hardness of his hipbones against my stomach. "If you want to stay, and Seth is okay with Carter, then—"

A heavy banging sound thunders throughout the house.

Sebastian's head jerks toward the front door. "What the hell?"

"*Daphne!*"

"It's Spencer!" I bite out, scrambling beneath Sebastian's arms.

More banging. "*Daphne! Daphne I'm sorry!*"

197

I run into the foyer and see that Daphne is already at the top of the stairs.

"Just go back to your room!" I yell at her.

She stops, uncertain. "But—"

"Amelia is right," Sebastian says, coming up behind me. "Stay upstairs."

Bracing my palm against the cool wood of the front door, I peer through the long, thin entrance window. Spencer, catching sight of me, pounds on the door again, this time so hard that the walls on either side of the frame shake.

"Don't answer it, Amelia," Sebastian warns, seizing my arm and dragging me back.

"I wasn't going to."

"Daphne! Talk to me!"

Daphne skitters down the stairs. "If we don't answer it then eventually someone is going to hear him yelling and call the police."

Sebastian's hard gaze cuts to her. "Good. He could use a night in a jail cell."

I shake my head. "No one is going to hear him. The nearest house is a half a mile away."

"Amelia, it doesn't matter. We can't let this go on all night. Just let me talk to him and he'll go away. I know it," Daphne says, reaching for the door knob.

"Stop—"

Ignoring me, she opens the door to reveal Spencer—eyes half-mast and swaying on his feet within the silver halo cast by the porch light.

"God, Spencer! What are you doing here?" she demands.

He smiles at her and garbles out, "I just came to say I'm sorry, baby."

"It's a little too late for that," says Daphne.

"It's never too late." He shakes his head and awkwardly tries to grab her.

"This time it is," she insists, stepping back out of his

reach. "You and I are over for real."

His face contracts in anger. "You can't do that. You're mine, Daphne. You said—"

"But I'm *not* yours. Not anymore. We ended things and I never should have started them up again."

"No!" Spencer pulls at his hair. "You're wrong!"

Okay, this is getting too crazy.

"Spencer, you need to go home," I tell him as I push Daphne aside and take her place in the doorway. "We'll even call you a ride because you shouldn't be driving. Just wait down in the driveway, okay?"

"Get out of my face. I need to talk to Daphne!" he yells, balling his hand and punching the wall next to the door.

"Spencer, man, get ahold of yourself and listen to Amelia," Sebastian tries.

More punching. "*No! No! No!*"

"Just go down the driveway and wait." I start to close the door, but Spencer grips it with one hand and shoves his way inside.

"Get out!" I shout, stepping in front of him in a vain attempt to block him.

It all happens so fast then. I know that Daphne is screaming and Sebastian is trying to leverage himself between us, but Spencer is too big compared to my small frame. And, even drunk as he is, he's too fast for me to dodge him. In one violent swoop, his arm connects with the side of my head and sends me stumbling backward into the wall.

"You son of a bitch!" Sebastian roars, charging forward.

"Stay out of this, Holbrook. It's none of your business!" Spencer tries to deflect him, but Sebastian easily grabs hold of the collar of his shirt and propels him back through the door.

"When you laid a hand on my girlfriend it became my business," he growls. "Now are you going to leave here on your own or am I going to have to make you?"

"I'd like to see you try," Spencer slurs, rocking unsteadily.

Sebastian releases his grip and gives a solid kick that sends Spencer tumbling down the front steps. He turns back to me, sides heaving. "Are you okay?"

Dazed but not seriously hurt, I carefully climb to my feet. "I-I'm going to be fine."

"I'm so sorry, Amelia!" Daphne cries, squeezing my arm and helping me the rest of the way up.

I rub at my head just below the temple and say, "Both of you—it's okay. I'm okay."

Sebastian pulls me close, cupping my head against his chest protectively. "It's not okay. Don't ever do something like that again, Amelia! He could've broken something or worse."

Still down on the ground, Spencer sees us in the open doorway and spits out nastily, "Fine. You can keep the slut and her sister too. I don't need any of you!"

Through gritted teeth, Sebastian tilts his head away from me and calls out, "I'm sure we'll figure out a way to live without you. Now, get your sorry ass out of here or we're calling the cops."

Spencer stands and juts his chin forward. His glassy eyes blink and he snarls, "You'll regret this, Daphne Bright. You wait and see!"

Tears are swimming in Daphne's eyes. Her whole body is shaking. In a voice so low, it takes me a moment to make sure I've heard her right, she whispers, "I already do."

CHAPTER TWENTY-ONE

Bash

I slip the financial aid applications into my bag before leaving the guidance counselor's office.

"Hey, what are you doing over here? Isn't your first class on the other side of the building?" Amelia greets me, a stack of brightly-colored paper flyers in her hands.

"Seeking guidance of course," I say trying to keep my voice casual. I don't want to get her hopes up. After all, college might not pan out and I don't want to disappoint her. "How's your head?"

Amelia rolls her eyes at me. "For the ten millionth time—it's fine."

I smooth her dark hair back so that I can examine the faint bluish bruise that's flowered to the side of her eye. Every time I see it, my chest tightens with unanswered fury.

"I still wish you had let me call the police. Even just to get Spencer pulled over for drunk driving. That idiot deserved it."

"I told you already that we just want to be done with him. Calling the police would have freaked Daphne out more than she already was. It was easier to just let it go."

"But you're still going to tell your parents about what happened, right?"

She nods. "Daphne swears she's going to talk to them at dinner tonight."

Then she stands on her toes and gives me a kiss chaste enough for the school hallway we're in. Wanting—no, *needing* more—I tug her into a shadowed alcove beside the lockers and cradle her face in my hands.

"You won't talk to him today at school, will you?" I say against her mouth.

She kisses me back and I can feel the soft smile that curves her lips. "Jeesh—I already told you I wouldn't. Though I might have to see him next period."

I don't like that at all. "I thought it was your free period?"

Amelia drops flat on her feet and makes a face. "I'm meeting with the Spirit Club."

"Why?"

"Student government has to help make plans for the winter pep rally next week. That means getting together in the gym with the cheerleaders and the basketball team and the captains of the football team—"

"Which means Spencer," I finish for her.

"Right," she says, nodding her head.

"Well..." I squeeze her waist. "Don't even look at him."

She laughs. "I won't, but you honestly don't have to worry. Mr. Brickler is going to be there along with about twenty other people. I don't think Spencer is going to wreck his reputation by confessing his undying love for my sister or crying or anything even remotely like that."

I breathe out. She's right. "Okay," I say. "Then I'll see you at lunch?"

One more kiss. "Of course."

"And what about after school? Are you free today because I don't have work."

Amelia's face falls. "I actually have my first official captains meeting to discuss the upcoming season. And, trust me, I'm not looking forward to it. Coach Sachs is going to be so mad when he realizes I've barely played since the summer."

I groan. "And I thought I was the one with the busy life..." Then I pause, realizing something. "When it's tennis season am I going to get to see you in one of those cute skirts?"

"I usually just wear shorts."

I toss my head back. "Ah, now that's a crying shame."

She laughs and swats at my arm as she backs away from me. "For you, I might wear a skirt."

"Yeah?"

"Yep," she says as she gives a little shake. She's wearing an ivory sweater and pink and green polka dot leggings that don't do much to hide her curves.

"You're killing me!" I complain.

"That's the plan!"

I get one last smile before she rounds the corner and is gone from my sight. But that final look—the one where the corners of her brown eyes crinkle and her smile goes lopsided—carries me down the hall and follows me into my economics class.

As I take my seat, I know I'm probably grinning like a lovesick fool and that everyone in the classroom is going to notice, but I can't even make myself care.

I think of the financial aid forms I picked up from the guidance counselor's office and all the colleges that Seth and I looked at on Saturday night. For the first time it feels like it might be possible.

I can actually do this.

I can make plans beyond how I'm going to afford the water bill or food for next week. *Real* plans for the kind of life I want to live—the kind of life I want to be able to provide for Carter. And Seth is right about the custody dispute with my aunt and uncle. No judge is going to take Carter from me when I can prove beyond a shadow of a doubt that I'm going places—that I'm not just some hillbilly whose barely going to graduate from high school.

Bang!

At first, the sound doesn't really register with me. In that empty and flat snap of time, I think a transformer has blown and I expect the lights to shut off.

Then I hear the first scream and the terrible realization explodes inside of me. That's *gunfire*.

I'm out of my chair and running before I can think better of it. Teachers are yelling. People are shouting. Panicked shrieks are coming from somewhere down the hall.

Fear splinters through me as I race toward the locker bay. There, I'm swarmed and driven back by a stampede of terror-stricken students running away from the cafeteria and the gym.

The gym.

That's where Amelia's Spirit Club meeting was going to be.

Bang! Bang!

"Bash!" It's Seth. He shoves past a fallen stepladder and grabs the bottom of my shirt to pull me from the crowd. "To the door!"

"I can't. Amelia is back there!" I push him off and fight my way against the tide of bodies as I desperately search for her familiar face.

"Amelia!" Even in this mess, I can hear the brokenness in my own voice. It echoes inside my head and billows straight into my lungs.

What had I said to her before? About wanting to worry, wanting to let her own my heart? Was that only two nights ago?

Bang! Another gunshot fractures the chaos.

Faster, the fear rings in my ears and keeps on ringing.

"Amelia!"

I turn the corner and skid to a stop. *Oh God.* It's too much to take in all at once and despite the frenzy burning its way in my chest, my eyes slip shut, but only for a fraction of a second until the adrenaline coursing through my veins pumps harder, taking over and forcing me into the gym.

"Amelia?" I howl, commanding my body to move, my eyes to search.

It's awful.

Blood spreads in slick black pools across the gym floor and vomits over the concrete steps that climb up through the center of the bleachers. Everywhere I look, I see pain and hurt. It blurs my vision and messes with my head.

A gun is lying just an inch away from a lifeless hand. I can't make out the face—it's just blood and gore—but I recognize the football jacket and Spencer's threats echo inside my mind. *You'll regret this.*

"Amelia!"

There.

I run, making a path between the door and the basketball hoop, and I drop down beside her.

"I've got you," I say hoarsely as I gather her quaking body in my arms.

She's moaning. Her breaths are shallow and stuttered and she's trying to crawl away from me. Blood is soaked through her leggings all the way into her boots.

"No, Amelia!" I push her long hair away from her forehead and force her face to mine. *Don't look at anything else but me. Please don't look.*

Her eyes are red and vacant with anguish. Unseeing, she squeezes my forearms, her nails making burrows in my skin, and screams.

"It's okay… it's okay…" I choke out these same words over and over as I brush her hair back. And each time I say it, it hurts worst than the last.

We both know I'm lying.

Nothing is going to be okay.

Not ever again.

PART TWO

Tell me what else should I have done? Doesn't everything die at last,
and too soon?
~Mary Oliver

CHAPTER TWENTY-TWO

Bash

The images are strange—faltering and choppy.
Blood. The sound of sirens assaulting my ears. Fear choking me, squeezing my heart. Her limp fingers slipping through mine. And yelling—so much yelling.

"Bash?"

I come to awareness at the kitchen sink, my ears filled with a swishing sound. What am I doing? Everything is too bright. Why am I staring out the window at nothing? I glance down and see that the tap is on and there's a glass full of water in my hand. Was I drinking that?

I turn the water off, then I set the glass down and look around and notice Carter. He's sitting at the kitchen table with a bowl of cereal in front of him. He's dressed for school, but I don't have any recollection of helping him get ready.

My head hurts and I wonder if maybe I'm losing my mind. Or maybe I'm trapped inside of a dream. A *nightmare*, I correct myself.

"Bash?"

I try out my voice, almost surprised when it works. "Yeah, bud?"

He gazes at me for a second before asking, "Why are you acting like this?"

"Like what?"

"Like you're sad?"

Fiery pain spikes my chest, slicing into my heart. I have no idea what to say to him. How to explain evil to a seven-year-old. How to tell him about Amelia.

"It's a terrible tragedy. Our thoughts and prayers are with the people of Green Cove this morning."

The sound of the television grabs my attention and draws me into the living room. They're talking about us—about Green Cove.

"That's right, Stuart. Police are saying three are dead and one person is injured."

The reporter is standing in the parking lot of the high school.

"Green Cove, South Carolina is the latest community in our nation to be rocked by a mass shooting. Here, at this high school you see behind me, eighteen-year-old Spencer McGovern reportedly demanded that students get on the floor of the high school gym before opening fire on Monday morning and killing three people, including himself."

The television clicks off to a black screen.

"Shit, man. I didn't know you were awake yet," Seth says guiltily, his eyes turning to me. The remote is in his hand.

I gesture to the television. "Has it been like this?"

He nods his head and swallows. "Nonstop."

I run my hands up and down my face. "Oh."

"You need to eat something," Seth says, his expression strained. "I got Carter ready for school. I wasn't sure if he should go or—"

"No, it's good for him to go. He needs things to be as normal as they can be."

"And your aunt was calling your phone all night. I finally answered around three in the morning to let her know you and Carter were fine."

Fine? I don't feel fine.

"Bash?" Carter asks from behind me. His face is red and he's blinking past me to the television. "What's wrong? Why was Green Cove on the TV?"

It takes a full minute to work up the courage to speak. "Nothing—" I start, trying to ignore the blistering ache in my chest, but it's no use. My voice shakes so much that I can't go on.

I can't do this.

I can't lie.

"Bash?" Carter is waiting.

I press the heels of my hands to my eyes but nothing will stop the flood this time. It takes over my whole body, driving me to the floor. I don't even know who I'm crying for— Myself? Her? All of us?

CHAPTER TWENTY-THREE

Amelia

Brittle grey morning light is sneaking in through the curtains, taunting me, luring me from the depths of sleep. I don't know how long it's been. Days? Weeks?

Wait.

Days... weeks... since *what?*

A sharp, cramping sensation ratchets up my side and I reach down to feel a bandage taped below my navel. What is that from? And why can't I think straight? My head feels dull and gauzy, caught somewhere between here and a faraway dream world.

Slowly, the sounds from outside my window come into focus. Shouts. The rumble of an engine. A clanging I don't recognize.

Pushing aside the comforter, I force my feet over the side of the mattress. They dangle for a moment and then I'm up on wobbly legs. I hold my aching side tightly, my fingers splayed across the white bandage, and I lean into the window sill.

There is a bustle of activity below and it takes me a minute to sift through it all—the news vans parked between the pine trees past the long driveway and the mob of strangers just beyond the front gate.

I don't see Daddy's car but I do see a woman I don't know staring up at the house. She's holding a teddy bear in one hand and a candle in the other.

As I watch her, a sick, nagging feeling begins to gnaw at me. *Why is she here?*

Nothing is making any kind of sense to me.

I can remember a hospital... A cold floor. A pale ceiling. A deafening noise. Beeping machines. Hands prodding my stomach. Apologies whispered in my ear.

But I can't remember *why*.

I turn around and stare at my bedroom. Everything is in the correct place, but something isn't right. Where is everyone? Why am I not at school? Where's Nancy? Daphne?

A memory swells within me only to be sucked away before I can grab hold of it, like a rimy word melting too soon on the tip of my tongue.

"Daphne?" I fumble toward the closed bedroom door and teeter into the hallway. "Hello? Anyone?

As I grapple with the knob of her bedroom door, a strange and wintry kind of panic begins to seep into my chest, filling in the spaces between each of my ribs.

Daphne's room is the same as it's always been, except... *What's wrong?*

A fragile image, breakable as glass, is struggling to the surface. Something about Daphne and...

The bed.

My sister never makes her bed, yet there it is—perfectly made up—right in front of me. Even the throw pillows are arranged nicely over the shams.

I take a tentative step into the room. "Daphne?"

"I didn't know you were up yet."

I swivel around to see Nancy hurrying down the hall. She worriedly brings her hands to her face. "You shouldn't be out of bed like this, Amelia."

"Why?" I was cold just a second ago, but now I'm starting to feel clammy. I peer into the bedroom, looking around the corner to Daphne's closet. "Where is she?"

Nancy's shoulders and face crumple in harmony. "Amelia... no, sweetheart. This is the sedatives talking."

"Sedatives?" I shake my head, thinking again of the

hospital. *What is it?* My fingers absently brush the bandage around my middle.

"Shhhh, they said you'd be woozy for a few more days." She tries to pull me into an embrace.

My heart is pounding hard now. I push away so that I can look again. "Where is she? Where is Daphne?"

"Amelia, you're weak as a kitten. Let's get you back into bed first," she coos, attempting to walk me out of Daphne's room, "and then we'll talk. Remember that the doctors want you resting as much as possible."

"I don't..." A chill rushes up my spine, making my whole body tremble. I grab onto the doorway, my nails hooking into the curves in the painted wood. "Where's my sister?"

Daddy comes running up the steps. He sees me clawing at the door to Daphne's room and his face goes slack. "Oh darlin', not again."

Nausea swims inside of me. "Daddy?"

He continues to stare at me. "You need to let Nancy and me get you back to your bed."

"But I don't want to go to bed."

Daddy reaches for me, but I stumble back away from him and fall against the wall, the weight of memories pouring over me like fast water.

The hospital.

Red and blue pinpricks of light against a sober sky.

Sebastian's arms around me.

A sound like the world ripping into pieces.

Daphne's body on the floor beside me.

And all at once, I can remember what I already knew three days ago. What I knew the moment Spencer McGovern stood across the school gym, pulled a shiny black handgun from his backpack, and took aim.

"No!" I wail, crawling on my hands toward my sister's bedroom. If I can just get in there, it will be okay. I'll see that she's safe in her bed, tucked under the covers where nothing bad can ever happen.

"Oh dear, I'll go get him," Nancy says, slowly backing away.

"Good idea," Daddy replies as she scurries off. Then he grabs my shoulders and tries to get me to look at him. "Now, Amelia Laine, you're starting to panic again. Take a deep breath and try to calm down."

But I can't calm down and I can't breathe. The water is coming on too fast. My lungs are screaming for oxygen but I'm stuck in the rip current. I know I need to come up for air, but I just can't *move*.

Is this what it's like to die?

Is this how my sister felt?

Take me with you, I silently plead, closing my eyes and wishing for the bitter blackness to sweep me away once and for all.

"Amelia."

I lift my head and see Sebastian coming for me. The instant I feel the warm touch of his skin against mine, the surface of the water breaks and I can breathe again.

"I've got you," he says, catching me to his chest and pulling us both onto our knees.

"Sebastian, you have to help me," I sob, thinking of how Daphne was on the gym floor—with one hand curled up under her chin and her eyes closed. I grip his shirt and pull his face to mine. "She might be sleeping!"

Sebastian's face is ashen and seriously set. "Amelia she's not asleep."

I knew it was a stupid thing to think. There was too much blood and her skin was so pale that she looked like a creature from another world—like a mermaid dragged from the depths of the sea. But I want to believe it so badly that I can't see straight.

Take me with you...

This time I think I've even said it out loud.

But no one is listening anymore.

CHAPTER TWENTY-FOUR

Bash

I stare down at the swirls of color on the page. "What's this?"

"It's you!" Carter says. He leans over and points to a circle with brown lines coming out of it. "See your hair right here?"

"Of course I see it. This guy looked familiar but I thought he was too good-looking to be me."

Carter shrugs his shoulders. "It's art."

I chuckle as I find a free magnet so that his drawing can be on the front and center of the refrigerator. "Well, I love it. Thanks, bud."

"Mrs. White told us to draw our hero."

I twist around, emotion pinching inside of me. "And you drew *me*? Why?"

"Because you're my hero," he says proudly.

I swallow and look back to the drawing. Funny—these days I feel wrecked and broken—not much like a hero.

"Nate drew George Washington," Carter says. "But I don't even know George Washington. *You* take care of me."

"Hey—what about me?" Seth interrupts. "I'm like Mr. Mom over here. Jesus—it's Friday night and I'm making a meatloaf. I think that deserves at least a drawing, don't you?"

I laugh but it's actually pretty accurate. Seth has been staying with us for almost two weeks, helping out with Carter, making lunches and dinner, giving him rides to school so that I can go over to Amelia's in the afternoons to try to coax her out of the silence she's been in since the shooting.

"Seth," Carter says, his tone serious. "I'll make you a drawing if you promise that I don't have to watch one of your boring movies tonight."

"They're called rockumentaries, and, kid, you should be grateful that I'm introducing you to the greatest rock bands of all time. It's a privilege."

Carter scrunches up his face. "I don't even know what that means."

Seth shakes his head. "It means that you're lucky I'm here to assist your bro with your music education. Now grab that pot holder over there and let's get this baby into the oven."

An hour later, the three of us are on the couch with Jinx watching a documentary about Iron Maiden. Beside me, Carter yawns.

"C'mere," I say, putting my arm over his shoulders and pulling him half onto my lap.

"Can I ask you a question?" he whispers, his eyes anxiously blinking up at me.

"Yeah, bud. Ask me anything."

"Did you see her today?"

I struggle to control my reaction because I know the *her* he's asking about is Amelia. "Yeah," I say, my throat tightening painfully. "I stopped by her house this afternoon."

"Is she okay?"

I don't know how to answer that. She's not okay. She's functioning, but she's not *my* Amelia. She's too thin. Her face is still pretty, almost porcelain, but the shadows under her brown eyes grow darker every day.

"She's getting there," I answer hesitantly.

"Do you think she wants to come over? We could take her on a shark hunt like we promised. It's winter break now and there's no school so I thought she might like that!"

"I don't know if that's a good idea."

"Why not?" Carter asks. "She's never at tutoring anymore either."

"Remember we talked about this, bud? Amelia's probably not going to be around for a while."

"I know." His expression falls. "You said a bad thing

216

happened to her and she's sad right now."

"That's right. Remember when Mama died and you felt real sick?"

"Like I was gonna throw up all day long," he says. "Is that how Amelia feels?"

"Kind of."

"And is that why you stopped working so much at Kane's? Seth says your boss is a big butthole."

My chest rumbles with laughter. "Seth shouldn't have told you that, but yeah, I had to cut my hours down to be able to help Amelia if she needs me, and while I was looking the other way, my boss hired someone else. But I don't want you to worry about my job, bud. I'll get another one," I say though I'm not sure that's true. I've been looking for something with good hours all week with no luck. "Carter, we're going to be fine and Amelia is going to be fine soon too."

"I know but... it's still not fair. I wanted to tell her that I finished the book she brought me right before Thanksgiving."

"I'll tell her for you."

"That's not the same thing," he says on a sigh. "I miss her, Bash."

I touch his hair, feeling the cool strands against my fingertips. "Me too, bud."

CHAPTER TWENTY-FIVE

Amelia

I'm on a pillow on the floor of my room staring up at the ceiling fan. Round and round it goes. Huh—isn't there an old saying like that?

Like every afternoon for the past couple of weeks, Audra is here. She's talking, but I'm not really listening to her. Blah, blah, blah. Like I want to know about anyone at school. Like I want her to tell me about the prayer circle they had on the last day before winter break or the assembly to honor the victims.

I close my eyes, mad at myself for even thinking it.

Victims.

I hate that word. I actually looked it up the other day and one of the definitions is *someone who has been sacrificed*. Is that how Spencer saw us? Was Mr. Brickler a sacrifice? Was Daphne?

"Did you hear what they're sayin'?" Audra is still talking.

I'm done with this. I'm about to tell her that I'm too tired to hear this crap and she should just go home when she continues, "About Spencer?"

"What about him?" I croak out.

Her blue eyes meet mine. I can see the relief there. Relief I guess that I'm not comatose or mentally planning out my suicide. "It's all over the news."

I don't watch the news. Most of the vans are gone from in front of our house now—off to document another tragedy and turn those people's lives inside out all for the sake of journalism—but I know that "The Green Cove Shooting"

218

still makes the nightly rounds. I know that the gun people and the anti-gun people stand in front of cameras waving my sister's picture around like they have something important to say.

All those people and all those reporters act like they knew Daphne and now they have a right to sadness.

But that grief they're toying with? The grief of a community? A nation? The whole world?

It's mine.

Because not one other person can feel like this—like they'll never be able to look into a mirror again without remembering. Not one other soul feels like their heart has been cut out of their body and beaten down to nothing but blood and pulp.

"Amelia?" she prompts.

"I haven't watched the news," I tell her, letting my eyes drift to the fan. *Round and round.*

"Well, he had traces of enough steroids in his system to gag a maggot and Spencer's parents are sayin' that he was on a prescribed medication, but it looks like he stopped takin' *those* pills months ago. They didn't know that at the time, of course, but now they're countin' up pills or whatever and the numbers don't add up. He was, like, supposed to be on some sort of antipsychotic—starts with an 'r'—but I can't remember the name of it."

"Why?"

"His parents are tellin' the police that he was supposed to be seein' a psychiatrist but he stopped going in August because it was too much with football practice and he didn't want anyone on the team to know. Can you believe that? Maybe if someone else had known he was strugglin' then maybe things would have been different."

"Don't," I say, looking at her.

Audra jerks her head back. "Don't what?"

"You're making excuses for him."

219

"No, I'm not doin' that."

"You are. You're acting like Spencer couldn't help himself. Like he didn't *want* to hurt anyone," I choke out.

"No, I'm not. I'm just tellin' you that Spencer was sick. He killed himself that day too. And maybe if he had stayed away from the gym candy and had been takin' his prescribed meds like he was supposed to then..."

I'm angry for Daphne. For myself. "Then *what?* He wouldn't have shot me? Would Daphne still be alive? Or what about Mr. Brinkler? Spencer shot him in cold blood just for trying to help us! Can your *maybes* bring them back or take that gun out of his hands? No, they can't. So just... don't try to analyze him or explain it away."

She sighs. "Maybe I shouldn't be bringin' this up, but I know his mom has tried reachin' out to ya'll."

"So?"

"I thought you might give her a chance."

"Why would I care what that woman has to say? There's nothing she can say that makes up for the fact that she raised a murderer."

Audra is quiet for a long time and then she says, "Amelia, I didn't mean to make things worse. I'm just tryin' to talk to you and make sense of all of this."

"I get it, but there is no sense to any of it. And I don't want to hear about Spencer or his mother," I say, my eyes going back to the fan. "What's the point?"

Round and round it goes, and where it stops nobody knows.

***

"What is it?" I ask, bending closer.

Daphne is crouched over her clasped hands. She looks up at me, her light brown eyes glittering with elation and says, "Open your hands."

"Why?"

"Because I want to show you something."

We're outside, sitting cross-legged in the dirt with our knees touching. Above us, the branches of an old oak create a mossy canopy that ensnares the sunlight.

"Where are we?" I ask my sister. In the distance I think I can see a white farmhouse but I'm not sure.

"That's not important right now. Amelia, open your hands for me."

This time I do as she asks and she places something warm and soft on my palm then folds her hands around mine to keep them closed.

"What is it?" I ask in wonder, trying to peek through the cracks in my fingers. I can feel the thing's rapid heartbeat fluttering against my skin and it reminds me of rain.

Daphne laughs. "It's a bird, silly. What did you think it was?"

And then I'm awake, my sister's voice fading as the dappled sunlight of a luminous and sunny afternoon is swallowed by the darkness of my bedroom.

My mind whirs as I try to keep hold of the tendrils of the dream. Why would Daphne have that bird? Did she catch it? Or maybe it fell out of a nest and she found it on the ground?

I close my eyes, desperate to get back inside the dream world, but my body rebels. I'm too fuzzy even for sleep. I'm too dim to dream of her again.

I need water.

I shuffle from my room and down the stairs. All around me, the house is mute and black. It feels vacant—like no one lives here anymore.

On the bottom landing, I can see the shadow of the Christmas tree in the living room. Nancy tried to get Daddy and I excited about Christmas this year, but the whole thing is a ridiculous waste of time. How can we be expected to care about ornaments and presents and stockings when we all know Daphne is cold and six feet under the earth?

When I get to the kitchen, I drink three glasses of lukewarm water so quickly that water dribbles down my chin and neck. I consider the food in the refrigerator, but even though I haven't eaten anything but crackers since yesterday,

I'm not really hungry. Especially not for this sympathy food.

People keep showing up here with their stupid casserole dishes and their sad cards and their dying flowers and their freaking honey baked hams and we're supposed to play along like those things mean something to us. Like a piece of well-cooked pork is supposed to make us less depressed.

I slam the refrigerator closed and turn to head back to the stairs. That's when I notice a sliver of warm light spreading from under the door to Daddy's office. Hesitantly, I poke my head inside.

Daddy is in the big leather chair behind his desk. He's slumped forward, looking down at something in his lap. A half-empty bottle of amber liquid is beside him and I watch as he lifts the bottle to his lips and tips his head back for a long swig.

In those first few days, he was Mr. Put-Us-Back-Together, trying to get me out of bed, encouraging me to eat something. Then around week two, he gave up. He stopped shaving and going to work. Now he spends his days locked behind his office door doing who knows what.

His face is drawn and his greying hair is sticking up in all directions. God, when was the last time he showered? Or consumed something beside liquor?

"Daddy?"

He looks up, startled when he sees me, and he tries to hide the bottle behind his chair.

"Where's Nancy?" I ask him.

He gestures sluggishly around his head. "Probably at church."

"But it's night."

"Who knows? She's always there lately."

Lately.

I start to turn away but he calls me back into his office. "Amelia—"

"Yeah?" I stop beside the desk. Now I can see what he

was looking at in his lap. It's a picture of Daphne and I with our arms around each other and I can remember exactly when it was taken. Nancy had driven us to Charleston and we'd gotten our nails done for the first time. I picked pink polish and she picked red. In the photo, both of us are showing off our fingernails to the camera and sporting wide matching smiles.

"She was so happy," I murmur, kneeling so that I can look more closely.

"She was always happy."

Daddy takes my face in his hands then and he stares down at me for a long time, his eyes searching every single one of my features.

Who are you seeing?

Is it me or is it her?

CHAPTER TWENTY-SIX

Bash

I wake up thirty minutes late. My mouth is smushed up against the mattress and my hair is plastered against my eyelids.

The digital clock next to my bed tells me that it's already nine fifteen, which means that I'm supposed to pick up Amelia in exactly ten minutes to take her to her doctor's appointment.

"Shit," I grumble as I look in the bottom dresser drawer for a clean pair of jeans. I can't believe I overslept like this, but I guess that's what happens when you stay up until four in the morning trying to figure out a way to pay the electric bill with zero dollars in your bank account.

It's deep winter in the Lowlands and the floor of my room is freezing cold. Still barefoot, I hop onto a pile of dirty laundry and bounce from foot to foot while I step into my jeans and yank a brown hoodie over the t-shirt I slept in.

There isn't enough time for coffee, but after pulling on my boots, I dash into the kitchen hoping to dig up a banana or a Pop-tart. In the middle of the kitchen table I spy a note written in Seth's messy handwriting.

Took Carter out for donuts. He says to tell you we'll pick you up a chocolate cream one for you.

No time to wait. Grabbing one of Seth's granola bars, I tug my phone from the wall charger and make a dash for it. I'm mid-bite when I wrench the front door open and nearly step on my aunt.

She's stooped over a small pile of presents, writing a note

on the backside of a sealed envelope.

"Oh! Bash, you surprised me!" she exclaims, springing to her feet and clasping her hand over her heart.

"What are you doing here?" I ask gruffly as I eye the presents. There are five of them wrapped in Christmas paper. Shiny red bows and laughing Santas wink up at me merrily.

"Well, I just..." Aunt Denise looks uncomfortable and I suppose that makes sense. The last time we were face-to-face, things didn't exactly go smoothly. And since then, the only communication we've had has come in the form of that letter from her attorney.

She exhales sharply and I watch the puff of her breath melt into the cool morning air. "I haven't seen you or Carter in so long and Mike and I missed you on Christmas. I knew I'd be in the area so I thought I'd try to catch you while you were at home."

It's a lie. Nobody is "in the area." This is Green Cove—halfway between Charleston and No Man's Land.

"If you came to the house trying to dig up dirt on me to prove to the courts how bad I am for Carter then you'll be disappointed because he's not even here."

She makes a pained face and shakes her head. "No, that's not why I'm here. I wanted to bring by your Christmas gifts."

"Oh." I look down at the presents again. I'm unsure what to do.

"And I'll admit that I was hoping to see Carter," she continues, nodding toward the house.

"Aunt Denise..." My shoulders slacken. "This really isn't a good time. Like I said, Carter isn't here and I'm on my way to get my girlfriend."

"How is Amelia? Mike and I have been watching the news every night and praying for her. I can't even fathom how something like that happened here in Green Cove," she says. "Her poor sister and her family. She has to be devastated."

Amelia *is* devastated. And now, because of me, she's also

225

going to be late for her doctor's appointment at the hospital. "It's been hard but she's getting through it. Anyway," I say dispassionately as I pull the door closed and use my key to lock it. "I really do have to go. I'm late."

"Right. I'll get out of your way."

My aunt looks so disappointed as she descends the porch steps that I almost call out and tell her if she waits a few minutes, Carter and Seth will probably be home. Then I remember that this is the same woman who is suing me for custody of my little brother and I keep my mouth closed.

"Will you give him his gifts?" she asks, stopping a couple steps from her car door and looking back to the house where I left the presents sitting by the front door. I'll have to text Seth about them later.

"I'm not sure," I say honestly. "I don't know if it's a good idea considering everything."

She nods. There are tears welling in her eyes and her nose is red. It's possible that both are products of the cold, but I don't think so. "Mike and I miss him." She sniffs. "And you, Bash. I'm sorry that you're angry with us."

I lean my hand against the top of my Bronco. The silvery frost coating the chipped paint stings my skin. "I'm not angry." My head drops forward. "I'm tired."

"But that's why we want to help you. Carter is too much for you."

I pick my head up and look at her. "Don't you get it? *Carter* is not too much. My girlfriend being shot, her sister dying, my school being swarmed by reporters and the FBI and a dozen psychologists, and getting a threatening letter in the mail from your lawyer... *Those* things are too much."

"Bash..." Her face contorts. "I know you don't understand where we're coming from, but you and Carter are my family and I'm trying to do the right thing here. I'm trying to do what I think Jean Anne would want me to do."

"Don't you dare bring my mother into this," I warn.

"But can't you see that this is about her as much as it's about you and me and Carter? I loved my sister—I still do—and I want what's best for her kids. And right now, I firmly believe that raising Carter is a burden that you don't need," she pleads, walking closer. "If you would just come to the house and sit down with Mike and I, I think we could figure something out without having to go to court. I don't want that anymore than you do."

"Then drop the case!" I shout so loud I'm sure Paul and his mother and the rest of the neighborhood think I'm having a fit. "That's all you have to do, Aunt Denise. See how I've solved the big problem?"

She sighs. "I can't, Bash. You don't want to hear this because you're only eighteen years old, but I think one day you'll see where we're coming from."

"I might be eighteen years old but I feel forty. My life is falling apart." I'm struggling not to choke up. "I trusted you and now you're suing me. And the first person I've let myself give a shit about since Mama died is going through a goddamn hell and I don't know how to help her. Can you understand how that feels?"

I can see the guilt written all over Aunt Denise's face. She tries to grab hold of my hand, but I evade her and climb into my truck.

"This isn't going like I want," she says, staring off.

I shrug. "Then leave it alone with the lawyers and let's just go back to how things were."

She takes a couple breaths. "It doesn't work like that. They're already working on getting a court date set up."

I start the truck and crank on the heater, hoping it will warm up fast and I can stop feeling this way—cold and frustrated and miserable. Then I turn to the open door, looking up at my aunt.

"Maybe you're right," I tell her. "But Carter is the *only* thing I'm sure of in the world. And staying together? What

227

you said before was wrong. It's not a burden. It's a privilege."

***

I know it's cowardly of me, but when the doctor peels back the final layer of gauze, I look away.

"The swelling is just about gone," he says.

I peek slowly, like I'm sticking my big toe in ice cold water. Amelia is flat on one of those padded medical tables that's covered in a piece of white paper. She's laying back with one hand down and the other curved over her head.

The doctor is on a wheeled stool leaning over her, holding her shirt up and prodding at her stomach. "Yes, this is looking very good," he says.

I step closer and crane my neck. The line that cuts from her bellybutton to her hip bone is pink and jagged, but it looks nothing like it did that day. I shudder thinking of the warm and sticky blood that coated my hands and how I worried that she'd die right there on the floor of the gym and that would be the last memory I'd ever have of her.

"Do you think I'll be ready for tennis?" Amelia asks. Her eyes are staring straight up at the fluorescent light panels that checker the ceiling. "The season starts back soon and I'd like to be on the court as soon as I can be."

She shouldn't be worried about tennis. She should be crying or angry or *anything* but thinking about getting back on the team. But this is how she's been ever since those first days after Daphne died. It was almost better when she was crazy sad and crying all the time. Now she's... *off*. It's like the power's been cut and the back-up generator hasn't kicked on yet.

"You'll still need to take it easy for a few more weeks, but this is healing up beautifully," the doctor says, moving her shirt back into place and kicking his stool toward the blue formica counter. "I'm very happy with the progress so I'm going to leave a bandage off, but you'll still need to keep the area clean."

"And tennis?" Amelia presses.

"You don't need to push yourself," I say.

She doesn't quite meet my eyes. "I'm captain of the school team, Sebastian. I've got to play."

"No, you've *got* to get healthy. You were shot a month ago."

"I was *grazed.*"

"That's still shot."

The paper crinkles as she sits up and swings her legs over the side of the exam table. She crosses her arms over her chest and pointedly does not look at me. "What do you think about tennis, Dr. Faris?"

The doctor is bent over the counter writing something on his clipboard. "As I said, you still need some time to heal. But give it a few more weeks and as long as everything progresses as it is now, I don't see any reason why you shouldn't be able to play tennis."

"So mid January?"

"That sounds about right." He nods and stands up. "I'm going to finish up your paperwork, Amelia. Someone will be here in a few minutes with the new instructions for wound care."

"Okay."

Twenty minutes later, we're in the Bronco, headed in the direction of her house. "Do you want anything?" I ask since we have to drive through the small downtown area and I've haven't eaten anything but a granola bar today. "Food? A coffee?"

"No," she says and goes back to staring out the window.

"All right."

Other than the rumble of the engine, it's quiet. This silence has become our new norm. No more 'this or that' games to pass the time. No more laughter. No more sharing ideas or stories. I desperately want to tell her about the conversation with my aunt this morning and the court case that's looming over me, but I don't even know how to start.

"Everything back there was cold and white," she says after a long time.

"At the hospital?" I clarify.

Still looking out the window, she nods. "They told me that Daphne hung on until she got there."

I start to say something but she interrupts me. "Do you think that white ceiling was the last thing she saw? They won't tell me much and I keep trying to think about what it must have been like for her. Was she scared? She must have been. She was all alone, Sebastian."

"She wasn't all alone."

"She was," she says in a barely audible voice. "Do you think she wondered why I wasn't with her? Do you think she was in pain?"

The guy behind me honks, but I don't give a shit. I cross two lanes and pull off the road, the whole truck quaking when the wheels jump the cement curb.

"I don't think she was in pain."

"How do you know?"

"I don't," I say. "And maybe this is just me digging my heels in like Mama used to say, but I don't think she suffered. I think that asshole shot her and that was it. Her body might have held on until the hospital but I think her soul had already escaped."

Her lip trembles. "Did you see her?"

I shake my head because I refuse to tell her how it really was. I refuse to fill her head with details about the blood and the ripped flesh and the pungent scent of gunpowder that clogged my nostrils that day.

"I just wish I knew for sure what she felt," Amelia says, her eyes shiny with tears. "Twins are supposed to know, aren't they?"

This is breaking my heart. I unbuckle both of our seatbelts and pull her into my lap. She resists at first, but then she gives in and crumples into my chest.

I know I shouldn't think it, but it feels good to hold her like this, even if she is crying. I run my hand over her neck and down her back, feeling her whole body shake with each breath.

"I don't even remember the last thing she said to me. Was it at breakfast? On the way to school? How can I not know that, Sebastian? What kind of sister doesn't remember?"

I kiss her hair and murmur, "Amelia, you weren't thinking about it. None of us were. It was just a normal day."

"But that's it," she says, wiping at her eyes.

"That's what?"

"It wasn't a normal day, was it?"

"What are you talking about?"

"I'm talking about Saturday night. About all of my suspicions. I should have known Spencer was dangerous. I *did* know, but I didn't do anything about it."

I brush her hair from her face and hold her chin up so that she's looking at me. "That's not fair."

"Why isn't it fair? How many times did you tell me to talk my parents about Spencer?" she cries and jerks her head away. "How many chances did I let slip by?"

"Amelia..." The helplessness I feel is tearing me up inside.

"It's the truth Sebastian! Now people are saying Spencer was off his medication and that he needed help and it's like... *I* knew that."

"No one knew for sure."

"Yes I did! Maybe I didn't know everything, but I could tell there was something wrong with him and I still did nothing to stop him."

"You were going to talk to your parents," I remind her.

"Too little too late," she snaps, pushing away from me and shifting back to her own seat. "What good are my intentions if Daphne is still gone? I can't bring her back now. I can't turn back time and go back to those last few weeks."

"You couldn't have stopped him. Even if you'd told someone, it's not like they would have locked him up for being a possessive boyfriend or an asshole."

"They might have done *something*!" She throws her hands up. "Maybe Spencer would have gotten the help he needed or maybe his father would have locked his goddamn gun cabinet! But we'll never know, will we? Daphne is *dead*," she shouts. "And she will always be dead."

The naked pain in her voice nearly suffocates me. It's torture. Worse than torture actually because it's like watching someone else being flayed alive, their skin peeled from their body piece by piece, and not being able to do a single thing about it.

I reach for her again, taking hold of her hand, but I have no idea what to do or say to make this better for her. She's right. Daphne is dead and that is forever. And in the face of that loss, anything I can say or do seems inadequate.

"Amelia, I'm sorry."

"Nevermind," she says, turning back to the passenger window.

"Nevermind?"

I let go of her wrist and she waves her hand in front of her face. "I mean… just forget it, okay? I shouldn't have freaked out like I did. I was just being stupid."

"There's nothing to forget. And you're not being stupid."

She shakes her head. "I just want to go home. I'm fine now," she says and I'm surprised by the sudden tonelessness of her tone. "I promise."

"You sure?" I ask, my heart sick.

She nods.

We both know she's not fine, but I let it go, turning the car key and merging back onto the road.

I hate pretending, but the thought of losing her looms

over me. Because right now this whole thing feels flimsy as a house of cards. One tiny breeze and everything will come crashing down around us.

CHAPTER TWENTY-SEVEN

Amelia

So guess what?

I got into Emory today.

I haven't been able to make myself open the thick cream-colored envelope that lays on the counter in front of me, but I know it's an acceptance letter—it's too thick not to be— and I'm not sure what to do about it.

Before, we all would have celebrated. Daddy would have grilled steaks. Nancy would have started calling her friends, boasting about me and my big brain. I know that Daphne would have squealed and done a happy little dance right here in the kitchen. That was how it should be, but that's not how we live now, is it? There will be no steaks, no calls, and especially no dancing tonight.

This is supposed to be a big deal, the kind of moment I keep tucked away for rainy day trips down memory lane when I'm eighty years old. *Emory.* This is what I always thought I wanted—a brilliant future waiting for me with a shiny, red bow on top. I should be happy, but I can't even remember what happy feels like.

"What is that?" Nancy asks, bending over my shoulder to eyeball the envelope in my hands. "It's from Emory."

"Mm-hmm."

She sets two brown paper sacks full of groceries down on the counter. "Aren't you going to open it?"

"Maybe I will later."

She purses her lips. "Amelia, that looks like it might be an acceptance letter."

"Fine." I throw her a look of annoyance as I rip open the letter.

It is with great pleasure that we inform you of your acceptance into Emory University.

"I got in," I say in a flat tone, not even bothering to finish it. I don't want to do *this*. All I want is to ball the letter and watch it roll off my palm and into the trashcan.

Nancy bends over and hugs me. I probably should stand up and hug her back or something, but I don't move. "Of course you did! Congratulations, dear. Your father is going to be so proud of you."

I snort. "I doubt Daddy will even notice."

Nancy looks away briefly, then she says, "Nevermind that. We should celebrate. You could invite your Sebastian."

Did I land on an alien planet? "You want me to invite Sebastian? What do you mean—like, for dinner?"

She starts to put away the groceries. "That's right. He's been around so much lately, I thought it would be nice. And his little brother—what's his name? Is it Christian? Carl? Do you think they'd like that rosemary chicken I made for Marjorie Bachman's baby shower last year? Oh, and we could make that peach cobbler recipe that you liked so much. "

Chicken? Peach cobbler? The thought of Nancy in the kitchen acting so *normal* stops my breathing. I feel my back stiffen and my shoulders get tight.

"Are you joking?" I bluster. "I'm not inviting Sebastian and his brother—and it's Carter, by the way—over to this crypt of a house to celebrate anything!" I wag the letter in front of her face. "It's not like I'm going to Emory."

Nancy face pales. "Why not, Amelia? You worked so hard to get in and I thought..."

"I'm not going to Emory or Vanderbilt or Wake Forest or anyplace else," I snap, the anger inside of me growing bigger. "And were you kidding about Sebastian? You've never invited them before because it wasn't *appropriate*," I say, mimicking the snobbish tone she'd used at Thanksgiving.

She looks down shamefully and whispers, "Amelia, I'm trying here."

"I don't want you to try!" I shout and let the letter fall from my hands to the floor. "Just stop, okay? Just stop everything!"

I run out of the kitchen up the stairs intent on crawling into my bed and cuddling with Frère Jacques—the poor rabbit is probably more salty tears than stuffing these days—but instead my feet take me to my sister's room.

And the weird thing is that it still smells like her.

It does. And except for the bed, everything is exactly how she left it that morning—the map above her desk is still dotted with paper flags. There's a notebook opened on the floor. Her black and gold cheer jacket is draped over the back of the chair.

With trembling legs, I walk to the closet and move my hands over the clothes hanging there, taking in more of Daphne's scent.

She loved winter, I think absently.

It doesn't often get below freezing here, but over the past few weeks, a gauzy layer of frost has coated the ground in the mornings and I know that she would have been excited to wear all of her sweaters and boots to school.

I sink to my knees to find her favorite pair. Brown leather with brushed silver buckles on the sides. There they are, tucked in the back of the closet just below her jeans.

Not thinking, I slide my right foot into the boot and then the left. Of course they're a perfect fit, molding to my toes and heels like I've worn them a hundred times before.

My unsteady hands reach out and pull a thick dark green sweater off the hanger. The neck is high and chunky and comes all the way up, over my chin and mouth. As I adjust the cuffs of the sweater, I catch sight of myself in the mirror on the closet door. For the briefest splinter of time, I can imagine a different girl is looking back, and the relief I feel almost levels me.

"Hi," I whisper to my reflection.

Pretending isn't even that hard. I shake my dark hair out, letting my long bangs fall to the side because that's how she liked to wear them. Then I press my finger to the cool glass and I outline my nose and my brow bone.

Who are you seeing?

Is it me or is it her?

CHAPTER TWENTY-EIGHT

Bash

I'm hunched in front of my locker, trying to get my head straight for a quiz we're taking during first period.

Students are buzzing behind me. That's nothing new, but there's something in the *way* they're buzzing that gets me to look up. Right away I notice a circle of people clustered at the far end of the hall. In the center of the circle is a girl with her back to me and the moment I see her standing there, my heart stops beating.

It's Amelia.

I stumble closer, barely believing my eyes, but they aren't lying to me. There she is, her dark hair pinned half-up with the bulk of it falling down her back, just past her shoulder blades. She's wearing jeans and brown boots and a slouchy bag is hanging from one shoulder.

My nerves are misfiring. My head is spinning. What the hell is she doing here? Why wouldn't she have called me?

The students surrounding her are hugging her and talking all at once.

"Have you talked to Spencer's parents at all?" Some guy asks her. "They did an interview on CNN last week. Did you see it?"

Amelia shakes her head. "No."

"My dad has a friend who works for the *The Post and Courier* and he said Spencer's mom has written you and your family a public apology letter."

She staggers back, her expression uncomprehending. "What?"

"You haven't read it yet?"

"No—what letter?" she asks, her voice cracking with despair. "I don't…"

Pushing my way toward her, I call out her name. "Amelia!"

Our eyes connect and for half a second and I think everything is going to be okay. Then she shakes her head and spins in the opposite direction, slamming through the crowd, knocking people aside. One girl actually trips and falls into a locker. Amelia doesn't stop. She runs for the nearest exit and I follow, trying to ignore the sounds of gossip travelling at the speed of light down the hall.

Did you just see Amelia Bright?

She completely lost it.

So sad.

She's obviously a mess.

Amelia is outside, maybe thirty feet from the school entrance, leaning up against a brick wall with her eyes shut tightly and her face tilted up toward the cloudless morning sky.

"Hey," I say, creeping closer, the way you might approach a startled animal.

Her chest heaves as she takes in a gulp of air. "Was it like this for you?"

"What do you mean? After my mother?"

She nods.

"No," I tell her. "The only ones who knew what had happened were Rachel, Seth, and a couple of my teachers."

She blinks at me. "Who's Rachel? Is that your ex-girlfriend?"

Shit. I am a verifiable idiot. This is definitely not the right moment for the ex talk.

"It doesn't matter," I say, interlacing our fingers and pulling her against me. "I'm more worried about you. Are you okay?"

239

She shudders and I can feel her heart pounding through her skin. "I can't believe I ran off like that. They're going to think I'm a head case."

"No, everyone will get it."

"I just... They started talking about Spencer's mother and some letter," she says, shaking her head. "I felt like they were smothering me."

"They *were* smothering you," I say, taking her face in my hands and ducking so that we're the same height. "And I hate to break it to you, but things are probably going to be like that for a while."

"Because I'm a novelty like some circus act," she says flatly.

"No, because you've been through a tragedy and you have friends and you're popular."

She sputters, "That's not—"

"I know, I know." *That's not friendship. That's nothing but a business transaction'* she told me so many months ago. "Maybe you're right about all those people back there. Maybe it's not true friendship, but either way, you have an effect on them."

"You're crazy."

"I'm not. They look to you." I shrug and glance back toward the school entrance. "And in their own way, they care. And they definitely care about Daphne and what happened here. It changed everything."

She drops her gaze. "I know, but I just want one day where it's not like that. One day to be okay."

I narrow my eyes at her. "Is that why you didn't tell me you were going to be here?"

"I guess so," she admits, pulling back and readjusting her sleeves and the strap of her bag.

"Amelia, I should take you back home."

She looks off blankly and sighs. "I don't want to go home. I need to be here."

"You don't need to be anywhere you don't want to be," I

240

say and jog to keep up as she briskly climbs the front steps of the school. "It would be understandable to take more time."

"You don't get it, Sebastian."

"What don't I get?"

"I don't have the luxury of time," she says and exhales sharply.

My skin prickles with edginess. "Why not?"

"I mean, tennis has already started back up and as captain I really need to be here for that. Not to mention that student council elections are coming up and it's critical that I help the incoming officers get acquainted with our system and—" she stops. "What? Why are you looking at me like that?"

"Nothing." I shake my head in confusion. "Do you really think student council is *critical*?"

"Well, a lot of people have worked really hard to make the council effective."

What? I can't keep up with her unpredictable moods anymore. One minute she's crying and falling apart, the next she's acting like nothing is wrong.

"Amelia, I've gotta admit… I'm lost here."

"What do you mean?" she asks over her shoulder.

"I mean—why are you acting this way?"

"What way?"

I grab her wrist and pull her to a stop. "Like everything is fine."

"Because I told you before—it *is* fine."

I stare hard at her. "It didn't look like that five minutes ago."

She steps back and twists her arm out of my grip. "God, Sebastian!" she pants in exasperation. "Is it such a crime to want to come to school and have everyone leave me alone? Am I such a bad person for wanting one normal day?"

My sense of dread mounts. Something is happening here. Something not right.

"Amelia…"

"Well, butter my butt and call me a biscuit!"

We both bring our heads around to see Audra sprinting toward us. She knocks into Amelia, throwing out her arms and spins the two of them around.

"As soon as I got out of my car, I knew you were here today. It's all anybody is talkin' about. And here I thought for sure you would've at least texted me," Audra pouts.

Amelia pulls back a little and frees her hair from beneath Audra's arm. "Hey, Audra."

Audra makes a frowny face and pokes her chin out. "*Hey?* That's all I get? I've been missin' you somethin' fierce. And how 'bout you, buckaroo?" She tilts her head back to look at me. "Happy to see our girl here?"

I don't answer because I'm getting the distinct impression that "our girl" is no longer happy to see me.

But Audra doesn't pick up on the tension and goes on, happily telling Amelia about school and classes this semester, and how much the tennis team is sucking without her. Amelia nods along, going through the motions like she cares, but I can tell she'd rather be anyplace but here.

And then the first warning bell rings and Audra starts to tug her away from me, but I hold her back.

"Audra, can you give us a second?"

"Sure thing. See you in third period, chica!" Audra says, waving and stomping off.

"What?" Amelia asks quietly, not meeting my eyes.

"*What?*" I repeat, trying to keep my voice down to avoid another scene. "I think we should talk."

"What's left to talk about?" she asks numbly.

"I don't think you're ready to be here yet."

She snorts and cocks her face to one side. "Well, that's not really your call, is it?"

"Amelia, I'm only trying to help you."

"And I appreciate it, but you've got to give me some breathing room. All of *this*—" she looks between us, her mouth puckering distastefully, "—is making me feel claustrophobic. Just like all those people who were smothering me."

"Oh." Stung, I immediately drop her hand and take a step back. "I didn't mean to push you."

"I know." She squeezes her eyes closed and shakes her head. "Look... I don't want to argue anymore but I've got to go or I'm going to be late."

Now I'm unsure what to do. This conversation feels punctuated with landmines and I have no idea how to navigate it. "Okay. Do you want me to walk you to your class?"

"I'm not going to class." She shakes her head. "As a returning *victim,* I have to go to the office and check in with the counselor first."

"That's good. You should be talking to somebody."

"Actually, it's stupid, but I don't have a say in it. They're making me." She rolls her eyes, but there's something off in the gesture.

"Okay. Well, I'll see you later then?"

She nods, but it still feels hollow and somehow wrong.

"Bye."

"Bye."

I watch her round the corner and I realize that even though Amelia is back, she's still a thousand miles away from me.

CHAPTER TWENTY-NINE

Amelia

"How do you feel about being here, Amelia?"

I blink, trying not to give anything away. "Do you mean in your office or just here in general?"

"Here in general." Mrs. Gaspard, the school counselor sits back and folds her hands over her lap. I think she's trying to appear relaxed to put me at ease. It's not working.

"I haven't even been here an hour yet."

"Well, coming back, surrounded by so many memories— even just being in this very building—it's got to be difficult for you, no?"

Are we really having this conversation? "I think I can manage."

"That's fabulous to hear." There's a cup of coffee on her desk. She picks it up and takes a sip. "And how do you think your classes will go? Will you be able to catch up on your school work?"

I shrug. "I guess so."

"Great," Mrs. Gaspard says, setting the coffee down. She rests her elbows on her desk and leans in closer like she's confiding in me. "Your teachers are sure to help you out, Amelia. If you run into any problems, all you have to do is speak up or come and talk to me. I'm here for you whenever you need *anything*. Just try and think of me as your school concierge," she says, laughing at her own humor.

I nod. God, I hate this so much, but coming to her office for a fifteen minute check-in three times this week is part of my return to school. The principal insisted on it. I assume it's part of the "Focus on Mental Health" plan he initiated in the wake of the shooting. Another part of the plan is apparently papering the walls with encouraging posters. In the office alone there are three pictures of kittens telling me that everything will be okay.

Mrs. Gaspard shuffles some papers on her desk and clears her throat. "And your friends?"

I wipe my mouth with the bottom of my sleeve. "It's... you know... fine."

"Reengaging isn't always simple," she says in a compassionate tone. "You might have difficulty."

"So far everyone is being great. Very helpful," I answer, my voice lighter. I need to do a better job of selling cheerful because it's not like I'm going to tell this woman anything real. What could she possibly understand? Like everyone else, she wants to pry and handle my misery like a coat that she can put on and discard whenever she feels like it.

"It's important that you feel like you have a network of support. A web, if you will," she says, interlacing her fingers to demonstrate this, "to catch you if you need catching."

"That's smart," I say, faking a smile.

She smiles back. "Well, I truly hope that you'll utilize this office whenever you need to. We're here for you, Amelia. All of us at school are cheering you on. And of course, we were so sorry about what happened. Your sister Daphne was... well, she was a wonderful girl and is greatly missed."

"Thank you," I say, standing from the chair and scooping up my bag from the floor.

"Don't be a stranger," she says when I'm at the door.

"I won't be." *Like I have a choice...*

After that, the rest of the morning blurs by.

Classes are a joke. I'm so far behind it seems pointless to even be here, but I go through the motions—taking out my notebooks and scribbling down things my teachers are saying. The truth is that I know it won't matter. My teachers feel sorry for me—*poor Amelia Bright, the girl who lived*—and they make it clear I'll pass with flying colors even if all I do for the rest of the semester is draw pictures of flying tacos on my test papers.

In Spanish, both Audra and Sebastian attempt to talk to me, but I feign a headache and spend the bulk of the period in the first floor bathroom staring blankly at the graffiti on the back of one of the stalls.

The hallways between classes are the worst part of the day. Every time I have to go get a book from my locker, it's the exact same thing. I'm like a minnow swimming through a sea of sharks, dodging questions and strange and sometimes awkward displays of sympathy, like when Marcus Green, a guy I've talked to maybe once before, stops me and tells me how much he misses Daphne and that she'd been the star of all his wet dreams when we were in the ninth grade. Um, thanks? Ew...

When the lunch bell rings just after fourth period, I know that the cafeteria—with all that noise and all those people—is going to be just as bad as the hallways. I know everyone means well, but when they talk to me or ask me questions like *what do you remember about that day* I feel like my insides have evaporated and I'm nothing but a suit of too-big skin drooping off a flimsy skeleton. I can't face it, so when no one is looking, I duck out and go hide in my car for some quiet.

That's better, I think as I gaze out the window at the sun bouncing off the hoods of all the shiny cars and I eat pretzels from a small plastic bag one by one. For the past two months, all food has tasted like ash, but at least if I eat something crunchy, I can enjoy the sound of eating.

On the seat beside me, my phone buzzes over and over. I don't have to look to know that it's Sebastian and Audra. It's been like this all day. Audra mother-henning me to the point of insanity and Sebastian... well, I'm not sure what to call it, but it's like he's trying to *solve* me. Like I'm a challenging equation or a knot that he can somehow free. I want to tell him the truth: I *am* a tangled knot and I'm pinched so tight that no amount of pulling or reworking is going to unravel me. He should just cut his losses and give up on me now.

The phone vibrates again and this time I scroll through to see what I missed. As suspected, my incoming texts are full of their tense concern.

Where are you?
Are you feeling any better?
You okay?
Anything I can do?

I know they're both trying to help but it's too much and, eventually, I get sick of the sound and simply power off my phone.

Time clicks by. The sky changes—the clouds huddle overhead, darkening the earth and stealing the sun's warmth. I know that lunch must be over and classes have probably started up again, but the thought of going back in that building makes me sick.

Then why bother?

The thought is casual at first and I don't take it seriously. But when I catch sight of my eyes in the rearview mirror, I think, *really, why bother?*

The teachers aren't going to give me trouble and if they do, I can always go talk to my buddy, Mrs. Gaspard. She did say she'd help me with anything, didn't she?

Traffic is nonexistent and the drive home is quick—ten minutes at the most. Nancy's and Daddy's cars are both parked in the driveway in front of the free-standing garage. I don't think they even notice that I live with them in this big, rambling house anymore, but I don't want even the possibility of questions or to risk raising any red flags, so I slip in through the front door and silently creep up the stairs.

Barricaded in the safety of my room, I fall onto my bed

247

and pull the covers up over my face until it's as dark in front of my eyes as it is in my head. The silence of the house is somehow deafening. I think of how Nancy used to fume when Daphne had her music turned up too loud and I literally ache.

Daphne would always comply, but the moment Nancy's feet hit the top steps, she would be back at the volume knob, bouncing her head to the beat and rolling her eyes at our stepmother's lack of what she called *music appreciation*.

And once I start to think of my sister, I can't stop. There's Daphne when we were eight pumping her legs fast and getting her swing going so that she could toss herself off and arc through the sky to land giggling on the warm grass. And Daphne at eleven trying on a white training bra and posing in front of the mirror with her hands on her hips. Daphne at twelve, talking to me excitedly as she braided Audra's blond hair. At fourteen, swallowed by sunlight, shouting my name from the stands at a tennis match. At sixteen with her new driver's license in her hand getting a congratulatory hug from Daddy. At seventeen, nestled beside me in bed.

Love you.

Love you more.

The sound of steps on the floorboards in front of my room curdles the memories.

"Amelia? Is that you? Amelia?" Nancy calls my name again as she tries to jiggle the knob of the door. Well, she's out of luck because I've locked it.

"It's me."

"Why are you home?" she asks and there's an edge of nervousness to her voice. "I thought this was your first day back. Did it not go well?"

"It was fine. We just had early release," I gasp out, rolling over and pressing my face into the pillow so I won't scream.

"I see." She pauses. "Would you like to go to church with me?"

"No. I'm tired," comes my muffled voice.

"It might do you good. There's a group I go to and it might be refreshing to talk about everything. I know it's helped me."

"Um, I'm really not well enough, but thanks."

"All right then," she says reluctantly. "Your father is... he's in his study. There's food in the refrigerator if you get hungry."

"Okay."

And then she leaves and the hours pass by. Afternoon fades to twilight and I drop the blankets from my head and push the air from my lungs into my now dark room. I stare at the wall that Sebastian and I painted, pretending it really is sky, and I wait for my eyes to grow heavy and my head to get lighter. I fall asleep and dream of water so deep and so black that no matter how hard I swim, I can never reach the bottom.

CHAPTER THIRTY

Bash

"I have one word of advice for you."

I look up and see Seth standing at the opposite end of the kitchen table with a guitar resting on the toes of his shoes. His brown hair is pulled back into a messy knot at the crown of his head and held in place with a rubber band.

"What?"

He gestures over the table at all the papers I've spread out. "Shredder."

"I wish. These are bills. And *this*," I say and pick up an envelope, "is a notice of the court date with my aunt and uncle."

"What does it say?" he asks as he sits down.

I furrow my brow. "It says that I have ninety days to figure out a way to hire an attorney and keep Carter."

"Shit."

"That sounds about right."

Jinx saunters into the kitchen and hops onto Seth's lap. She certainly does stay in the house more now that Seth is pretty much living here.

"Anything I can do?" Seth asks as he picks up a bill and examines it.

"Yeah, you can buy some cat food for your friend there."

"You know that's not what I meant. I have some money saved from shows and you know I'm happy to pitch in."

"You're already helping enough, Seth, especially with Carter," I remind him. "And that money is supposed to float you after graduation if you want to get on the road and play."

He shrugs and shifts his knee so that he can tune his guitar without disturbing Jinx. She still gives the instrument an indignant look. Cats, man. "Things change."

I sigh. I know Seth means it, but I just can't make myself ask anything more of my best friend.

"There's always Paul," I say, looking out the window to my neighbor's house.

Seth stops tuning and stares up at me. "You're joking."

"It'd be a one time thing. Just let him and his guys use the house one time for whatever it is they want and then I could breathe."

"Whatever it is they want to do?" He laughs bitterly. "They want to cook meth here. I don't think there's any doubt about that."

"But Carter..." My eyes dart to the hall that leads to his bedroom. He's sleeping soundly right now because he doesn't know how close he is to losing the only life he knows. "If I can keep him fed and with me then isn't it worth it?"

"Bash, are you trying to convince me or yourself?" Seth asks. "And, Jesus, I thought this conversation was over and done. I thought you were going to apply to colleges and we were going to take the world on like gangbusters."

"I never sent out the applications."

Seth's eyebrows lift. "Well that's your first mistake."

I inhale slowly. "With everything happening with Amelia I didn't know what to do."

"Dude, I get it. But now Amelia is back."

Is she?

"It's time to get serious," he continues as he piles the bills. "First, let's get these organized and figure out which ones have to be taken care of now and which ones can be put off a little. Then let's find you a new job."

I laugh. "And how do you figure that'll happen?"

"That's actually kind of a funny story," he says, smiling

wryly.

"What the hell did you do?"

He blinks innocently. "Nothing bad. I happen to know a guy in Atlanta who knows a guy who—"

"Knows a guy?" I guess.

"No," Seth says snidely. "This guy makes graphics for bands to sell at their merch tables and he also runs a shirt company."

"And?"

He shrugs one shoulder. "And I may have sent him some of your stuff a few days back."

"Why would you do that?"

"Because I knew you wouldn't do it yourself."

He has a point. "Okay, so what happened?"

"He emailed me yesterday to let me know he's interested as long as you're willing to sell at the right price. And he asked if you had any more designs."

"You're serious?"

"As a heart attack." He fiddles with one guitar string. "And I'll share the email with you as long as I can do the talking. I'm not letting you sell those drawings for five dollars a pop. You're worth more than that."

"You've got yourself a deal," I say, my chest expanding with relief. "And thanks."

Seth tilts his chin so he can get a better view of the guitar strings. "Don't thank me yet. I haven't told you my other condition."

"Which is?"

"College."

"What about it?"

"Those applications, including the financial aid forms. We're mailing them out first thing Monday morning," he says it like it's already a done deal.

"It's too late," I tell him.

"Too late, my ass. When we looked, almost every single

deadline was March first. You still have time left and I'm not going to sit here and let you waste it."

"You're not going to *let* me?"

"Someone's got to give you a swift kick to the ass and it might as well be me."

"Says the guy with the man bun."

He fingers the back of his head. "Hey now. Don't knock it till you've tried it. I'm told that women are going crazy for this look."

"Have you been reading Cosmo again?"

He cracks his trademark grin. "Only for the recipes."

I laugh. "I know it's not enough to say it but thank you. For everything. You're a good friend, Seth, and occasionally you can be Jedi-wise."

He gives me a look. "Dude."

"What?"

He shakes his head and goes back to his guitar. "Don't get mushy on me."

CHAPTER THIRTY-ONE

Amelia

I'm so lost in thought that the tapping on my car window doesn't fully register right away. Then it becomes full on knocking and I turn with a start to see Sebastian bent close over my window, a mop of dark brown waves tumbling into his eyes. I wave hello and he circles around the hood and gets in the passenger seat.

"I figured I'd find you out here," he says, pulling off his backpack and stowing it on the floorboard in between his legs.

I've been eating lunch every day in my car for weeks now. He was bound to notice. I'm actually surprised it took him this long to come find me.

"It's quieter," I say by way of an explanation.

"You don't have to tell me why. That place is..." Sebastian looks out the window toward the school.

"It's getting better."

He turns back to me, his grey eyes settling on mine. "Is it?"

I shrug. In a way, school *is* better. It's been a month and the novelty of my *triumphant* return has finally started to wear off. Every day that passes, I have to pretend less that I give a damn about how sorry so-and-so is for my loss. And I no longer have to return so many stupid and sad little smiles or listen to theories and speculation about Spencer and the *I completely understand what you're going through* lines. Those are the worst. *No*, I want to shout back, *you do not know what I'm going through!*

How could they understand? How could anyone fathom what it's like to swim through a guilt so big that it could swallow down entire oceans?

"It's okay," is all I tell Sebastian.

He nods and looks away. I know what he's thinking because I'm thinking the same thing—I don't remember it being this hard to talk to each other before.

"So…" I try, shifting in my seat.

"So."

Our eyes meet and we both start to smile.

"How's tennis going?" he asks, leaning back against the car door.

"It's okay," I say again because it's easier than telling him the truth—that tennis, like everything else—feels like it belongs in someone else's life.

I'm going through the motions, but school… my college plans… heck, even my clothes seem like they don't fit anymore. All those leggings that I used to love to wear and taunt Nancy with remain folded neatly in the bottom of my dresser drawer while I rotate through Daphne's jeans and long-sleeved shirts. And, God, I know I shouldn't do it. I know that the clothes thing is weird and Mrs. Gaspard, the school counselor, would probably have a field day with it, but I can't seem to help myself.

"I brought you something." He reaches into his bag and pulls out a beat-up hardback book.

I stare down at it, brushing my fingers across the white cover and the title, *Fragile Things*.

"Is this—?"

"It's the same one my mom gave me. The one she found," he says, flipping it open to show me the title page. "See? It's not in great shape but it is signed by Neil Gaiman."

I glance between the sprawling black ink signature and the words on Sebastian's sneakers. *All your tomorrows start here.*

"I thought maybe you'd like to read it," he's saying, "but if you're not interested, there's no pressure."

"No," I say, holding the book more firmly, "I want to read it. Thank you."

He looks pleased by this. "It's a short story collection so you can skip around or read them in order or whatever you feel like."

I'm nodding. "Okay."

"Most people would tell you to start with 'A Study in Emerald,' but I prefer 'How to Talk to Girls at Parties.'"

"Okay." Sebastian is so clearly excited about the book that I laugh.

He sits upright, startled.

I blink. "What?"

He shakes his head, his eyes blazing with emotion. "Nothing. Just, you laughed and I haven't heard it in a while. Or seen this," he says, touching my cheek. "You have this one dimple right here."

"Oh."

We're looking at each other and I'm suddenly aware that I'm with my boyfriend and we're all alone in my car. And I notice his Adam's apple and the stubble on his chin and the little creases around his mouth and the soft, shiny dark hair dripping into his eyes, and my breathing gets faster.

Sebastian swallows. Then, so slowly, his hand moves to the side of my face to cup my jaw. He leans in a fraction—a test, I think, to see how I'll react.

I'm petrified, but I slip forward on my seat, getting close enough that our breaths mingle and I can feel the heat coming off his body.

"Is this okay?" he asks, bending even closer.

In answer, I nod.

And then we're kissing and the world is falling away. My head is filled with the taste of his mouth and the feel of his fingers tangling in my hair. I'm unsteady. Wild. I desperately pull on his shirt, sliding my palms up over the hot skin of his stomach. Sebastian shudders and his arms tug me closer, hoisting me over the center console onto his lap.

His lips are on my neck and then my throat and his thigh is pressing in between my legs. I let my head fall back and my eyes close. In my chest, my heart thunders a round of applause. This is right. I feel so good and so, so alive.

The last thought snaps at me like a rubber band.

Alive.

What am I doing? How can I possibly feel this way? How can I let myself kiss someone like this when my sister is dead?

Daphne will never kiss another boy.

She'll never feel her heart pound or the rush of her blood beneath her skin.

She'll never feel anything.

Ever again.

"Stop!" I gasp out.

Sebastian immediately releases me.

I scuttle off his lap and back to my seat. My pulse is crazy. "I just... I can't. I'm sorry."

He takes a shaky breath and pushes his hands back through his hair. "Amelia, don't be sorry. It's okay."

I almost wish he'd be angry with me. In a way, it would be easier if Sebastian were that kind of guy—the kind of guy who demands, who *wants*. Instead, he's spent months being patient and understanding with me. He never seems mad. Never bitter. I should be happy, but it just makes me feel like I'm the one who's being unfair.

"I'm not sure when..." I trail off, feeling increasingly uncomfortable about all of this.

He reaches out and his fingertips brush over my lips carefully as though I'm breakable as an egg shell. "It's nothing. Just being here with you is good."

"But it won't be that way forever. Eventually you'll get sick of waiting around."

He looks down and takes my hand in his, turning it over

so that our palms are pressed together. When his words come, they are slow and steady. "Let's not worry about forever because right now, all I want is to be near you. It's more than enough for me."

We're both quiet for a long time. I watch his fingers lace through mine and his thumb make lazy circles on the back of my hand. Then, out of the blue, he clears his throat and says, "So I have a question for you. What are you doing this afternoon?"

"I have practice."

He nods like he was expecting that. "And what time is that done?"

"Probably like four thirty. Why?"

"Because, Carter got a really good grade on a reading test."

"Really? That's great," I say, genuinely pleased about this.

"Yep, and he wants to celebrate with ice cream. I thought you might want to come with us."

"Oh."

His expression wavers. "If it's too soon—"

"No," I say almost too quickly, "I'd like to."

He squeezes my hand tighter. "Great. I'll find out where he wants to go and text you this afternoon. And just so you're prepared—Carter is going to go apeshit when he finds out you're coming with us. I swear, the kid asks about you constantly."

"I want to see him too. But," I say, suddenly thinking of something. "Don't you usually work on Fridays?"

"About that..." Sebastian shrugs his shoulders evasively. "I quit my job at Kane's."

"You did?"

"They had already cut my hours and... well, I have something to tell you." He blows out a breath. "Actually, I have a lot of things to tell you, but they'll wait."

"For what?"

He smiles at me. "Ice cream."

***

I should have known when the rain started coming down at the end of sixth period. Maybe I did know but I just didn't want to carry the thought all the way through.

Because here I am, taken off guard, when Emily VanHeusen storms into the locker room carrying a ball bag and two orange plastic cones and announces that practice is going to be in the gym because the courts are wet. "Coach wants us there in five minutes or he says he's taking off heads," she says, her long blonde ponytail swinging behind her.

"Okay," I mumble and look back down to finish lacing up my white sneakers.

Audra is staring. I can feel her eyes on me from the other side of the bench.

"What?" I ask when I can't stand it anymore.

She's quiet for another moment, waiting for the other girls to finish getting dressed and clear out of the locker room. When we're alone, she asks me, "Are you sure you can handle practice there? You know—in the gym?"

"I've handled everything so far, haven't I?"

"But this is—"

"Just another practice," I say, dropping my foot and brusquely reaching for my racquet bag. "I've been back long enough. I think if I was going to lose it, that would have happened already, don't you?"

Audra's mouth bobs open, but she wisely closes it and goes back to minding her own business and I leave without saying goodbye. In the gym, Coach Sachs is already pacing the length of the court and calling out orders. From the look of things, he's splitting us into groups of four to run conditioning drills.

"Hustle now! They tell me the basketball team gets the

court in fifty-five minutes," he shouts. "And what do you think that means?"

"That you only have an hour to try to kill us?" Brayden Wright jokes. He's on his knees placing strips of masking tape in a hexagon shape on the gym floor.

"That's right," Coach Sachs yells back. "Don't think that because it's raining cats and dogs out there, y'all have it easy. You best give your hearts to Jesus right now 'cause your butts belong to me."

"Where do you want me?" I ask him, ignoring the painful ache that presses into my breastbone as I step onto the basketball court.

"Why don't you check everyone in," he says and absently hands over his clipboard, "and then join up with Brayden and Eric on the hexagons for footwork." He glances behind me. "And Audra, I want you running stairs for a solid ten. Then you can be on the med ball rally with Emily and Sanchez. Got it?"

Gripping the clipboard in my hands so tightly my knuckles go white, I glance up to begin taking roll, but a shadow makes me stop short.

Spencer McGovern's dark form is looming before me.

I gasp for breath and the clipboard clatters from my hands. I know this is a trick of the mind. I know that Spencer is dead. I know that he can't really be here, but suddenly I'm not *here* anymore either. I'm back in that November morning, still flushed from kissing Sebastian in the hallway, trying to find a seat and barely listening as Daphne complains about what the humidity is doing to her hair.

"I'm just going to cut it off," she says.

"You are not going to cut it off," I reason, sliding onto the bleachers next to where Mr. Brickler is sitting.

In the very next moment, she screams from behind me. "What are you doing?!"

I barely register Spencer's face or the black thing in his hand when a single loud pop reverberates in the air around me. Before I realize what is happening, an excruciating sensation rips through my body, overtaking all of my senses. I can't think. I can't breathe. I force my eyes down, barely comprehending the dark and wet liquid seeping from my side.

"What—" I drop to my knees and then forward, but I don't even feel myself hit the floor. I'm too lost to the raw shock of pain and... the fear. Red hot fear is what I feel most of all.

Another gunshot. Followed by another and another. The smell of gunpowder and burning flesh surrounds me but I'm already losing hold on reality. I'm floating away.

Daphne.

She's beside me on the floor. Her lips part as broken, rasping breaths leave her mouth.

I try to crawl toward her, but nothing will move like I want it to. I'm suddenly freezing. My eyes are losing focus, but I fight to keep them open, terrified of what will happen if I succumb to the darkness...if I lose sight of my sister.

"Amelia!"

I hear my name, but I can't respond. I'm too numb. A black wave washes over me and a trickle of icy water slides down my throat.

Take me with you.

"Amelia?" Audra's voice finally breaks through and slings me back to the present.

I realize that I'm bent over and panting. Practice has stopped and the entire tennis team is staring at me.

Coach Sachs comes forward, his eyes fixed on me. "Emily," he yells. "Go and get the nurse!"

I shake my head and stumble back. "No, I'm... I'm okay."

"Amelia," Audra says, grabbing me. "You're not okay."

She's right and now everyone knows it.

"I can't be here," I choke out the words as hot tears pool on the rims of my eyes.

"Aw, honey, I know." She drapes her arm over me, knocking her racquet gently against my hip. "Let's just go to the locker room and have ourselves a little break."

261

"No." I'm crippled by the sound of my pounding heart. "I can't... I can't breathe."

"Just try to relax. Next week, we'll be back on the courts outside and you'll see, you'll feel one hundred percent better."

I shake my head. "There's not going to be a next week, Audra," I say, grabbing my racquet bag. "I quit."

She and Coach Sachs yell after me, their voices blending in with the roar of blood rushing by my ears. I turn the corner and keep going, my legs breaking into a run, but it's no use. Guilt nips at my heels.

I *lived*.

And no matter how fast I go, I can't escape the truth of that. The memories whisper across my arms and back, bringing up goose bumps on my flesh, haunting me like a shadow that I can never outrun.

CHAPTER THIRTY-TWO

Bash

"Is that her?" Carter stands up a little straighter.

"Nope," I say, looking back to see the door swing closed behind a woman with three blond-haired children in tow.

He sinks back down to his normal height. "Oh."

"But I'm sure Amelia will be here any minute," I reassure him.

"And then I can show her my test!" He holds up his latest reading test and points to the glittering gold star sticker his teacher stuck on the top of the paper.

"She's going to be really impressed."

"You think so?"

"I know so."

The ice cream shop smells like waffle cones and melted chocolate. While I check my phone to see if there's a text from Amelia, Carter goes back to eyeing the glass cases that are full of an assortment of ice cream and gelato flavors.

"Hey, bud, while we're waiting…" I take a breath and wipe my hair off my forehead. "There's something I've been wanting to talk to you about."

"What is it?"

I don't want to involve Carter in all of the mess, but I've decided that he has a right to know some of it. He's in this as much as I am, and I need to be sure that I'm fighting for him as much as I am for myself.

"Aunt Denise and Uncle Mike came to me a while back."

"Uh-huh?"

"And they wanted to know if you would prefer living with

them."

He looks at me, puzzled. "Live with them instead of you?"

I nod. "You're a popular kid. It seems like everyone wants you."

Carter tilts his head. "Well, I like Aunt Denise's house because she has a Playstation, but I don't think I want to stay there *all* the time. I like living with you and Seth and Jinx."

"That's what I thought, but I wanted to be sure," I say, my hand going to his shoulder.

"So I don't have to go live with them?"

"I'm working on that, bud. I don't want you to worry about it at all, but if you ever have any questions, you know you can ask me."

"I do have a question."

"Okay?" I ask, steeling myself.

"How do you say that one?" Carter turns back to the freezer and points to a tiny slip of printed paper in front of an orange-colored tub of ice cream. "Mango haba—"

My relief is so great, I almost laugh. Kids are so resilient. "That one is called mango habañero," I tell him.

"What's a habeñero?"

"It's like a spicy pepper."

He makes a face. "In ice cream? That's kinda weird."

"Or maybe it's kinda delicious. You never know until you try," I say and look around. Now that the scary custody conversation is out of the way, I'm back to worrying about Amelia. Where could she be?

"There are a lot of flavors I haven't ever heard of," Carter says with suspicion.

"Do you want to go someplace else?"

He shakes his head. "No, this is good. You never know until you try, right?"

I laugh. Carter and I haven't been to this shop in a while, probably since before Mama died, but it looks pretty much the same. There's still a chalkboard menu on the back wall

264

that details the flavors in funky lettering. The counters are the same bright purple I remember, but they've updated the art on the buttery yellow walls and hung mismatched strands of twinkling Christmas lights from the ceiling over the long coolers.

I'm sure that one of the chain ice cream joints in town would be a lot cheaper, but when he aced his reading test, I promised Carter we could celebrate and this is where he wanted to come. He said he knew Amelia would love it and he's probably right, though I'm beginning to doubt she's going to show.

I look down at the string of unanswered texts I've sent her in the last half hour.

Are you on your way?
Carter asking about you.
Hey did you forget we were meeting for ice cream?

Still no response.

I don't know why I'm even surprised. Lately, she's been bailing on me more than she's been following through.

Heaving out a breath, I stuff my phone in my back pocket and fold my arms over my chest. "You know what, bud? Why don't we just go ahead and order."

Carter looks between the ice cream freezers and the door. "But what about Amelia? Isn't she coming?"

I keep my voice low and steady. "I don't think she can make it."

"Oh, okay," he says, hanging his head.

I hate to see him disappointed. I wish I could get him to understand that Amelia isn't herself, otherwise she'd never let him down like this. But how can I explain that to a seven-year-old when I can't even seem to grasp it myself?

"C'mon, hoss. I'll let you get two scoops," I say in an attempt to cheer him up. When that doesn't do the trick, I add, "And sprinkles."

"And whipped cream?" he asks looking up at me, the start of a smile forming on his lips.

"Whipped cream?" I stagger back like this is a huge request.

Now he's smiling. "*And* a cherry."

I clasp his shoulder and give it a squeeze. "Why not?"

He jumps up and presses his palms against the freezer glass, eager to make the oh-so-hard decision which two flavors he's going to choose. Behind me, the door chimes and even though the rational side of my brain knows it's not going to be her, I look. Because there's still some part of me—maybe my heart—that's holding out hope that things will be okay.

But the truth is, I know I'm losing her.

Or maybe she's already gone and I just don't want to admit it to myself.

CHAPTER THIRTY-THREE

Amelia

The evening is dull and damp. I pull the thin jacket I'm wearing a little tighter over my tennis clothes and keep walking.

My phone vibrates again with another text from Sebastian. I ignore it and push on. I have no idea where I'm headed, I just know that I don't want to go home and I don't want to face Sebastian and Carter. Really, I don't want to be anywhere.

A patchwork of neon lights bounces off the puddles on the pavement and catches my attention. I look around then, realizing that I've walked so far, I ended up in front of The Tap Room.

I should turn back. I'm soaking wet and my car is still at the school parking lot. By the time I make it all the way back there, it's going to be full dark and I'll freeze out here in nothing but shorts and a light jacket.

But instead of turning the other way, I look again to the bar.

There's something about the lights and the sounds coming from inside that draw me closer to the door. This is crazy and I know it. The old me never would have contemplated the idea of walking into a dive bar like this, but the old me doesn't exist anymore, does she?

So I sidle through the door and walk right up to the bar like I've done it a thousand times before. As I take a seat on one of the dark wooden stools, the bartender looks up from wiping down the counter. His name tag says Tommy and he's got friendly eyes and a bushy beard that completely covers the bottom half of his face.

Tommy steps to the counter, and like we're play-acting our way through a scene in a movie, he throws the towel over his shoulder and asks, "What'll it be?"

I swallow back my uncertainty and say, "I'll have a beer."

He chuckles. "What kind, sweetheart?"

Oh crap, I have no idea what kind of beer I want. *Budweiser? Coors?* Those make sense, right? I quickly glance around and notice that the guy sitting next to me has a mug of beer in front of him.

"I'll have whatever he's having," I say with as much confidence as I can muster.

"Sure thing."

A moment later, Tommy returns and slides a small napkin and a glass mug my way. As I grab the handle, foam drips down the sides and over my fingers.

"Did you lose a game?" he inquires.

It takes me a second to understand he's referring to my wet tennis clothes.

"Nope. I lost a lot more than that," I say and tip the beer back, planning to drink to Daphne. To the life she'll never get the chance to live.

As anticipated, the beer tastes nasty. I chug it quickly, hoping that once I've downed the entire glass, I won't care that I'm drinking the equivalent of horse piss.

"Slow down there, slugger," the guy sitting next to me says. He's about twenty-five, wearing a red plaid button down shirt and worn jeans. The hair sticking from beneath his baseball hat is dark and greasy-looking. "If you ain't careful, someone will have to carry you outta this place. I've seen it before."

Ignoring him, I call Tommy back over. "I'll have another," I tell him, hoping that I'm not pushing my luck. He didn't ask for my ID when I ordered the first drink, but who knows when he might get curious about my age.

Tommy nods, but instead of another beer, he comes back with a shot glass and sets it down on the bar top in front of me.

When I gape up at him, he shrugs and says, "You look like you could use it."

I shake my head in appreciation. "You have no idea."

He fills the glass to the brim and waits while I gulp the entire shot in one go. It scorches its way down my throat, leaving a tingly and not unpleasant feeling in its wake.

"Another?" Tommy asks, poised with the bottle above my glass.

I nod and wait for him to fill the glass again.

"What's your name?" The guy sitting next to me asks.

I turn and blink at him. I guess he's not as greasy as I first thought. His face is nice enough and his eyes are sleepy and warm.

"I'm Sarah," I say, liking the way the lie sounds.

"Well, nice to meet you Sarah. I'm Wesley." He tips the rim of his baseball hat to me. It's a goofy gesture and I laugh.

Wesley smiles. "You have a nice laugh."

"Thanks," I say, wincing as the second shot slides home.

"Do you want to dance?"

"I'm all wet," I point out.

He smiles. "I don't care a thing 'bout that."

I look out over the dance floor where a few couples are swaying in front of an old-school jukebox. *Why not?*

"Okay, sure," I tell him and hop off the barstool. I stumble a little and Wesley's hands find my waist, guiding me to the dance floor.

It's strange pretending to be someone else, but it's kind of exhilarating at the same time. It's like I'm starting with a clean slate. I have no memories here. There's no one who knows my real name or my story.

"You're a good dancer," Wesley says, throwing his arm

out to spin me around.

I twirl away and roll back. "You're not so bad yourself."

It hits me that tonight things can be easy. I can forget. I can be free of the despair that has been suffocating me for months. I don't have to feel like I'm sleepwalking through my own life because I can be someone else entirely. Someone *happy.*

"I took dance lessons," Wesley tells me.

"Noooo…"

He grins and pulls me flush against his body. I notice that he smells kind of like an ashtray, but I don't let myself care. This is just for fun.

"I did," he says, nodding. "I can show you the cha-cha or the waltz."

"How about the foxtrot?"

"You betcha."

"The Charleston?"

He breaks into a short jig and I throw my head back and laugh as I try to mimic him.

An hour later, we're still on the dance floor, pulling off ridiculous moves. I'm dry, but now the room is starting to spin.

"I need a break," I shout to Wesley. Then I wobble away from him to seek balance against my stool.

"Water?" Tommy asks me from behind the bar.

I swallow and nod. My face and chest are too warm and I'm starting to get a little woozy. While I greedily drink the ice cold water, Wesley comes and finds me. I can't really understand what he's asking me, but I realize I don't like the way he's rubbing his hand up and down my arm.

"Let's go to my place. It ain't far," he whispers into my ear.

"Ummm…" Leaving with this guy is not a good idea, but my brain is too hazy to offer up much of a protest. "I don't think so."

"How 'bout the back room? Let me show you how to play pool."

"I think I know how to play beer pong," I mumble, confused and feeling light-headed.

"Do you now?" He laughs and takes my arm, leading me away from the bar and past the bathrooms. We walk through a door into a long, dark hallway.

"Just this way, Sarah," he murmurs, letting his fingers brush against my bare thigh.

I don't like that. I don't like *this*.

"I think… I think I need to go back," I say. I try to push him out of my way but my arms feel like wet noodles that I have no control over.

"Don't fret. That's where I'm takin' you," he says as he opens a door and pushes me into a small, black room.

Through the dark, I make out shelves on the wall that are filled with cardboard boxes and stacks of clean glasses.

"Why isn't anyone else here?" I ask, a dim and blundering suspicion welling in the pit of my stomach.

"C'mere," Wesley says, his heavy-lidded eyes shining at me.

"No."

I'm done flirting now. I try to leave, my fingers clumsily seeking the doorknob, but Wesley yanks me against his body. I feel his hard-on pressing into my leg through his jeans and I jerk back, shocked.

He laughs and even in the dark I can see a cruel glint in his expression. "What's wrong, Sarah? I know you like that."

He's too strong. I don't think I can get past him.

"I need to find my friend," I say, my voice shaking.

"What friend is that?"

When I don't answer, he chuckles and traps me in against the wall with his arms. "Don't lie, sweet girl. You're all alone tonight and we both know it."

I whimper when I feel the tip of his tongue on my neck.

271

"Leave me alone." I try to shout, but my voice comes out weak and scared.

"I had my eye on you the minute you walked through that door like a drowned rat. We both know you wore those short shorts hopin' to find somethin' special tonight." He rubs his nose against my skin, breathing deeply. "And, lucky girl, you found me."

Then his enormous, chapped hand grabs my thigh and I cry out. "No, please."

"Hush," he tells me, roughly groping under my shorts.

A fierce surge of panic bites through me. I try to pull away but he shoves me back against the wall. My head knocks a shelf and dislodges a glass. It crashes to the floor and wakes me up even more. *This is bad. Really bad.*

"Stop," I plead.

Wesley clicks his tongue against the roof of his mouth like a reprimand. "I ain't gonna give up that easily, Sarah. You best give me what I want. Hear me now?"

He grabs hold of my waist, his fingers digging into my side and forces his mouth on my own. I want to fight. I *try* to fight, but every time I slap his back or push my hands against his chest, his grip tightens and his hips thrust harder, pushing me back against the wall.

His lips are all over me. He removes one hand, fumbling at his belt buckle and the button on his jeans and I know it might be my only chance. With every ounce of strength I have left, I rear back and bring my knee straight up, connecting solidly with his groin.

With a pained grunt, he crumples to the floor like a balloon losing its air.

I scramble sideways, kind of crab-walking along the wall until I feel the door behind me. Wesley is still on the floor, but I can see that I don't have a lot of time before he regains his composure.

His head comes up and he growls at me, "You bitch!"

I don't wait around to see what happens next. I bolt into the the hallway, knocking a broom down in front of the door, and I start to run.

It's not until I bang into a wall that I realize I have no idea how to get back to the main part of the bar. I look left and right. How did I get here? I can hear bar music but I can't tell which direction the noise is coming from. All the doors look exactly the same like I'm trapped in some messed-up carnival's Funhouse.

From somewhere behind me, I hear Wesley cursing furiously. I'm still disoriented but I'm not confused enough to risk him finding me here in the hall, so I turn to my left and hope that it's the correct way. As I run, the music gets louder which gives me hope that I'm close. I open the last door on the right, stumbling over my own feet into the lights and noise.

I careen toward the bar, crying. Tommy asks me if I'm okay, but that only makes me cry even harder. God, I'm a sticky, sniveling mess.

"Do you want me to call someone for you?" he asks.

I shake my head and grab my racquet bag from where I left it under the bar stool. I find a twenty dollar bill and shove it toward him. "I'm fine."

"You don't look fine to me."

"It's nothing," I respond, keeping my face down and making a beeline for the door.

"You're not driving are you?"

More head shaking on my end.

"Be safe out there," Tommy calls as the door falls shut behind me.

Out on the sidewalk, I take off into a sprint. *I need to get away from here,* I think as moonlight chases me down the sidewalk. I bump into some guy who's walking out of a restaurant, but I don't even stop to apologize. It's not until I'm blocks away from Wesley and the bar that I pause to catch my breath. As my heartbeat dips back down, I reach into my bag for my phone.

It only rings one time before he answers.

"Hello?"

"Sebastian? Can you come get me?"

CHAPTER THIRTY-FOUR

Bash

She's standing exactly where she said she'd be. Her head and shoulders are bent and her long hair is loose and blowing into her face. Her legs are bare and even from the car I can see that she's shaking.

I pull the car parallel to the curb and unlock the door. As she climbs unsteadily in the passenger side, I crank up the heat. "You look like you're freezing."

She gratefully holds her hands over a vent and stretches out her fingers. "Because I am." Then she looks in the backseat and blinks in surprise. "Carter is back there," she says like I might have missed that.

"Seth has a show tonight in Summerville and I didn't think it was a good idea to leave him at home by himself."

"Right," she says. "God, I'm sorry. I shouldn't have called you for this."

"You mean for being drunk?"

"I'm more tipsy than drunk."

"Whatever," I say. I reach over her and start to pull the seatbelt over her chest. Like a little kid, she obediently lifts her arms higher so that I can buckle her in.

"You're mad," she observes.

"I'm not mad. I'm—" I take a breath and exhale. I don't know what I am. There are so many things I want to ask her... so many things I'm confused about but I don't know where to begin.

"What?"

"For starters—why were you at a bar by yourself?"

"Because I felt like having a drink."

"You felt like having a drink?" I repeat back to her.

"Yes, I wanted a drink and I wanted to be alone for a little while," she says, her voice growing in volume with each word. "Is that really so hard to understand?"

I put my finger to my lips and glance in the backseat, relieved to see that Carter is still sleeping.

"Sorry," she whispers, wincing. "I forgot."

"Like you forgot that you were supposed to meet us for ice cream?"

"Oh, crap… Sebastian, I meant to text you back and tell you—"

"Or like you forgot to tell me why your face is red and you've obviously been crying? Or maybe why the leg of your shorts is ripped and why there's a button missing from your jacket?"

She looks down at her clothes and bursts into tears.

Shit.

"Amelia… I…"

"No, you're right," she hiccups in between choked breaths. "This day has been a mess." She stops and shakes her head. "I'm sorry."

"I don't want you to be sorry. I want to know what's going on with you."

"I suck."

This gets me to smile a little. I reach over to push her hair from her face. "You don't suck."

"I do suck. I don't know why I was there," she whispers, tears still streaming down her cheeks. "Practice was a disaster. I quit the team."

"You quit tennis?"

She nods and scrunches her eyebrows down. "Yeah, and I guess I wanted to be somewhere where no one knew who I was, and I was walking and I saw the sign and… I went in and sat on a stool not really expecting to get served. The next

276

thing I knew, I was three drinks in and there was this awful guy."

This gets my hackles up. "What guy?"

She shakes her head. "Nothing happened. I just realized I didn't really want to be there after all. I don't think I want to be anywhere, Sebastian."

My heart races as I pull her close and press our foreheads together. All the pieces of the last few months and the ones before that are whirling in my head. I can't get things straight yet, but I can control this moment with this girl.

I tell her it will be all right. I don't know if she believes me but she lets me kiss her crying face and rub her arms and tuck her tightly against my chest. And a while later—it could be seconds or hours—I notice the crying has stopped and her breathing has fallen into a steady rhythm.

I lay her back carefully against the seat so I don't jostle her awake. Then I look in the rearview mirror at Carter, who is still in a coma in the backseat, and laugh to myself as I pull onto the road. I'm like a chauffeur for the living dead.

The dark, wet streets pass by quickly. Within ten minutes, I pull into the driveway and turn off the ignition.

Amelia groggily lifts her head and asks, "Where are we?"

"My house."

She yawns. "Oh."

"I wasn't sure what to do," I admit. "I didn't drive you home because I didn't want your parents to find out you'd been drinking."

"I doubt my father will notice I'm gone. And Nancy… well, it'll be all right."

"I can take you there if that's better."

"No," she says softly. "I'd rather be here. Is that okay with you?"

"Of course," I tell her. "Just wait here while I get Carter into bed and I'll be back for you."

"I can walk myself," she murmurs, her eyes drooping a

little.

I chuckle. "Amelia, just wait for me here."

She gives a small, contented sigh and snuggles against the seat. "Okay."

Once I'm certain Amelia's going to stay put, I sling Carter over my shoulder and take him inside. He barely even stirs as I lay him down in his bed and pull his comforter up, but when I'm at the door he calls out to me.

"Bash, where's Red Dead Fred?"

I look back and see the bear on the floor, halfway under the bed. I pick it up and put it under my brother's arm.

"Night, bud."

Carter makes a sleepy, chewing sound and rolls over to face the wall, taking the bear with him.

Amelia is still in my car like I asked so at least that's something. I open her door and start to lift her up.

"Is it morning yet?" she asks sleepily.

"Not quite," I tell her as I get my hand under her legs for leverage. "Go back to sleep.

"Uh-huh," she mumbles, turning her face into my chest.

I carry her up the steps and into the house.

"Why are you being so nice to me?" she asks, her words mushy with sleep and hard to understand.

"Why do you think?" I ask as I lay her down gently on my unmade bed and remove her jacket. She's wearing a simple white tank and tennis shorts. Not the best pajamas, but I think they'll work.

"I think you like me."

I laugh and move to her feet to pull off her shoes and socks. "I think you might be right."

She curls her toes in my hand and rolls over, burrowing under the comforter. "I think you love me," she murmurs.

I think you might be right.

I fold both her legs on the bed and cover her with my comforter. Then I pick up her tennis bag and search through it until I find her cell. Normally I'd never think about going through Amelia's things, but since she's in no shape to text her parents, I figure I get a free pass.

I scroll through her contacts, pausing when I see Daphne's name still listed next to a picture of her grinning and giving the peace sign to the camera. I find Nancy's entry and I type out a quick text letting her know that Amelia is staying at Audra's tonight. Yeah it's a lie, but I doubt they'd be happy about her staying here. Next, I send Audra a text to explain the cover story.

Amelia is on her side with her arm curled beneath her chin, snoring softly. I lay down beside her and brush her hair off of her face so that I can get a better look at her. I let my eyes trace her jaw and the soft shape of her mouth. There are two little lines between her eyebrows that make me sigh. Even deep in sleep she doesn't look completely at peace.

I rub my thumb against those two little lines. If I only knew what to do for her. If only I knew what to do in general.

I think you love me, she'd said.

She may have been completely out of it, but she was still right. I do love this beautiful, broken girl beside me. But one thing the world has taught me is that sometimes love isn't enough.

***

At first I think it's a dream. A good dream—the kind that I want to go on for days and days.

I feel her kiss my eyelids in turn and then my mouth. Her breath falls over my jaw and her tongue skims to the base of my neck. Then her fingertips brush down my side and dip under my t-shirt and that's when I come to, realizing that I'm not dreaming. I'm awake and Amelia is in my bed on top of me.

I open my eyes and see that my bedroom is full of dull, greenish light. It's not morning yet, but it's close.

Amelia is above me, her hair falling over us both like a heavy velvet curtain. She still has on her tennis clothes—a thin white tank over a sport bra that leaves hardly a thing to the imagination and those torn shorts. Her eyes are bright and clear—like two stars climbing high into the night sky.

She bends down and kisses me on the mouth. The taste of her is intoxicating and for a moment I get lost in it. Then I remember where we are and what happened last night, and I find her hands and trap them on top of my shirt. "Amelia, stop."

Her swollen lips form a question. "Why?"

"You were drinking."

She shakes her head. "That was hours and hours ago. I swear I'm not even a little buzzed now."

"But—"

"I miss you," she whispers.

It's such a small and simple thing to say, but it moves through me with the power of a hurricane, knocking down houses and tearing up trees by their root systems.

I release the air in my lungs in a gush and let go of her hands. "I miss you too."

Amelia smiles. I run my fingers through her hair and down the side of her neck. She shivers beneath my touch. I take her face in between my palms and we're kissing again, only this time it's not so gentle.

A flood of heat ignites under my skin and both of our shirts become a thing of the past. In a tangle of limbs and hitched breaths, we switch places. I kiss my way down her neck and over her chest and she closes her eyes and presses her head back into the pillow. Her hands move below my waist, seeking blindly.

I stop and look down at her. She's breathing hard and her skin is flushed pink in the soft light.

"Is this not okay?" she asks, her fingers sliding slowly beneath the waistband of my boxer shorts.

My entire body quakes. I close my eyes and shake my head. "Of course it's okay. But—" I'm still unsure if this is a good idea.

"Please, Sebastian?" she pleads softly, her lips barely brushing against my own. "I just want to feel something other than sad. And if you have something then..."

I think of the small box in the drawer by my bed. I'd bought it on impulse, not really expecting anything. "I do, but are you positive?"

Instead of answering, she kisses me and it's the kind of kiss that speaks the words for her. I meet her bold touch with a desperation of my own, claiming her mouth and peeling the rest of her clothes from her body.

Never breaking the kiss, Amelia twines her arms around my neck and presses herself against me. I graze my fingers over her satiny skin, paying attention to every detail of her and loving the small gasping sounds she makes into my mouth when I find something she likes.

"This?" I ask, my hand traveling over the sloping curve of her hip.

She nods and kisses my chin, urging me on. For a long time, we explore each other like that, tasting and savoring.

And then, like the last piece of the puzzle slipping into place, it happens. One moment Amelia and I are a world apart and in the next heartbeat, we're as close as two people can be.

281

CHAPTER THIRTY-FIVE

Amelia

A distant sound tugs me from sleep. I rub at my eyes, forcing them to let in the blaring morning light, and I realize I'm not where I'm expecting to be.

The navy walls are covered with vintage punk posters and a few original sketches. I look to my side, but the only sign of Sebastian is in the form of an imprint on the dark green sheets.

I take slow breaths and turn back into the pillow, letting myself relive last night. I barrel through the memory of the storage room at the bar and my clammy fear and focus only on Sebastian.

Smiling, I close my eyes and exhale. I don't know what I thought it would be like, but whatever I'd imagined, it was better. Perfect even. There was nothing to be afraid of, nothing to worry about. Somehow I'd known exactly what to do, rising and falling to him naturally like the tide following the moon.

The telltale sound of pipes cutting off water snaps my eyes open. I suddenly realize that I'm completely naked beneath this downy comforter and that makes me self-conscious despite the fact that after last night, there's nothing left to hide.

I quickly pull the top sheet around my body like a wrap and set my feet on the floor.

My racquet bag, I see, is on a chair next to the desk. I tiptoe over to it and dig through the contents for my phone.

No matter how little my parents notice me lately, I definitely should have let them know I'd be out all night.

"Huh." I see that there are outgoing texts to both Nancy and Audra so I guess Sebastian took care of that too.

The bedroom door bursts open and my head shoots up.

Sebastian steps through the door and tosses a wet towel into his clothes hamper. "You're up."

The sight of him, damp from a shower and wearing nothing but a pair of loose jeans, causes my heart to lurch.

Oblivious to my perusal, he looks down at the phone in my hand. "I hope it's okay that I texted Nancy from your phone last night," he says. "I didn't want her to worry."

"Yeah, it's… thank you." Nerves fluttering, I awkwardly stuff the phone back in my bag and pull the sheet tighter around my body. "Thank you for everything."

He pushes his hair back. It's still wet, the ends just starting to curl behind his ears. "I feel like I should be the one thanking you. Last night was…"

I glance down and then up, my lips curving in a shy half smile.

"There it is." He bends forward and kisses the dimple on my cheek, a move that makes my breath catch. Then he kisses the corner of my mouth and buries his face into my neck. My hand automatically goes to the base of his skull. His skin is cooling and smells so good—like soap and fall leaves.

Groaning, he stands up and gives my upper arms a reluctant squeeze. "I'll make coffee and then take you to your car, okay?"

"Okay." My eyes move over the floor of his bedroom, searching for my discarded clothes. "I'll get dressed."

He cocks an eyebrow at me and runs one finger over my collarbone. "You sure you want to do that?"

More smiling and bashful staring. Good gravy, we're ridiculous.

"I'm sure."

"Okay then." He gives me a reluctant shrug. "Coffee it is."

Sebastian leaves to go get the coffee started and I dig around his room for my clothes.

"How in the heck did you get all the way over here?" I mumble at my underwear as I scoop them up from the bookshelf.

It's not until after I find my ruined tennis shorts and my top tangled up in his comforter that I realize I don't want to get back in those clothes. They remind me of Wesley and the bar and everything I want to forget about yesterday.

Thinking that Sebastian probably has a shirt and a pair of gym shorts that will work for me, I amble to his dresser. In the second drawer down I find a pile of shirts. Beside that is his sketchbook and I pick it up and turn it over in my hands.

I pause, wondering if this is intrusive of me. I mean… he did let me look at it before so it's not like I'm actually snooping without permission. Eventually curiosity wins out and I sit down on the mattress and cautiously start to flip through the pages.

His drawings are as beautiful as I remember. I deliberately study the long, bold strokes and the expert shading. Whether Sebastian is willing to admit it or not, he has real talent and I wish that he'd pursue it. But who am I to talk about pursuing anything? I have no idea what I want to do with my life now. My stomach twists as I think back over all the college acceptances I've gotten in the mail and have balled-up and tossed into the trash.

Pushing those thoughts aside, I continue to move through the sketchbook, noting landscapes that I recognize and a couple of drawings of myself. Then I get to a page that makes my heart and everything around me freeze in place.

I've seen the drawing before but I must have forgotten about it. It's Daphne and me lying side by side in the grass of the school courtyard. She's wearing huge sunglasses and laughing. Our fingertips are barely touching.

As I take it in, my throat constricts and a hot tear slides down my cheek.

My sister will never see this sketch.

She'll never hear about last night or tell me about her own magical night.

She'll never make it to Olney, Illinois to see those silly albino squirrels she was so crazy for.

She'll never do anything.

Without warning, the pain hits. It's too big to contain, spilling out over me and stealing my breath. Tears fall freely down my face now.

I sniff and look around Sebastian's room but everything is different, like I'm seeing it through fogged glass. What felt right just a few minutes ago suddenly feels strange and filled with a heavy uncertainty.

With shaking hands, I stand from the bed and set the sketchbook back down in the dresser drawer. As I do, a piece of paper falls from the last pages. I recognize it immediately as something I've seen in Daddy's office a hundred times: a summons to appear in court.

I know I shouldn't read it—that I have no right to invade Sebastian's privacy in this way, but words like custody and minor in question catch my attention.

I taste bile in my throat. This can't be right. Sebastian is being sued?

***

He's standing at the counter busily pouring coffee into a mug.

"Not only do I have coffee ready," Sebastian says, his back still to me. "But I made toast too. A real gourmet meal."

I look around the kitchen. "Where's Carter?"

"I told him he could play a video game. I figured that would give us time." He finally turns around and sees the expression on my face and the redness around my eyes.

285

"What's wrong?"

I hold up the court summons. "You didn't tell me about this."

His whole body tenses. "You haven't exactly been available."

"What's that supposed to mean?"

He swallows hard and rakes a hand through his hair. "That wasn't supposed to come out like that. I... I don't know. Amelia, you've been going through a lot and I didn't want to bother you with this."

I look down at my hands, feeling guiltier than ever. I could work up an argument, but what's the point? I know he's right. I've been so lost in grief, I failed to notice that Sebastian was going through his own struggle.

"I still wish you would've told me," I whisper.

"I know, and I wanted to tell you, but the timing never seemed right."

"What are you going to do?"

"Right now I'm trying to find a lawyer. I can pay for most of the retainer, but I still can't find anyone who wants to take the case. I'll figure it out though. I just have to do it by May 11th."

"What happens on May 11th?"

"That's the date I have to appear before a judge."

"Oh." I set the paper down on the kitchen table. "I really am sorry."

He shrugs, his face unreadable. "It'll be okay. So... coffee? Toast?"

I shake my head. I don't want coffee or toast. I don't even want to be here anymore. That sick, unsettled feeling is growing in my belly.

"Amelia, now what's wrong?"

I don't say anything. How can I possibly explain this to him?

Sebastian hesitantly asks, "Is it... is it about last night?"

286

"I..." I take a breath. "I don't know. Maybe."

He lets that sink in for a minute then turns away from me. "I thought we were good. I thought we were together."

"I'm not sure what that means anymore," I admit.

He looks back to me and asks in a plaintive tone, "How can you say that?"

I don't know what I'm doing, but it's like fire is burning up my arms. It's a weird sensation. I'm confused and scared and I'm... mad. At myself. At Sebastian. At my parents. At Spencer McGovern and his mother. I'm mad at everyone.

The hole in my chest—the one that's been there since Daphne died—is still there. Last night didn't change it. It didn't fill it or make it disappear, and I was stupid and naive to think otherwise.

"I just think it might have been a mistake. I'm sorry."

"You're sorry?" he asks me in exasperation. "You call me last night to pick you up and you come here and you initiate sex and now—"

"I was drunk." The words pop out of my mouth before I can even consider them.

He staggers back. "What?"

"I... I was upset yesterday and you know I was at a bar and..." I shrug. The lie stings, but it's somehow easier than telling the truth—that I have no idea what's wrong with me and I'm not sure I ever will.

Sebastian looks gutted. His face is pale and he can barely lift his eyes to meet mine. "You were drunk?" he repeats, needing even more confirmation of my betrayal.

I hate this. I nod anyway.

He falls into a chair and drops his head. "I thought..."

"I'm sorry," I tell him again, hating myself, hating all of this. He's angry. Hurt. I know I should stop, but I can't. "I know you must be mad right now."

His laugh is bitter and accusatory. "I can't even be mad at you, can I? You've been through something horrible. Your sister is gone and I want to help, but you keep pushing me away and…"

I know what's coming next. I know that he's about to give up on me and I can't even blame him for it. I'm a mess. A lost cause. I've faked and lied and burned everything good in my life down to the ground. I abandoned ship. It only makes sense that he would bail too.

Sebastian blows out a long, defeated breath and says, "I don't know what else to do for you."

I turn to hide my face. "I don't need you to do anything for me."

"Why? Because you're just fine?"

I realize I'm probably making a terrible mistake but I can't handle it. I can't handle how he's looking at me like he can see all the way through me. It makes me feel exposed and raw in a way that I've never felt before.

I'm done. All I want is to slink home and crawl back into my bed and stay there forever like some princess in a story. Forgotten about, I'll sleep for an eternity and vines and moss will grow right over my bones. But first, I have to end this conversation.

"Look," I say to him, trying to sound a heck of a lot steadier than I feel. "It's not that I don't care about you."

He blinks at me. "Amelia, if you cared at all… if you felt even the tiniest bit of what I feel for you, you wouldn't be doing this."

My eyes are wet. My lungs are starting to heave for oxygen. "It's not that simple."

"Why isn't it that simple?"

"Because it can't be." I'm crying again.

"Why not?"

Why not? The question pokes at the frustration and anger inside of me. I take a step toward him and wag my finger. "Because you don't understand what it's like for me!"

"You don't think I understand what it's like to lose

someone?" he shouts back. "Take a look around my life, Amelia. My whole existence is about losing people. My mother, Carter, and now you!"

"If you think you can just wave a magic wand and make me better—"

His eyebrows cave on his forehead. "What are you talking about? When did I think that?"

I shake my head. My thoughts are muddled and I'm not making sense anymore. "Just stop—okay? I can't do this with you anymore. It's too much!"

Sebastian is breathing hard. He looks down at his lap for a long time. Finally, he asks, "So what are you saying? It's over?"

"I... I think so," I say to him, my chest aching. "Eventually you'll see that this is for the best. You and I are making each other miserable, Sebastian."

He picks his face up and I can see the pain there. "I make you miserable?"

Struggling not to cry more, I tell him, "I didn't mean it like that. I just think it'll be better if I'm alone."

"At least let me give you a ride home," he says, his voice hoarse.

I give a hard shake of my head. "No, I'll text Audra to come get me."

He won't look at me anymore. "Fine."

I glance at the untouched coffee mugs sitting on the counter and the toast he put on a plate for me. God, this is so uncomfortable.

"I know you don't want to hear it," I say, "but I am sorry."

Sebastian nods, accepting that, and my heart pounds out a protest. Fight me, I think, suddenly panicked as the weight of what I've just done settles onto my shoulders.

"I wish—I wish things were different," I continue. "But I can't do it. I can't pretend anymore."

"I don't want you to pretend," he says to me. "All I want is for you to be okay."

"Okay?" My laugh is like acid. "I'll never be okay again. My sister isn't just gone. She's not on vacation or in the bathroom doing her hair. She's dead. For the rest of my life, I'll be a twinless twin."

"Amelia... don't."

"Why not? It's the truth, isn't it?" I croak out, my voice breaking. "Daphne is dead and the absence of her is so loud that I can't hear anything else. I don't know what to do, Sebastian. Tell me, what am I supposed to do?"

He finally looks up, his grey eyes pinning me in place. "You listen."

CHAPTER THIRTY-SIX

Bash

I am a fool.

I went all in and I lost. As Mama would say, the wheels on the metaphorical bus have come flying off and now I'm left stranded on the side of a road without a ride.

"Do you know how to say turtle?"

Startled out of my stupor, I look across my desk to Audra, who is flicking through the paperback Spanish-English dictionary in her hands and trying to translate the paragraph we've been assigned. I guess I should be grateful that Mr. Gubera didn't pair me with Amelia, but as soon as he called out her best friend's name, I knew my life was back to being a cosmic joke. The universe hates me.

"Hello, Bash? Turtle?" Audra presses.

"Tortuga."

"Got it," she says, nodding her blond head and scribbling down the word.

Amelia is on the other side of the classroom working with Asher O'Brien, who I didn't realize how much I disliked until he was sitting next to my ex-girlfriend, obviously trying to find reasons to touch her.

"You okay there, buckaroo?" asks Audra.

I clear my throat and swipe a hand over my hot forehead. "Yeah."

Not buying it, she glances over her shoulder to Amelia. "At least she's here today."

That's true. As much as I flinched when I saw her walk through the door of the classroom, I was also relieved. Her attendance is hit or miss these days and when she misses, I worry. I don't want to worry about her, but I do it anyway and maybe there's a part of me that always will.

It's been nearly a month since she broke up with me and every day is a fresh hell, a kind of study in agony as I rock violently between missing her and resenting her.

In the beginning, I wanted to forget because it was easier that way. I couldn't look at her. I couldn't even bear to think of her or what she'd become to me, so I shoved her into a tiny shadowed room and put a padlock on the door.

And it even worked for a short while. But what I didn't count on is that there are some thoughts that are too powerful for locks and keys. Thoughts that are strong enough to break through walls and claw their way out of their steely cages when you're least expecting it. Thoughts that can detonate like bombs, obliterating anything around them.

I think you love me.

I do love her but it isn't enough, is it? Poetry and song lyrics might want us to believe that finding love is like uncovering buried treasure, but now I know the truth. There's no joy or celebration in love. There are no happy endings. There is simply me and her and a crushing pain. What's left after that? An entire life of mute should-haves and second-bests.

I'm angry. And I know how twisted and unfair that is. After all Amelia has been through, I have no right to feel any venom toward her, but it's there—outrage and anguish at war within me, my heart stretched too thin by the hectic pull of loving her and losing her all in the same breath.

"You're a wreck, aren't you?"

I blink at Audra, thinking I've misheard her. "What?"

"I can tell, you know, that you're a wreck," she says. "I've seen wet cats that look happier than you."

Humiliated that I'm so transparent, I shrink down into my chair. "It doesn't matter."

She tips her head, letting her long blond hair fall to one side. "Maybe, maybe not."

I despise the tiny kernel of hope that I feel in my chest, but this is what my life has been reduced to—hanging on to any shred of Amelia that I can get my hands on. "What's that supposed to mean?"

She looks at me, her face grave, and says quietly. "She's a mess too."

My gaze flickers.

Amelia Bright ruined me and I can't look at her.

But I can't look away either.

***

Bash: It's official. I'm a gator.

I send the text to Seth and look back at the acceptance letter in my hand. I'm a little shocked, but it's all here in black and white. I got into the University of Florida starting the summer session and not only that, I qualified for financial aid. Between that and the money I'm now bringing in from my t-shirt designs, I have no arguments left. I'm going to college.

My mind starts racing with everything I have to do before June. I look around the cramped house thinking that I'll have to start looking for renters. I'll also need to see about getting boxes and a small moving truck. Oh, and I guess I need to figure out exactly where I'm moving to. Family housing was my first thought, but if Seth wants to keep on living with us, I can always look at apartments or cheap houses.

"Bash?" Carter pops his head out of his room. "Have you seen my folder? I have to look at my spelling words and I can't find it."

I fold the letter and tuck it into my back pocket. "I think you left it in the kitchen, bud. Actually, why don't you come on out here for a minute."

Carter looks confused, but he complies. "Is everything okay?"

Like Seth, he's been worried about me for obvious reasons.

"Yeah, everything is fine. I was just thinking about doing something we haven't done in a while."

"What is it?"

The start of a smile turns my mouth. "A shark hunt."

His eyes widen. "Really?"

"Yep. I think it's the perfect day, don't you?" Carter nods enthusiastically and I say, "Go grab your boots and bucket and I'll get the folder. I can read you the spelling words on the way."

"Okay!"

Thirty minutes later, we're tumbling in the truck down the dirt road that takes us out to Blackwater Creek. It's a fine spring day in the Lowlands and the sun is beating down through the tree canopy and speckling the pavement with its honeyed light. Carter is in the backseat talking about school and making predictions about the upcoming hunt for shark's teeth.

"Does this mean that you're not sad anymore that Amelia doesn't want to be your girlfriend?" he asks me.

"Who told you that?" I ask, looking in the rearview mirror.

He shrugs. "I'm seven but that doesn't mean I'm stupid."

Fair enough. My eyes go back to the road. "I'm still sad, but I'm getting better."

Carter nods. "Seth says you have heartburn."

I laugh. "I think you mean heart*break*."

"Isn't it the same thing?"

"Not quite."

He thinks about that, shuffling the information away for later and says, "My teacher was sad two weeks ago, but that was because her pet rabbit died."

"That is sad," I say and shake my head. "Carter, I'm sorry

if I've been out of it. I think... I think I'm turning a corner and I actually have something to talk to you about."

"What's that?"

"How would you feel about moving this summer?"

His mouth drops open in surprise. "You mean, leave Green Cove? Where would we go?"

"Believe it or not, I got into a college down in Florida."

"In Florida?"

I nod. "And I'm hoping, if you agree that it's a good idea, we could go there."

He's quiet for a while. "I heard they've got Disney World down there. Can we go?"

My eyes still on the road, I smile. "We might be able to make that happen."

"What about our house?" he asks me.

I give a half shrug. "We'll rent it to someone else and find a new place to live."

"But won't Aunt Denise and Uncle Mike miss us if we move to Florida?"

I'm not expecting him to say that and it throws me for a bit of a loop. "I don't know. Do you miss them?"

He chews on his bottom lip and nods.

"Oh." I'm not sure what to tell Carter. Things with my aunt and uncle are still a disaster. I'm biding my time, hoping that in May the judge assigned to the case will examine all the circumstances and honor my mother's wishes. I haven't looked beyond that—to a future without any family at all—or let myself wonder what that might mean for Carter. "I'm not sure, but we'll try to work something out, okay?"

He nods. More lip biting. "And what about all of our stuff? And Jinx?"

I hadn't really considered the cat, but I know we can figure it out. We can figure out anything as long as we stick together the way Mama wanted. All your tomorrows start here.

"We'll take all of our stuff with us and find a place that lets us have a cat," I tell him with certainty. "Anything else you're worried about back there, hoss?"

He looks out the window and by the time he turns back to me, he's almost smiling. "Do we get to pack up Seth too?"

CHAPTER THIRTY-SEVEN

Amelia

When we were young, Daphne and I had this game. One of us would be blindfolded and the other would be the leader—in charge of directing and giving orders so that the person with the blindfold didn't bang into walls or fall down the stairs and break a leg or anything like that.

Occasionally, if Daphne was the leader and she wanted to make the game really tricky, she'd go for minutes without speaking, hoping that I'd be able to follow the sounds of breathing or just understand intrinsically how to get to her. I hated that—that feeling of not knowing the right way, of being lost and sightless, my arms held out and my sister hovering somewhere just beyond my reach. And yet, that's how I feel now—confused and waiting alone in the dark for instructions that never seem to come.

Over the last five weeks, I've spent more time in my bed than anyplace else. The rest of the house is off-limits because all it does is remind me of Daphne and how I failed her. And school is out too, because there I'm faced with Sebastian and all the mistakes I made with him. No way. What's the point anyway? It's better to stay here in bed, where I can shut everything and everyone out. If only I could—

The door to my bedroom suddenly creaks open and interrupts my brooding.

My breathing changes, but I don't bother to open my eyes because I know exactly who it is from the sounds her feet make.

"Hi, Audra."

The footsteps pause. "What are you doin'?"

"Sleeping."

Audra snorts. "Sleepin'?"

My eyes stay closed and I keep perfectly still. "Yep."

"You can't be asleep."

I feel my bed sink as she sits down beside me. "Why not?"

"Well… you're talkin' so I know for a fact you're not asleep. Not only that, but it's lunchtime and it's your birthday."

"See, I think that's even more reason to be asleep," I mumble.

"Amelia."

"Uh-huh?"

"I let you sulk all the way through spring break," she says.

"Uh-huh."

She prods me with one hand and sighs heavily. "You don't answer my calls or texts. And you barely come to school anymore."

"The teachers don't care what I do and I prefer my bed. I'm thinking of having this made my permanent address."

"You can't spend your whole life in bed."

"Really? Watch me."

Another sigh and then, "What am I goin' to do with you?"

She lays all the way down beside me. I feel her breath on my face and reluctantly open my eyes. Audra is there, right in front of my nose looking straight at me with her clear blue eyes.

"Hi," I say.

"Hi," she says back. "Are you okay?"

Am I okay? My body feels bruised and my mind is as frigid as an arctic lake. "Umm… My heart feels like it's being split in two and put through a meat grinder."

Her mouth curves. "So you're sayin' you're great?"

Defiant, I swallow back the tears gathering in my eyes and nod my head.

She fastens her eyes on mine. "Really now?"

I can't do it anymore. Awash with loneliness and regret, I close my eyes and surrender to the tears. Audra wraps her arms around my middle and hugs me.

"I'm eighteen today," I tell her through my sobs, my eyelids fluttering.

Audra nods in agreement.

"And Daphne... Daphne is never going to get older. She'll never have another adventure or fall in love or get married or have babies. She's forever seventeen and it's my fault!"

"How is it your fault?"

I suck in a breath and try to think of how to tell her in words. "I should have fought harder! I should have known about Spencer and—" Hiccups overtake me and I can't continue.

"You could say the same for me, couldn't you? And do you blame me?"

I shake my head.

"Do you blame Daphne?"

I'm appalled. "Of course not."

"Then your theory is crap. You've fooled yourself into believin' that the rules are different for you than they are for everyone else."

"But it's not fair," I moan.

"Damn straight it's not fair! But sometimes we just have to say screw fair and right and move on with what we've got. I mean, look around—there's no customer service desk here. There's no place you can stomp back to and demand a full refund or ask to make an exchange. Bad store policy or not, this world is all we've got. And it's flawed and confusin' and really stinkin' hard sometimes, but it's ours."

"How can you say that?"

"Because it's what's real, Amelia. I'm what's real. You're what's real. And while you're barricaded up here in your tower, the earth is down there movin' on without you. And I swear on all that is holy that no one would hate that more than Daphne."

Audra is right. I hate that she's right, but she is and I know it. And with her arms around me, I cry big, gulping sobs until I'm so hollowed and emptied out that I don't think I could cry anymore even if I wanted do.

A long time later, Audra whispers, "Let's do somethin'. Let's go someplace."

My hair is a tangled bird's nest and my face is puffy and damp. "Where would we go?"

Audra takes a breath. "I have an idea. I also have a bottle of wine I stole from my parents' stash and a bag of Red Vines."

"You have Red Vines?"

She shrugs. "It's your birthday. I figured I'd go all out and we could binge on processed sugar and stolen wine and tell the rest of the world to kiss our go-to-hells."

I laugh and Audra stands from the bed and tugs on my arm. "Come on, Sugartits. I think you've wallowed enough for one lifetime, don't you?"

**

This is weird," I say.

"Why is it weird?"

I roll over, the warm grass crunching beneath my arms and look at my friend. Her long hair is fanned out around her like a golden mane.

"It's like two in the afternoon," I say, "and we're at the cemetery eating candy and drinking white wine straight out of the bottle."

Audra cocks her sunglasses and gestures to the marble headstone with Daphne's name etched in long and thin block letters.

"Well, it's your birthday and it's her birthday."

"So what? You're like a matchmaker for the dead?"

"If that's what you want to call it." We both laugh and then get quiet. In the distance I hear the beating of wings as a bird seeks a higher place in the trees that border the cemetery.

After a few minutes, I tell Audra, "I haven't been here. Not since the day of the funeral."

She says, "I come here a lot actually."

"You do?"

She nods. "I know Daphne's not really here, stuck in some graveyard with a bunch of old and crusty dead people, but it's nice to think I'm talkin' to her all the same."

"What do you say?"

"I just tell her stuff. Mostly the dumb stuff, you know, about school and tennis and my parents." A short pause. "And you, Amelia. I tell her about you."

Intrigued, I prop myself up higher on my elbow. "Like what?"

Audra cants her head. "Oh, I tell her the basics—how I think you're doing, how you broke up with Bash, and how sad you've been." She pauses. "And I tell her how much I miss you. How much I miss you both."

My throat burns and my eyes fill with tears, but for once not because I'm sad—not really. I'm all right. And it's a strange, rattling and screwed-up feeling, but it's one I'm hoping to hold on to for a little bit longer.

I peel a Red Vine from the bag that Audra brought and lean back in the grass and stare up at the shifting, bleached-out clouds and the swatches of blue sky overhead. "Do you think she can hear you?"

"I don't know. I hope so and sometimes I even think she gives advice."

"Oh yeah?" I ask, chewing.

"Yeah."

"What would she say just now if she could?"

Audra ponders this for a moment. "She'd probably tell

you to get your butt in gear and get your life and your boyfriend back."

I laugh out loud. "And how should I go about doing that? There's no way Sebastian is going to give me another chance—not after the way I royally screwed everything."

And then I tell Audra the truth. I tell her about that cold and perfect night in March, when everything had fit into place, and about the morning when I'd pulled at the seams and watched it fall apart.

"So you see," I say, finishing gloomily, "there's not a chance."

"I don't know about that."

"How do you figure?"

She shrugs noncommittally. "I just think that for some people, the story is never over."

Unsure how to respond to that, I focus on the other piece of advice. "As for getting back my life, that's out too. I didn't follow up on any of my college acceptance letters and now it's probably too late. And I'm not even sure that's what I want anymore." I give a heavy sigh. "I honestly don't know what I want."

"Okay, so college isn't happenin' just now. Let's not even get that far, Amelia. You have a whole summer ahead of you just sittin' there waitin' to be enjoyed."

"So?"

She makes a face and scoffs. "So?"

I laugh. "What are you saying?"

"I'm sayin' that there's always you and me and the open road."

"What do you mean?" I ask in wonder. "Like your road trip? You're not serious... I thought that was off?"

"The thing is, I still have to make it out to San Jose State by the end of August. I can go by myself and just drive straight on through. Or," she says, pushing the sunglasses onto her head so that I can see her eyes, "you can come with me and we can hold on to all those plans Daphne made for the best summer of our lives."

My mind races. I think of the little pieces of colored paper swirled across the map in my sister's room like a rowdy invitation. Then I think of sunrises and sunsets I haven't lived through and of songs I haven't yet heard, and of inside jokes and warm kisses and hot chocolates I still have to drink and the kaleidoscope of jangling late-night stars I want to see. In a small voice I confess, "I'm scared."

"What are you scared of?"

"Of living my whole life without her."

"You know what Daphne would have said about being scared."

I turn my face toward the great big bowl of blue sky and I sigh through my nose. "If it scares you then it's probably worth it."

Beside me, Audra holds up the wine bottle and drinks down the last of it. "Cheers to that."

***

When the sun has sunk below the trees and the light is nearly gone, Audra drops me off at home. I tell her goodbye and I walk through the front doors and up the stairs. This time, when I step into my sister's room, it's not to fall apart, it's to listen.

I move slowly among Daphne's stuff and my fingers brush over the music box Grandma Rose got her for our seventh birthday. I pause to wind it and watch the tiny pink ballerina spin in circles to Fur Elise.

Then I stop at her desk and I touch the Polaroid camera she found at the thrift store and my eyes glide up and over the paper flags she carefully placed across the map of the United States. There are quotes scattered across the rest of the bulletin board—phrases she cut out of magazines or saw in books. As I read them, I realize Daphne wanted adventure for sure, but mostly she wanted to simply live. She wanted to be happy and listen to music and laugh with her friends.

I pick the camera up and turn it over and I think about how I always had plans for this big and meaningful life I was going to live someday. I never stopped to consider that *someday* may never come. But that's the truth, isn't it? There are no guarantees. You don't know when you might take your last breath. Things happen. You could get in a car accident tomorrow, or choke on a chicken bone twenty minutes from now, or drown in a swimming hole. You could go to sleep one night and never wake to see the morning light slip in through your window blinds. Or someone could take your life away from you in a blink of an eye just because they can.

My sister is dead and I will go on missing her forever. That's the kind of hurt that can't be ignored or forgotten or buried underground because it's inside of me, stretching wide like an ocean. And I can stand here, always clinging to the shore and looking out over the water and wondering what lies on the other side, or I can try to find a way across.

Here in Daphne's room, surrounded by all her things, I know with biting clarity exactly what she would say. She'd tell me to build myself a freaking boat.

I almost laugh out loud as I look back to the map and let the thoughts start to boomerang around my head. I'm going to go on that trip with Audra. I'm going to find adventure and big, wide open spaces, but first there are some things that I have to do here.

As soon as I hit the bottom of the stairs, sweet and buttery smells waft toward me. Intrigued, I follow them into the kitchen.

"What's this?" I ask. I don't think anyone has cooked in this house since November, but the signs of cooking are all over the counter—dirty bowls and measuring cups. And I swear I smell a roast cooking in the oven.

"Darn it, I was hoping to surprise you," Nancy says as she straightens from whatever it is she's working on. "There's a roast cooking. It should be ready in a half an hour."

"We're having dinner here?" I ask, stunned and scarcely breathing. "I figured you'd be at church tonight."

"It was time for a little break," she says simply. "You know I've been going to a grief group there?"

I shake my head. I didn't know that actually, but in a way it makes sense.

"Two nights ago someone from my group talked about getting back to the normal, everyday things and something about that rang true for me." She takes a breath. "I don't know that I'm ready for normal, but I can certainly make dinner today of all days."

Then she steps back from the counter and reveals a round cake iced with chocolate frosting and two pink and white striped candles in the center. She halts when she sees me looking down at the cake and asks tensely, "Is this okay?"

"Is that a birthday cake?" I ask, even though I know the answer already. It obviously is.

Daddy enters the kitchen before Nancy can answer me. He still needs to shave and there are dark grey circles under his eyes, but at least he showered so that's progress. Perplexion flashes across his face as he glances between Nancy and me, taking in the scene.

"I didn't think anyone would want to celebrate," Nancy starts to explain. "But it felt wrong not to at least acknowledge the day somehow."

Realizing that I'm holding my breath, I let it out. Nancy is right, just like Audra was right. I don't feel like celebrating my birthday, but I do want to celebrate Daphne's. She deserves that much.

"I think that sounds like a fine idea," Daddy says in a scratchy voice. He turns to Nancy and wraps his arms around her waist and kisses her gently on the top of her head. It's such a normal gesture, but it's one I haven't seen in a long while.

"It's her favorite," Nancy says softly.

"Red velvet," I say, smiling despite the tears welling up in the corners of my eyes.

"And chocolate chips sprinkled on top," she adds, tilting the cake slightly so I can see.

"I think she would have loved it and encouraged us to eat it before dinner."

"You think?" she asks me.

Daddy and I both nod as we sit down at the counter.

Nancy smiles a sad smile. Then she gets out the serving plates and finds a lighter. "I know that none of us really feel much like singing," she says, her hand poised above the candles, "but do you want to go ahead and make a wish, Amelia?"

Daddy turns to me questioningly. "It is your birthday too, darlin'. It'd be a shame to let a wish go to waste."

"Actually, I want something better than a wish. Daddy, can I ask you for a huge favor?"

CHAPTER THIRTY-EIGHT

Bash

"I thought that was you."

I sit up in suddenness and blink at the person who has discovered my lunchtime hiding place in the library. It's Rachel, my ex-girlfriend, in all her blue-eyed and long-legged glory. She's cut her hair recently and the choppy, strawberry-blond ends fan across her chin.

"Hi, Rach."

"What are you working on?" she asks as she knocks her bag to the floor and slides into the chair next to me, getting close enough that our arms touch. "Still doodling?"

"Yeah, I guess. Just working on some new designs for shirts."

"Seth told me about that," she says, eyebrows raised. "And about you getting into school in Florida. It's pretty impressive. And here I always thought you'd end up as a professional groupie for Seth's band." She says band with finger quotes because, like most of the school, she doesn't give him nearly enough credit. "But I guess I was wrong. Bash Holbrook is going to be a college boy."

"Thanks," I say, embarrassed. "How about you? What are you doing next year?"

She shrugs. "A little bit of this and that. You know Mandie's, that sweet shop over on Brady Avenue?"

I nod. "Sure do. Carter is head over heels for their apple cakes."

She smiles. "Well, I got a job there and the owner says he'll make it full-time after graduation."

"That's great."

"You should come in and see me this afternoon. You could bring Carter and I could slip him some apple cakes and we could talk."

It's an innocent enough suggestion, but there's something in the soft way she says it that has me thinking that Rachel is asking me to do a lot more than talk.

It's not that I don't consider taking her up on it because I do. I'm tired of feeling lost and being so goddamn angry all the time. I don't want to be tortured anymore and it should be a simple thing to do—to let go. Rachel is beautiful and, despite everything that went on between us, there's something familiar and comforting about her. The problem is: no matter how I turn it over in my head, she's not Amelia.

"We can't today, but maybe another time."

Rachel slowly looks over my face then seeming to decide something, she points to my sketchbook and asks, "Do you mind if I look?"

It's strange. Rachel and I dated for almost a year and she never asked to see my sketches and I never offered, but now that she's sitting here with her big blue eyes on me, it seems so obvious that she should see them.

"Sure," I answer.

She takes her time working through the pages. "You know… I didn't know."

"Know what?"

She looks up at me and bites her lip deliberately. "That you were this good."

"Thanks—I think?"

"I would have encouraged you more."

"I doubt it. You didn't like anything that occupied my time."

She laughs—an honest and relaxed laugh. "You're probably right about that. But I'm at least vain enough that I would have asked you to do one of me."

She turns the sketchbook toward me, showing me a charcoal drawing of Amelia that I did from memory. In it, she's leaning against the window of my truck, her face turned up and her features mostly washed out by moonlight.

Then Rachel says, "Bash, did I ever tell you what happened with us?"

My guts lurch in surprise at the question. "You didn't need to. It was pretty straightforward," I say. "You dumped me."

"Actually, you dumped me."

I give my head a shake. "Technically maybe, but that was because—"

"I know, I know," she interrupts. "I cheated on you."

Shifting uncomfortably, I wave her off the topic. "This is history, Rach. We don't have to do this. I know that you didn't want to deal with Carter and—"

"Carter had nothing to do with it," she says firmly. "Maybe I wasn't the best with him, but I liked Carter just fine. And see, I *loved* you."

My mouth opens a little. Rachel and I never said the word love. "Rachel—"

"Let me finish," she says. "I loved you, but then your mama died and you were so closed off and it got to where I couldn't even talk to you. I wanted to be there for you, but every time I tried, you barely seemed to notice me. And I know what I did was wrong—I'm not making excuses for that—but I'm telling you how it was. I never wanted to be with that other guy. I only wanted you to see me."

"Why are you telling me all of this?"

Rachel hesitates. "You know I'm not the type to be gracious, but I've watched you. And I'm not saying it didn't kill me a little to see you with someone else, but..." She sighs and her eyes go to the drawing of Amelia. "Bash, there was a time not that long ago you didn't think you'd ever smile again. But you did. And maybe if I had been stronger or if I'd had more hope, I would've been around long enough to be the one you were smiling at."

***

"You know what Mrs. Ruiz says?" Carter asks.

"What?"

"That Florida is crawling with shark teeth," he says and then frowns. "But I don't think she meant that the teeth were really crawling. I think she meant they're everywhere along with arrowheads and all kinds of other cool stuff."

"Then we'll have to schedule a shark hunt as soon as we're settled in the new place."

"Can you tell me about it again? The new house?"

"I've only seen pictures same as you," I remind him.

"I know, but I like to hear you talk about what it's going to be like."

"Okay," I say, smiling. "It's painted yellow with a dark blue door. And it has three bedrooms."

"One for you and one for me and one for Seth," he supplies.

"That's right. And we're going to set up your room just like you want it."

"And I can even get those glowy stars for the ceiling?" he confirms for the hundredth time.

"Absolutely. Now, one thing you have to remember is that the kitchen and living room are a little small."

"But that's okay," he says, nodding, "because it's got a big backyard. With a fence and trees and lots of other places for Jinxy to hide."

I laugh. "Exactly."

I'm almost shocked at how well everything is coming together. The house in Gainesville is going to be ready for us the first week of June. And I think I've found a renter to take over the Green Cove house who can move about a week later.

The timing is so good that I'm starting to worry that it's too good. Usually, when things are going well in my life, it's a sign that everything is about to turn to shit.

"Do you think there might even be room for a dog?" Carter asks as I make the turn onto our street.

"A dog? You might be pushing your luck there," I say. And then I catch sight of something unsettling. "What in the—?"

Carter asks, "What is it?"

I shake my head hard. "Nothing, bud."

But it's not nothing. There's a silver mercedes parked at the end of our driveway and for a terrible moment I'm afraid the county has sent out another social worker, but then I realize there's no way in hell a social worker would be driving a car like that.

Then who?

Whoever he is, I think he must be waiting on pins and needles for me, because I don't even have the truck parked at the curb before the door to the Mercedes opens and a suit steps out with a briefcase clutched in one hand.

I do a double-take. It's Amelia's dad, but I have no idea what he's doing here. The last time I saw him he was rotting in his office with a bottle of bourbon. Now he's showered and shaved and wearing polished shoes and coming forward with his right hand outstretched.

"Hello."

All of a sudden, him being here hits me with full force and my heart misses a beat. "What's wrong? Is Amelia okay?"

Mr. Bright drops his hand and makes a placating motion. "Yes, yes, everything is fine with Amelia," he says. "I was hoping you and I could have a chat."

A chat? With the father of my ex-girlfriend? Thoughts speed around my head—none of them good—but I'm not sure how to extricate myself from this situation, so I cross my arms across my chest, control my expression and say. "Sure

311

thing."

Mr. Bright takes in the change in my body language and raises his brow. I think he's about to ask me something, but Carter interrupts by hopping down from the truck and asking, "Who are you?"

"My name is Bill Bright, and you are?"

My brother straightens his spine. "I'm Carter Holbrook."

"Nice to meet you, Carter. Amelia told me you were quite a kid but she didn't mention how tall you were."

"Like Amelia Bright? Do you know her?"

"Yes, sir." Mr Bright smiles down at Carter. "She's my daughter."

"Is she here too?" Carter asks uncertainly, looking around Mr. Bright for any sign of her.

"No, I'm afraid I came alone. I have something I'd like to talk to your big brother about if that's okay?"

"What about?" he asks in curiosity.

"Well..." Mr. Bright raises his eyes to meet mine and I take the hint.

"Carter, why don't you go play a videogame?" I suggest, giving his shoulder a quick squeeze.

"But before you said no videogames until after dinner and homework."

"If I changed my mind are you going to argue with me?"

He shakes his head vigorously and races ahead of us to the door. "It was nice to meet you Mr. Bright!"

"Nice meeting you, Carter," he says before turning back to me expectantly.

I'm not sure what to do here. "Would you like to come in?"

"That would be nice."

Feeling completely off-kilter, I awkwardly lead Mr. Bright through the front door and down the hall to the kitchen. Seth is standing over the counter holding a half-eaten hoagie.

312

"Hey man, I was thinking—" He stops talking when he sees that there's someone behind me. "Oh, sorry. Hi?"

"Seth, this is Mr. Bright, Amelia's dad. And this," I say, motioning between them, "is my friend Seth."

Seth swallows down the bite he'd been working on and wipes his hands on his jeans so that he can greet Mr. Bright. "Nice to meet you." He looks back and forth then snatches up the paper plate with his hoagie. "Well, I guess I'll give you guys some space."

"Thanks."

When we're alone, Mr. Bright sits down at the table and, unsure what to do, I offer him something to drink.

"Water is fine," he says, getting situated and pulling some papers out of his briefcase.

Water I can do, I think, reaching into the cabinet nearest the sink. I'm careful to inspect the glass to make sure it's not gross or spotty, which I know is probably ridiculous. It's not like Amelia's dad hasn't already noticed the threadbare sofa he passed or the empty pizza box on top of the trash can or the scuff marks all over the kitchen table.

"So what's all this?" I ask, placing the glass of water down. "Did I win something?"

He looks up from his papers, confused. "Excuse me?"

"Sorry, bad joke. I…" I shake my head. "Why are you here?"

"It's pretty simple actually. I've come to offer my legal services to you in the custody case for your brother. That is, if you want them."

I'm too shocked to speak right away. I drop down to a chair.

Mr. Bright keeps talking. "Before agreeing to anything, you need to understand that custody is not my area of expertise. That's not to say that I've never dealt with the family courts, but this is not my specialty. Amelia said that your court date is already set for May 11th, which doesn't give us a lot of time. I could ask for an extension, but then you'll be living in uncertainty for longer."

Still reeling, I shake my head. "Wait—you really want to help me? But how? Why?"

"My daughter told me that you needed counsel and..." He shrugs. "She speaks very highly of you. The fact that you managed to win her over tells me enough."

"Thank you, but you should know that Amelia and I broke up."

"I am aware of that Sebastian—or do you prefer Bash?"

"Uh—Bash is fine. And if you really mean all this—about taking Carter and me on—I can pay you," I say, not wanting him to think I expect a hand out. "I've been saving up the extra money I make from t-shirts."

"T-shirts?"

"Yes sir. I've been selling my designs to a website."

"An entrepreneur?" he asks, nodding in approval. "That will go a long way with the court. And as for payment, we can discuss the details later. Right now, I'd like to focus all of our energy on developing a strategy. I'm going to ask you a lot of questions and I'm going to need complete honesty from you. Bash, I can't help you if I don't know what we're up against. Do you follow?"

"Yes sir."

He sits back and appraises me. "Tell me son, are you ready for this fight?"

"I'm ready."

***

About the worst thing in the world to wake up to is the sound of sirens cutting through the night.

I'm out of bed like a flash, my brain trying to catch up as I make a dash for Carter's room. He's perfectly fine—sleeping with his arms and legs thrown out like a starfish. His bear and blanket are dangling precariously off the side of the bed so I step forward and move them closer to his pillow.

Seth must have heard the sirens and had the same idea as me because he appears in the open door.

"He's okay?" he whispers.

"He's fine," I mumble, exiting the room and closing the door.

"I wonder what they're for."

"I have no clue."

The sirens are getting closer and more are joining in. Swirls of blue and red interrupt the dark calm of the living room. Seth strides to the window over the couch and uses his fingers to separate the blinds.

"Holy shitballs," he exclaims. "They're right next door!"

"No," I say, but sure enough, there are at least three cop cars with lights blaring outside my nextdoor neighbor's house.

"They must be here for Paul."

"Do you think it's bad?" I ask, thinking of Paul's mother, Sandra.

"Considering all the crap he was knee deep in, I'd say, yeah, it's probably very bad." He moves his fingers, letting the blinds fall back into place. "But there's only one way to find out."

We're not the only neighbors outside at four in the morning. Mrs. Larson from two doors down is standing in her driveway and Mr. and Mrs. Ward have pulled camp chairs from their carport and are set up on their lawn to watch Paul and another guy be escorted from his house by four officers.

"Hell, that's Levi Palmerton," Seth hisses.

With Levi and Paul in handcuffs and secured in the back of the police cars, the activity dies down quickly. We find out that they've been arrested on some serious felony counts and are most likely going to go away for a long time. I start to worry about Sandra, but she finds us all watching on and tells us that she's the one who turned Paul and Levi in.

"Serves them right for getting into a fistfight in my house," she says, pulling her puffy purple bathrobe tighter around her chest. "Paul thought I'd just sit back and watch, but I called the police and when they showed up... well, the jig was up. Both of those boys are on something and I'll tell you, Paul did not choose the best places to hide his drugs or his money. When the good Lord was handing out brains, I do believe he forgot about my son. Now I've got to go inside and start cleaning up. Those officers weren't neat when they were searching the place."

"Do you need help?" I ask her.

"You're a sweet thing, but cleaning will help me keep my mind off things and Lord knows I need that right now."

After that, Seth and I wander back inside but we're both too amped up to go back to sleep.

As Seth is pouring out two cups of coffee, I say what I've been thinking since we saw Paul being dragged out of his house. "That could have been me."

Seth shakes his head. "Nah, you aren't Paul."

"Maybe not, but I thought about it—easy money, the chance to stop worrying so much. You know I did, Seth."

"But in the end, you always do the right thing because it's who you are and because you put Carter first." He pauses. "Speaking of—is Amelia's dad really going to help?"

I blow across my cup, making ripples in the dark coffee. "That's what he says."

"What, you don't believe him?"

"No, I believe him," I say. "But I can't wrap my head around the fact that someone is watching out for us. I'm afraid it's a sick joke."

"It's not a joke. He's helping you out because his daughter loves you."

I shoot him a hard look. "She broke up with me."

Seth shrugs. "More like she broke up with herself. You

should tell her about college and how you're doing something with your life. Take it from me—girls dig that shit."

I close my eyes, not wanting to hear this. Not wanting to think again of Amelia and her crinkling brown eyes and her soft, shiny hair. She's too much. It's too much—that sense that I'm done for and I might never feel anything that good ever again.

"Don't go there," I tell him, my jaw twitching. "Rachel already tried."

"Rachel?"

"Yeah, she came at me this afternoon with some bullshit about smiling and hope." I sigh. "But it's over and me telling Amelia that I'm moving away isn't going to change that, which is fine. I'm finally used to her being gone and out of my life."

He gives me a skeptical look.

"It's true," I say, my voice suddenly husky. "She's been my weak spot, but I'm through waiting around and I'm through with hope. It's nothing but a waste of time."

Seth takes a sip of his coffee and thinks that over. "That's too bad, man. The world is a shitty place without any room left for hope."

CHAPTER THIRTY-NINE

Amelia

My thoughts are a mess. My tongue feels swollen in my mouth.

Good gravy, what the heck am I doing? I think as my eyes dart around the large front porch and over a hanging bench and an impressive collection of potted ferns. The wooden porch slats are painted a shiny dark brown and I can actually see parts of my reflection in the paint. What are you thinking? I silently ask my blurry face.

"It's not that I don't appreciate what you're doing today and I'll drive you all the way to Jupiter if that's what it takes, but are you sure about this one?"

I pick my head up and find Audra's eyes waiting. I try to smile. "No," I tell her truthfully, "I'm not at all sure."

"But you're doing it anyway?" she guesses.

"Do you think it's crazy?"

"No way. I thought going to Charleston this morning was a little crazy. I think this is brave."

"I don't feel very brave," I say, glancing up. Then, bracing myself, I ring the doorbell beside the massive red door and take a step back.

A dog barks from inside the house. Footsteps sound. Finally, after what feels like a very long time, a woman with mousy brown hair peeks her head around the door, her slow and cautious movements reminding me that she's spent the last five months dodging photographers and journalists.

"Can I help you?" she asks warily, barely looking at us.

"Mrs. McGovern?"

But the woman doesn't answer. She clutches the doorframe harder and her whole body begins to tremble. "Amelia Bright?"

I can't speak past the lump growing in my throat so I nod.

She covers her mouth with her hand and closes her eyes to trap her tears. Then she nods her head and steps back to usher us inside the house. "I've been praying to talk to you every day," she tells us as she shoos away a buff-colored labrador retriever and leads us into a small sitting room. "But I never expected those prayers to be answered."

When we're all sitting, she pulls her cardigan around herself and asks, "Can I get you girls something to drink? I've got sweet tea or lemonade?"

"No we're okay," I answer heavily, trying not to be overwhelmed by the pictures hanging on the mossy green walls.

There's a family portrait above the black tiled fireplace. In it, Spencer is around twelve years old and is smiling at the camera with a mouth full of metal braces. Then there is a collage of senior pictures in simple black frames—Spencer sitting down in the grass, Spencer holding a football under one arm, Spencer in a tuxedo with his hair gelled back from his forehead. But it's a small 5X7 photo that makes me gasp.

I stand shakily and walk over to better study it. I've never seen this picture before. My sister and her killer are side by side with their arms around each other. Daphne is smiling brilliantly and the homecoming crown glitters on the top of her head. Spencer looks handsome in a suit and a tie that matches the color of Daphne's dress.

How could things have gone so wrong after this? How could these smiles have changed so drastically?

Behind me, Mrs. McGovern says, "I wasn't sure what to do with that one. Actually, I wasn't sure what to do with any of them. Leaving them up feels wrong, but taking them down… Spencer's father can't understand why I don't burn everything after what he did." She sniffs. "We disagreed about a lot of other things and he left in February and moved to Atlanta. I haven't heard much since."

I turn around and swallow uncertainly. "I'm sorry."

She stares at me, her body rigid. "Oh, sweetheart, I'm sorry. I don't know how I can ever account for your loss, but I'm grateful that you came here. The last months have been impossible. But I want you to know that I pray for you and your family every day."

My breath is stalled somewhere in the back of my throat. I've hated Spencer so much that I let myself get used to that hate—that boiling, black feeling like a nasty pothole on the surface of my heart. I became comfortable with it and in a way, I needed it because it was easier to be angry than feel the hurt.

But, looking at the sad and guilty face of Spencer's mother, I realize that no matter what happened, this woman lost her son. Her world was irrevocably changed the exact moment mine was. And at least I can go to sleep at night knowing that my sister was honored and mourned. Spencer's mom has been suffering in this empty house all alone in her pain. And, better than anyone, I should know that there's no rule book for missing someone. You just do.

"I wish I could turn back the clock," she says, her voice quivering on a sob. "I wish I had known more about what Spencer was thinking. I was his mother. It was my job and I failed. I should have been able to save him and your sister. I'm so sorry."

I don't think about it any longer. I cross the room to her and I take a deep breath and I say the words I know she needs me to say, "It's not your fault."

She can't speak yet, but she wraps her hands around mine. Her skin is cool and smooth and I can feel the ridges in her fingers between my own.

I'll never not ache for Daphne. And I'll probably never forgive completely or understand. That feels like an impossible sort of thing. But maybe the universe is bigger than what I can hold within my heart. At least, I hope it is. I really hope so.

***

"One more stop to make," Audra says, sliding the car into park.

My stomach shudders and dips as I turn to the car window and squint out at the doughy white clouds. I have no clue what to expect out of this meeting. "Believe it or not," I say, "I think I'm more nervous about this one than I've been all day."

"Girl, you've got this."

"Do I?"

She twists her mouth to the side. "Heck yes. All you need to do is talk to him."

"And tell him what? He was counting on me and I let him down in so many ways."

"You tell him that you're sorry."

"I might be sorry, but he still has every right to be mad at me for basically abandoning him this semester."

Audra rolls her eyes and laughs, but it's halfhearted. "He's not goin' to be mad at you."

"He might be."

"Fine then," she says as she reaches around the steering wheel and puts her hand on the car key. "Should we just leave?"

"No," I say quickly and climb out. "I'm going."

"I'll be here," she yells after me.

Good grief, I'm nervous. After everything else, you'd think this would be like nothing, but as I trudge up the steps and down the long, wide hallway, my heart feels like it's a passenger on an elevator headed straight for the basement level.

At the door, I hesitate once more to gather my courage, then I slip quietly inside. He's there at a table not far from me, head bent low, dark hair flopping down into his eyes. I don't call his name. I hang back against the wall for a minute and watch him with his new tutor—a sophomore from my school. I think her name is Riley Adams.

It must be close to five minutes before I'm able to make myself walk across the cafeteria toward the table.

When I'm close enough to be noticed, the girl, Riley, glances up. She's startled to see me there. "Amelia?"

"Hi. Um, it's Riley, right?"

She nods, seemingly pleased that I know her name. "I tutor here in the afternoons."

I shake my head, slightly embarrassed. "Yeah, I used to do the same thing. Carter was my star pupil."

In response to that, Carter grunts and folds his arms over his chest.

I wince. This is exactly the reaction I'd been worried about. Audra was so sure he wouldn't be angry, but I knew. He has every right to shun me.

I stand in awkward silence for a few more seconds before sucking it up and gesturing to the spot on the bench next to Carter. "Would it be okay if I joined you two?"

"Of course," Riley says, and when Carter still says nothing, she nudges his arm and he gives a reluctant nod then slumps down in his seat.

"So, Carter, what are you reading?" I ask in a light tone that completely defies the hot anxiety brimming inside of me.

He ignores the question and looks back down at the book in his hands, which is a library copy of a book about sharks.

Riley, finally understanding that something is rotten in the state of Denmark, answers for him. "Actually, we just started a new book today because Carter moved up to the next reading group in his class."

"Wow, go you!" I clap my hands together.

Still nothing.

Riley meets my eyes and twists her mouth in a silent apology. I can feel my cheeks starting to flush.

"So... Amelia," she says, slowly standing from the bench. "I was wondering if you could take over for me for a minute? I just remembered that I forgot to make a phone call."

I nod to her gratefully. "I would love that. As long as it's okay with Carter."

Another grunt.

When Riley is gone, I look back to the top of his head. "So, would you mind reading for me?"

It takes him a minute but he lifts his shoulders and opens the book and says, "I guess so."

He then proceeds to read the entire first chapter without any help from me.

"Holy smokes, Carter. That was awesome!" I gush. It's the truth. I'm so proud of him that I feel close to tears. "You've improved so much."

I can tell that he wants to smile at my words, but he won't let himself. Instead, he tilts his head and bites down on his bottom lip. "Thank you." Then he wrinkles his nose and his eyes flicker to mine. "I can read more if you want me to."

That's something at least. Trying not to be too obvious about my excitement, because I can tell that would be uncool, I shrug and say, "You're amazing so of course I want you to read for me, but only if you feel like it."

He nods. "I'll read."

I smile. "Great."

Carter reads the next two chapters easily. When he's finished with them, he closes the book and blinks up at me and I know that this is my cue to get this over with and pull the Band-Aid off.

"Carter," I say solemnly, "I understand why you're angry

with me. And I don't blame you at all if you can't forgive me, but I do want you to know how sorry I am."

He doesn't say anything at first. He fiddles with the pages of the book and sheepishly chews on his lip. Then, finally, he glances up at me and says, "My brother says you aren't his girlfriend anymore."

"That's true."

"But then he told me that your dad is helping us."

"That's true also."

He makes a face. "So why aren't you his girlfriend? Did Bash do something? Did he make you mad?"

"No, not at all."

He sighs and shakes his head. "I don't understand teenagers."

It's such a ridiculous thing for a seven-year-old to say, I burst into laughter.

"Why is that funny?"

I wave my hand in the air. "Just trust me."

He lets my laughter fade then he glances over his shoulder and leans closer so that I can hear him whisper. "I want to tell you something."

"Okay?"

"It was more fun when you were around. I like Riley, but I like you better."

I sit back, smug. "I shouldn't admit that I'm happy to hear that, but I am."

He smiles, reluctant at first, but eventually showing me all of his teeth. "I wish you could be my tutor next year, but we won't be living here anymore."

My heart twists. "I heard about that."

"We're going to live in Gainesville, Florida in a yellow house."

"Oh yeah?"

He nods eagerly. "And there's a big yard with lots of trees."

"Wow."

"And, I'm getting a dog."

"You are?"

"Well, Bash hasn't said yes, but he hasn't said no either and that usually ends up meaning yes."

"I see."

He pauses then looks down at his lap and back up. "Can I ask you something, Amelia?"

I draw closer. "You can ask me anything."

"Did my brother make you sad?"

"No, he didn't. But I think I might have made him sad because I've been so sad."

Carter nods, thinking that through. "Because your sister died?"

I force myself to swallow the lump in my throat. "Yes."

"I understand. You know my mama died?"

"I do."

"I still get sad about that because all my friends have their moms around but I don't. And she was the best," he tells me. "She could count all the way to like four million and she could sing songs and do the Donald Duck voice."

"She sounds pretty special."

"She was. And when I get sad about it and I miss her, Bash reminds me that it's actually a happy thing because Mama is an angel now which means she can be everywhere all the time watching over us. I bet she's here with us right now."

"I think you're right."

He smiles and impulsively wraps his arms around my waist and squeezes me tightly. Then he looks up at me and says, "So maybe your sister is an angel too?"

CHAPTER FORTY

Bash

"The goal is to settle this dispute fairly," says the judge. "We are all here this afternoon because each of you has a vested interest in the minor, Carter Holbrook. Let's try to remember that before we go any further."

I nod, my heart like a heavy stone in my chest.

The room is windowless and cold. I look across the wide stained-oak conference table at my aunt. She's sitting with her shoulders curled inward and her hands in her lap. Her eyes are wet with tears. Sitting beside her, my uncle is stoic and stiff in a grey suit. This room is a like a funeral parlor for families.

I thought we might be in an actual courtroom with a judge's bench and a witness stand, but Mr. Bright told me the county doesn't really do that for custody hearings anymore.

At the end of the table, the judge talks a little longer, explaining the process and how she's had the chance to look over the paperwork and meet with the social worker who came to my house in the fall. She clears her throat and asks Mr. Bright a question.

"Yes, it's right here," Mr. Bright says, sliding a piece of paper to her.

The judge adjusts her glasses and looks over the paper. "Okay then. And Carter is in the hallway in case I need to speak with him—is that correct?"

I nod. I hated dragging him to this, but Mr. Bright said that we had no choice. The judge might want to talk to Carter and ask him questions about what his life is like and where he'd like to live.

"Then I think everything is in order. Now let's start with—"

"Wait!"

My heart speeds up. *Wait?* I raise an eyebrow at my aunt. "Wait?"

My uncle is looking at her too. "What's wrong, Denise?"

She presses her head into the sleeve of his suit jacket and begins to cry. "I can't do this."

What does she mean by that? I'm almost afraid to speak. Mike is rubbing her arm and their attorney is saying something in her ear. She buries her face in her hands and cries harder.

I look at Mr. Bright and start to ask him something, but he lifts his hand, warning me to wait and let this play out. He's the attorney and I'm no one so I figure I should follow his lead.

My aunt and uncle's attorney begins to ask for a break, but Denise puts a hand on his arm to stop him. "I don't need a break," she says, squinting at me through her tears.

"You're sure?"

"I'm sure."

The judge passes her a tissue, which she gratefully takes. My brain is going haywire. I have no idea what's going on but maybe that's because I've never been in a fight for custody before now. Maybe this happens all of the time. Maybe this is some kind of trap, like a ploy for sympathy from the judge.

And then, before my thoughts can settle down, my aunt looks up and says to me, "I'm sorry, Bash."

"Wait—what? You're sorry?"

She nods. "I know that it must seem like we doubted you—and maybe we did a little—but I'm happy you've proved us wrong. All this time, I kept thinking, what would Jean Anne want, and… now that I'm sitting across from you, I know that she'd tell me this is a mistake."

Now I'm really turned around. "What do you mean? What's a mistake?"

"This," she says, looking around the room. "Mike and I want to drop the suit."

I don't want to look a gift horse in the mouth, but I'm still confused. "Why?" I ask, shaking my head. "What changed?"

"Let's just say that your girlfriend is very persuasive. She came to see us last week."

"You mean Amelia?"

My aunt nods. "She told us how hard you've been working and she let us know that you got into college down in Florida. I'm so proud of you for that. And your mama—well, she would be too."

"But Amelia and I... we're not even... How did she...?" Everything is happening too fast and I can't really wrap my head around it. I turn to Mr. Bright and ask, "Did you know about this?"

He clears his throat. "I had an inkling that she was up to something, but I wasn't positive."

Something else occurs to me. "Were you the one who told her about college?"

He shakes his head. "No, I can assure you that was not me."

Seth. I think of my best friend waiting out in the hall with Carter. I'm not sure if I should wring his neck or throw him a parade.

"Is it that easy?" I ask Mr. Bright.

He glances at the judge, who looks around the table and says, "I told you that the goal today was to come to a fair resolution. If Mr. and Mrs. Maxwell both agree that they do not want to pursue the suit, then I see no reason why we need to drag this out, do you, Mr. Holbrook?"

I shake my head ferociously. "No, ma'am."

Aunt Denise lifts her hand somewhat hesitantly. "I do have one request."

"All right," I say warily.

"Mike and I only ask that you call us if you need help."

I raise my eyebrows. "That's all?"

"That's all, Bash. I just…" She stops and lets out a slow, deep breath. I can tell she's trying not to cry and that pulls at my heart. "I only wanted what was best for Carter and you, but after talking with Amelia, I realized I got a lot of things wrong."

"Aunt Denise, you don't have to explain yourself."

"But don't I?" She presses her lips together. "I was so wrapped up in missing Jean Anne and wanting to keep a part of her with me, I lost track of what mattered. But you're my family and I want us to try again."

Uncle Mike leans forward. "I think what your aunt is trying to say is that she hopes we'll hear from you boys when you move to Florida."

I swallow and nod my head.

"Our door is always open, and maybe Carter could visit on school breaks."

I gaze around the room, my eyes passing over the expectant faces of Mr. Bright and the judge. This is probably bad court etiquette, but I'm beyond caring about that. I stand up from my chair and walk around the table to where my aunt is and I hug her. And I can tell that it's the right move. She hugs me back and cries into my shoulder, and then it's Mike's turn.

After that, things move quickly. The judge and attorneys sort out the paperwork, hands are shaken and it's a done thing.

Months and months of stressing out and it's over in a matter of minutes.

Seth and Carter are waiting for us in the hall with a pile of crayons and a stack of coloring books between them.

Seth throws me a concerned look when he sees that I'm holding my aunt's hand. "Already?"

"It's over."

He and Carter both stand up. "And?"

I look at my brother. There are tears stinging the backs of my eyes. "We get to stay together."

His eyes brighten. "You mean it?"

Seth and I grin broadly at each other. Then I put my arm around Carter and crush his small body to my chest. "Yep," I say, kissing the top of his head. "You're all mine."

He pulls his head back. His eyebrows are pinched together. "Was I never not yours?"

***

It's been a whirlwind of a day. As we leave the courthouse, I have no idea what to say to Mr. Bright. Thank you hardly seems adequate.

"So this is it," Mr. Bright says, turning to me .

"I guess so."

We both stare down the steps in silence for a moment. Seth and Carter are about a dozen yards off waiting to go for ice cream. After the events of the afternoon, I'm ready to buy Carter a scoop of every flavor.

"We're going for ice cream," I tell Mr. Bright. "Would you like to join us?"

"I appreciate the offer, but I think I'll head on home."

"We're meeting my aunt and uncle there," I tell him, still surprised at how this all turned out.

Mr. Bright smiles. "That's wonderful to hear. It's not often that you get to leave the court and go have ice cream with your opponent."

I start to laugh.

"So, when do you start school?" he asks me.

"I don't start until the second summer session, but we're heading down there a day or so after graduation because I have renters lined up for the house here. I want to make sure we're completely cleared out in time."

He nods. "That's great, son. Do you need any help?"

"No, sir. I think you've helped me enough already." I stop and shake my head. "You have no idea what this means to me—to not have to worry about this anymore. Thank you isn't even enough."

"I didn't really do anything," he says, chuckling.

"But you did. And Amelia too."

I'm still digesting the knowledge that it was Amelia who went to my aunt and uncle. It seems insane, but she did it. When? Why? So many questions and I'm not confident I'll ever get all of the answers. And maybe I don't even want them. Because thinking about her leads to missing her, and missing her leads to loving her, and loving her leads to losing her. All over again.

Mr. Bright says, "Really, it's me who should be thanking you. These last few weeks..." He blows out a breath. "Well, I guess I could say that they've brought me back to life. I needed something to fight for. After I lost Daphne I think I lost myself too. We all did."

"Will you tell Amelia that we won?"

"I will. She'll be mighty happy to hear that you get to keep Carter with you. She cares an awful lot about the both of you."

I'm at a loss for words.

"I know it's not my place, son," Mr. Bright continues, "but as a father I've already missed too many opportunities and whether it's meddling or not, I'm not going to miss anymore. Amelia... you know she's something special."

I swallow back the lump growing in my throat. "She is."

"And I know that kids will be kids and all that, but my girl misses you. And she might not be ready to admit it yet, but I hope when she is, you won't let her go on missing you."

CHAPTER FORTY-ONE

Amelia

I'm back in the dirt with Daphne. This time we're sitting side by side and our legs are bent like tents over the soft earth.

It's a hot day. I'm blinking at the dazzling patches of yellow sunlight that press down through the mossy branches of the big tree.

"I told you this would work," Daphne is saying. The same little bird from before is perched on her shoulder with its neck tucked backward into its feathers.

"Daphne, where are we?" I ask, my eyes straining to make sense of the geography. I swear I can hear the sound of waves, but this place doesn't look close enough to the beach. "Is this Green Cove?"

Daphne shakes her head and laughs. "Forget about that and put your arm out for me. This is more important."

I do as she says and watch, awestruck, as she tenderly urges the small bird from her shoulder to my fingers.

"She's so light." I slowly bend closer so that I can look into the bird's beady black eyes without spooking her.

"Of course she is. How else would she fly?"

I sit back up and look questioningly at my sister. "What am I supposed to do with her?"

Daphne smiles. Then she touches my elbow, lifting my hand toward the sky and says, "You let her go."

***

"What about that scarf—the one with the embroidery on the ends? I always liked that one paired with your purple Tory Burch dress."

I look up from my newly-purchased oversized olive green duffle bag. "Nancy, I'm going to be riding in a car for two months, not going to the Women's Auxiliary Cotillion. I have to fit everything I'm taking with me in this bag so I'm not wasting any space on dresses."

My stepmother sighs as she sorts through the pile of leggings I gave her to refold. "I'm still not sure how I feel about this. Where will you girls sleep?"

We've been over this ten times already. "Audra and I are camping some places and we've got motels mapped out for the others."

She shakes her head. "Camping and motels? Are we sure that's safe?"

"No," I say heavily, "but I don't think we're sure anything is safe, are we?"

She takes my meaning and swallows and goes back to folding, but I know Nancy well enough to know that she's not done. And after she's finished the leggings and is moving on to my camis, she says, "It's not that I don't approve."

I tilt my head. "You mean you're not going to disown me for turning down Emory?"

"*And* Tulane and Wake Forest and Vanderbilt and College of Charleston."

"Nancy."

"I know—you're not ready and you can always apply again next year."

"That's right."

"And I understand and so does your father. We think this time with Audra will be good for you, but we're going to miss you, that's all."

I look at Nancy again and think of her and my father all alone in this house.

"I feel bad about that. Are you and Daddy going to be okay here?

"I think so."

333

"Maybe you should take a trip," I suggest.

She smiles a little. "Who knows? Maybe we will do just that."

A couple more minutes pass. My bag is almost full. All I need to do is figure out which shoes I'm taking. That thought makes me reach down into the depths of my clothes to double-check that I remembered socks.

"One day," Nancy says, gently touching my cheek. "You'll have a daughter of your own and you'll know."

"I'll know what?"

"That all I want is for you to be happy."

I stop what I'm doing and pull my hands from the bag so that she'll know I heard her. "I'm working on it."

***

"Jesus, Audra!" I say into the phone. "You were supposed to give me a list of movies to get me excited about the road trip."

"Are you tellin' me you're not enjoyin' *Jeepers Creepers*? It's a classic."

I glance at my laptop where the movie is paused. "Um, it's horrifying."

She gives a breathy sigh. "Spoiler alert: road trips aren't all fun and games. I want you to be prepared when we get a flat tire on the highway at three o'clock in the mornin'."

"Then I should be reading an auto manual," I tell her. "As of now, if we get a flat tire, I'm going to be useless because I'll be too busy being scared out of my mind thinking we're about to wind up as the main course in some kind of demonic ritual."

Audra laughs. "M'kay, I'll come up with a better list."

"Please do. Oh and I'll have your packing list ready by tomorrow."

"Of course you will," she laughs. "Let me guess, you're

already all packed up, aren't you?"

"Pretty much. Nancy wants to take me to Target tomorrow to buy a poncho, a heavy-duty flashlight, and a good rope."

"What? Why does she think you need that stuff? We're not doin' Outward Bound or murderin' anyone that I know of."

Even though she can't see me, I shrug. "She says it will make her feel better to know I'm prepared for all kinds of emergencies."

"Whatever," Audra says. I hear something rustle in the background and then she says, "Hey, can I call you back in a few? My mom is callin' me downstairs."

"Sure. I'm actually tired so we'll just talk tomorrow, okay?"

"Sounds good."

"Night."

"Night, Sugartits."

I laugh and end the call. I have zero interest in finishing this movie so I turn off my computer and and look around my room. Have I packed everything? I still have ten days before we leave, but I'm nervous that I'm forgetting something critical.

Should I take an extra jacket? It's going to be summertime, but you never know. And what about books? I've got my Kindle, but after nearly three months I'll probably want to read one or two of the books from my shelves. The Kindle is the most convenient, but sometimes I just want the comfort of holding a book in my hands and feeling the pages.

Wuthering Heights maybe. And—I stop, my eyes lighting on a cracked white spine. *Fragile Things*, the book of short stories that Sebastian loaned me, is on the bottom shelf. We broke up right after he gave it to me so I put it there, hoping to forget.

I pick the book up and open it. There's the author's signature, but on the next page there is an inscription I hadn't seen before.

Maybe some things are fragile, but your heart is not one of them. It is invincible. ~Mama

I touch the words, wishing that I'd met Sebastian's mother. She was right. His heart is invincible, but that doesn't mean that I didn't try my best to break it.

In a sad and slow kind of way, I think about those early days with him. Carter's school and the party. Our midnight trip to the beach when, whether I wanted to admit it to myself or not, I fell at least a little in love. I think of the way he smiled at me in the dark, and our almost-kiss in his kitchen the day Carter was sick. And then I think of the water tower—the night that I tripped over the edge and dropped into the void. I never stood a chance after that.

I sit down on my bed and start to read the book. I read for a long time, getting at least three-quarters of the way through, before stopping.

I don't know what I want anymore, but I know what I *don't* want. I don't want to be scared. I don't want to be angry. I don't want to be that girl who can't say the words she should have already said out loud. I don't want to always look at things from a distance so that I can hold on to this idea that they're so perfect and flawless. I want to be close enough to see the cracks and all of the dark spaces. And if it's true that all of my tomorrows are really beginning right this minute, I know exactly how I want them to go.

With my pulse throbbing, I pick up my phone and I type out the text and press send. I don't even take a breath while I wait.

Amelia: Cheetos or Fritos?

They don't sound like much, but those three words make

336

up a love letter. This game had been *our* game and by giving it another chance, I'm really asking him something else—if *I* can have another chance.

Bash: **Cheetos**

I let go of my breath. It's not much, but at least he answered, right? And then my phone vibrates again.

Bash: **Strawberry jelly or grape?**

Amelia: **Strawberry**

Bash: **You don't even want to think about it?**

Amelia: **I don't need to. There's no competition. I don't even understand why they make grape jelly when there's strawberry.**

Bash: **I bet the grape people would say otherwise.**

Amelia: **The "grape people?" Do they really exist? I thought they were just a myth made up to scare kids.**

Bash: **Oh yeah. The grape people are a terrifying race of subterranean beings who break into houses and raid pantries, stealing all the grape jelly and wine.**

I laugh. And then I take a big breath and I do one of the scariest things I've ever done. But, like Daphne said, if it's scary, it's probably worth it.

Amelia: **Forget me or Forgive me?**

Anything could happen here, I think as I nervously bite my fingernails. I have just long enough to wonder if he's even going to respond, when my phone goes off in my hand.

Bash: **Forgive. I could never forget you.**

CHAPTER FORTY-TWO

Bash

Here I am, on an uncomfortable seat with a wasp buzzing around my head, about to become official.

The afternoon is sweltering, a fact made worse since I'm in head-to-toe black. As are all of my classmates.

Principal Johnson is on the sun-washed stage talking about the year and explaining to the restless crowd how hard we've all worked for our diplomas. I turn my head over my shoulder to look for Carter. He's sitting about a dozen rows back in between Aunt Denise and Uncle Mike.

"Before we hear from our valedictorian, Shayna Webb, I'd like to call us all to a moment of silence to remember the students and faculty we lost this year."

Everyone gets quiet.

"As you all know, we at Green Cove High School have had a very difficult year," Mr. Johnson says, struggling to keep his voice steady. "We have prayed together and we have cried together in our classrooms. I don't think words could ever be enough to explain our sadness or ease our mourning, but I will say this: at least we have each other and the support of our wonderful community.

"Despite devastating circumstances, I have been so proud to see you students lifting your hearts to each other, displaying empathy and kindness, and working to build a better future. We cannot go back, which means we must go forward, and I hope when you leave this campus today, you go out into the world carrying the lessons you've learned and remembering the people who touched your life and were taken too soon."

He pauses and looks out over the heads of the crowd. People are quietly crying and sniffling. My spine is tingling, some impulse telling me to seek out Amelia.

"Please join me in remembering our friends and the teacher we have lost."

She's four rows up and just as my eyes find her, she turns around and looks at me straight on. A scant, humid breeze pushes her hair forward and into her face, but she doesn't move or brush it away. She keeps looking at me and I keep looking at her. Tears are leaking from her eyes.

There was a time when I wished that I'd never fallen in love with her, when I thought I should have known better. The pain was a monster that hurt too much. But I finally understand that Amelia could never be a mistake because when I found her, I found myself.

We're at the end of high school and everything we've ever known. The past is a condemned building we're being evicted from and the future is nothing but a forwarding address to a place we've never been. As I sit here in my itchy cap and gown and look into Amelia's eyes, I know that, like everything else I want, she's uncharted territory.

Loving her is strange and confusing and damn risky.

And if I had the chance, I'd choose it all over again.

***

The next morning we start packing up the U-Haul trailer way too early. It's like the zombie apocalypse hit with me chugging coffee and Seth blaring music to stay awake, and boxes and crap everywhere you look. It's not fun, but by midday, it all starts to feel worth it because the crap is mostly gone and the boxes are all taped up and ready to go.

"We're almost done," I say, surprised at how close we are.

"Lunch and then we finish Carter's room?" Seth asks,

letting out an exhausted breath. He pulls a blue bandana off his head and stretches out his neck.

"Sounds good."

Carter is staying over in Charleston with our aunt and uncle while Seth and I finish up things here. The plan is to stop and pick him up tomorrow on the way down to Gainesville.

"I don't know about you," Seth says, "but I want one last pulled pork sandwich from Ryan's Smokehouse. Who knows if they can barbeque down in Florida. I have my doubts."

I smile. "I like where your head's at. Ryan's it is."

We grab our wallets and the keys to Seth's Honda because the Bronco is already loaded up. The moment we walk out the door, I put my hand in front of my face to block the sun.

"Hell, it's bright out here," I say. And then my eyes adjust to the light and I freeze. Amelia's silver Prius is parked at the curb and she's climbing out.

"Hi," she says hesitantly when she sees us.

Seth looks at her and then back to me and I catch the hint of a smile on his face. "You know, Bash... why don't I go ahead and pick up sandwiches and bring them back here?"

I don't trust myself to speak yet so I nod.

Amelia waves to Seth and we both watch him back out of the driveway. Then her eyes dart up to mine. She tugs on the bottom of her white dress and I notice that beneath it she's wearing leggings with blue and yellow zigzags.

"Hi," she says again.

Hi, I think.

Amelia chews on her lip and looks at the boxes piled near the open end of the U-Haul trailer. "I see you guys are packing up." When I don't respond, she takes a breath. "So I looked for you after graduation, but it was a madhouse and I... um... I wanted to return this." She stretches into her car and comes back holding a small white box tied with twine and my copy of *Fragile Things.*

341

I walk closer. "Did you read it?"

"Yeah."

"What did you think?"

She looks down at the grass for a moment and fidgets. "It was beautiful, Sebastian. I loved it and I know you do too so I wanted to make sure you took it back before you left."

I don't want to take anything back. "Keep it."

"Are you sure?" she asks doubtfully.

"Yes. I think I owe you more than a book after what you did with my aunt and uncle. And your dad."

Amelia's skin flushes. "It was the least I could do. I want you and Carter to be happy and..."

I wait.

"And I'm sorry," she says it fast, like the words are fire in her mouth. "I made a mess of things and I don't know why."

"Amelia—"

"Wait, I need to finish," she says, her brown eyes pleading with me. "You should know that I wasn't drunk that night. I lied to you because—well, I can't explain it. But I loved being with you, Sebastian, and I'm so sorry. And you probably won't want it, but I got you this."

She thrusts the box at me and takes a step back.

I look down. "You didn't have to get me anything."

"I wanted to. It's a congratulations and an apology and... just open it, okay?"

I untie the twine and lift up the lid. Inside there is a thick, brown leather cuff with a metal plate fastened to the side. I pick it up so I can read the words inscribed on the plate.

All your tomorrows start here

I look up, speechless.

Her cheeks are still pink and her eyes are reflecting the gold of the sun. "There's a lady over near Walterboro who makes them. If you don't like it, I can probably take it back, or..." She starts to reach for the box but I quickly take the cuff out and snap it onto my wrist.

"I don't want you to return it. Thank you."

Amelia smiles. "You're welcome."

I glance at the house. "I actually have something for you, but I wasn't sure... " I shake my head. "It was never the right time."

She swallows awkwardly. "Oh, okay."

"But it is now. If you can wait right here?"

She nods and I dash into the house. I find the small roll of paper on top of my bare mattress and I'm glad that I decided not to pack it. I'd been thinking of driving to her house and leaving it in the mailbox with a note, but this is better.

When I return, Amelia has moved so that she's beneath the shade of a laurel tree.

"Here," I say and hand her my gift.

She carefully unrolls the paper and looks at the painting.

"You've seen it before," I say nervously.

Amelia doesn't speak at first. She keeps looking. Then she takes a long breath and says, "I haven't seen it like this."

I used a previous drawing I'd done of her and Daphne as my guide, but in this one, instead of lying next to each other, Amelia is on the grass and Daphne is in the sky looking back at her.

"You painted it?" she says it like a question.

"I used watercolors," I respond. "I'm not great with a brush, but I'm working on it."

Amelia shakes her head. A single tear streaks down her cheek. "You're better than great. This is beautiful and I'll love it forever." She falls into silence and wipes at her eyes. Then she takes another big breath and laughs a little and says, "I don't want to say goodbye to you."

I reach for her hand, hold it for a moment and then let it go. My insides are in a million pieces. If this is it—if this is the last chance I get—I want to make it count, but I don't know how to do that. Before, when things were bad, I'd been so sure I wasn't enough that I gave up too easily. I let go of

343

the idea of love before it let go of me because it was easier than admitting I was terrified. I don't want to make that same mistake again.

"Amelia..."

She sighs and then smiles sadly at me. "I know. Endings are hard because you want to get it right."

My heart constricts. "Maybe it doesn't have to be an ending. Maybe it can be a beginning. But I can't always be the one reaching for you. I need—"

Before I can say anything else, she closes the distance between us, grabs my arm, and kisses me. And she kisses me like I'm not wearing sweaty, moving-day clothes and we're not standing in my front yard saying what could have been a goodbye. And I put my arms around her and I kiss her back in the same way because she tastes like sunshine and honey and forever and I don't want to lose this feeling.

"Amelia, I should have done this before, but I didn't and now that you're here I don't want to waste any more chances." I hold her face between my hands. "I love you."

"But I broke your heart," she whispers.

I shrug and kiss her again. "You break it, you buy it."

***

The morning sunlight is hurting my eyes. I roll to my side and see Amelia, propped up on one elbow, looking down at me.

She's still wearing the white dress and the leggings she had on yesterday and her hair is mussed from sleep and her eyes are a little droopy, but when she sees that I'm awake, she smiles.

"Hi."

"Hi," I say back, smiling too. We're on a mattress on the floor of my empty room. "Were you watching me sleep?"

She shrugs. "Maybe."

"That's kind of stalkerish."

She shrugs again.

"And it's also kind of hot."

And then, not caring that I'm exhausted because we were up talking for most of the night, or worrying about the threat of morning breath, I sit up and press my mouth to hers.

I hear a whistle and then Seth, who is walking by my door, shouts, "Get a room!"

"We're in a room," I yell back.

"Whatever."

Amelia laughs and untangles herself from me. She reaches into her bag and collects an ancient-looking Polaroid camera.

"More pictures?" I groan. She must have taken twenty pictures of my house last night.

"Carter is going to be happy to have all of those when he wants to remember what this place looks like."

"I do have a phone that takes pictures," I remind her.

She's looking down at the camera, adjusting something on the backside. "Yeah but... I think there's something to be said for the instant gratification of being able to hold a memory in your hand."

"The film's got to be damn expensive." She laughs and I ask, "What?"

"That's pretty much exactly what I told Daphne when she found it. But she was right. This camera is special and I know it's not practical, but I'm going to use it to document all the places that Audra and I go to this summer."

I smile and run my finger over her shoulder.

She puts the camera up to her face and snaps a picture of me.

"Hey—I wasn't ready," I complain.

"I don't care. I want to remember this moment exactly as it happened," she says and pulls the picture from the end of the camera and waves it in the air while it develops.

"Fair is fair," I say, grabbing the camera from her hands and snapping a candid shot of her.

After that, we both get quiet. I stare at the picture in my hands, waiting for the image of Amelia to appear.

"I don't want this to be it," she says finally.

I pick my head up and look at her. "This isn't it."

"But I'm leaving with Audra and you're moving. *Today*, I might add." She sighs. "It just seems like terrible timing. Like we missed the boat or something."

"We didn't miss anything," I say and take her hand. The cuff she got me is still on my wrist where I intend for it to stay. "I love you and whether we're together this summer or next year or five years from now, I already know I want all of my tomorrows to start with you. I'm here whenever you're ready."

She blinks. "But you're going away and..."

I know what she's trying to say because she said it last night too. And as I look at her face, I can see the doubt and the uncertainty there, but also the hope. And the hope is what gives me courage.

This is it. Whatever piece of forever we get, I'm not going to let it go without a fight. I take a breath and I turn her hand over and press it to my heart so she can feel it beating.

"So follow me."

EPILOGUE

We stop the car where the sky meets the ocean.

"Ready?" Audra asks from beside me.

I turn to my best friend. My fellow adventurer. Her clothes are a little grimier than they were two months ago and her hair is a little messier, but she looks happy. As do I.

"Yep," I tell her. "Let's do this."

We step out and I feel the salty Pacific breeze whip up around my bare legs. I think about the road behind us and all of the checkmarks we've put on my sister's list. I think about the cheesy singalong songs we've heard too many times and the bad tacos we ate back in St. Louis and then I remember all of the stars we've counted and pictures we've taken and the smiles we've shared.

And when the sun kisses my eyes and I see the water, sparkling and endless, I think of Sebastian and our whispered late-night phone calls and the promises given and taken this summer. I wonder what Daphne would say about me being in love with him—because there's no doubt in my mind that I am. And I wonder what she would make of my next adventure. I like to think she'd approve. After all, I'm ready to do something that scares me—follow my own heart exactly where it leads.

No regrets, I think as Audra takes hold of my hand. Together we step to the edge of the rocky cliff and look out at the wide sky.

I will always miss my sister, but I know now that wherever I go, whether it's to California or Florida or Antarctica or the moon, I carry her with me.

Love you.

Love you more.

And with the future spread out before me and the world spinning all around me, I open my mouth and I scream.

THE END

ACKNOWLEDGEMENTS

Sometimes writing is a solitary thing, but more often than not, it takes a village. When we came up with the storyline for *The Bright Effect*, I don't think even we knew how much we would rely on the feedback of others or how many brains we would end up picking. This book is both familiar and uncharted territory for us, and more than anything, we knew that Bash and Amelia's story was special and that we needed to get it right. We could not have have done that without some important people.

Our biggest *thank you* by far goes to Autumn's mom, Heather Doughton, who we think might know this story even better than we do since she's read the book AT LEAST 50 times (and we are not exaggerating). From the very beginning, she cared so much about Bash and Amelia and her thoughts and ideas molded them into the characters they became. She cried, she encouraged, and she pushed us to do better, and we love her for that!

Special thanks to other early readers and editors: Kaylee Gwyn, Elizabeth Hilburn, Susan Simmons, Michelle Flick, Lisa West, Renny Meister, Angie McCune, Sarah Smith, Nicole Quiett, and Sarah West from Three Owls Editing.

We'd also like to extend our eternal gratitude to our families who endure sub-par dinners, piles and piles of dirty laundry, and zombie-like moms when we are lost in our writing caves. We love you and couldn't do this without your support.

And to our readers. You are everything. You make our dreams come true every single day and if the world were a party, you would all be first on our invite list.

Cheers,
Autumn & Erica

ABOUT THE AUTHORS

Autumn Doughton writes books. Fun books. Books for you, your best friend, your favorite barista and that girl you knew back in the tenth grade. She likes to write about the things she knows about. Things like being confused. Being afraid. Falling in love.

When Autumn isn't writing, she's usually chasing after her three cats, two daughters, two dogs, two chinchillas and one lovely husband. You can find her in Florida, where it's salty, sunny and humid. Bad for the hair. Good for the soul.

Find out more at www.autumndoughton.com

~

Erica Cope lives in the Midwest with her husband, three children, three dogs, and three cats (apparently she has a thing for the number three).

She has an unhealthy addiction to coffee, a bad habit of binge watching shows on Netflix and eating pretzel M&Ms for breakfast.

When Erica isn't writing you can find her pretending to play her guitar, reading or baking something delicious.

Find out more at www.ericacope.com

STEERING the STARS

AUTUMN DOUGHTON
AND ERICA COPE

CHAPTER ONE

HANNAH

To: Hannah<<u>vaughn.hannah@hotmail.com</u>>
From: Caroline<<u>cbmckain@gmail.com</u>>
Date: August 24
Subject: Leaving on a jet plane...

Or more accurately, just left on a jet plane...

I just got home from the airport but I already miss you!
Message me when you land and take lots and lots of
pictures. Remember that I'm living vicariously through you.

-Care

It was raining.

This shouldn't have been a surprise because the first thing I'd read about England when I started doing my online research was that it rained, like, all of the time. But as I looked out the curved plane window over a sludgy sky and a tarmac slick and black with rain, my throat grew uncomfortably tight.

The flight attendant's voice came over the intercom. *On behalf of the airline and the entire crew, I'd like to welcome you to London, where the local time is eleven-oh-*

seven.

The plane wheeled closer to the gate and I felt the woman next to me lean over my back, crowding my space. I could smell her perfume and feel her breath creeping across the skin of my neck.

"It's raining," she said like this wasn't totally obvious. We'd been next to each other since New York, and by now I knew that her name was Deena. She was from Rhode Island and she had three grandkids and a dog named Pugnacious. He was a pug and according to her, he loved to dress in wool sweaters and even in pants. Pants on a dog? I had my doubts.

"Yep."

"I was hoping for good weather," she said as though a little offended. She was patting down her grey curls and sniffing.

What could I say? "Mmm-hmmm."

Before she could push the weather issue, the plane came to a full-stop, the seatbelt light clicked and everyone on board, including Deena and I, started to pack up.

I gathered a rainbow of pens and balled up my sweatshirt and stuffed them all into my messy backpack. Deena bent over to put away a half-eaten pack of Tic-Tacs and the book on the history of saltwater taffy that she'd barely even looked at.

She turned to me as we stood, both of us slightly stooping so we wouldn't bump our heads. "It was good to meet you. Good luck with your sister and your new school."

"Thanks and you too," I said, cramming into the center aisle.

The rest of deplaning was a slow and silent ordeal. We dragged ourselves and our neck pillows and pudgy carry-ons past the cramped seats and through a twisting florescent-lit loading bridge until we spilled into a busy customs terminal. I blinked, trying to adjust to the new space, and took a breath. When I turned my head to tell Deena goodbye, I saw that she was already walking away, pulling her red rolling suitcase behind her.

Suddenly alone, I rubbed my thumb across the star-shaped pendant hanging from my neck and started reading the signs. I needed to figure out where I was supposed to go next.

Was it only two days ago that Caroline had asked me if I was scared to be moving for the whole freaking year? At the time, I'd been cutting tags off all my new clothes and had been too amped about London and my new school to feel anything but excitement. But, as I navigated the customs line, answering questions about whether or not I was smuggling meat or dairy products into the country, my stomach began to slither and hiss like a pit of disturbed vipers. Yep. What I was feeling was something close to scared.

A guard in a dark blue uniform stamped my passport and shooed me along. I shifted my bags, swallowed, and walked through a set of sliding glass doors. They whooshed shut behind me and I scanned the crowd, not knowing exactly where I should be looking. I was anxious. Uptight. Dad had said that Felicity would be the one picking me up from the airport, but would my half-sister even recognize me? Should I have made a sign or worn a flashy red hat? What if she didn't show and I wound up homeless and living down by the Thames in a cardboard box?

"Hannah!"

My out of control thoughts screeched to a halt and I spun around. Felicity, my father's daughter by a first marriage, was walking toward me with a purposeful stride. She was easy to recognize with her wide pool-blue eyes,

354

perfectly sloped nose, and even features. Her fashionable suit and heels hinted that she had come straight to the airport from work. That's when I realized that I had no idea what she did for a living.

How strange was that?

We shared DNA.

This was technically my *sister* and I couldn't tell you her job title or her favorite animal or what kind of music she liked to listen to.

Hell, I didn't even know her middle name.

"Hannah!" Felicity called again. The sleeves of her tailored green jacket bunched in at the shoulders as she lifted an arm to wave me over.

I took in a deep breath to feed my nervous lungs and walked a little faster. "Hi!"

"How was your flight?"

"Fine. I mean, not really. It was cramped and horrible and way too long but you know how that goes. By the end I was hoping the flight attendants would just hand us all parachutes, open up the door and let us jump out." I tried to smile but it was all wonky on my face. My cheeks felt weird and I knew the amount of teeth I was showing was downright obscene.

Her forehead wrinkled as she looked me down and up. "You've certainly changed since I saw you last."

"Ah, gaining a few cup sizes in the boob department will do that," I said as I patted my chest. This was a total joke. I was flat as day-old soda and I figured I always would be. My mother was a dancer turned dance teacher and she'd passed on her hipless, buttless, boobless body to me, but not her grace or athleticism.

Felicity looked confused.

"I'm joking," I clued her in.

"Of course." She forced out a laugh. *Can you say*

AWKWARD? "Well, it truly is great to see you." More uncomfortable laughter.

"Um, you too." The snakes in my stomach hissed.

"Well then…" Felicity leaned forward and we did one of those hugs where your bodies don't really touch. When she pulled back, one of my duffel bags was swinging from the crook of her arm and she was shaking her head. "I'm sorry Michael and the girls aren't here to meet you."

Michael was Felicity's husband, and "the girls" were Grace and Chloe, their five-year-old twin daughters. I had never met any of them.

"That's okay. We have the whole year to get to know each other.

"I assure you that everyone is looking forward to having you stay with us. The girls haven't been able to stop talking about it, and I should probably warn you that they've started decorating your room with their latest artwork. It's quite abstract."

"I'm sure I'll love it," I said, fidgeting with a loose thread dangling from the hem of my wrinkled t-shirt. Her suit and perfect hair were making me feel all kinds of shifty. Like I should have tried harder and worn a nice blouse or put on lipstick or at least fixed my ponytail. "This is… just… thank you again for having me. I still can't believe that I'm actually here. In London."

"I'm looking forward to it. I've never really had a sister and I suppose neither have you."

With these stilted niceties out of the way, we got busy situating my suitcases on a sort of rolling cart, finding a SIM card that would work in my phone, and exchanging some of my American dollars for pounds.

Felicity warned me the car ride from the airport would be a long one so I settled into the front seat, trying not to be freaked out by the fact that she was driving from the right side of the car and I was sitting on the left without a steering wheel in front of me. But it was weird and I caught myself cringing every time a car passed us.

"How are your parents?" she asked, shifting the car into third gear and jerking her left foot off the clutch. Even in heels she seemed to know what she was doing with a car.

"Good I guess. My mom's studio has taken off. She started to offer aerial dance and it's become, like, the thing," I said, using air quotes, "for middle age women in Libby Park."

"What's aerial dance?"

"Basically, these ladies wrap themselves in sheets and hang from the ceiling like they're part of Cirque du Soleil. Kind of like yoga but a foot off the ground." I shrugged. "It's weird but at least she's busy. And Dad's company opened up a new development in Missouri last month. It's been a bit of a mess so he's been travelling a lot to get things in order and make sure the foreman on the project knows what he's doing."

"Is astronomy still his hobby of choice?"

"Yep," I told her with a nod. "He's nerdy as ever and has been known to wake me up at three in the morning to ask if I'm interested in seeing a conjunction or Neptune in opposition. The answer is always a resounding *no.*"

We shared a quiet laugh. "And what about Henry?"

I thought about my brother, who, I realized with a start, was Felicity's brother also. "Oh, you know… he's Henry. Since he's going to be a senior this year he thinks he knows pretty much everything. The reality is that he knows about as much as a slice of banana bread."

Felicity's blue eyes darted to mine and back to the road. The car lurched into fourth gear. "Which is?"

"Absolutely nothing."

She humored me with a chuckle. "And your boyfriend?

Dad mentioned he was some kind of big hockey star?"

"Lacrosse," I corrected before twisting to look out the rain-splattered window. I definitely did not feel like talking about Owen. Not now. And definitely not with Felicity. "So, where are we?"

She bobbed her head. "Brentford and Gunnersbury Park are up ahead."

Whatever that meant. "Huh."

A weighty silence stretched out between us. The snakes inside of me had calmed, but I was still nervous. I scratched my elbow. I coughed. I studied the other cars on the road for a while. Then I sifted through my bag and pulled out my phone to double check that the new SIM card was in working order. When my email loaded, there were two new messages from Caroline and one from Mom. Nothing from Owen.

Felicity cleared her throat. "You must be excited about your new school. Dad tells me you want to be a writer."

More than anything in the whole world.

I put the phone face down in my lap and flopped back against the seat. "Yeah, Warriner is supposed to be the best. I've thought about it every day for the last three months and I still can't believe it's real."

Last spring, I'd stumbled upon an essay competition for aspiring teenage writers based in the London area. The prize was a partial scholarship and a position at The Warriner School, a school with a killer creative writing department.

It was a longshot. It was such a longshot that I didn't tell anyone—not even Owen or Caroline—when I sent off the essay and my application packet.

Then it happened.

In May, I received an envelope in the mail—the big, fat, good kind of envelope—and it was time to come clean.

Mom and Dad were furious for about five minutes and then they were sad and *then* they started talking logistics. I suggested looking for a boarding house or some kind of city dorm (if that even existed), but they straight-up laughed in my face. Staying with my half-sister was the only option.

I knew I had a great thing going at home, where I had the perfect boyfriend and friends and I was a shoo-in for assistant editor of the school newspaper. But, the truth is that getting into Warriner and making the move to London was an adventure. And after a lifetime in Oklahoma, an adventure was exactly what I wanted.

Yep. This whole thing felt like the plot twist I needed—like a golden ticket to another kind of life. A more exciting life.

"It will certainly be different from Oklahoma," Felicity observed.

I caught a glimpse of my reflection in the car window. I was smiling softly. "That's the plan."

****

To: Hannah<<u>vaughn.hannah@hotmail.com</u>>
From: Caroline<<u>cbmckain@gmail.com</u>>
Date: August 25
Subject: Hello?

omgggggg!!! Not to sound pathetic or anything but, WHY HAVEN'T YOU MESSAGED ME?! It's been well over a day. Were you whisked away by an Ed Sheeran look alike? Or better yet, Ed himself? *wink, wink*
Can't wait to hear about what your sister is like! Write me soon. And by "soon" I mean RIGHT NOW!

Caroline

To: Hannah<vaughn.hannah@hotmail.com>
From: Cecilia<vaughn_cecilia@yahoo.com>
Date: August 25
Subject: Checking in

Hi Jellybean!

I hope you're settling in and getting to know your sister. So proud of you.

Love you,

Mom

To: Hannah<vaughn.hannah@hotmail.com>
From: Caroline<cbmckain@gmail.com>
Date: August 26
Subject: Earth to Hannah

Testing...

Is anyone out there?

To: Caroline<cbmckain@gmail.com>
From: Hannah<vaughn.hannah@hotmail.com>
Date: August 27
Subject: Hannah phones home

Sorry! I know I promised to email every day and I officially suck. My only excuse is that it's been crazy getting settled and figuring things out. Supposedly, English is our common language but everything is confusing. For instance, cookies are biscuits, pudding seems to be more like bread, chips are called crisps, and french fries are called chips. What gives?

The city is both amazing and scary. It's so much bigger than we even imagined and I'm almost afraid to go out and get lost. Yesterday, I did brave a bus and check off some big things like Harrod's and Big Ben and Westminster Abbey. And, yes, I tried to distract the guards by picking my nose but they didn't take the bait ;)

So far no Ed sightings, though I am vigilantly on the lookout as promised.

Hannah

_____

To: Owen<kilgoman24@gmail.com>
From: Hannah<vaughn.hannah@hotmail.com>
Date: August 27
Subject: hi

I made it. Just thought you might want to know.

_____

To: Hannah<vaughn.hannah@hotmail.com>
From: Caroline<cbmckain@gmail.com>
Date: August 28
Subject: Details please

Sooooo jelly!

How's your sister? Her husband? Your nieces? The house? Your room?

Have I mentioned that I am stuck in Libby Park and am living vicariously through you???

#sorrynotsorry

To: Caroline<cbmckain@gmail.com>
From: Hannah<vaughn.hannah@hotmail.com>
Date: August 28
Subject: Re: Details please

My sister (that is so weird to say) seems great but we haven't actually spent much time together. Things are a little awkward which I guess is normal considering we're strangers. Her hubs, Michael, seems nice enough but he works a lot. Chloe and Grace are LOUD and STICKY but the cutest. You know how I wondered how I'd be able to tell them apart? Well, Chloe just got hot pink glasses so that solved that. Both of the girls are in love with my makeup case and my nail polishes and have been trying to talk me into painting Professor Pufferton's nails.

And, the house is this really cool Georgian style walk-up, which basically means it's like a two-story apartment.

#yourewelcome

Hannah

To: Hannah<vaughn.hannah@hotmail.com>
From: Caroline<cbmckain@gmail.com>
Date: August 28
Subject: Re: Re: Details please

Ummm… Who is Professor Pufferton?

To: Caroline<cbmckain@gmail.com>
From: Hannah<vaughn.hannah@hotmail.com>
Date: August 28
Subject: Re: Re: Re: Details please

The cat.

To: Owen<kilgoman24@gmail.com>
From: Hannah<vaughn.hannah@hotmail.com>
Date: August 29
Subject: Seriously?

The silent treatment is getting old. I know that you're hurt but call me or email me, okay? At this point, I'll take a smoke signal or even an owl. ANYTHING.

And, before you even ask, I haven't told Caroline what's going on. Please, please don't talk to her until I have a chance to explain. You know how sensitive she is.

To: Hannah<vaughn.hannah@hotmail.com>
From: Cecilia<vaughn_cecilia@yahoo.com>
Date: August 30
Subject: School forms

Jellybean,

When you go in to school tomorrow, don't forget to take that packet of paperwork I put in the zippered pouch of the lime

green suitcase.

XOXO

Mom

To: Hannah<vaughn.hannah@hotmail.com>
From: Caroline<cbmckain@gmail.com>
Date: August 30
Subject: The longest year

Tomorrow is the first day of school. I know I'm supposed to be optimistic, but I have it on good authority that it's going to SUCK. How could it not? Seriously. A year. A whole year of you living in England and me staying in Oklahoma. I still can't believe it...
I know I sound like a sad sack but I do hope you are having a blast (even though I kinda hate you right now for abandoning me...JK...sorta). Just promise me that when you win the Pulitzer one day you'll remember me.

-Caroline

PS: And, don't forget your umbrella!

To: Caroline<cbmckain@gmail.com>
From: Hannah<vaughn.hannah@hotmail.com>
Date: August 31
Subject: Re: The longest year

Remember you? You'll be my date.

364

And, I'm telling you that your day is NOT going to suck! You are going to walk into Northside High and show everyone who is boss (or at least who discovered an awesome frizz-reducing conditioner this summer). I'm sure by the time lunch rolls around and Derek Warren is shoving Pixie Stix up his nose, you won't even miss me.

As I type this I'm staring with dread at my new school uniform. I was going to send you a picture but I don't want any official evidence that I ever had so much wool and polyester on my body at one time.

TTYL

Hannah

——————————

"Phew," I wheezed as I walked into The Warriner School, twisting rain from the ends of my hair and wishing that I had paid more attention to Caroline's email and carried an umbrella.

The heavy door fell shut behind me and I did a quick scan of the office. To be honest, it was like any school office, with walls the color of masking tape and dark brown Berber carpet and the faintly antiseptic smell of new paper and lemon cleaner. The school crest was front and center, stenciled in white, blue, and gold paint just above a large reception desk where an older woman with short grey hair was quietly typing on a computer.

Students were around. It seemed like the usual first day stuff—mostly kids waiting in chairs outside of what I guessed was the headmaster's office. I noticed one kid in particular. He was slumped over with his head cradled in his hand, drawing in a sketchbook. From this angle, I couldn't see his eyes, just his hair—a mess of tiny black curls—plus a bit of dark skin with the hint of broad cheekbones, and a wide, almost pretty mouth. But his looks weren't what caught my attention. It was the drawing. It was abstract—a series of concentric circles, all layered on top of each other—and it was completely amazing.

A shrill voice jolted me out of my head. "You're late."

"Excuse me?" My shoes squelched as I turned left and spotted a girl about my age leaning against the wall with her arms crossed in front of her body. Her outfit mirrored my own—boxy blue blazer with red piping and an embroidered patch over the breast, white collared shirt, a shapeless skirt, and dark tights that ended in clunky leather oxfords.

"You're late," she repeated.

I wiped cold raindrops from the tip my nose and stammered, "S-sorry. With the rain and being new to the city, getting here took longer than I thought it would."

Motionless, the girl stared at me and clicked her tongue.

Confidence drained from me like water pouring from an open faucet. I felt my shoulders slump and my breathing change. I wasn't normally the type to be intimidated easily, but this girl… well, she was intimidating. Maybe it was her perfectly parted dark hair or her unfriendly expression. Everything about her came off so severe, she might have stepped right out of a pamphlet for a deeply religious school or some kind of military camp.

Even though I wanted to curl up into a ball and roll right back out the door, I forced myself to smile and stick out my hand. "I'm Hannah."

"I know who you are." The girl uncrossed her arms but she didn't take my outstretched hand. "You're Hannah Vaughn, sixth form transfer student from America," she went on, assessing me with critical eyes. "I'm Ava

Cameron, one of the lower sixth prefects."

I'd read *Harry Potter* and researched enough online to know that prefects were class officers that were able to hand out detentions or demerits. Sort of like hall monitors on steroids.

"Ah, hi?" I tried. "Nice to meet you?"

Deep creases appeared at the sides of her mouth. Maybe that was her best attempt at a smile?

"As a prefect and a fellow member of the writing program, I've been given your schedule and have agreed to acclimate you to our school."

Lucky me.

She produced a piece of paper and pointed to it. "On Mondays, you begin with a double period of economics. Then, a fifteen-minute break and maths."

"And when do I take my writing classes?" I asked, leaning in and trying to decrypt the complicated-looking schedule. "That's why I'm here."

Annoyance flitted across Ava's face. "We move into specialties after lunch. But as I was saying…after maths, you should report to the dining hall for a thirty-minute lunch period. After that, you take accelerated composition in the McCabe Building."

A body pressed into my space and a head covered in sunny blonde curls poked over my shoulder to get a look at the schedule. "Brilliant! You have that class with me.

I blinked at the head. It belonged to a ruddy-cheeked girl with a wide, gap-toothed grin. "Um, hi?"

She stepped around to my front and grabbed for my hand. Once she had a good grip, she shook it vigorously. "I'm Tillie Hoover."

"I'm Hannah," I said and my relief was palpable. At least Tillie here didn't look ready to sentence me to latrine duty or tar and feather me.

"Oh, I know. And let me tell you, it's been ages since we've had anyone new and exciting around here. I can't wait to show you around and introduce you—" Abruptly, she stopped and lifted my hand up to eye level. "Oooh, I love your varnish! What's the shade called?"

I figured she meant my nail polish.

"Oh, I think it's called Afternoon Breeze," I told her, curling my fingers to my palms. My nails were short and square and painted a soft robin's egg blue. The bottle had been a going away gift from Caroline. She'd held it up to the outside of my house and said, *Just in case you forget the color of home, all you have to do is look down.*

"It's fantastic," Tillie said, nodding. "I looked all summer for a shade of blue that wouldn't make my skin look waxy but I never found one.

"If you like, I could bring it in for you."

Warm brown eyes squinted at me. "You would do that?"

"This is not a beauty school," Ava injected. "And painted nails break uniform code.

Tillie scrunched up her nose. "Oh, bollocks. That rule is never enforced."

"Still," Ava said, gruffly clicking her tongue against the roof of her mouth. "Didn't you read the student handbook, Hannah?"

"I tried." And I did try. "I just didn't manage to make it past paragraph two before falling into such a deep sleep that I woke up with drool caked to the side of my face."

Tillie giggled but Ava was undeterred. "I know things are done differently in *America,* but here we do have rules."

Oh God. I could sense exactly where this was heading. This was the smugness Henry had warned me of repeatedly. *Remember that they hate Americans,* he'd said, chucking me on the chin as we'd traded goodbyes at the airport. *They think we're a bunch of ignoramuses with a cache of guns and red Solo cups. Be sure to prove them wrong.*

I needed a reset button. That's all.

If I could only go back three minutes and start this conversation all over.

I blinked and looked around. To my total embarrassment, everyone in the office was staring. The kid with the sketchbook had stopped drawing. Even the receptionist was looking this way. I wondered if I should offer to pop some popcorn for them to munch on.

"It's just nail polish," I whispered.

Ava gave her head a shake. "Transfer students always think they'll be given preferential treatment."

"No, that's not what I meant."

Tillie rolled her eyes. "Oh, please get off it, Ava."

Ava pursed her lips and widened her stance. "I'm not on anything. I simply think it's a matter of—"

"Girls, I see you've met our new student!"

A man emerged from behind the reception desk. His clothes were tailored, his skin was bronzed like he'd spent the summer lounging on a beach in the south of France, and his hair was long and styled with a bit too much gel to be considered casual.

"Miss Vaughn, is that correct?"

"Y-yes." How did all these people already know my name? Had the administration sent out some kind of missive to the entire school?

The man shook my hand. "Your essay was just wonderful. We're so pleased that you won the writing contest and were able to join us all the way from America. Aren't we, girls?"

Ava's nasty expression flattened to something just this

side of friendly. "Of course, Mr. Hammond. Tillie and I were just about to accompany Hannah to her first course of the day."

Whoa. I looked back at the man, who I now realized was Ethan Hammond, the head of the writing department. *This* was him—the man who had chosen my essay and sealed my acceptance to Warriner.

"Mr. Hammond?"

He smiled. "The very one. I believe I'll be seeing you this afternoon in my classroom."

"Oh... I mean..." *Way to make a good impression, Hannah.* "I'm looking forward to it."

"We have a rigorous curriculum but I am always available if you have any questions or concerns. And I won't bite. At least not on the first day." He laughed loudly at his own joke. "I'm certain Ava and Tillie will make sure you feel comfortable as you familiarize yourself with school grounds."

"Absolutely, Mr. Hammond," Tillie piped up. And, no, I didn't miss the dreamy way she said his name.

His green eyes crinkled at the corners as he tipped his gaze toward me. "Hannah, I know you have a lot to think about at the moment, but if you permit, I'd like to suggest squash to you. We have a mixed team—that's boys and girls for one sport. I'm not supposed to actively recruit students—you understand," he said, leaning toward me conspiratorially. "School rules. But just between us, we are desperately in need of players this year if we hope to make any progress with the team. Ava and Tillie can share the specifics with you if you find yourself in the least bit interested."

"Squash?" I looked around. Most of our audience seemed to have lost interest, but the black kid with the sketchbook was closely following the entire exchange. His lips were clamped and his cheeks were puffed out as though he might burst into laughter at any minute.

"Quite a few of my writers participate," Mr. Hammond said seriously.

"*Squash?*" I asked again.

Tillie nodded encouragingly. "You know... squash?"

"No."

She wrinkled her nose. "With racquets? And a ball?" When I didn't respond, she shook her head in frustration. "For your sport?"

At that, I laughed and flapped a hand dismissively. "Oh, thanks for the offer but I don't play sports."

Her eyes rounded. "But you must!"

Mr. Hammond said, "You may want to reconsider. Nearly every student at Warriner participates in an athletic. It's not a written requirement but it is highly encouraged. We like to think of it as way to engage your peers as well as the faculty."

Sure, I signed up for new experiences when I moved to London but running around and getting sweaty was not one of them. "I don't think..."

Ava spoke over me. "For girls, we have lacrosse, netball, and hockey."

Mr. Hammond lifted a finger. "And don't forget about squash."

"Right," she added, turning back to me with unhappy eyes. "*And* squash. I'm one of the team captains this year."

"I'm not captain, but I play on the team," Tillie told me.

Mr. Hammond cocked his head. "So what do you think?"

I rocked back on my heels, hoping they would read my discomfort and realize I was about as sporty as a station wagon. But that didn't happen. If anything, his stare

371

became more expectant.

"Hannah?" he asked.

OH. MY. GOD.

Squash?

My heart was drumming and I could feel tiny beads of sweat forming up near my hairline. Blood rushed behind my ears.

I should have said no and laughed in their faces but I felt trapped. Panicky. Desperate to make a good impression on my teacher. Desperate to make a new friend in Tillie Hoover.

Adrenaline rushed through me and my traitorous mouth formed the word before my brain could fully process the seriousness of the situation. "Okay."

Tillie clapped with delight.

"Brilliant!" Mr. Hammond flashed me a megawatt smile. "We'll discuss our practice schedule this afternoon. The official squash season doesn't begin until late November and until then we only meet on Mondays, Tuesdays, and Fridays. And as for uniform—don't worry too much as I'm sure we'll be able come up with something in your size for today."

Uniforms?

The practice schedule?

Squash season?

My stomach was going sour. "Great."

"Wonderful," he repeated, nodding and heading for the exit. The moment the office door shut behind him, Ava rolled her eyes and the boy with the sketchbook really did start to laugh.

For my part, I couldn't move. I just stood there with a vacant expression on my face, staring after my new teacher.

"Oh God," I wheezed.

What the hell?

Was it possible that I agreed to play SQUASH?

"You don't even know how to play," Ava's disgusted words found my ears.

"No," I confirmed. "But I guess I'm going to figure it out."

CHAPTER TWO

CAROLINE

To: Caroline<cbmckain@gmail.com>
From: Hannah<vaughn.hannah@hotmail.com>
Date: August 31
Subject: SOS

This is my official signal for distress. School is not going well. I repeat, SCHOOL IS NOT GOING WELL. I have so much to tell you about but have no time to explain right now.

-H

_____

After I finished reading Hannah's email, I groaned and dropped my phone to the bed. I did a few calculations, trying to think if it was already tomorrow there or the middle of the night, but eventually gave up. I'd have to check that time zone app thingy I downloaded before she left me because my brain wasn't working properly.

It was too early.

My caffeine levels were down to zero.

And it was the first day of school.

Normally I loved the first day. Maybe it was just me being an overachiever, but there was something about the smell of fresh paper and never-before-used pencils and new books that took me to my happy place. But not this year. This year I was dreading the first day of school like it was nobody's business.

As I rolled over and burrowed further beneath the covers, an awful, queasy feeling came over me. The thought of having to endure junior year without my best friend was making me physically ill. I knew it was the age of cell phones and Facebook, but *still*. There was no doubt in my mind that this year was going to, in a word, *suck*.

Okay, so maybe I was being a little dramatic, but there was definitely something wrong with me. I took stock of my symptoms. I was sick to my stomach and every few minutes I would feel like I couldn't breathe, but I wasn't running a fever—was I? I touched my forehead but my skin felt fine. Gah, this whole thing was crazy and stupid and I couldn't explain exactly why I felt like this. I just wanted desperately for it to stop.

Swallowing against a dry throat, I thought about staying in bed and not doing anything for the rest of the day. Maybe even the rest of the year. As it was, I certainly didn't have the energy or the desire to get up and get ready.

After a few more minutes and a lot more wallowing, Aspen, my red and white Siberian husky, decided she'd had enough. She pounced on me and placed her paws on either side of my body and licked my face until even my eyelids were drenched in slobber. I tried to deflect but it was no use.

"Geroffmee!" I shouted as we tumbled to the floor in an avalanche of pillows and blankets.

I glanced back at my bed. Well, I guess that was one way to force me out of bed.

Aspen circled me until I pushed to my feet and tramped down the stairs to let her out into the backyard. I leaned against the doorframe just watching her frolic and sniff the grass. It was starting to rain but she didn't care. In fact, she seemed even happier. She just shook her body and bounded to the other side of the yard. I found myself jealous of her ability to adapt.

Jealous of a dog.

Yep. I was officially pathetic.

I left Aspen outside and wandered back upstairs, trying to convince myself that a shower would help my rotten mood. It didn't.

Ten minutes later, I wrapped myself in a towel and I stared at my reflection in the full-length mirror. I was close to tears and everything inside of me was still all dark and twisty. Was this what it felt like to be depressed? Was I hurtling down the road to becoming an emo teen who wore all black and listened to crybaby music?

I wasn't entirely sure, but I was positive that despite knowing my father was just down the hall, I'd never felt so alone in the world. And, all things considered, that was saying something.

I still couldn't believe that Hannah had left this town. Oklahoma. *Me.*

My best friend was off having an amazing adventure in London and I'd totally morphed into an ugly, green-eyed monster. Maybe the knowledge that I wasn't as happy for her as I'd previously thought was what was making me feel sick.

I reminded myself that if the roles were reversed and I had been the one who'd won an essay competition and was offered a place at my dream school, I'd probably have abandoned Hannah without a second thought.

It was London after all.

Buckingham Palace.

Big Ben.

Platform 9 ¾.

Okay, so probably not the last one, but she'd promised to see King's Cross Station and I figured that was close enough to count.

She was the writer though. She was destined for greatness and adventure and a big life. But me? I wasn't sure what I was yet.

"Caroline!" my dad called from the hall.

"Getting dressed!" I hollered back.

"Ten minute warning."

"I'm hurrying," I lied as I stared at the wildly-patterned leggings, cream-colored top, and bright teal scarf that I had picked out last week with Hannah's help. The shirt was okay, but those leggings? Yeah, who was I kidding? That just wasn't happening. Not even on a good day... and today was not a good day.

I threw the leggings and scarf in a pile on the floor next to my desk before pulling out a pair of well-worn jeans and a plain top from my dresser drawers.

As I dressed, I thought more about my predicament. It's not like I could reasonably be mad at Hannah for jumping at the chance to leave. Logically, I knew this was an opportunity of a lifetime. But knowing that didn't change the fact that I was stuck behind in boring Oklahoma. Sure, Libby Park was pretty and quaint. It had been voted the "Top Historic Town in the Midwest" three years running, but that didn't make it cool. Certainly not London-cool.

Even steadfast, always-there-in-a-pinch, Owen Kilgore had been radio silent for days. He was off doing new and exciting things too. After a lot of pushing from his parents, he had agreed to transfer to Holy Cross this year because their lacrosse team was much better than Northside's and it would definitely boost his college scholarship prospects.

Nope, I couldn't blame either Hannah or Owen for leaving, but that didn't mean that I had to like it. No matter how I looked at the situation, I was officially and completely alone. And, as I tried to wrangle my mass of curly red hair into a simple ponytail, I decided I wasn't happy about it. Not one bit.

"Caroline! If you aren't out in five minutes, you'll be walking to school!" Dad yelled up the stairs.

The threat was actually pretty tempting, but a flash of lightning followed by a thundering boom quickly changed my mind. If it wasn't raining cats and dogs, walking would have been a much better alternative to sitting in my dad's old beat up work truck that smelled faintly of oil, grime, and cigarette smoke for ten minutes of what was sure to be awkward silence.

"Fine," I mumbled under my breath before shouting, "I'm coming!" as I grudgingly stomped down the stairs. He was waiting for me at the front door with one hand already on the doorknob and his toolbox in the other. He was wearing a plain white shirt with a red flannel shirt over it, dirty blue jeans, and his work boots. He must have a job today. That was, so far, the only bright spot in this very gloomy morning.

I'd seen pictures of my dad from when he was in high school. Back in the day he looked just like Val Kilmer in all of his *Top Gun* glory. Sadly, these days the only thing he resembled was a broken man in grease-stained jeans.

"What took you so long?" he said, looking down at the toolbox in his hands instead of up at me. He never looked me in the eyes any more. Even though it hurt, it wasn't hard to understand why he couldn't. With my mess of red curls, the dusting of freckles across my nose, and my pale green eyes, everyone said I looked just like my mom.

"I couldn't decide what to wear," I grumbled. I really wished it wasn't raining. The eight blocks on foot would probably be worth it just so that I could pop by Starbucks for a Pumpkin Spice Latte right now. Even when the world sucked all around me, I could always count on PSL to remind me that there were still bits of happiness out there.

For the last two years, I'd ridden with Hannah and her brother. But this year, I'd be depending on my dad for rides until I could manage to buy myself a car. I'd piled on the babysitting jobs over the summer to save up and I was almost there. Just a dozen or so more nights of getting my hair pulled by the Rennert boys and I should have enough. It would probably only be enough to snag a junker but I wasn't going to complain. I'd take anything.

Before she left, Hannah had advised me to ask my father for help, but I wasn't about to go there. Dad couldn't spare the couple hundred dollars I needed or handle an extra insurance payment. God, he could barely cover the bills as it was.

He was a contractor who was scarcely able to stay afloat in work. And it had been that way ever since Mom died.

Plus, the old Victorian house we lived in wasn't exactly cheap to maintain. *Even to these standards*, I thought as I looked around.

Mom had had huge plans for this place… historic tours or maybe even a bed and breakfast that would one day be featured in a five-page spread in *Architectural Digest.* But, like everything else, the house and the dream had faded when she had. Now I just hoped that the walls and the roof would hold through the winter.

"Well, c'mon before we're both late," he muttered as he handed me an umbrella.

"Thanks," I said as I took the umbrella from him. I grabbed my bag from the hook in the hall and dragged my feet out the door. The world outside was cloaked in a grimy grey. I blamed Hannah for this too. As if it wasn't enough that she had abandoned me, it truly seemed that my bright and sunshiny best friend had taken the sun and all of its warmth with her.

"Good morning, Mr. McKain," a familiar voice rang out, surprising me. I looked up to see Henry, Hannah's older brother, walking up the sidewalk toward us holding a cup from Starbucks. Could it possibly be a delicious Pumpkin Spice Latte? My heart thumped with anticipation.

Henry had on hoodie with Northside Buffalos written in red lettering across the front. The hood was pulled up, but his face still glistened with stray raindrops. He and Hannah had that weird sibling quality where they looked alike but not really. They both had light brown hair that faded to soft gold at the tips and wide-set eyes that seemed to shift between smoky blue and grey. Today Henry's eyes seemed more grey than blue as though they were reflecting the dreary sky and my mood.

"Caroline? Are you okay?"

"I-I…What are you doing here?" I asked, secretly hoping that the coffee cup in his hands was for me.

"Um, it is the first day of school, right?" he said as he handed me the coffee. My *hero!*

"Yeah," I answered, taking the cup from him gratefully and letting my hands absorb the warmth. Mmmm, it was definitely a PSL! Fall in a cup and so good for the soul.

"So—I'm here."

"You're still going to give me rides?" I asked, dumbfounded.

"Of course I am. Why wouldn't I?" Henry frowned, which drew my attention to his mouth and square chin. He hadn't bothered to shave this morning and I could see a light smattering of stubble along his jaw. Hannah always complained if Owen didn't shave, but if I was being totally honest, I kind of liked the scruffy look. It was rugged and... hot. Not that I was supposed to be thinking of Henry as hot. What was wrong with me this morning? He was Hannah's brother *and* a taken man.

"I, uh... I just figured with Hannah gone, you wouldn't bother."

"You know I'd never let ya down," he said with an easy smile. "Remembered your favorite coffee and everything."

"Okay great, so Henry will take you to school," Dad said, not even bothering to hide the relief in his voice. "See you this evening, Caroline. And thanks, Henry."

"Right. Bye, Dad." I waved to his back as he hurried away.

"Should we get going?" Henry asked, bringing my attention back to the fact that we were still standing out in the rain and, unlike me, he didn't have an umbrella.

"Yeah, sorry." I raised the umbrella, stretching it as high as I could in an attempt to shield us both from the downpour. Henry, quite a bit taller than my five feet two inches, laughed as he took the umbrella from me and held it high enough for both of us. He rested his hand on the small of my back and my body suddenly rippled with an involuntary shiver.

"Cold?" he asked.

"Mm-hmm," I mumbled. Better to fake a chill in September than admit that my body just spontaneously combusted at his mere touch.

"So are we picking up Elise too?" I asked hesitantly.

Elise and Henry had been dating almost as long as Hannah and Owen had, which meant *forever* in my opinion. But, unlike Owen, I didn't particularly like Elise Rivers. Call me crazy but blond, big-breasted and bitchy was not my idea of someone I wanted to spend time with. But I wasn't a guy so what did I know?

"No," he said a little harshly before adding, "We broke up."

What? My brain was screaming with this new information. Though I'd never thought Elise deserved him in the first place, this was an unexpected development. Of course, I wasn't sure that any man, woman or beast on the planet could ever really deserve Henry Vaughn. "Really? What happened?

"I caught her messing around with some jackass from Holy Cross at a field party a few weeks ago," he said.

"What?" I sputtered. "Hannah didn't mention it."

"I didn't exactly hire a skywriter if you know what I mean."

"Right." I shook my head. "God, Henry, I'm so sorry."

"No worries. I've had time and I'm fine with it," he said with a casual shrug, but I could tell he was still hurt by the betrayal.

If I didn't like Elise before, I really hated her now. I wanted to press the issue, squeeze out all the dirty details but I could tell Henry didn't want to talk about it, so I let it drop. I'd definitely have to ask Hannah about this later.

The ride to school was a little awkward. Maybe it was because we'd been discussing Elise, or maybe it was because it was just the two of us and we'd never hung out without his sister. Not that we were hanging out. Henry was just giving me a ride to school and that was all. Actually, the more I thought about it, the more I thought that Hannah must have put him up to it. Yep, that would explain why he showed up this morning. She must have read my sad email and begged her brother to rescue me.

So, that begged the question: was a pity ride to school better or worse than having your dad drive you to school? I couldn't be sure. Both options made me feel pretty pathetic though I knew which one I *preferred.* It was a no brainer. I'd take the pity ride with Henry any day. Especially if it came with a pumpkin spice latte. I took a sip of my glorious caffeinated coffee.

"Have you talked to Jellybean much?" Henry asked, finally breaking the silence as he pulled into the school parking lot. Jellybean was a nickname Hannah's family started using when she was a baby, and it stuck.

"Yeah, I got a message from her this morning."

"Cool."

"Yeah, cool." I didn't know what else to say and the uncomfortable silence inside the car was becoming unbearable so I figured it was time for me to make my exit before this got any weirder.

"Well, thanks for the ride," I said awkwardly. I did a wave/shrug thing before turning to fumble with the door handle. Then, *of course,* my foot caught on the strap of my bag which caused me to tumble out of the car. N*ice. Real smooth, Care.*

"You okay?" he asked, jumping out of his side of the car with obvious concern while at the same time trying not to chuckle at my expense.

"Yeah, I'm good. Fine. Golden."

"At least you saved your coffee," Henry said, pointing to my still upright cup.

"Right. You gotta have priorities. So… see you later. Or not. Whatever. Bye!" I scrambled like an idiot to make an escape.

Yep. I should've just stayed in bed wallowing. Too late

now.

Little did I know that my day was about to get even worse and it wasn't even officially 8AM yet…

"Ah, Miss McKain!" Mr. Kant, the school counselor, waved when I entered the building. He was panting like he'd been walking too fast and he had a phone gripped in his hand. "I'm so glad I ran into you before first period. I was going to have to come and find you."

"Um, okay?"

"Let's head into my office. We have a slight problem."

Dread filled me. What could possibly be wrong? I had never ever *ever* had a problem at school. The only time my name was called during announcements was to commend me for perfect attendance. And the only reason Mr. Kant even knew me was because he ran a peer counseling club and Hannah and I had both been members freshman year.

"Can you tell me what it is?" I asked nervously as I followed him to the administration office. I had a photography class first period and it looked like I was going to be late.

"Just a moment." We walked past a group of students who Mr. Kant assured he'd see in turn, and ended up in a corner office. I tried to make myself as comfortable as I could on one of two stiff wooden chairs situated in front of his desk. You'd think a counselor would have comfortable chairs to be, you know, counseled in. But I'd only been sitting for about five seconds when my butt and back started to hurt. I noticed Mr. Kant's chair was plush and comfy looking.

After sitting down, he wheeled himself over to a filing cabinet and started rifling through a drawer full of papers. My nervousness kicked it up a few notches.

"The first day is always hectic so we try to help out in different ways," he told me. "I'm working on clearing

384

scheduling kinks."

"Okaaaay?"

"It seems that the photography elective you signed up for last year is full so you'll have to switch to an alternative class," he dropped this information in my lap as though it wasn't a big deal.

But it was. It was huge. I was not a go-with-the-flow kind of person. I didn't just change class schedules on a whim. I calculated. I weighed options. I planned. And I had *planned* on taking that class.

"What do you mean?" I asked, fighting against the desperation in my voice. "I signed up for this class last year. It was supposed to be *guaranteed*."

Mr. Kant, a.k.a., "The Troll Messing With My Schedule," swiveled his chair away from the files to face me and said, "I think you understand that nothing in life is guaranteed."

"But…" my voice trailed off and I shook my head. "I don't know how this happened. I was supposed to have this class to work toward being a yearbook photographer." Hannah had encouraged me to go for it. I was already decent with a camera but I needed the class to even be considered for the yearbook position. If I didn't take it this year, there was no way I'd get the position next year.

"You are only a junior," he said, like I was unaware of what my grade level was. "And you are aware, of course, that seniors get scheduling priority. Next year, that will be you, and you can organize your schedule how you like."

"But we're talking about *this* year."

"Yes, we are."

"Can't you just slip me in? It's just a photography elective. It's not like it's a core class," I argued. What was happening to me? I *never* argued with adults. I was a model student. I was a sit-in-the-front-row and never-even-tardy kind of girl.

This wasn't fair.

I'd signed up for that class last spring. Hannah and I had talked about it extensively. She'd left me one of her cameras specifically for this purpose. I was counting on this. It was the only thing I had to look forward to this semester.

"You're right. Photography is an elective, and you have other options for an elective. Good options."

"Please don't do this to me," I said, now dangerously close to tears. I could feel my throat tightening and my eyes burning. "I'm begging you."

"If I made special arrangements for *every* student then where would we be?"

"But it's not for *every* student. It's just me."

Mr. Kant, who I was now upgrading to "Jerkface," didn't seem even remotely sympathetic to my plight. He sat back in his chair and sighed. "That's what everyone says."

"But I have a perfect record!" I wasn't about to give up yet. "I've never even so much as skipped a class. I get straight As!" Okay, so there was that time last year when I got a B in Calculus, but it was a B+ so that's practically an A. I mean, *hello,* it was *Calculus!* "You can't make just a tiny exception?"

"Miss McKain, I'm sorry but I can't."

"But—"

"I really can't," he said, shaking his head. "You're going to have to choose something else for that time slot."

"Okay, fine. Whatever," I conceded. Now that I knew I was getting nowhere fast, I wanted to get out of this office as soon as possible. Hopefully before I burst into tears in front of all the other students who were waiting to speak to the school counselor.

He considered whatever was on his computer screen

and said, "Your choices for first period electives are Intro to Theater or Marine Biology."

I choked on a laugh. "You're joking."

"Afraid not, Miss McKain." A note of real annoyance crossed his voice, as though I was purposely being difficult. So what if the line of students outside of his office was growing restless? I wasn't the one who screwed up my schedule. This wasn't my fault. "Now, are you going to pick a class or will I have the honor?"

Theater or Marine Biology? These were not good options in that they both sucked.

I couldn't help but feel like if Hannah were here, none of this would be happening. She'd have somehow convinced Mr. Kant to give me the class because she had that kind of power over people. I called it the Hannah Effect. And, if all else failed and she couldn't get Mr. Kant to relent, she'd probably have dropped another class herself so that we could suffer through *Romeo and Juliet* or learn about the mating habits of squid together.

"I'm waiting," he said impatiently, giving me a pointed look.

I found myself wondering, *what would Hannah do?* Costumes and bright lights or salty water samples and dead crab carcasses to examine?

"Theater," I said quickly. I just might have to get a bracelet custom embroidered with *WWHD?* to get me through this year.

"Excellent." Mr. Kant nodded and typed the change into his computer. He printed out the new schedule and handed it to me. "You're all set."

"Fine," I told him ungratefully as I stared down at the slip of white paper. It looked innocuous enough, but it was solid proof that major suckage was ahead.

"Intro to Theater," I read quietly, my insides going icy

cold. Theater. *Theater.* That meant acting. Being on a stage. In front of other people.

Was I crazy? For all of my life, I'd made a point of staying off the radar. I didn't go to school dances. I didn't date. I didn't make a spectacle of myself. If you searched "wallflower" in the dictionary, I was confident that my name would be listed under the derivations.

Fingering the paper schedule, I realized that my sudden burst of Hannah-infused gusto had been a huge blunder. I swallowed and lifted my chin, but before I could tell Mr. Kant that I'd been joking and really wanted to spend first period learning about red algae and sea turtles, he looked past me to the line of students waiting outside his office, waved his hand and shouted, "Next!"

****

The walk down C hall—a hall I had never once been down—seemed painfully long. My stomach was in knots and my head was killing me. I located the classroom by the number plaque nailed over the door. I had every intention of sliding into a desk in the back row. Preferably in a dark, dank corner where I could blend into the shadows and no one would notice my presence.

Except there were no desks.

None.

There were just two rectangular tables surrounded by a few mismatched metal chairs. There weren't nearly enough seats for the number of students already gathered in the classroom, but nobody seemed to mind. They were sitting on the floor and the windowsills and on a handful of bean bag chairs that were scattered throughout the room.

There was so much chaos everywhere I looked that my stomach started to feel swishy.

Bright, sparkly costumes were draped over hangers and haphazardly thrown onto rolling racks. Posters of Broadway shows were pinned cockeyed to the walls with bright red and blue thumbtacks. On a low circular table near the back window there was a box full of random props. I spied a pair of purple goggles, a plastic microphone bedazzled with rhinestones, and a green wig that looked like it belonged in a Dr. Seuss book.

The whole scene made me want to turn and run, but before I could backtrack, a tall, willowy woman glided through the door, effectively trapping me inside.

"Hello, actors and welcome to Intro to Theater!" she greeted us enthusiastically. "My name is Nina but—" she bowed her head and sighed, "—alas, the administration insists you all call me Mrs. Cobb."

A few people laughed. I nervously backed myself up safely against the nearest wall and tried my best to be invisible.

Nina, or *Mrs. Cobb*, could have been twenty or fifty for all I could tell. She was wearing all black—loose gaucho pants, a flowy blouse, and pointy-toed shoes. The only splash of color was a bright orange and pink skinny scarf that actually looked more like a knitted necktie than anything else. Her hair was long and dark brown with heavy bangs that fell in a blunt line straight across her forehead.

"Let's circle up!" she called out, pushing at the thick frames of her glasses. "We're going to play a couple of getting-to-know-you games. Maybe even try a little improv on the first day."

Circle up? Was she serious?

The rest of the class got busy pushing aside the tables to make a wide enough space in the middle of the room to accommodate everyone.

"Is she going to make us all join hands?" I asked the air.

"She probably will," said a cute boy I semi-recognized. "Before the bell rings, we'll all be singing 'Kumbaya' and telling each other our deepest fears."

"No... not really?"

He laughed at my expression. "No, you're safe. She's just going to go over the basics today. If she actually calls anyone up for improv, it will be with volunteers."

"Thank God. I'm not nearly caffeinated enough." I took a breath. "Um, by the way... How do you know all this?"

"I'm actually assisting for the class," he told me.

"Oh." Well, that explained it. I looked him over again, taking in his sculpted hair and dark brown eyes. He was looking more and more familiar to me. "Are you...?"

"Miles Sloan," he offered.

That's right. Northside was a huge school, servicing Libby Park and two other nearby towns, but after a while you started to notice the same people and put them into categories. Miles was one of the drama kids and I was pretty sure he'd played Captain Hook in last spring's *Peter Pan* show. I hadn't seen the play—just the posters—but I remembered Hannah talking about it. "I think you were lab partners with my best friend last year."

His eyebrows moved. "In chemistry?"

"Yeah."

"Hannah Vaughn?"

I nodded. "Yep."

"Ah..." Something sparked for him. I saw it move across his face. "I remember... You used to wait for her after class. You're the friend."

The friend. That's how I was known.

"Hannah's an angel," he continued. "She saved my ass

390

in that class."

She had mentioned something about covering all the lab assignments because Miles was cute but far from the brightest bulb in the chandelier. "She's good at that."

The tables were still being moved around. Someone had knocked over one of the garment racks and another girl caught her sweater on a fake sword so now a huge cleanup effort was being coordinated. I was fine hanging back like this with Miles.

"So, how is Hannah doing?" he asked.

"Oh, she's good. She's in London this year."

"For the whole year?"

I wanted to say, *Yes, and thank you for the reminder.* Instead, I mumbled, "Uh, yeah."

"That's awesome. I bet she's having a blast," he said, smacking his lips. "She does the writing thing, doesn't she?"

"She does. She's actually in a great writing program there. It's like…" I searched for something more to say. "It's a really big deal."

"Very cool."

And it was. It was the coolest. That was what I had to keep reminding myself.

In the center of the classroom, Mrs. Cobb lifted her arms and swung them around her body. "We are ready!"

We all sat down and she explained the rules of the getting-to-know-you game. We would go around the circle, each telling two truths and one lie. The people sitting on either side of us had to guess which of our statements were true and which one was false. Shockingly, I'd actually played this at a sleepover in the fourth grade. I remembered it being like a very tame version of Truth or Dare.

"Should you really be playing this game?" I whispered to Miles. "Since you're the teacher's assistant, it seems

kind of unfair. Shouldn't you be… I don't know…
assisting?"

He smiled at me. "The teaching assistant title is a loose
one. Mainly this is just Mrs. Cobb helping me fill in one of
my elective spots," he confided. "I'm already in her
advanced class this afternoon and I'm also a member of the
drama club. For this class, I'll have to help with grading
and do some busy work, but I'm hoping once we get into
the play, I can use the time to practice lines and run through
my scenes."

"The play?"

Miles didn't get a chance to answer. The game had
moved fast around the circle and we were up.

The "facts" I told about myself were lacking in drama
and beyond lame. The first truth I shared was that I had
never left the state of Oklahoma. The second was that I had
an unhealthy addiction to coffee and pretzel M&Ms. The
lie I told was that I was allergic to nectarines.

Miles picked out the lie right away, but since he was
the first student to talk to me aside from Henry, I decided
not to hold it against him.

"How did you do that?" I asked him when the game
and the rest of "circle time" was over and we were
retrieving our bags from where we'd all dumped them by
the windows.

"How did I do what?"

"Figure out my lie so easily."

"The key to lying is to not hesitate. Works every time."

"I'll keep that in mind," I said, smiling at him.

He grinned back.

Talking to Miles wasn't the same as having Hannah
here—not even close—but it was pleasant. His jeans were
way too tight and he had on copious amounts of cologne,
but he seemed nice enough. Maybe we would become

friends. And, maybe this class wouldn't be so bad after all.

"Thank you all for joining in today," Mrs. Cobb said over the scrape of tables and chairs being moved back into position. "Tomorrow, we'll talk about elements of acting and the fall production. As you all know from the form you were given when you signed up for the class, participation in our show is mandatory. This means your afternoons from mid-September until December will be occupied!"

"Did she really just say that?" I asked Miles.

He just laughed. That wasn't the response I was hoping for.

"I mean it," I pushed. "I signed up late so I didn't see anything about a play…"

"You'll be fine."

"But I won't be," I said firmly. "I don't do stuff like school plays. I can't even give speeches in class."

"It's okay," he said in a reassuring tone. "Participation is required, but there's no way everyone is going to get a part. Especially not in this class."

"Are you sure?"

The dismissal bell rang out shrilly and students started to push past us.

"I'm sure," he told me. "You have to go through the audition just so you understand the process and get the experience, but that's all. The people who don't get speaking parts will be put in the chorus or given a job backstage. There's plenty to do." He lifted his hand and started to list the tasks on his fingers. "Make up, costume stuff, design work, and there's even going to be set building."

"You said… *the chorus?*"

Miles moved his head. "It's a musical. I don't know which one yet, but, between us, I'm hoping she picks *West Side Story*. I've always wanted to play Tony."

"Ummm…"

It was bad enough that I had to take a theater class but now I was going to be expected to audition for a musical?

"Do you sing?"

In the shower, but that was about it. "No…"

"Play an instrument?"

I thought of my mother's piano, sitting at home gathering dust. "I used to play piano but—"

"Well, there you go," Miles said. "Caroline, I've got to get moving, but I'll see you tomorrow. Okay?"

"Sure," I replied absently. My mind was already someplace else.

As I wandered out of the classroom, I considered the possibilities. Maybe I could run away. Or perhaps I could still get that spot in Marine Biology. Because, all things considered, researching the mating habits of squid didn't sound so terrible anymore.

Steering the Stars is now available!

CPSIA information can be obtained
at www.ICGtesting.com
Printed in the USA
LVOW01s2141261115
464290LV00012B/110/P